Louie Louie™
Me Gotta Go Now

By Dick Peterson
With Jim Ojala Editing

THALIAN PRESS

© 2006 Richard Peterson.
All Rights Reserved. No part of this publication may be reproduced, or transmitted in any form by any means, electronic or mechanical, including photocopy, recording, or any information storage or retrieval system, without permission in writing from the copyright holder.

First published by AuthorHouse 01/10/06

ISBN: 1-4208-5610-3 (sc)
ISBN: 1-4208-5609-X (dj)
Library of Congress Control Number: 2005904870

Printed in the United States of America
Bloomington, Indiana

Typography and book design by Jim Ojala
Cover design by April Mostek
All photographs from author's personal collection.
Album covers courtesy of Dave Voorhees,
Bop Street Records, Seattle, Washington
"Louie Louie™" and "The Kingsmen™" are registered Trademarks and are printed by permission

Published by: THALIAN PRESS
Sherwood, Oregon
in conjunction with
AuthorHouse®
Bloomington, Indiana

LOUIE LOUIE™: ME GOTTA GO NOW
by Dick Peterson

Edited by: Jim Ojala
*Additional editing by: Paige Nicklaus, Karen McGhee,
Sherry Holland & Mischelle Day*

This book is printed on acid-free paper.

January 2006 — First Edition

This book is dedicated to Paige, Teal and Karris who have supported my dauntless, and at times seemingly never-ending, effort to realize my ambitious and speculative dreams. It has been through their love, friendship, encouragement, prayers, strength and understanding that I continue, with determination, to pursue my insane aspirations of endless nebulosity.

I also dedicate this work to my mother Lillie Kizer for her love and faith. To Nancy and Gordon Fraser, without whom this book would never have been possible.

To Meredith MacMullin, Mike Mitchell, Tim and Laurie Griffin, Phil and Ceci McCrea, Gary and Cathy Daichendt, Jack and Becky Loughridge, Ed Kleven, Dan and Michelle Harrington, Laura Ben-Porat, Cheryl Hodgson, Billy and Roberta Meshel, Brian and Cindee Beirne, Kim and Stephanie Nicklaus, Sherry Holland, Jim Ojala, Mischelle Day, Shonda Kearns, Lamont Dozier, Todd and Karen Saunders, Millie Bessey, Carl and Patsey Sanders, Rick and Tracy Beeks, Steve Bonner, Steve Doctrow, Tiffany Youhanna and Maestro Gerard Schwarz.

My fellow Musketeers, past Kingsmen and those we recognize as honorary Kingsmen: Mike Mitchell, Barry Curtis, Lynn Easton, Norm Sundholm, Steve Peterson, Todd McPherson, Craig Bystrom, Marc Willett, Pete Blecha, Jerry Dennon, Jack Ely, Bob Nordby, Don Gallucci, Gary Abbott, Kerry Magness, J.C. Reick, Turley Richards, Pete Borg, Jeff Beals, Steve Friedson, Fred Dennis, Andy Parypa, Kim Nicklaus, Jim Johnson, Del Meyer, Bob Ehlert, Hermie Dressel, Shelly Berger, Bill Lee, Dick St. John, Roger Hart, Karen McGhee, Pat Bukieda, Scott Edleman, Jeanette Bazis and of course, Mr. X and his wonderful family.

FOREWORD

THROUGHOUT the years we Kingsmen have told a seemingly limitless number of stories about "Louie Louie", the Kingsmen and our experiences, to friends, family, acquaintances and interviewers. I can't count how many times I have heard, "You should write a book," or "That would make a great movie." It would seem that everyone is interested in "Louie Louie" and the controversies it has created. I have one friend in particular, Jim Ojala, who is an editor, writer and publisher from Seattle. He has relentlessly been after me for years to "write the book." I received an email from my "good friend Jim" that stated, "Enclosed please find the first paragraph to your book, 'Louie Louie.' Now you fill in the rest and finish the damn thing!" The pages you are about to read are the result of his clever email and it's inspiration. Upon completing my manuscript I sent it back to Jim for his critique. Encouragingly, he took on the task of editing my manuscript. I thank my friend with great and loving gratitude.

The dialog and running conversations created in this book were created to tell the story of The Kingsmen, our relationship to "Louie Louie," the legends, claims and myths that created this fun controversy and were generally paraphrased and generated for story telling and an accurate illustration of historical events. Quotes were not intended to be absolute and unequivocal but historical re-enactments. I apologize for any misspelled names of friends and family, places and people that made up the craziness that has become the legend of Louie Louie.

—Sherwood, April 2005

The Kingsmen™ Discography – Singles

1. *Louie Louie/Haunted Castle* (Jerden 712) 1963
2. *Louie Louie/Haunted Castle* (Wand 143) 1963
3. *Money/Bent Scepter* (Wand 150) 1964
4. *Little Latin Lupe Lu/David's Mood* (Wand 157) 1964
5. *Death Of An Angel/Searching For Love* (Wand 164) 1964
6. *The Jolly Green Giant/Long Green* (Wand 172) 1964
7. *The Climb/The Waiting* (Wand 183) 1965
8. *Annie Fanny/Give Her Lovin'* (Wand 189) 1965
9. *(You Got) The Gamma Goochee/It's Only The Dog* (Wand 1107) 1965
10. *Little Green Thing/Killer Joe* (Wand 1115) 1966
11. *The Krunch/The Climb* (Wand 1118) 1966 (promo only)
12. *My Wife Can't Cook/Little Sally Tease* (Wand 1127) 1966
13. *If I Need(ed) Someone/Grass Is Green* (Wand 1137) 1966
14. *Trouble/Daytime Shadows* (Wand 1147) 1967
15. *Children's Caretaker/The Wolf of Manhattan* (Wand 1154) 1967
16. *(I Have Found) Another Girl/Don't Say No* (Wand 1157) 1967
17. *Bo Diddley Bach/Just Before the Break of Day* (Wand 1164) 1968
18. *Get Out of My Life Woman/Since You've Been Gone* (Wand 1174) 1968
19. *On Love/I Guess I Was Dreamin'* (Wand 1180) 1968
20. *You Better Do Right/Today* (Capitol 3576) 1973

The Kingsmen™ Discography – Albums

1. *The Kingsmen™ In Person* (Wand LP-657) 1963
2. *The Kingsmen™, Volume II* (Wand LP-659) 1964
3. *The Kingsmen™, Volume 3* (Wand LP-662) 1965
4. *The Kingsmen™ on Campus* (Wand WDM-670) 1965
5. *How to Stuff a Wild Bikini* (Wand WDM-671) 1965
6. *15 Great Hits* (Wand W-674) 1966
7. *Up and Away* (Wand WDM-675) 1966
8. *The Kingsmen™-Greatest Hits* (Wand WDS-681) 1966
9. *The Kingsmen™-A Quarter To Three* (Picc-A-Dilly PIC-3329) 1980
10. *The Kingsmen™-Ya Ya* (Picc-A-Dilly PIC-3330) 1980
11. *The Kingsmen™-House Party* (Picc-A-Dilly PIC-3346) 1980
12. *The Kingsmen™-Greatest Hits* (Picc-A-Dilly PIC-3348) 1981
13. *Live and Unreleased* (Jerden 7004) recorded 1963, released 1992
14. *Since We've Been Gone* (Sundazed 6027) recorded 1967, released 1994
15. *The Kingsmen™-Plugged* (Kingsmen™ CD #1) 1995
16. *Garage Sale* (Louie Louie™ Records–no catalog #) 2003

These are partial discographies reflecting only original US releases, and do not include reissues or overseas releases which together total over 100.

OVERTURE

WORLDWIDE, hundreds of millions of people recognize the opening strains of "Louie Louie" the instant they hear them. Whether listening to the Kingsmen singing on radio or CD or tape, or watching actors performing in *Animal House* or *Mr. Holland's Opus* or *Dave*, people of all ages and from every background break into knowing smiles the moment that raucous riff first tickles their ears. On a multitude of levels, "Louie Louie" has embedded itself deep within our collective consciousness and become a permanent element of our cultural identity. Yet, few know the true story behind this legendary recording and its aftermath.

We all have our own special stories to tell. Mine is one of an innocent, square, naïve, extremely sheltered boy who was just 17 when he came of age as a member of one of the most talked-about rock 'n' roll bands of all time, The Kingsmen. The Kingsmen gained fame from a recording ("Louie Louie") once widely banned from the airwaves. Critics alleged with absolute confidence that the record "Louie Louie" featured obscene lyrics and that the group The Kingsmen spewed vulgar profanities in their live concerts. For over 18 months, J. Edgar Hoover and the FBI shadowed the band, investigating the allegations and looking for opportunities to arrest and punish the teenage transgressors. But *was* the song dirty? *Were* the boys guilty? *Who* was right and *who* was wrong? *What was* the truth? Read on.

J. Edgar's paranoiac suspicions notwithstanding, here follows the insanely humorous story of a band of ordinary guys who one April day in 1963 ventured into a recording studio just trying to earn enough money to afford the teenage staples: gas, girls and admission to the drive-in. Within the next year, to our complete surprise, we found ourselves besieged by extraordinary, unimaginable troubles. Labeled "a bunch of dirty little boys" with "dirty little minds" singing "dirty little songs," we were attacked by federal and state authorities as "subversives" bent on corrupting the moral fiber of the youth of America." We consoled ourselves with the knowledge we were earning far more money than teenage boys should ever be allowed to have.

When trying to think up a moniker for their group, most bands agree on a name because "it sounds good" or maybe "it has a ring to it" or, more intellectually, "it's the essence of what we are." Our famous/infamous name, in contrast, was the pure inspiration of founding members Mike Mitchell and Lynn Easton after seeing the brand name "Kings Men" on a bottle of Lynn's father's aftershave. In the 1990's, Northwest grunge pioneers Nirvana made it big singing a song named after a teenage toiletry; in the 1960's, Northwest garage-band pioneers The Kingsmen made it big naming themselves after an *adult* toiletry. On top of that, "Smells Like Teen Spirit" and "Louie Louie" are arguably two of the greatest records in rock 'n' roll history. Go figure.

Could it be that a passel of all-American boys from Portland, Oregon managed to completely change our moral character overnight and become the bad boys Establishment powers made us out to be?

What are the lyrics in "Louie Louie" about?

What truth can be found in the countless articles and books that endlessly examine the rumors that circulate about the Kingsmen and our history?

Why do reporters and authors continue to rely on rumors piled on rumors piled on rumors as their information source without taking the time to actually interview the band? From the first day those rumors started, people have assumed they know the real story of "Louie Louie." I've been a Kingsmen now for over 40 years, and I was a member when the mayhem began, and I'm telling you right now, the world *doesn't* know the truth about "Louie Louie." I know. I was there.

The band originally formed in 1959 as a three-piece folk group—*The Kingsmen*—featuring bongos and two guitars and singing covers of Kingston Trio and Peter, Paul and Mary hits.

As a new decade began, the band graduated from playing at grade school dances to performing at high school proms and sock-hops. By 1963, the Kingsmen had become a five-piece rock band and had a steady gig appearing every Tuesday through Saturday night at The Chase, a teen night club owned by Ken Chase, a disk jockey at the number one Top-40 radio station in Portland, KISN. When I joined the group in December of that year, they were just starting to become known beyond Portland and vicinity, in particular across New England thanks to the perverse sense of humor of a madcap disc jockey at a Boston radio station. On air one day he played this crude, strange-sounding record with lyrics no one could understand, something called "Louie Louie." Exactly what it was — other than a bunch of loud noises — he wasn't certain, but he played it anyway as part of a joke, as a gimmick. That gimmick turned into one of the enduring legends in rock history and, ultimately, led to the writing of this book.

None of this could be foreseen in late 1963 when I auditioned for the band and passed muster. With my addition to the musical mix, the Kingsmen completed their metamorphosis into the loudest, most electrified full tilt rock 'n' roll band in the known universe.

Soon after the nation ushered in 1964, the saga of "Louie Louie" as a cultural phenomenon began. In January, barely a month after I joined the group, a media fire storm engulfed us and America's forever-rebellious teenage population took us to their bosoms and turned us into anti-establishment heroes. We ignored the criticisms as best we could; we welcomed the adoration with open arms, literally and figuratively.

Starting from a world of such innocent fun and becoming the most notorious band in the land sounds like a contradiction, doesn't it? Indeed it was, but I'm getting ahead of myself. To better set the stage for this tale, I'll begin with a look back at a few life-forming experiences from my youth. That should give you a good perspective for viewing my unlikely role in the legend of "Louie Louie."

PRELUDE

MY story begins in 1951, a time of national innocence when divorce remained a four-letter word. Young and attractive, a single mom raising three small children, my mother might as well have sported a big scarlet *D* on her chest. Such was the shame that divorce then brought in Portland, Oregon.

She juggled several jobs at once to keep my sisters Nancy and Gayle and me fed and dressed in what could best be described as "only slightly worn-out, but regularly and diligently scrubbed" clothing. Our standard-issue shoes invariably developed holes in their soles which she filled with pieces of cardboard inserted in just the right way to prevent matching holes from wearing through our socks. Heck, just because there was a hole in the bottom of your shoe, that didn't mean you had to throw the whole thing out. The top was still good, and with a thick enough piece of cardboard you could squeak through a whole entire summer until the autumn rains returned (as they always do in Portland) and soaked the cardboard through and through to ruination and you finally had to trade in your treasured footwear for another "like new" pair and begin the annual ritual all over again.

One of Mother's jobs had her working at the local Fred Meyer, a sprawling supermarket-department store hybrid that carried everything from soup to nuts to tire chains to women's undies. "Freddie's" is where fate declared she'd meet a young, handsome, blonde-haired, blue-eyed, workin'-his-way-through-school, soon-to-be-a-doctor Karl Peterson.

Karl hailed from Gig Harbor, Washington. A small, quaint, idyllic, picturesque sliver of a place. The town was nestled around a boot-shaped Puget Sound inlet west of Tacoma on the weather-protected east side of the Olympic Mountains. Back then, it claimed some 720 citizens, give or take a few salty dogs, sea dogs and assorted denizens, some of whom weren't exactly sure *where* to call home. Growing up along the shores of Gig Harbor was very much a Pacific Northwest version of Mark Twain's Tom Sawyer and Huckleberry Finn growing up along the banks of the Mississippi River. Twain chronicled Tom and Huck's exploits; readers of this tale will have to make do with me as their guide.

In the early '50s, the Harbor was populated mostly with Norwegians, Swedes, Croatians and a few Native Americans—members of the Nisqually tribe, to be exact. In their oral tradition, the Nisquallies traced their heritage back in time well beyond the single century that had passed since the first pioneer settlers arrived in the area. Almost everything in Gig Harbor was centered around either fishing or logging. In fact, the two biggest celebrations of the year were the early summer day when the fishing boats left in search of fortune in the salmon-rich North Pacific waters off Alaska and the fall day months later when they returned with their fortunes. Sadly, not every fortune-seeker who left Gig Harbor in June returned in October. The North Pacific's frigid waters can be a cruel mistress.

Karl, his sister and brother were all born in this picture-postcard, Norman Rockwell-sort-of town, and young Karl was raised there with no inkling he'd ever leave. That was before his father suffered an early and needless death for wont of proper medical treatment, and a grieving Karl became acutely aware of the need for a doctor in his town. So, with the Good Book in hand and a promise to his fellow residents to return as a doctor fresh off his lips, Karl said good-bye to friends and family and headed south to Portland for college and medical school.

After serendipity brought them together on the cosmetics aisle at Freddie's, my mother and Karl dated for a few years before marrying just as I approached five. I had reached six by the time Karl Jr. appeared and seven when the stork dropped off the unexpected Heidi, expanding our family to seven and matching in number my years. All the while, Karl continued his medical studies. After what seemed like forever, he graduated, becoming "Doctor Karl," and finally we were going to move to Gig Harbor. Often at bedtime, he'd captivated my sisters and me with his colorful tales of his childhood, and we brimmed with excitement at the thought of making his hometown our new home. My mother may have been responsible for that gleam in his eye but, judging from the way he talked about Gig

Harbor, there was no question that its waters were the lifeblood that flowed through his veins. He made it sound like the greatest place on earth, and in spring he was taking us to his Shangri-la.

I had a best friend in Portland who was going to be difficult to leave. His name was Farnsworth, but I called him "Fawnie," and we were inseparable. In the better-than-real world created by our boyish imaginations, he was Roy Rogers and I was Hopalong Cassidy. We had the official Roy and Hoppy cuffs for our arms, the handkerchiefs for our necks, the hats for our heads and the cap guns for our hands. When we loaded our six-shooters with a roll of caps and pulled the trigger, they sounded absolutely real, just like one of the genuine Colt 45s our heros wielded. Well, they sounded absolutely real to us, anyway, and what else mattered? Everywhere we went we galloped, clapping our hands against our sides to make the sound of our horses, Trigger and Topper. What true happiness! Every once in a while, one of us would make that sound with our lips that a horse makes when it whinnies. Fighting the bad guys and always winning, shooting our cap guns and falling wounded to the grass in uncontrollable laughter only to rise and fight again—such was the order of our endless days. We thought ourselves invincible.

Fawnie lived directly across the park from me, and every morning during the summer we'd meet in the middle, at *our* tree, to play away the day together. Saturdays, for a quarter, we'd go to the movies in the hope of catching a Roy Rogers or Hopalong Cassidy movie, for that would give us another week of inspiration for our cowboy fantasies. Before the feature film, there was always a serial, like *Buck Rogers* or *Copperhead* or *The Masked Marvel*. Their spine-tingling adventures kept Fawnie and me sitting on the edge of our seats and compelled us to return the following week to discover how the hero managed to survive the perilous situation the previous episode had left him in with yet another incredible, unforeseen, death-defying feat of derring-do. Even during school months, we'd meet at our tree in the park and walk to school together. We were best friends as only boys that age can be.

We were 6 years old when Fawnie was diagnosed with what my parents told me was "a terminal disease." I watched without understanding as he slowly went from running to walking, from walking and gasping for air to sitting in a wheelchair, from sitting in a wheelchair to lying in bed. I didn't think that "terminal" meant he was going to die; I always thought he'd eventually get well. Roy always won in the movies, so why wouldn't Fawnie in real life? Every day after school, I ran to Fawnie's house and did any and every silly thing I could think of to make him laugh as his condition continued to deteriorate. I jumped around like a crazy man making monkey noises, opened his copy of *Little Red Riding Hood* and made up a silly, stupid story about "Miss Hood" and her associates. Laughing was Fawnie's favorite thing to do, and laugh he did. I could always make *Roy* laugh.

We were moving in a week, and I was beginning to wonder whether Fawnie, in his condition, was going to be able to find a new Hoppy. I really didn't want to move away and leave him alone without knowing that someone would be there in my place to make him laugh. I knew it would be almost impossible for him to find new friends when he was confined to bed. My mom, trying to ease my concern, said I could call him from time to time and that I could visit him later that summer. She even suggested that Fawnie could come up to Gig Harbor for a visit when he felt better. It bothered my friend and me to the core to know that I was moving. Yet, in the best Roy-and-Hoppy cowboy tradition, we made a pact to see each other as often as possible and always remain best friends.

I remember my last week in Portland. The sun shone bright as I knocked on Fawnie's front door. To my surprise, I looked up to see his father slowly opening the door. *How unusual*, I thought. *He should be working at this time of day.* I could see Fawnie's mother through the screen door, weeping and struggling to catch her breath as she gasped in a shaky voice, "Fawnie just passed away."

"What does that mean?" I asked.

"He's gone, Dickie, he's gone," she said sadly. "You'd better go home now. I'll let your mother know about the arrangements."

As the front door closed, I sat down on Fawnie's front porch and began to cry. The walk home took forever. Not running as I usually did made it seem as though the trip had tripled in distance. When I finally reached home, my mother had already heard the devastating news. After talking with Mom and Dad about death and funerals, I decided not to go to Fawnie's service. I wanted to remember him laughing and running through the park with me—Roy and Hoppy, together forever, dispensing justice in the trouble-free, make-believe days of cowboys and Indians. I didn't want to think of him as dead. Rather, I resigned myself to the belief that he'd gone someplace else and that someday we'd meet again and once more ride the range together.

Gayle, Nancy and author   *Hoppy*

IT was still dark when we left Portland heading for our new start in Gig Harbor. The big blue-grey '51 Buick Roadmaster was packed to the windows with kids and toys. About an hour outside of Portland, we stopped for breakfast at a small diner. It had a big neon sign you could see from a mile away, begging travelers in large flashing red letters to "EAT NOW." I sat by the partially-opened, hardly-ever-washed window as a light breeze from outside blew the dingy light-yellow curtains slowly back and forth in front of my sleepy eyes. Resting my elbows on the cold red Formica-and-chrome restaurant table, I cupped my chin in my hands as thoughts kept running through my head of the Hoppy outfit I'd carefully folded and painfully left behind lying on the floor of my bedroom back in Portland. I watched the sun start to rise and wondered *How am I going live the rest of my life without Roy?*

Author, Karl Jr., Nancy and Gayle

Author, Nancy, Karl Jr. and Gayle, Gig Harbor

Gayle, Author and Nancy, Gig Harbor

INTRO

I'LL never forget driving into Gig Harbor for the first time. As we approached the town limits, Daddy, fisherman extraordinaire, played us perfectly, pulling the car over, not saying a word, choosing the ideal place to park—a viewpoint from where he knew we could see the entire harbor. Before the dust kicked up by the lumbering Buick's sudden stop could settle, we all scrambled out in a mad race to be the first to catch a glimpse of our new hometown. As usual, I emerged last from the car.

As my parents leaned closely together, taking in the stunning vista, I ran up from behind and squeezed my head between their legs.

"Hey, let me see!" I demanded, and Mom and Dad complied.

A sharp, sudden "Whooooa!" was my profound sound of choice. Then I just gaped. The captivating splendor of the Harbor stunned us all to silence. At last, Daddy broke the spell.

"Well," he said to my mom, "what do you think, honey?"

Slowly she turned her head and looked up at him. With smiling eyes, Mom gave her approval. "Beautiful."

"Yeah, beautiful," parroted my sisters in unison.

Gig Harbor was magical beyond any of the visions I'd created in my mind as Daddy told his nightly stories—a fairy tale come true. Unlike today, there were few houses on the water back then, and towering spruces and firs and cedars and hemlocks extended their reach over long stretches of shoreline nearly to the water's edge. A glistening grey beach separated the variegated green forest from the most beautiful deep blue water I'd ever seen.

Raising his arm and pointing his finger to our left, Daddy started.

"There's the marina," he said with pride.

A fleet of white fishing boats, most all of them the same shape, filled the marina's slips and moorings. Every vessel boasted a distinctive set of colored accent stripes running its length, giving each a sense of individuality. Reds of various hues, light and dark blues, different shades of green, some violets and golds—a full rainbow spectrum of colors beckoned to me. I was dying to run off to the marina and check things out for myself.

"Can we go down there, Daddy?" I asked. "Can we, huh, can we?"

"In a minute," he answered.

He continued pointing out the different sights, bringing to life the images he'd created in my mind through his stories—the boat launch, Grandma's house, the sand spit—but we were anxious to get to our new house. When Nancy could take it no longer, she pulled on Daddy's pant leg and said, "Come on, Daddy, let's go!" interrupting his nostalgic, emotional experience.

"Okay," he said, reluctantly giving in. With a tear in his eye and a break in his voice, he softly added, "This is your first day in Gig Harbor. Take a good long look, kids, and never forget this day. *Never ever* forget this day...."

I looked up at Daddy and sensed the enormity of *the good Dr. Karl Peterson*'s attachment to and affection for this place. Though only seven, I knew Gig Harbor was more than just a place special to him; it was the source of life between each beat of his heart. I desperately hoped that, in a short time, it would be that for me as well.

It didn't take long before Nancy begged again, "Let's go!"

"Alright, we can go," Daddy laughingly answered.

"Dibs on a window!" Nancy shouted as she ran back to the car.

"I want a window, too," Gayle complained, following right behind.

"Dickie," Mom said, "you ride up front with us. That way you *all* can have a window. We'll put the babies in the back between Nancy and Gayle."

The seven of us piled back into the Buick, rolled down the windows and started down the hill toward the water. As he drove, Daddy continued to identify the many different but familiar landmarks he'd told us about—Mrs. Fuqua's movie house, the school, his brother Bubby's gas station, Herb's post office, Brian the Cop's house—all people and places from his bedtime stories. As we passed the grocery store, he said to Mom, "That's Finholm's

Grocery. I'll take you in later and introduce you to Mrs. Finholm. We'll set up a charge account. She's going to love you to death!" Everything was nearly too much for me to absorb. As we crossed a small bridge at the end of the harbor, Daddy gestured toward the park.

"That's where we have picnics on holidays and Sundays after church," he said proudly. "Most of the town turns out. You'll make a lot of good friends there."

I was sitting wide-eyed on the edge of the front seat when he reached across Mom and tapped me on the shoulder. I looked over.

"That's also where the Tarzan swing is," he said, wearing a devilish grin. "I'll take you there later."

I thrust my head out the window and looked back at the park, trying desperately to catch a glimpse of the swing, but we were traveling too fast and all I could see as we negotiated a bend in the road was a broad grassy area, a big log shelter and a soaring stand of trees.

We followed the water's edge for another few hundred yards, then turned into a driveway.

"Here we are, kids," Daddy announced.

The first thing I noticed was a gigantic willow tree in the front yard with thin, leafy green branches that drooped to the ground, hiding what I figured must surely be a huge trunk.

Perfect place for a fort, I thought.

Climbing out of the car, I saw before me a white house with dark green shutters. Tall white rose bushes framed a porch leading to a front door whose color matched that of the shutters. I paused for a moment, absorbing the magic of it all. As Mom and the girls worked at opening the front door, Daddy looked back at me and quietly hinted, "There's a swing set around back."

I raced off in the direction of the backyard. Turning the corner, I expected to see grass and a swing set. Wrong. I couldn't believe it. Was I dreaming? Was someone going to spoil the moment with that dreaded phrase "Wake up, Dickie. Time for school!" Was I really looking at A BEACH IN MY OWN BACK YARD? Wow! This was paradise, the perfect place to live, and it was all mine—or, more accurately, all mine to share with my siblings.

Sure, there was grass there, and a swing set, too, but who cared about those anymore? I had a beach! I ran down toward the water and was nearing the waters edge when I heard my mother yelling through an open window in the kitchen.

"Dickie, don't go near the water!" she called out.

How do parents do it, and moms in particular? It's like they have some sort of built-in fun-killing radar that sends them a signal whenever you're about to do something great. Dismayed, I plopped down on the grass, my legs dangling over a two-foot drop-off created over time by the weather and changing tides. I stared in wonderment at the spell-binding, almost spiritual scene before me. Before too long, Daddy joined me.

"You know" he said, sitting down beside me, "when I was your age, I used to come down to the beach and skip stones for hours. Feel like skipping a few now?"

"Sure," I answered, "but they're pretty small to jump over."

"Not *that kind* of skipping," he said, smiling. "Here, let me show you what I mean."

The shoreline was carpeted with stones, and I watched him as he jumped down on the beach and started searching for just the right one.

"You need to find a flat round one like this."

He bent over and picked up a wafer-shaped black stone about the size of a half dollar as he continued to explain.

"You put your finger around the rock like this and throw it across the water so it stays level with the surface. Here, watch!"

The stone sailed out of his hand and grazed the water's face, jumping and skimming and hopping along the top, creating little circles wherever it touched. I was amazed.

"One, two, three, four, five, *six* times!" Dad counted. He was so excited. "A sixer!" he exclaimed. "Now, you come try."

I hopped down to the beach and selected a stone.

"Watch this!" I said confidently as I flung with all my might. "One, two, three," I counted, and then it was gone. It was as though the water had sucked my stone down. I looked up at Daddy, expecting disappointment.

"Three!" he shouted encouragingly. "That's better than my first throw. I'll bet if you work at it you could throw a ten'er with an arm like that."

"Really?" I said, beginning to smile.

"You bet!" he replied. "Let's try it again."

We stayed on the beach throwing stones, getting sand in our shoes and having a blast until Mom finally called us into the house. My arm was starting to fall off, and, in truth, I needed a break. The fisherman extraordinaire not only hooked me—he landed me in the boat. I loved that day. It still remains one of the favorite moments of my life.

I spent most of that summer playing at the park. It was only a few city blocks away, and most of the kids between the ages of 7 and 13 from my side of the Harbor gathered there every morning right after breakfast. It was exactly as Daddy promised. The park was home to a swamp complete with frogs and muck (a favorite with boys my age), a rock-strewn softball field and a large log shelter to protect gatherings from the not-too-uncommon and universally-expected precipitation on cloudy days. Trees grew everywhere, with huge maples and taller still old growth firs lining the river's edge. Best of all, there was the giant Tarzan swing that Daddy pointed out that first day. Since before he was born, it had been thrilling the children of Gig Harbor the same way it was now thrilling me.

The rope was big—several inches thick, I'd guess—a relic from some fishing boat that long ago had been re-rigged. The top end was tied to an upper branch of a strategically-located Douglas fir. A long piece of twine was tied to the bottom end, and that, in turn, was used to tie around your waist. The twine was much more manageable than the heavy thick rope, and tying it around your waist freed your hands for use in climbing up the ladder and scooting into place for take off. About 30 feet further from the water stood another giant fir with pieces of wood nailed to its trunk to form a make-shift ladder. From the top of the ladder, you slid out on a plank spanning two thick, sturdy branches. Sitting on the plank, you reeled in the twine, bringing the big rope over close enough for you to grab hold of it. Then you put the big rope between your legs, sat on the knot tied at its end and slipped off the platform.

"Woo-hoo!"

Away you swung like Johnny Weissmuller on his way to saving Jane, your stomach rising in your throat. The rope's sweeping arc carried you far out over the water—it seemed like miles to me—and, when you let go, you flew through the air for another 40 feet or so before you hit the cold water, your arms and legs flailing away in a swirling egg beater-like motion. Splash! This was a favorite sport of Harbor children of all ages. On weekends or after work, our parents sometimes joined in the fun, excusing themselves by saying something to the effect that "We have to make sure the swing's in good working order and not dangerously in need of repair." Yeah, right! We knew the truth, then and now. It was, plain and simple, a fun thing to do; it was a local tradition, and a great one at that; it was proof that in our town at least, a child still lived on in the heart of every adult. All that was needed to bring it out was a giant Tarzan swing.

On the water, Gig Harbor provided safe moorage for a fleet of boats; on land, Gig Harbor provided safe homes for a gathering of families, especially for ones like ours with small children and budding aspirations. Looking back, it seems like a whole 'nother era, a time of easy friendships, kept promises and living dreams. As a child, you could leave home after breakfast and not come back until dark, and your parents would never worry about where you were or what you were doing. They always knew you were safe. The only rule was, if you went somewhere, you couldn't go by yourself, so we operated on the buddy system.

Harbor parents could always find their children. The swarm was easy to locate. We were either at the park playing, or on the docks fishing, or in the woods exploring, or on the beach digging or, if the tide was low, in the mud flats getting filthy with all of the other kids. If anyone wanted to know where we were at a particular moment, they simply asked around. Always, someone in the Harbor had seen the gang at one time or another during the day and could supply directions. And don't forget, our moms all had that fun-killing radar thing going for them.

Harbor summers seemed to go on forever, at least until we were dragged to the store for a new set of school clothes, which announced to us all that our season of freedom was about to end. Until age 14, I was blessed with the same assortment of new clothing every fall: two pairs of corduroy trousers, three short-sleeved shirts, a heavy winter coat and a new pair of shoes (all of which were promised to fit by year's end). My shoe experiences were especially memorable. I always ended up with the thickest-soled, stiffest-topped, loudest-sounding pair of clodhoppers west of the Atlantic Ocean. Their soles were so formidable, they refused to bend even the slightest bit for the first few months I wore them. Throughout the fall, they made a sort of *clop, clop* sound. After an entire summer of bare feet and shorts, my new back-to-school shoes felt like cumbersome, heavy anchor weights on my feet.

Above my shoes, choking my legs, stretched these rolled-up-at-the-cuff, long-legged cords. Thick and stiff, they made a *zipping* noise when you walked as one leg passed the other. *Clop-zip, clop-zip, clop-zip*—I sounded like a one-legged man in a parade playing a washboard in the rhythm section of a bad bluegrass band. Forget about sneaking up on a friend with your school clothes on, let alone on a frog—it couldn't be done. The collective racket you made walking home from school with a pack of your newly-outfitted schoolmates could be alarming. For years, my parents duped me into believing this was the sound of *quality* clothing. I know now it was not the sound of *quality* clothing, but rather the sound of *hearty* clothing. Harbor schools overflowed with students sporting the *heartiest* attire in existence, the proof of which could be easily heard.

We had one grade school in the Harbor, Lincoln Elementary, located on the opposite side of the water from where I lived. On fair weather days we had the choice of either rowing a dinghy across the water, walking along the roads or hopping a ride on the bus. Living in the rainy Northwest, we mostly rode. We liked taking the rowboat best, however, for then we could fish for dinner on the way home. Unlike today, on a good day then (which was most of the time) we could count on catching a salmon; on a bad day we might snag an octopus instead. Dad loved octopus, but the rest of us hated it and were grossed out by the ugly, slimy, smelly creatures. Miraculously—"accidentally on purpose"—most of those repulsive, chewy little beasts slipped off our lines and back into the water. Oops!

A white three-room schoolhouse, Lincoln stood in constant need of paint and repair, showing its age. A flight of wide, worn wooden steps led up to the front door. At the entrance was a cloakroom with hooks on the wall for hanging our coats, a wooden bench running its length for sitting while changing our shoes and a large three-sided wooden keep for storing the firewood. Five rows of desks sat on the classroom's timeworn, creaky wood plank floor. Each row represented a different grade. The row nearest the windows held first graders, and every year you moved one row further away from the view outside. The desks and dust had been there for generations, and many of our grandparents had used these same desks, as evidenced by the carvings of their initials and names on the undersides of the wooden tops. When lifted, these hinged desktops revealed your personal storage compartment. We kept our tablets, extra pencils, workbooks and crayons in there.

The upper left sides of our desktops had holes in them, used by past generations for their ink bottles. Stealthily tying an unsuspecting Bernadette's super-long ponytail through the hole in my desk was always a favorite prank of mine, one guaranteed to create a commotion when she stood. The scratched-and-dented surface of the desk was slanted down toward you for ease of use and had a groove across the top for securing your pencils so they wouldn't roll off into your lap or onto the floor. Pleasantly and unadjustably, all of the desks in each row were bolted to two wooden runners that ran from the front desk to the last, linking them together, kind of a one-size fits-all sort of a thing.

The school's central heating system consisted of a solitary wood-burning potbelly stove parked in a front corner of the classroom. It was seen to glow red on crisp winter days, and the back of the room could be unpleasantly cold at such times, though the front of the room baked. Behind the teacher's desk hung a slate blackboard, complete with a wooden rail filled with assorted lengths of chalk—some of them colored, most of them white—and a few well-worn black-and-white-striped felt erasers. The back wall boasted a pull-down, pastel-shaded political map of the world. A well-seasoned American flag displaying 48 stars stood on a wooden pole by the door in the front. Every morning, with our hands over our hearts, we stood and faced the flag, reciting the Pledge of Allegiance and proudly including the words "...one nation, under

God, indivisible...," certain that America was just that.

The playground outside was a rock lover's dream, a stony patch of dirt—some days a dust bowl, other days a sea of mud—where generations of laughing, squealing children had somehow managed to play baseball and dodge ball and tag, skip rope and climb monkey bars, all without noticeable complaint.

I know it sounds as though we didn't have much in those days, but not so. We had everything. With so much to do, we were completely unaware of whatever possessions we lacked. Those were simple and happy and magical times in the Harbor.

Gig Harbor 1950's

LETTER "B"

MUSIC entered my life in a most unusual way. In the happy Washington home I prefer to remember, money problems alone could spark conflicts between Mom and Dad. We lived in a cash-poor community where people relied on each other's cooperation. Since the days settlers founded our little town, a thriving barter system had kept the wheels of local commerce well oiled during good times and bad. Daddy was constantly coming home with a big bag of fresh picked corn, his reward for treating Mrs. Olson's troubled feet, or with a fresh chinook or silver salmon, his payment from Mr. Johnson for removing a sliver from his wife's ear. Mrs. Johnson was notorious for pressing that ear of hers against the town's wooden walls. No rumor-monger she, Mrs. Johnson shamelessly professed to keep all material she thus collected to herself, save, of course, for when she religiously shared select tidbits daily with "just those women I can trust to keep things secret." Mrs. Johnson's ear kept us well stocked with salmon.

In the Peterson household, the same issue always arose: Mom would need money to pay a bill or buy something for us children, and Daddy would come home feeling enthusiastic about his treasured payment for the day, a six-month supply of earthworms. "Good for fishing," he'd say. Good for fishing, yes, but bad for keeping the lights on, or putting oil in the furnace, or making sure the kids were clothed, or making Mom happy.

One evening in my 10th year, as we sat at the dinner table, Daddy asked, "Which two of you want to take piano lessons?"

Silence filled the room. Toddlers Karl Jr. and Heidi were too young to be indentured as future concert pianists, so he wasn't addressing them, and infant Kary (yes, Mom had dropped another one) was younger still, so he was disqualified. That left my two older sisters and me as the unwitting, unwilling targets of Daddy's latest barter deal.

I tried desperately to turn invisible, but failed. I tried to make myself smaller than the bowl of soup before me, and failed at that as well.

"Okay," Daddy said upon hearing no reply from any of us.

Reaching across to the center of the table, he removed three toothpicks from their holder, broke them into different sizes and held them up in one hand with equal lengths showing above his clenched fist.

"You're the oldest, take one," he said, turning to Nancy.

Wearing a smile that betrayed both shyness and a sense of privilege, Nancy glanced around the table before choosing her *straw* with a flourish. I drew mine next, leaving Gayle no choice but to accept whatever fate the last remaining straw carried with it.

"Okay, Nancy, okay, Dickie," Daddy said, addressing the losing pair, "tomorrow after school I'll drive the two of you up to Mr. Thorstensen's house and introduce you to your new piano teacher."

"Piano lessons?" I whined. "That's for girls! Let Gayle take my place."

"You won," Daddy said in a righteous tone of voice. "Besides, I think you'll like it."

"Won?" I cried. "You mean I *lost*!"

"No, I mean you *won*," he replied with another of his mischievous looks on his face. "You don't *have* to take piano lessons, you know."

"Good!" I interrupted, feeling relieved.

"You *get* to take piano lessons," he corrected me, thus sealing my fate.

I passed the following day hoping Daddy would forget about the prison term he'd sentenced me to the night before. To my chagrin, right after school, I heard him calling out from the kitchen.

"Nancy, Dickie," he announced, "it's time to meet your piano teacher."

Great, just what I wanted to do! I thought to myself.

"I'm watching *The Lone Ranger*," I pleaded. "Can't we go after it's over?"

"Sorry, no, we need to leave now," he answered. "Mr. Thorstensen's expecting us."

Mr. Thorstensen's house sat perched atop Peacock Hill with a view that was nothing short of spectacular. From the front porch you could survey the entire Harbor area and see for miles and miles beyond—across Puget Sound to Point Defiance and further still, on to the eastern horizon where Mount Rainier rose majestically over emerald-clad mountains and hills. A rustic cedar shake roof topped the house, and weathered white clapboards sheathed its sides. A covered wooden porch 10 feet deep circled the Thorstensen home, and a worn gravel driveway led to the rear. There, noisy little stones formed a walkway that funneled visitors to the old, raised-panel wooden door on the back porch that served as the main entrance. White eyelet curtains framed the inside of the window centered on the door's upper half. Its glass pane extended far enough down that, with effort, a boy my height could peek in, just barely.

Daddy knocked on the door as, ever so curious, I stood on my tip-toes and peered in the window. I could see past the kitchen through a painted wooden archway into the part of the living room where Mr. Thorstensen was sitting. Hearing our knock, he closed the book he was reading, rose out of his rocking chair and walked slowly toward us. I backed away from the window as he opened the creaking door and warmly invited us in.

"Goot evening, Docta Petason," he said in a thick accent. "Please come in."

"Thank you," said my father. "How's your back feeling?"

"Much betta," Mr. Thorstensen answered.

As we stepped through the doorway and took off our coats, Daddy introduced us.

"This is my son Dick and my daughter Nancy"

"Zo nice to meet you children," he said.

As usual, shy, shy Nancy just stood there in her braided pigtails, saying nothing.

"Thank you, sir," I said, never shy and always ready with something.

"Zo polite," he said. "I zink vee vill get along yust fine."

We followed him into the living room where Nancy and I fidgeted on Victorian furniture only an adult would call comfortable while he talked about the further tortures awaiting us. This Mr. Thorstensen had moved to Gig Harbor while our Dr. Peterson was going to med school, and Daddy was curious about his background and why he'd chosen to live in this town of all places.

As the two of them talked about Mr. Thorstensen's Scandinavian background and other matters, my eyes wandered around the room, ogling the unusual objects and curios. In my reverie, only an occasional reference to piano lessons penetrated through my ears and into my consciousness.

Museum-quality antique furniture filled the house, and area rugs in colors and patterns that nicely complemented the rooms covered the well-polished hardwood floors. Artwork dotted the walls, surrounded by dark wood shelves that climbed to the beamed ceiling above. Every shelf teemed with books and personal memorabilia, making where we sat as much a private library as it was a living room.

Continuing their search, my eyes reached the front of the room where, facing the window, stood the most imposing piano I'd ever seen. Ours at home I'd heard Mom call an "upright." Only two feet deep and maybe five feet high—six at the most—it stood flush against the wall and required little effort to ignore. Mr. Thorstensen's piano, in contrast, had to be at least seven feet long and nearly that wide and totally commanded the space around it. A wing-like raised top revealed the piano's inner workings: rich, dark brown wood everywhere and row upon row of brass and silver-colored strings streching above a bank of hammers. Now *this* was a piano, not an *upright* piano or a *spinet* piano but a *grand* piano, the Real McCoy. This instrument no one could easily ignore, but I was determined to try.

Mr. Thorstensen showed us the book we'd be using and pointed out that he expected us to practice half an hour every day.

Half an hour a day! I worried to myself. *I can't do that! I play with the guys after school. No way Dad will ever make me take piano lessons and miss the after-school baseball games. Surely* this *will be the mark of Gayle's doom.*

They talked a while longer and, as soon as they reached an agreement, Dad told us to put on our coats. We exchanged the usual good-bye pleasantries and headed for home.

As soon as we were back to the car I started.

"Daddy," I said, "can we talk about this? You know, the guys and I always..."

"No!" he interrupted. "You won and you get to take the lessons. You'll like it."

"No I won't!" I said defiantly, as I spied Nancy's tongue sticking out of her smirky little face. Throughout the two-minute ride home I sat in silence with my arms folded and my eyebrows scrunched all the way down to my pouting lips. I was determined that I was going to hate these lessons and equally determined that everyone around me would enjoy every minute of my oh-so-pleasant attitude with me. In short, I was being a brat.

IT didn't take long for me to figure out a way to avoid the drudgery learning to play the piano entailed. I noticed that when Nancy came home from school, she did her homework first and then sat right down at the piano to practice, usually finishing about the time I arrived home from playing baseball or chasing frogs with my buddies. I discovered that if I stood behind her for a few minutes and watched carefully, I could memorize the keys she was playing and, through some sort of aural osmosis, pick up the rest by ear. By the end of the first week, when the time for my next lesson arrived, I could play the exercise as well as she. I didn't need the book, and I didn't need to practice except a little here and there. I quickly decided, *This piano thing is going to be a piece of cake.*

My lessons were on Saturdays, just after dark, and on clear evenings I rode my bike up Peacock Hill. It was a steep, hard climb, but I got to coast a thousand miles an hour on my way back down as I rode for home, satisfying my youthful, boyish need for speed. That made the hard work of peddling up more than worth the effort.

One momentous evening, several weeks into the ordeal, the weather turned cold and clear. So far, our lessons had amounted to little more than finger exercises. First, up five notes, down five notes, one finger at a time with the *right* hand, then, up five notes, down five notes, one finger at a time with the *left* hand. The first real piece Mr.

Thorstensen expected us to play was "Beautiful Dreamer," for which he prescribed hours of practice at home. Mastering this piece proved more of a challenge than any of the previous assignments. I had to actually learn a different sequence with each hand, put them together and make the result sound like the same melody Nancy was playing. Fortunately, Nancy required several lessons to learn the piece, and I found Mr. Thorstensen using most of my lesson times going over the lines and spaces on the sheet music. If you took music lessons you remember the routine: *E-very...G-ood...B-oy...D-eserves...F-udge....*

One evening, he wanted to see how well I was progressing. As Mr. Thorstensen sat down next to me on the piano bench, I opened the book and began to play. It proved easier than I'd expected, no problem at all. I'd listened to Nancy destroying the tune for weeks and figured I surely could do as well as she. I'd finished my debut performance and was starting to puff up with pride at my accomplishment when a weighty, pregnant pause stopped me. I waited, and waited some more, for Mr. Thorstensen to say something, *anything*.

"Dat vuz...," he finally began, his voice trailing off in search of the right word.

My heart pounded with anticipation, I felt the room growing hot.

"...unnnnbelieveable," he said at last, completing his sentence. He went on: "Vood you to play dis vonce again to me, please?"

"Sure," I said with an air of confidence.

I'm off the hook! I thought to myself. *I did it once, and I can certainly do it again.* The weight of the world suddenly lifted from my deceitful little shoulders.

I plunged right in and thought I was doing well until Mr. Thorstensen calmly stopped me from further torturing his well-developed ear.

"I vood like for you to please to shtart from measure 18," he requested.

"Oh? Did I make a mistake?" I asked, doe-eyed.

"No. But I vood like for you to shtart from measure 18, if dis is not too much trouble for you, Dickie."

Blood rushed to my face, turning it a guilty shade of red.

"That's okay," I gulped. "I'll just start over."

Before my hands could find the piano, he once again slipped his hand between the keys and my fingers.

"No," he said, "yust shtart from measure 18."

He raised his hand and pointed to the requested measure.

"Rrright here," he said with conviction.

"But, I can start over," I squirreled. The truth was, I had no idea which music went with what notes. I'd learned a pattern much like a politician learns a speech. If you interrupt the liar, he loses his place and has to start over.

"Rrright here," he said again. "Please."

I was so busted, I could do nothing but sit there with my eyes fixed on the book and my face on fire, burning with embarrassment, trying to appear like I was busy figuring out something important. Without turning my head, I snuck a look up at the clock.

Twenty minutes to go, I thought to myself. *Umm, too much time, can't find anything that important. What do I do now?*

The notes on the sheet were just a spattering of meaningless black dots to me. My mind raced in search of a new ploy to throw my mentor/tormentor off track.

Just then, Mr. Thorstensen got up from the bench.

"Git you coat und come vis me," he instructed.

Dutifully, fearfully, I trudged along behind him, having no idea what he was about to do to me. I followed him outside into the backyard and began to tremble as he turned on a flashlight and started down a walkway between two large green hedges easily 15 feet high. It was clear and dark and cold. I could see my breath as we walked and was beginning to wonder how much longer I'd still be breathing and capable of seeing the foggy looking stuff. We continued another 50 feet or so, without saying a word, stopping at last before a curious-looking mound covered with a tarp.

"Here," he said, handing me a corner of the stiff green tarp, "help me to pull dis back."

As we removed the cover, I saw what appeared to be a hole in the ground and wondered if he was planning to drop me in it for the remaining 20 minutes to teach me a lesson. Then I noticed something sitting in the hole—a big mysterious tube, about 12 inches in diameter and maybe five feet long. It was supported by a three-legged stand and had strange objects dangling from it. The tube swiveled in the middle and could also be tilted up or down. Mr. Thorstensen plugged in a long extension cord running from the house. Holding the tube with his left arm, he positioned it to where he wanted it.

"Dis is a telescope," he said in a calm and schooled voice. "Do you seeing dis lenz?" he added, pointing to an object on the side of the telescope.

"Yeah," I mumbled, my curiosity growing.

He slid a wooden box next to the telescope.

"Shtand on dis box," he said, "putting your eyes up to da lenz as you vood like camera und luke in dere, but careful not to touch da telescope vis your haands."

Cautiously, I did as he said. Putting my eye up to the lens, I was stunned, amazed and curious all at the same time.

"Wow!" I almost shouted. "What's that?"

"Dis is da planet vich is named Jupiter," he said in a scholarly manner.

Seen through the telescope, Jupiter appeared about the size of a dime held in your fingers at arm's length, whitish pink with light purplish stripes. Staring into the eyepiece, I couldn't get enough. He talked about the planet while I soaked in its magnificence.

"Vood you like to zee anoder?" he asked.

"Would I!" I exclaimed.

As I stepped away from the telescope, I looked up at the dark night sky and noticed a star that appeared brighter than any of the others.

"Is that star the one I was looking at?" I asked, pointing to it.

"Ya," he said, looking up, then pointing the telescope at another part of the sky. "But dat is not a shtar. Dat is a planet." He went on to explain the difference.

"A shtar is a ball of gas dat is burning. Da sun is a shtar. Planets, like Earth und Saturn und Mars, dey orbit shtars."

"Take a look a dis one," he said, turning the telescope back over to me.

Again I looked into the eyepiece.

"Saturn!" I said in a breathless whisper.

"Vedy goot. Zo, you know your planets, do you?"

"No, but I know what Saturn looks like because of the rings."

Saturn was beautiful—grayish, almost yellowish in color, with faint stripes running across its surface. Tilted forward, it looked like a Mexican sombrero, Mr. Thorstensen continued to speak, and I couldn't stop looking at the miracle in the dark sky.

"Saturn is a ball of gas like da sun," he said. "Howeva, it is not on fire. You cannot shtand on da surface. The rrrings are probably duurt und ice paaticles orbiting da planet. Most likely a moon or several moons dat collided into each aada und brrroke up into dese paaticles. But, we rrreally don't know vis all certainty."

He showed me a few other objects in the sky before announcing, "Time's up!"

I was hooked, and he knew it. With each new object he showed me, I had sounded like a monosyllabic wordsmith. "Wow!" "Oh!" "Gee!" "Man!" "Cool!" and "My!" comprised the full extent of my vocabulary at that moment.

"Zo, vat do you dink about da heavens?" he inquired as we covered his telescope.

"This is the neatest thing I've ever seen!" I answered excitedly. "I'd rather learn this...You know, I could call home and ask to stay a bit longer."

"No," he said as he turned and looked me directly in the eyes, "but I vood make you agreement."

"Agreement?" I said, wondering where this was leading.

"Ya. Every veek you know your piano lesson, I vill let you see in dis telescope vun night."

Oh, no! I thought. *Back to that torture again. How can I convince him to let me change my lessons to astronomy?*

"You don't deside rrright now. You vill let me know next veek."

As I helped him finish covering the telescope back up, I asked, "What if it's cloudy or raining?" I thought I had him there.

"Ve can make a mark in your piano book," he answered, "und I vill owe you a see on anoder evening. You vill dink about it. You betta get home, you ahh a little late and ve don't vant to vury your muda."

I didn't have to *dink* about it. I desperately needed to look in that telescope again. I wanted to know everything he knew about the mysteries of the night sky. I was stuck. My only choice was to practice that piano. From then on, I went up once a week.

"Do you know your lesson?" he asked me each time.

"I think so," I answered, somewhat confidently.

"Den let us begin," he countered.

My progress was slow, for my heart was not in the piano; my passion was the night sky. Mr. Thorstensen, however, was a clever man. After a few weeks, he could see I was doing my time like a prisoner in cell block number nine, and that Nancy was leaving me behind. He gave me marks in the book for night viewing, all right, but only out of compassion and as a way to keep me coming back. He saw something in that first "unnnnbelieveable" performance and was trying to stimulate and develop it.

"You have such a feel for da music," he'd say. "If only you vood shtudy."

One night after our standard opening exchange ("Do you know your lesson?"/"I think so."/"Den let us begin.") and subsequent time in the book, he stopped and looked straight at me.

"Vee vill stop dis lesson early tonight," he said. "I vood like to tell you a shtory vid de rrremainder of our time."

Stop early? Sounded good to me. No objections here.

He invited me to sit on the sofa as he walked to the wooden shelves and started looking through his records. In a calm voice he began telling me a story concerning Beethoven and a girl who was the inspiration behind his composition *Moonlight Sonata*. I'd gained so much respect for him that, despite his thick accent, I hung on his every passionate word, giving him my full attention. As soon as he finished his story of the unrequited love Beethoven was expressing in this sonata, he played a recording of the piece for me.

The music was filled with images of the story he'd just finished telling me. Note after elegant note was placed with such sensitivity and skill, the music painted a picture my imagination could see and my soul could sense. Through a rare and special gift from God, Beethoven had been enabled to express this creation. It touched something inside of me, giving me the impetus to breathe and wonder, *This is longhair!?*

In the era of Elvis and the Big Bopper, I was discovering that longhair classical music from centuries ago was more substantial to me than longhair rock 'n' roll music from my own time. Mr. Thorstensen had hooked me once again. Although I continued to attend fifth grade dances and listen to the latest Top-40 music, that day I set off on a journey that has taken a lifetime to bring me back to where I began.

Throughout that winter, at the close of each lesson, Mr. Thorstensen exposed me to symphonies, concertos, operas and sonatas—to an anthology of masterpieces and the inspirations that led to their creation. It didn't take long before I began hearing music in everything I experienced. I realized by having 50 symphonic musicians always playing in my mind regardless of time and place, I was never alone. For me, life had become a fully-orchestrated movie, and at times the sound was—and is—overwhelmingly moving. Nancy and I took lessons from him for the remainder of that school year. After that, I began to slowly fall away from structured piano lessons in favor of "making up" music according to my whim. I drove my sister crazy on the piano with boogie-woogie versions of Beethoven's *Für Elise* and assaulted her eardrums with the snare drum I played in the school band. Throughout the following summer, and for five years after that, I continued my pilgrimages up Peacock Hill, traveling down the paths of longhair music and astronomy with the extraordinary man who lived there. I treasured our unique friendship, loved to hear about the stories behind the music of the masters and loved even more to listen to his seemingly endless supply of longhair records. On clear nights, we viewed the stars in the heavens together.

On the surface—that seen by adolescent eyes—mine was an ideal childhood, a perfect mixture of a little music and astronomy here and there with baseball and fishing. Living in a small harbor town, going shoeless like Tom Sawyer and Huck Finn, swinging on the Tarzan rope with my step-father, a man I truly loved, Dr. Karl—beneath that calm surface, on a level better seen and understood by adult eyes, a separate, more turbulent reality prevailed. In that other world, the times were such that my mother was never really accepted by Gig Harbor. From the start, Grandma Ruby, Daddy's mother, disapproved of her precious little boy's selection of a bride. Once we arrived, it didn't take long for the news to spread about Mom being a divorcée and about Nancy and Gayle and me being stepchildren. Rumors worse than that were no doubt started and fueled by sweet little Grandma herself. Adult problems that started below the surface in time broke through to the top, became open wounds and festered to the point where not even I, with my rose-colored glasses, could deny them any longer.

After 10 life-shaping years in paradise, my idyllic, small town country life came to an abrupt end. My mother could deal with the bartering and endure the prejudice no longer. Being children, we gradually became accepted as home grown by the locals. However, eventhough Mom volunteered for everything from PTA Chair to heading the Historical Society, being a divorcée, she was never made to feel truly welcome. And thus, in July 1961, sporting another divorce, she packed up my two sisters and me and returned to the place where she felt most at home, Portland. Raising six children was expensive, and my parents decided my half-sister and two half-brothers would stay with Daddy in the Harbor. My sisters and me faced a big, ugly adjustment. We were moving to the Big City

Author, guitar and siblings, Gig Harbor

VERSE 1

FRESH from the straight-laced Eisenhower years of the '50s, the America I grew up with entered the '60s with a vibrant young JFK at the fore, our patriotic certitude unquestioned and our cultural rectitude a given. By decade's end, an assassin in Dallas had claimed our president, a war in Southeast Asia had shaken our confidence and convulsions in Selma and Watts, Birmingham and Chicago, Detroit and Cleveland had shattered our innocence. Somewhere in between came the Beatles and the Stones and a British Invasion, hippies and flower power and Haight-Ashbury, peace signs and protests, psychedelia and free love, Woodstock, Black Panthers and SDS'ers. In the critical moments when all of that was just beginning, the Kingsmen appeared with "Louie Louie."

In the '60s, as with generations of teens before and since, my generation came of age by flaunting our independence—shunning the old, worshiping the new, asking too many and too few questions. That muddled formula carried us through it all, though in our special case with profound changes that were both a blessing and a curse, changes that felt unique to us then and look much the same to me now.

In the '70s, it was the disco generation's turn to flex their muscles and turn the tables on us, which they did wearing polyester suits while dancing on lighted club floors beneath revolving mirror balls. What were they thinking? They were definitely speaking a different language than mine.

Oops. Here I go again, going off on a tangent and getting ahead of myself. It's time to return to my narrative.

AFTER leaving the Harbor for Portland, I buried myself in music. Throughout high school, I was a certified music geek, by all measures a square. To a man, my good friends were music freaks like me; we all dressed in the wrong clothes, sported unstylish haircuts, wore our belts in our jeans at the hip and drove our parents' sedans.

Clueless as to style and taste, I sat across the table in study hall from Shannon Burke. Popular and pretty, Shannon was far from the norm among her high school peers. Intelligent and nice, she actually spoke to those of us who occupied the bottom rung of the social ladder. Every school has students like us, I'm sure you know the type: *dorks.*

One morning in December 1963, Shannon sat down across from me in study hall.

"Don't you play drums?" she pleasantly asked in a whisper.

As if she didn't know. For the past four years, she'd seen me beat the tar out of them at countless school dances, assemblies, band concerts and lunch breaks.

"Why do you ask?" I quietly replied.

"Well," she said, "my boyfriend plays in a rock band, and their drummer was just drafted. They're looking for someone to replace him."

"Really?" I answered snobbishly, as though rock 'n' roll were beneath my calling.

Doesn't she realize, I asked myself, *I play TIMPANI in the Portland Junior Symphony?*

"I'm pretty busy these days," I softly continued. "I really don't know if I'd have the time."

She looked around to make sure no one was listening.

"Have you ever heard of *The Kingsmen*?" she asked in a soft voice,

She seemed to think the mere mention of that name would shake me.

"No," I whispered back, "I don't think so."

"What? Are you kidding me?" she exclaimed. "Why, they're the number one band in Oregon!"

"Oh?" I said, questioning her statement.

"Hey, they're really popular. They play every weekend!"

"Really?" I said, continuing in my condescending manner. "And just where exactly do they play?"

"Oh," Shannon responded, "they play at supermarket openings, at Lloyd Center Mall, at lots of stuff with KISN radio. KISN uses them for everything—dances, promotions, fashion shows, you name it—everything."

Like that was supposed to impress me. I was only into classical and some jazz; I'd jammed with a few friends who played rock 'n' roll, but I really wasn't into it; rock was nowhere to be found on my list of musical preferences. Then she spoke the sort of magic phrase that reaches the soul of every musician.

"Gee," she said, "they make at least 20 bucks a weekend—apiece!"

That caught my ear.

"Twenty bucks each?" I questioned. "Are you serious?"

I could fill my mom's car up with gas on six bucks, so that should give you some idea how far 20 bucks went in 1963.

"Okay," I coyly responded, trying to appear cool, "so what do I have to do to get the job?"

"Well, the band's holding auditions at my boyfriend's house this weekend. Take your drums over to his house and bash away! You know, jam with them for a while, see if you fit in."

"You mean audition?" I said. "Try out? I don't know."

Suddenly, she cut back in, still speaking softly.

"I told my boyfriend Norm all about you. He's the bass player in the band. I can set it up, I have the inside track. You can go in the evening after all of the other drummers are finished. That way, you make the final impression. You know Karen Duncan, don't you?"

Karen was another really, really nice, really, really great looking, really, really popular girl who went to our high school.

"Sure," I said, "I know who she is."

"Karen's going with one of the Kingsmen, too. His name's Lynn. He's the leader of the band. She thinks you're just the guy for the job too. Believe me, we both agree: You'd be perfect for their band."

"Why do you say that?" I asked, chuckling.

"Because you play loud, and they're *really* loud! Plus, they're just a bunch of nice guys trying to find other nice guys to play music with."

Wow! I thought. *She thinks I'm a nice guy? That's outstanding!*

"Okay," I said, giving in. "I'll do it. See what you can do."

"Great!" she answered. "I'll ask Norm to call you tonight."

Norm phoned that evening just as Shannon promised.

"Hi, Dick," he said. "This is Norm Sundholm with the Kingsmen."

He sounded old, like a college guy to me, more mature than the high schoolers I was used to.

"Shannon tells me you play drums and are interested in possibly joining the band."

"Yeah," I said. "Shannon was telling me that your drummer was drafted and you're looking to replace him."

"That's true," he said. "She tells me you're probably the loudest drummer on the planet. Have you ever seen us play before?"

"Sorry, no," I answered. "Maybe once, but there was too much chaos to hear you play. But I hear you guys are really loud."

I added the latter comment in an attempt to make brownie points.

"Yeah, I custom make all of our amps, and volume is something of a priority with The Kingsmen. You'll hear and see our equipment for yourself when you come over. How do you feel about Saturday night, say around 7:30?"

"Cool," I eloquently replied, relying on my older sister's hip vocabulary lessons.

Norm gave me directions to his house and, after a short conversation about equipment and some of the songs they played, we hung up the phone.

Filthy lucre, long green, bread, moolah, double sawbucks—call it by any name you choose—money proved a great motivation to me. For the rest of the week, all I could think about was the loot I stood to pocket and what I could afford to buy with 20 bucks a week. I found some catalogs and tore out pictures of musical equipment I planned to buy with my soon-to-be-acquired fortune. I left pictures of the drum gear I wanted to purchase lying all over my room.

For Christmas the year before, my mom had given me a brand new set of silver sparkle Gretsch drums with Zildjian cymbals—the best set-up money could buy. I had a hi-fi sitting right next to my drum set in the basement at home, and throughout the remainder of that week, every afternoon I went straight home from school, turned that baby up until the speakers were slapping the grill cloth, and bashed away, playing my drums along with every rock 'n' roll record I could borrow from my friends or steal from my sister's collection.

I had been dragged to an afternoon Elvis concert in Tacoma on Labor Day weekend in '57. The site was the picturesque Stadium

High School football field, and the stage was made up of two long flatbed trailers set side by side on the dirt track in front of the bleachers. When we arrived, Elvis's white limo was parked next to the stage, beside a small portable shack he used to meet and greet a select lucky few. I was impressed by the number of insane, screaming little girls and by one particular older girl—my mother. Mom and my sister Nancy were such rabid fans, at the end of the concert, when Elvis jumped from the stage onto the track and sprinted to his limo to evade his hysterical fans, the two of them raced on the track. I watched with great surprise as my mother reached down and grabbed a handful of dirt holding the impression of Elvis' shoe. She kept the treasured dirt in a small glass vial and gave it to me some years later. I continue to cherish my vial of the ground Elvis walked on.

Nonetheless, in 1963, when it came to rock 'n' roll music, I remained perhaps the most naïve and out-of-touch 17-year-old in existence.

NERVES nearly overcame me on the drive to Norm's house. I didn't know what to expect. To earn my position with Portland Junior Symphony, I'd had to audition, and I'd been involved in chair challenges in orchestras since fifth grade. But I'd never auditioned for a rock band before. I *had* jammed with a few friends and played a few dances in the school cafeteria in return for a pat on the back, but that wasn't the same as this. I was nervous, maybe even more so because I was beginning to actually *like* rock 'n' roll music. I found it fun to play, and the drum parts for the songs were not all that hard to learn—not nearly the same as trying to keep pace with the records I normally had blaring on the hi-fi, featuring jazz drummers like Charlie Persip, "Philly" Joe Jones, Grady Tate, Joe Morello and the unbelievable Buddy Rich.

It was twilight when my mother and I arrived at Norm's house. As I drove into the driveway, I saw several guys looking under the hood of a maroon Corvette. I was driving my mom's white four-door '62 Chevy Impala—not exactly the coolest of cars for a teenager to be seen behind the wheel driving. When I turned off the ignition, they all looked up at me and started to walk over to my car as I opened the door.

"Are you Dick?" one of them asked.

"Yeah," I answered, "and this is my mom, Lillie."

"I'm Lynn Easton," he said as we shook hands.

"Oh," I responded, "you're Karen's boyfriend."

"Yeah, and this is Mike Mitchell, Norm Sundholm and Barry Curtis."

As I was shaking hands with Barry, Lynn started opening the back door to my mom's car.

"Let's get your drums unloaded," he volunteered.

Shannon had told me that the Kingsmen were a democracy, but that Lynn was their leader and considered his vote a little more equal than those of his fellow band members ("All Kingsmen are created equal, some Kingsmen are more equal than others," if I may paraphrase George Orwell's famous line from *Animal Farm*). Having this image of Lynn already planted in my mind, I was surprised by his helpful gesture.

He looked like an Ivy Leaguer, and his blonde hair and button-down-collar shirt, pressed cotton trousers and friendly smile would've gotten him into any function at Harvard unchallenged. He was stout and slightly overweight, but presented himself well.

Norm's dad came out and took my mom in to meet the other parents, who were sitting in the kitchen.

"My directions were okay, I see," Mr. Sundholm said to my mother as they went into the house.

Normally, I was very particular about my drums and never let anyone else handle them for fear they might get scratched or damaged. If they were going to be marred by someone, I wanted that someone to be me. That night, however, I'd carefully packed my drums in black fiberglass cases, and I didn't mind or protest as everyone pitched in.

"Is that your 'Vette?" I said to Norm as we started unloading my drums.

"No," he said before correcting himself. "Well, it *might* be. I borrowed it from a dealer for the weekend. If I like it, I'll buy it."

"Looks pretty fast," I said.

"*Really* fast," he responded. "If I buy it, though, I'll put these new kind of tires on it. Ever heard of *radials*? They say they really stick in the corners."

Norm's priorities were those of a true teenager.

"Radials? I've never heard of them," I answered. "Is Shannon here?" I inquired, changing the subject.

"Yeah, she's in the kitchen with Karen and my folks."

Norm was a nice looking kid. He, too, was slightly overweight, but you couldn't properly call him fat. He had dark hair he combed into a pompadour and a well-carved dimple on each cheek that the girls really seemed to go for whenever he smiled. Norm was the electrical engineer type, sans pocket protector. He wore semi-thick black horn-rimmed glasses that incessantly slid down his nose. Norm constantly had to crinkle up his nose, squint his eyes and tilt his head back in order to see through his coke-bottle lenses. Whenever he did so, his front teeth would show, adding to his trademark mad scientist/Japanese guy look. He had two nicknames, *Jap* and *Ox*. You'll have a chance to figure out why as this tale unfolds.

Norm lived in Lake Oswego, a ritzy area on the south side of Portland, while I lived in north Portland on "the other side of the tracks." I'd assumed that, living in Lake Oswego, he had a great music room in which to practice. What was I thinking? There's a reason why people consider The Kingsmen the fathers of garage-band rock.

They piled my stuff in the Sundholm garage where all of their musical gear lay scattered about. *This is outstanding*, I thought as I surveyed their "studio." Oriental rugs overlapped each other on the floor and patchwork blankets hung on the walls—homespun efforts to deaden the sound—and microphone cables snaked in all directions at our feet. They had individual mics for each player to sing into; they had mics for the organ and sax; they had University PA speakers; they had a Hammond M3 organ; they had a rotating Leslie speaker unit to go with the Hammond; they had guitar and bass amps; and, next to the door that led to the kitchen, they had couches where their parents and girlfriends could sit and listen as the band rehearsed. In other words, they had everything a rock 'n' roll band could dream of having, *and all in their garage*. I decided that the couches were located next to the door so people could come and go without bugging the band.

"You can set up there," Norm said, pointing to the only empty space left in the garage.

"Okay," I acknowledged.

As I started to set up, I could tell they were quite impressed with my drum kit.

"Hey, nice drums!" said Lynn in a semi-surprised tone. "They look brand new. How long have you had them?"

"About a year," I answered. "Just wait until you hear them. They sound great."

"It doesn't look like you've carted them around much," he added.

They looked like that for good reason, for *two* good reasons, in fact. Whenever I transported my drums, I secured them in double cases. First, there was a set of hard-shell fiberglass *outer* cases which protected the drums from general banging around during transportation. Second, since the hard-shell cases were loose fitting, within them each drum was zipped into its own individual *inner* case made of soft canvas. These soft cases came lined with fleece-like material similar to what you find on the inside of new sweatshirts. Those soft-lined inner cases protected the drums from getting scratched while moving around inside the hard-shell outer cases.

Mike Mitchell was the first of my new friends to inquire as to my experience. He was, hands down, the best-looking member of the group. This tall, thin, polite, dark-haired teen was fashionably dressed with enough flashy jewelry to blind at first sight. Indeed, this young male fashion plate proved to be the Casanova/girl magnet in the group.

"How long have you been playing?" asked Mike as I continued to set up.

"Since fifth grade," I answered.

"How old are you?" asked Lynn.

"Seventeen," I answered. "How old are you guys?"

"We're all 19," said Mike casting a glance at his band mates.

I set up my drums facing the center of the garage. The large wooden organ was sitting to my left at a 90-degree angle with the Leslie rotating speaker cabinet separating us. Directly across from me, at the back of the garage, stood two of the biggest amps I'd ever seen. They were black, with dark white grill cloth covering the face of the cabinets. Each of them was at least four feet high, and they looked dangerously loud. This was entirely new to me, and I was properly impressed.

"Are those the amps you made, Norm?" I asked in disbelief.

He tilted his head in pride, exposing his front teeth and crinkling his nose as he surveyed me through his glasses.

"No," he answered. "Actually, those are just the speaker cabinets I made. They each have two 15-inch JBL D130's in a double-folded horn bass reflex."

Was that English? I thought to myself. I looked over at Barry, who was shaking his head and laughing.

"Don't feel bad," he said. "We don't know what that means, either. But whatever that mumbo jumbo is, it makes them loud."

Barry was the resident intellectual in the group. This thin, brainy, blonde-haired, average-looking boy had an agile sense of timing to his intellectual humor.

Laughing and pointing to the floor, Lynn added, "The amps are sitting down there on the floor next to the speaker cabinets."

"Yeah," Norm chuckled. "I can't put the amps on top of the speaker cabinets like everybody else does because the cabinets are so loud. The tubes don't like the intense vibration and they blow up!"

We all started laughing, and Norm seemed to get a strange, almost mad-scientist kick out of the whole proposition.

"Besides that," he added, with that crinkled-nose thing going on, "without some sort a shock mount, the amp would just vibrate off the cabinet and crash to the floor."

"Hey," he said, as though the proverbial light bulb had suddenly turned on in his head, "foam rubber might work!"

Norm's dad was standing by the door listening to our lighthearted conversation.

"Dad," said Norm, "hand me a couple of those foam rubber strips behind you."

Turning around, Mr. Sundholm picked up a few strips of foam rubber sitting on the shelves.

"You mean these?" he said, showing them to Norm.

"Yeah, that might work," said Norm.

The foam rubber pieces were each about two inches thick. Norm laid them across the top of the amp and cut them to the proper length. Next, he lifted the amp off the floor and set it directly on top of the cabinet. He then switched on the amp, which by now rivaled me in height. With that crinkly thing going on with his nose again,

Norm addressed the rest of us, wearing a satisfied smile.

"It'll take a second for the tubes to warm up," he said.

He took his bass out of a case that was sitting upright next to the monstrous black speaker cabinet and plugged it into the amp.

By this time I'd nearly finished setting up and was putting the last cymbal on its stand when Norm hit a note.

Booooooooooooooooooom!

Never before in my life had I heard *anything* that loud. It scared—no, *terrified*—me. The blast was so loud and the frequency so low, I not only felt the fillings in my teeth rattling, I felt like every cell in my body was separating. What it did to the garage walls, I'll leave to your imagination. For starters, think about the opening scene in the first *Back to the Future* movie where Michael J. Fox, playing Marty McFly, plugs his guitar into that giant amp, cranks up the volume and strums one note. The speaker/amp explodes, sending Marty flying through the wall. The scene that evening in the Sundholm garage was a prequel to that scene in *Back to the Future*. Maybe no walls were blown down that night in Lake Oswego, and maybe no one was sent flying through the air, but it was close. Now that I think about it, Norm Sundholm would've been a good stand-in for either of the movie's star's—guitar player Marty McFly or mad scientist Doc Brown—maybe not in appearance, but certainly in attitude.

For several moments, my brain went on vibrating inside my skull. I'm not kidding. I literally felt my hair being blown back by the wind created by the movement of the speakers. It was awesome.

"Well," said Norm as he lifted his head with his patented look, "the amp didn't move. Looks like that'll work."

The room broke out in laughter. Norm's mom, Astrid, came running into the garage with Karen and Shannon close behind.

"What was that!?" she frantically asked. "I thought the garage had fallen down!"

"No, Mom," Norm said, "I was just testing some foam rubber."

Totally innocent, deadly serious, from her own little world Norm's mother responded, "Oh, I didn't know foam rubber could be so loud!"

With that comment, we all broke up. It was exactly what was needed to break the ice. Once the room calmed a little, Mike started telling me about their show.

"We always start with '*You Can't Sit Down*'. Do you know it?"

"No, I don't know it," I answered.

"It's really easy," he said in an encouraging tone, picking up his guitar. "You start it with one big bang on the drums, and then we all play this…"

He played a couple of chords on his guitar—*dot. da. dit da.*

"So, it goes," he continued—*bang. dot da. dit da*—"then each one of us takes a 16-bar solo with a full turn around between solos. Want to try it?"

"Sure," I said, apprehensively.

Well, the truth was, Shannon had given me the title the week before, and I was all over the song. From the first *bang* we jelled. It was as though we'd been thrashing away together our whole lives. Playing rock 'n' roll with these guys was way more fun than anything teenagers like me ever got to enjoy normally. The joy of the moment shone on the rest of the guys' faces, too. You couldn't wipe the grins off of any of our faces all night long.

We were too loud to hear any mistakes we might be making. Besides, all that mattered to us was that we all started together and we all ended together. By our standards, that meant we were good. After playing each song, we all laughed.

"How can you play so loud?" Lynn asked me at one point. "I play the drums, and I've never heard anybody play the drums that loud before!"

"Yeah," Mike said, "I can actually hear the beat. That's incredible!"

What was more incredible to me was how loud Norm's amps were. It was like being hit with a wall of sound. I really liked it. These guys not only played loudly and well; they were *too fun* to play with. We popped every cut off and never missed a beat. At the same time, there was no structure to what we were playing. Yet we played as one mind all night long, making things up as we went along. I didn't want the night to ever end, I was having so much fun.

In those days, I stood five-foot eight and weighed about one-thirty soaking wet in my winter clothes. I started to laugh at Lynn's comment about my volume.

"It must be my thin wrists!" I exclaimed, holding them up for all to see. "No wind resistance."

Everyone laughed even harder.

About that time, Lynn said, "We have a gig at a skating rink next weekend and a dance for KISN radio on the following Wednesday night at Archeryland [a local indoor archery range]. If we can rehearse every night next week, and if you come watch us on Saturday, you should be ready to start at Archeryland. What do you think?"

I was thrilled.

"Cool!" I said as I looked over at my mom.

"Think I can use the car?" I asked her.

"I think so," she laughed.

Cool! I remember thinking. *Cool! Did I really say cool? I'll bet these college guys think that sounded stupidly 17.*

Norm chimed in, interrupting my thoughts.

"If you want to, you can leave your drums set up here so you won't have to pack them up every night after we've finished rehearsing."

"Fellas," said Lynn, "I think we've found our new drummer."

"Welcome to the Kingsmen," said Mike, offering his hand for me to shake.

I looked over at Shannon sitting on the couch. She wore a broad grin and was quietly shaking her head up and down in approval, obviously pleased. Barry and Lynn followed Mike's lead and, one by one, we all shook hands, laughing.

About that time Astrid yelled, "Pizza's here! Can you guys take a break for a few minutes and enjoy it while it's hot?"

Barry was the first to respond.

"Absolutely. I'm starving!"

As we started into the kitchen to inhale the pizza, Lynn asked, "Did Shannon tell you that we made a record earlier this year?"

"'No," I responded, impressed and curious.

"Yeah, we recorded it last spring, about eight months ago. Ken Chase and Tom Murphy at KISN played it for a while last summer. It did okay here in Portland, but nothing to write home about."

Lynn stopped by the door, reached in a box sitting on a shelf, pulled out a record and handed me a *free* copy of their song.

"'Louie Louie!'" I remarked. "Oh, I've heard this! My best friend John has this song by several bands."

"Yeah," Lynn answered, "it's been a pretty popular song with the kids around here for a few years. Every band has to play it. I can't wait to get back in a recording studio again. Recording is fun, and being on the radio gets us great gigs."

After eating, learning a few more songs and agreeing on practice times for the remainder of the week—as well as talking about maybe being good enough to record *hit records*—we called it a night.

As I drove home with Mom from my audition, I asked whether she was concerned about me traveling, and what would happen were we to score with a hit record.

She answered with perfect logic.

"If you guys record," she said, "it will take months before you'll have to travel anyplace far away like Seattle or Yakima. By that time, you'll be out of school. And besides, I don't think any of you know just how hard it is to get a hit record. I really don't see a problem. It looks like they're trying to make money and run the band like a business, and that's good. And, with KISN behind you guys, you should at the very least have lots of work through the summer. By then it'll be time for you to start college."

"They seem like nice guys, don't you think?" I said.

"They do," Mom answered. "And I like their parents, too."

"I wonder if any of them have ever been to a symphonic concert before," I said.

"Why do you wonder that?" she asked.

"I was just thinking about Mr. Thorstensen," I answered, "and what he'd say about me playing this rock stuff to make money."

"I think he'd be as proud of you as I am," she answered. "Music is music. You'll be doing what you love to do—making music. There's nothing wrong with that."

That night was unforgettable for me. I met four guys who became life-long best friends. It was also a night that completely changed the direction of the remainders of all of our lives.

𝄞 Verse 2

ARGUABLY the most talked-about recording session in rock 'n' roll history happened in Portland, Oregon the weekend of April 6, 1963 when this immortal, unforgettable, unintelligible version of "Louie Louie" was put to tape. [I'm sure of the date. It's written on the box containing the original master recording which I'm looking at as I write these words.] There are many accounts of the events surrounding "Louie Louie" and the first Kingsmen recording session. I've relived the scene on many occasions with most of those who were in the studio. One of the best times I've ever had took place with Lynn Easton, Mike Mitchell, Barry Curtis and Don Gallucci [the Kingsmen's keyboardist on the recording and later "Don" in the popular Portland band Don & The Goodtimes] just a few years ago. As the five of us sat in Don's living room in LA reliving old times, the subject of the "Louie" session came up. Don, Lynn and Mike, all of whom were there, began reliving that memorable day. I've often laughed my head off with the other band members reminiscing and reliving the countless stories and experiences this band of unlikely characters has managed to live through. Never before or since, however, have I laughed quite so hard as I did that afternoon as the tale unfolded. Based on the recollections shared that day, and on other anecdotes I've collected during my 40-plus years as a Kingsman, I offer this account of what went on in the studio that glorious day.

THE idea of cutting a record was first broached in 1963 between sets as the band took one of their regular breaks on an unusually warm and beautiful March night. If you've ever been in Portland in

March, you know that the weather then is normally unpredictable. Locals joke that "if you don't like the weather right now, just wait 15 minutes." There on the banks of the Willamette, you never quite know what the ocean breezes flowing up the Columbia River from the nearby Pacific Ocean are going to bring next.

On this particular evening, the band was playing for a dance at a roller rink. Lynn's dad came down to the dance wanting to share an idea that had been presented to him. After the second set, as the band was about to go on break, Lynn said, "Hey! Before you guys scatter, my dad wants to meet with the band for a few minutes. Can we all meet out back in five?"

"Sure," all agreed save one.

"What's this about?" asked Mike, setting down his guitar.

"A summer gig," answered Lynn.

"Hey, Lynn," Mike responded with a smirk, "did you check out Karen Powell? She really has a pit goin' on tonight."

"Yeah, God love her," Lynn answered, laughing. "Those Powell pits are dripping tonight! I don't think she's missed a dance yet."

"I'm going to say 'hi' to her and grab a Coke. I'll be out in a minute," replied Mike, always on the prowl.

Ken Chase, a DJ from KISN, had hired the band for that night and was hosting the dance. Mike ran into Ken at the candy counter, told him there was going to be a band meeting behind the rink to talk about a summer gig and asked if he wanted to join in. A few minutes later, the band and Ken gathered behind the rink.

"I have a friend," Mr. Easton started, "who's in the cruise line industry, and last week he told me their company is looking for a rock 'n' roll band to play on board one of their ships for next summer. He asked about you fellows and wondered if you'd like to cruise the Caribbean for a few months."

"Wow!" exclaimed Mike. "The ship has to be full of girls!"

"Yeah, in bikinis!" someone added.

Mr. Easton broke into a smile and continued.

"The money is pretty decent, and the fun factor is probably off the charts."

"Cool!" said Mike. "What do we have to do to get *that* job?"

"Well," said Mr. Easton, "we need to send my friend a professional tape recording so he can show the cruise line company what you boys sound like."

"Oh, great!" said Jack, "another good idea down the drain."

At that time the band was modeling itself after the Ventures—the Kingsmen circa 1963 were primarily an instrumental group, and vocals were more or less an afterthought. Jack Ely was a long-time friend of Lynn's and Mike's and was playing rhythm guitar in the band.

"Why do you say that, Jack?" Lynn responded, slightly annoyed, as the band usually was with Jack.

"Because we don't have a tape recording now, *do we*, Lynn?" snapped Jack.

"Now just hold on," said Mr. Easton, trying to keep the peace. "Ken told me about a studio downtown where you can record a few songs. It's called Northwest Recording Studio. I spoke with the owner, I think his name is Bob Lindall. Anyway, he told me his rate is $36 an hour."

Ken Chase interrupted.

"That would be great! You guys really do need to have an audition tape. I could do a lot more for the band if I had some tape on you guys."

"Yeah?" Jack responded. "Like what?"

"I have a friend in Seattle who owns a record company. I could send it to him at the same time Mr. Easton sends it to the cruise line company and maybe we could get him interested in putting out a record. I know I could get the station to back it. Hell, I'll push it to death on my radio show and you know T.M., Hart and Phillips will push it on their shows, too. They love you guys."

"How many hours does it take to record a tape?" asked Mike.

"If we're organized, we can do it in an hour," said Lynn. "We can record stuff we already know."

"Anybody got an extra 36 bucks layin' around?" Jack said comically.

"I'm more than willing to float a loan to the band until you boys can pay me back," volunteered Mr. Easton.

"Cool! Let's go for it!" said Mike.

"Next question is," Lynn said, "what do we record? What kind of stuff does the cruise line need to hear?"

"One of our Ventures songs!" said Mike with enthusiasm. "They always get a great reaction. Like 'Walk-Don't Run.' Everybody loves it."

"You gotta do 'Louie Louie,'" Ken suggested. "That thing always packs the dance floor and brings the house down."

"Really?" questioned Lynn. "Don't you think we should do something with a vocal?" [The group had always played "Louie Louie" as an instrumental featuring Mike on lead guitar.]

"I think we should do 'Jamaica Farewell,'" said Lynn. "It fits with the Caribbean thing, and the crowds like it."

"Yeah," said the usually silent bassist. "They like it because it's a slow song and they get to hold on to each other."

Everyone laughed.

"That would be a good one," said Mr. Easton, "and it has vocals."

"Yeah, Lynn's and Mike's!" said Jack with a hint of jealously.

"So, do the cruise line people want a vocal group?" asked Mike. "We're mostly an instrumental band."

"I'm telling you, 'Louie Louie' has to be done," said Ken adamantly. "It gets the best reaction all night. It's animal!"

"Yeah, but that's just because every band plays it," said Jack.

"Exactly!" continued Ken. "But not the way you guys do it. Your version is bashin'!"

"Well, we're the only band that does it as an instrumental," added Lynn.

"Well, it *is* Jamaican," confirmed Mike.

"I think you should do the vocal," suggested Ken. "Nobody's ever heard 'Louie Louie' outside of the Northwest, and certainly not the way you guys do it. 'Haunted Castle' would be a good one, too. That way you have a Caribbean song in 'Jamaica Farewell,' an original instrumental in 'Haunted Castle' and another Caribbean song in 'Louie Louie' that you kick the crap out of. If that doesn't get you the gig, nothing will. Those are the best three. Now, I've got to go. Let me know what you guys decide. But that's my vote—if I have one."

With that, Ken went back inside.

"Well, what do you guys think?" asked Mr. Easton.

"I have the record of 'Louie Louie' by the Wailers, and I know most of the words already," said Jack. "And I can get the rest of them down by next week."

"We all have their record," said Lynn, slightly agitated. "We learned the song from the Wailers' record."

"Hey, Ken should know," said Mike, trying to relieve the tension between the two bantering teens.

"Okay, it's settled," then said Mr. Easton. "Let's go back to work."

" 'Jamaica Farewell' Really?" said Mike as he scratched his head, walking back inside. "I still think a Ventures song would work better."

"Yeah, but 'Jamaica Farewell' has that Calypso thing I think that the cruise line is looking for," said Lynn as the two entered together. "And 'Louie Louie' is reggae. Those songs fit the Caribbean theme."

After the gig, while the band was packing up, Lynn told Ken he'd let him know what time this "recording thing" was going to happen.

"Lynn," Ken said, "I really want to be at the recording session. I know what sounds work best for radio and how to make the band sound right. You guys are ready to make a move."

"Great!" said Lynn. "I know we'd all appreciate your help and, besides, we're all kind of in this thing together, aren't we?"

"I'm in 'til the end," answered Ken.

As the week went on, the guys grew more excited about the possibilities that lay before them. Lynn's dad called the recording studio and set Saturday afternoon, April 6 for the fateful recording. Mr. Lindall, the owner of the studio, gave Mr. Easton the particulars.

"The clock starts from the second you start loading in your equipment," he explained, "and the clock doesn't stop until you've loaded it all out of my room."

"Okay," said Mr. Easton. "I understand, and I'll inform the band accordingly."

When the band arrived at Northwest Recording Studio, they found a set-up typical of such facilities built in the '50s: panels with acoustical sound tiles placed here and there on lathe-and-plaster walls. The control room had a mono tape recorder and a mixing board made up of large black round knobs that controlled the volume of each microphone. Unlike Hollywood recording studios, this Portland facility was designed and built to record things other than records. Despite its limitations, it was the best (and only) recording studio the city had to offer. Mr. Lindall, the owner, told everyone where and how to set up in front of their microphones, which, he informed the band, *no one* was allowed to move.

"Don't you think we should set up the amps and drums the way we can best hear each other, and then move the mics to the equipment?" asked Mike.

"No!" snapped Mr. Lindall. "I do this all the time, and I know where everything goes. The mics sound best right where they are. Put the two guitar amps in front of these mics on this wall," he said, pointing to the wall farthest from the studio door. "Put the bass amp directly across the room in front of this mic and put the drums under these mics by this wall." Pointing directly across the room from the drums, he added, "The organ goes over there. And please, *don't* move the mics. I've spent years getting them in just the right places. Believe me, that's where they sound the best. If you want something louder, move it closer to the mic."

Before he even finished his speech, the bossy engineer started to leave the room. "Take it or leave it!" summarizes well his attitude that day.

The guys looked at each other—intimidated and helpless and without options.

"What about the vocals?" asked Jack, setting down his amp.

Mr. Lindall stopped, turned around, walked over to the corner of the room and rolled out a mic—a U-87 on a six-foot boom stand—to the middle of the room.

"Put the singer in front of this. Singers can be anywhere. It's the instruments you should worry about."

"You're going to put the vocal in the middle of all of us?" questioned Lynn.

"You can put the vocal anywhere you like. I just told you, it doesn't matter." Raising his arms in the air as if to wash his hands of the whole mess, he started back into the control room, delivering one final message: "As soon as you guys are ready, we can run a test."

With eyebrows raised, the band finished setting up, then ran through "Jamaica Farewell" so that Mr. Lindall could hear the music and adjust the levels on his control board.

"Okay," Mr. Lindall yelled, "I'm ready to roll tape when you are. Somebody yell the take number into one of the mics before you count off so we can tell one take from the other."

"Okay," said Lynn. Turning to the others, he asked, "Did anybody talk to Ken?"

"I talked to him," said Mr. Easton, standing next to the control room. "He said he was going to be here."

"Shouldn't we wait for him?" asked Lynn.

"Better not," answered Mr. Easton. "The clock's running, and we only have an hour."

"Okay," said Lynn, "let's record 'Jamaica.' Maybe he'll get here before we move on to the next song."

"'Jamaica Farewell,'" Lynn yelled, "take one!"

"Stop!" yelled Mr. Lindall.

This band of novices invading his studio clearly knew nothing of recording protocol. The frustrated engineer turned stern instructor:

"*I* say 'rolling,' then *you* say the title and take. Then you count it off. You can't start until the tape is rolling!"

"Good idea," said Mike, breaking out in laughter, realizing the funny little man was right.

As soon as the moderately soft "Jamaica Farewell" was recorded, everyone started listening to the playback.

It was the first time the band had ever heard what they sounded like in a professional recording studio, and everyone was impressed.

"Sounds okay to me," said Mike.

"To me, too," said Mr. Lindall. Everyone seemed happy with the overall sound and performance.

"Let's do 'Louie Louie' next," said Jack enthusiastically. "I want to try out these words."

Their spirits renewed, the guys headed back into the studio to record the next song. Little did the band know, they were about to make history.

Pushing the talk back button, Mr. Lindall asked, "Are you boys ready?"

"Whenever you are," answered Lynn.

"We're rolling," said Mr. Lindall.

"Okay," Lynn shouted, "'Louie Louie,' take one!"

Since their rendition of the song started with a string of pounding chords on the Honer electric piano, the guys decided to go without a count off. They didn't need one—the song had one already built in.

Don Gallucci on the keyboard started the intro, and the band joined in with reckless abandon. Ken arrived half way through the first take and stood in the control room watching with a look of disgust on his face. As soon as the group finished, they could hear him yelling, "What the hell is this!?"

Don went to the control room door, opened it and stood there listening as Ken gave instructions to Mr. Lindall.

"There's not enough bass...The vocal's too loud...He stinks!" Looking over at Don, Ken added, "Why is Jack the one singing? I didn't mean for him to sing it. He sounds awful!"

"Well," said Mike, "he's the one that learned the words, and he sounds like that because he just had his braces tightened, and his mouth hurts."

"Oh, yeah?" answered Ken. "His mouth might be hurting him, but it's killin' me!"

"We'll turn him down, then," Ken went on. "It's the sound of the band that I really want, anyway. Which mic is his?"

At that point, Ken decided he should take control. As he reached for the knob to turn down the vocal mic, Mr. Lindall quickly grabbed his hand, interrupting the DJ.

"DON'T TOUCH THAT KNOB!" Mr. Lindall yelled. "It's taken me years to get these knobs set like this. I have them set perfectly. You're not the only ones that record here, you know. If you want less vocal, tell him to move away from the mic or raise the mic up so it doesn't get so much of his vocal. That's the only mic you can move. If you want something louder or softer, move it in the studio."

"Are you kidding me?" said Ken in disbelief.

"No, I'm not kidding you," answered the geeky engineer. "You can move that vocal mic or the amps, but don't you dare touch the other mics or my control board. I have other people coming in this evening and I can't lose these settings."

"Unbelievable!" said Ken in amazement. "What kind of recordings do you do here?"

"Mostly industrial recordings," Mr. Lindall answered innocently.

"Really?" responded Ken, shaking his head as he stomped to the door in frustration.

Ken stormed passed Don, who was still standing in the doorway with his mouth hanging open and a look of disbelief on his face.

"Close your mouth, Donnie," Ken said as he passed Don. "Let's go get it straightened out!"

With authority, Ken started suggesting a few changes.

"Turn up your bass!" he ordered.

"Up? I like up!" answered the more-than-willing bass player.

Walking over to loosen the boom stand holding the vocal mic, Ken raised it several feet into the air above the worried rhythm guitar player.

"And we need less vocal."

"Are you even going to be able to hear me?" asked Jack.

"Not if we're lucky!" joked Ken. "Try it again, and this time, play it like you would if tons of people were rockin' with you guys. We're making a hit here, boys."

With that, Ken returned to the control room.

"Rolling," said Mr. Lindall.

"Take two, 'Louie Louie!'" shouted Lynn.

Having Ken there gave the band much more confidence. After all, he knew what this process was all about, and he was going to make the recording perfect. With renewed determination, the band took off, crashing, banging and blasting away.

As soon as the band was finished, Ken yelled, "Great! I love it! What's next?"

"Wait a minute!" Mike said. "I made a mistake in the guitar solo. Can we do it again?"

"Yeah," said Lynn, "and a drumstick flew across the room just before the third verse!"

"Well, okay," Ken said, pushing the talk-back button, "but why don't you guys come in here? Let's listen to it first."

Mr. Lindall rewound the tape and in a concerned voice said, "It might be too loud for the tape. I didn't know they were going to play it that loud. They didn't play the last one that loud. We might have to turn it down and do it over."

"That's what I like about it!" said Ken. "It sounds out of control."

The band entered the control room and started listening to the tape.

When it came to his guitar solo, Mike grimaced.

"See," he said, "right there, I screwed up!"

"It goes by so fast, Mike, no one will even notice it!" argued Ken.

"Hello!" Jack jumped in. "Can't anyone hear that I started the vocal in the wrong place after the guitar solo? I lost my place and wasn't sure where to come in."

"Well, you guys certainly didn't drop the beat." Ken responded. "This sounds great. No one will ever hear any mistakes."

"Maybe you don't miss the sound of the cymbals when he dropped his stick," argued Mike, "but you can hear the mistakes in the guitar solo and the vocal."

"Mike's right!" agreed Jack.

"We better do it again," said Lynn.

"Believe me," argued Ken, "it all goes by so fast, no one will ever notice. Besides, it's a demo. It doesn't matter. The people hearing this are pros. They know the difference between a recording that's polished and a demo. I can show it the way it is, and the cruise line people will only listen once. The mistakes go by too fast for anyone to catch them. I say move on."

"How much time do we have left?" Ken asked, looking at Mr. Lindall.

"About 20 minutes," Mr. Lindall answered.

"And you still have two songs to record?" said Ken.

"No, answered Mike. "We recorded 'Jamaica Farewell' before you got here."

"Okay," said Ken, "how 'bout we do 'Haunted Castle' and, if we have time after that, we redo 'Louie?'"

"That sounds reasonable to me," Mr. Easton added, no doubt worried about maybe having to dig a little deeper into his pockets.

The guys agreed and returned to the studio.

"Bash it hard like you did 'Louie!'" Ken yelled after them.

It took less than eight minutes to get the instruments strapped back on and "Haunted Castle" recorded.

"Sounded great to me," said Ken. "Do you guys want to hear it back?"

"Sure," everyone agreed, setting down their instruments.

As soon as they'd finished listening to the take of "Haunted Castle," Lynn said, "I think it's a keeper."

"Me, too," agreed Mike and the rest of the band.

"You have about nine minutes," Mr. Easton said, "to get everything packed up and out of here."

"But what about 'Louie?'" asked Mike. "I really need to fix those guitar mistakes. Don't we have time to run it one more time?"

"Trust me, Mike," said Ken, "we can make the *real* record perfect. But, for right now, we have the demo we need, and it sounds so animal. It's fine. No one'll ever notice the mistakes. It's not like people will be analyzing the thing and playing it over and over or anything."

"It's just a demo, Mike," added Lynn. "We'd better get our stuff out of here. Our time's up."

"Well, as long as you think we have what we need," said Mike.

"Trust me, we do," said Ken.

"Is the vocal loud enough?" asked Jack.

"I think it's just right," answered Ken. "The thing sounds animal."

"I thought you wanted to play it on the radio," said Mike, still wanting another stab at it. "You can't play it like that."

"You're right, I do," Ken said, "but, until we record the real version, I'll use it as the background music for ads to your dances. That way, the mistakes won't come through."

"Okay," said Mr. Easton, trying once more to ease the tension. "I guess we're finished."

"But I really hate having a tape out there with mistakes on it," added Mike with a final objection, "especially guitar and vocal mistakes."

"I hear you, Mike," said Ken. "But, let's get a record deal and a cruise. We can record it better later. This is more than good enough for now. Besides, we're out of time."

The band hurriedly packed up and was out of the studio as the hour ended. Mr. Easton made his check out to Northwest Recording Studios for 36 bucks, and all was finished. Ken took the newly-recorded tape with him. To save time, he said he'd edit the tape, make copies of it for everybody at the radio station and bring the edited tape to rehearsal that night.

That evening, Ken hooked up a reel-to-reel tape recorder to the PA and played the tape in the garage where the band rehearsed. Oddly enough, it sounded live, and none of the parents caught the mistakes. As always, the good folks of River City were blind to reality when it came to their little darlings and their music.

Ken took the demo tape to Seattle and played it for Jerry Dennon, a friend who owned a record label, Jerden Records. Because 'Louie Louie' was already so popular with the kids in the Northwest, Jerry agreed to release it on his label. Jerry also liked the idea that Ken could help sell records by pushing it on KISN. Jerry and Ken also agreed to try to get a national label interested in the band. That's how the Jerden 45 ended up on a desk at Scepter/Wand, a record company in New York.

Jerry released the recording locally, mistakes and all, on his own label and Ken started pushing the record on KISN as being "hot off of the presses." The band had decidedly mixed feelings about the questionable, mistake-ridden recording being promoted in their territory. On the plus side, it was increasing the prestige and popularity of The Kingsmen.

Within a few weeks, Mr. Easton received word that the cruise line had turned them down. It was a big disappointment, but Mike felt vindicated—happy that they hated the tape as much as he did. He knew he was right about not wanting to send out a tape riddled with so many mistakes.

Around the time that disappointing bit of news arrived, the band had been talking about making changes in its musical direction. The news proved to be just impetus they needed to make those changes. Mike and Lynn wanted to add vocals and a sax to the mostly-instrumental band. They wanted to become more versatile, to be able to play the ever-changing Top-40 hits and to possibly expand their travel to cover more of the Northwest.

Through those early years, Lynn's comedic gifts and talent to emcee had become more and more evident to all. He was more comfortable in front of crowds and on the mic than he was behind the drums. With the exception of Jack, everyone wanted Lynn to front the band. Understandably, Jack was unhappy about the changes in direction. He was comfortable with playing rhythm parts in Ventures songs and was unsure of his ability to fit in with the changes the band was making. He finally announced that, since there was no longer the possibility of working for the summer on a cruise ship, he didn't want to be in the band any more—especially if Lynn was going to take over as lead singer and run the show.

All kinds of trash stories have circulated since the breakup about Lynn's alleged power trip kicking Jack out of the band, and about Jack wanting to go off on his own and form his own Kingsmen band. There are also stories about Lynn cheating Jack out of the name The Kingsmen. Those stories, all of them, are simply not true. Sure-enough there were arguments over the changes in musical direction and who was going to front the band, but Jack, not wanting to re-work the band in order to adapt to the changes in the industry, told the others in a huff that he'd been wanting to quit anyway. He was going to get married, he was returning to school to avoid the draft and he was growing tired of having the band come first in his life. No one tried to talk the disgruntled rhythm guitar player out of quitting. Several years would pass before Jack, after seeing our success with subsequent recordings, played in another band.

Shortly after Jack quit, Ken opened a teen club, *The Chase*, and the reshaped band happily worked in the club all summer long. Ken promoted The Chase and managed to push "Louie Louie" to the top of the local charts on KISN. Through June, July and August, the teen club was packed to the rafters with wild and semi-unnatural teens, gyrating to the beat of "Louie Louie." By September, the record had pretty much run its course in the Northwest. But forces were at work elsewhere that would change all that. Little did anyone suspect that by January '64, eight months after the tune was recorded, the platter would once again heat up due to a lyrical controversy thanks to Ken's production prowess.

VERSE 3

NOW that you know my take on that famous recording session, it's time to focus again on my participation in the "Louie Louie" story.

Starting the day after I passed muster at my audition, we practiced almost every night in the Sundholm garage. On one of those evenings we were in the middle of practicing our version of "Walkin' the Dog"—the smash hit by Memphis DJ Rufus Thomas ["Walkin' the dog"/"I'm just a-walkin' your dog"/"Well if you don't know how ta do it"/"I'll show ya how to walk the dog"]—when Norm's dad came in and said, "Hey, there's a strange guy on the phone who wants to talk to one of the Kingsmen."

"Okay," said Lynn, "I'll take it."

The rest of us took a break while he was on the phone.

Before too long, Lynn returned to the garage laughing.

"You guys will never believe this!" he said.

"Who was it?" asked Norm.

"Some guy who claimed he was with a bunch of students calling from the University of Alabama."

"Alabama?" questioned Mike. "What did they want?"

Lynn kept on laughing, so Mike tried again.

"What'd they say?" he asked, rephrasing his question.

"He was hilarious!" Lynn sputtered, barely able to speak he was laughing so hard. He went on.

"When I answered the phone, this guy's first words were 'Ya'll the Kangs-men?'"

Lynn's version of a thick southern accent started us chuckling as he continued.

"'Ya'll the ones that sang that "Louee, Lou-eye?"'"

That did it. By now we were all laughing.

"Are you serious?" said Barry with a wide grin on his face.

"'Louee, Lou-eye?'" Norm said. "Are you kidding me?"

We were breaking up.

"What did you say?" asked Barry.

"I played along," said Lynn with a grin. "I told him, 'Yeah, but we pronounce it a little differently. What can I do for you?' and he said 'Way-ell, we been a hear'n yer record in the doe-erm on the radio from Boston and cain't seem ta geet da words right. So, I've been designated ta be the one ta call ya'll and settle the bet.' So I said, 'A bet about what?' and the guy on the phone said 'Do ya'll say "Stick my bone up in her harr?"' Then I said 'What are you talking about?' and he said 'In da lass verse, don't ya'll say "Stick my bone up in her harr?"'"

By that time everyone else was shaking with laughter. I was laughing, too, but, being the naïve nerd that I was, I had no idea what our new friend from Alabama meant by "Stick my bone up in her harr." I pictured a chicken bone stuck in a ponytail and wondered why anyone would want to do that. It sounded like something tribal or a childhood prank to me. I didn't get it, but Lynn's fake southern accent made it sound like something that must be funny, so I laughed along with everyone else.

Lynn was chortling as he went on.

"I said 'No!' and then I asked him again, 'What are you talking about?' and this guy said 'Well, how 'bout in the second verse? "Ever night, at ten, I lay her again?"'"

Kingsmen were collapsing all over the garage floor.

"So, what did you say to this nut?" laughed Mike.

"Was he for real?" added Norm.

"I told him 'You're close,'" Lynn said, "'but that's not quite it!'"

Our collective ribs were starting to ache. I was laughing at Lynn's accent; the guys were laughing at the commentary.

"You don't suppose he was serious, do you?" said Barry, shaking his head in disbelief as he lit a cigarette.

"How did you leave it?" Norm asked.

"I asked him 'Who's playing our record in Alabama?' and he answered 'Woo Woo!' So I said, 'Yeah, right!' and hung up the phone."

Convulsions struck the lot of us.

"Really!?" Norm asked. "Woo Woo? I wonder how they got the record?"

"Who knows?" said Lynn. "It was probably someone from here in Portland playing a joke."

"You think so?" questioned Norm.

"Absolutely!" answered Lynn. "'Louie Louie' isn't even out on the East Coast yet, is it? Or in the South?"

"That's funny," added Mike. "I'll bet it was Ken just playing with you."

"You know, I'll bet you're right," laughed Norm. "We'll have to think of something to get him back."

But we were wrong, oh so wrong. The call wasn't a joke, and there really was someone out there crazy enough to call himself "Woo Woo." Baby boomers reading this who grew up in the Boston area, you know who that was. Five baby-boomer musicians from Portland soon found out.

IN the '50s and '60s, the young in every major city had a favorite DJ or two whom they idolized. Portland and Boston were no exceptions. Out in the Rose City, teens tuned in to Ken Chase and Tom Murphy and Roger Hart and Mike Phillips and The Real Don Steele at KISN to keep them jumping, while back in Beantown, the city's airwaves were ruled by an anarchic weirdo ensconced in the control room at WMEX radio. Given his antics and influence and wit, Arnie "Woo Woo" Ginsburg deserves a spot in the pantheon of all-time great disk jockeys, right up there alongside Alan Freed, Wolfman Jack, Cousin Brucie, Hunter Hancock, Dick Biondi, Porky Chadwick and all the rest of that lunatic breed. He certainly gets the Kingsmen's vote.

Record promoters hoping to score a hit with a new release worked the DJ star system as best they could. Everyone knew that certain jocks in certain markets could "make" a record if they decided to push it. Pat O'Day at KJR in Seattle was one of them; another was Murray ("Murray the K") Kaufman at WINS in New York; and still another was this Arnie "Woo Woo" Ginsburg character at WMEX in Boston. Courtesy of Ken Chase's connections, the Kingsmen's version of "Louie Louie" had made it to wax on Jerry Dennon's Seattle-based Jerden label. Ever the entrepreneur, Jerry had managed to land a copy on Ginsburg's desk and, through the unlikeliest series of circumstances, Arnie was soon playing the record to death on WMEX.

Arnie's show reached all up and down the Eastern Seaboard. He was what was known in those days as a *book banger*. On the air, he blew whistles, rang cowbells, banged on drums, tooted his trumpet, pounded phone books on desks and did whatever else he could think of—and get away with—to excite his listeners.

One of Arnie's cleverest gimmicks was a half-hour segment of his show he called "The Worst Record of the Week." Arnie would listen to all the new releases sent to him by the different record companies and single out those he thought were the worst of the lot. Then he'd match them up against each other on air and ask his listeners to phone in their votes on which one they judged the worst. Come time for the next Worst Record contest, the reigning "champion"—that being the record that got the most phone-in votes from his listeners during the previous segment—was pitted against a new challenger. Whatever record won that vote continued on to face another new challenger in the next round, and so on and so on and so on.

What the gentleman who phoned from Alabama had failed to tell Lynn was that "Louee, Lou-eye," as he called it, was being played over and over again on Ginsburg's show, and that for weeks it had been successfully defending its title as champion Worst Record of New England.

Have you ever hated a record the first time you heard it; and then, after it gets played so much, before too long you start liking it; and then you continue hearing the record so often, you eventually end up loving it? Well, that's essentially what happened in Boston. After enough Kingsmen victories, it became camp to vote for "Louie Louie," and soon Woo Woo had to call Jerry in Seattle and ask him when the record would be released in Boston. He explained to Jerry that "Louie Louie" was making such a stir, WMEX was being swamped with inquiries from fans wanting to know where they could buy the horrible thing.

Jerry told Woo Woo that Jerden was just a small local record company, but that a major company, Scepter/Wand in New York, would soon be releasing "Louie Louie" nationally on their Wand label. Arnie told Jerry that he knew someone at Scepter/Wand. He promised he'd call his friend, VP Marvin Schlackter, and find out from him how soon the record would be hitting store shelves in Boston.

As promised, Woo Woo called Marv and told him about the conversation he'd just had with Jerry. He explained the amazing action that "Louie Louie" was getting, and Marv responded that the record in question would be out in a few days and asked that Woo Woo "just keep the fire burning." When Marv hung up the phone, he did so feeling a bit discombobulated. He hadn't the foggiest idea what Woo Woo was talking about, but whatever it was, he and Scepter/Wand were going to try to take advantage of it. Immediately, he called his assistant into his office and asked, "Do you remember a record that Jerry Dennon sent me a while back, 'Louie Louie?'"

"I think so," she replied. "But, if I remember it right, I think we hated it. Why do you ask?"

"The damn thing is taking off in Boston," Marv answered, "and Arnie is pushing the hell out of it. And Jerry Dennon told him *we* were releasing it. Find it and get this Jerry guy on the phone. We'd better try to pick it up."

Within minutes Jerry and Marvin cut a deal and Marvin scheduled a pressing. (And what a deal it was—Jerry got peanuts and the band got the shells.) About that time, Marvin's assistant found the record Jerry had sent. They put it on the record player to listen to it.

"What the hell is this?" asked Marvin. "Are you sure this is the record Woo Woo is talking about?"

"Yeah," she said, reading from the record. "That's 'Louie Louie' by The Kingsmen on Jerden—and that's Jerry Dennon's label."

"I just made a deal for that. Get Arnie on the phone," Marvin ordered.

"Arnie," questioned Marvin as he played the intro over the phone, "is this the record we're talking about?"

"That's it!" said Arnie. "Isn't it great?"

"You've got to be kidding!" responded Marvin.

"Why, isn't that the record you're releasing?" asked Woo Woo.

"Sure, that's the one. Just checking. Looks like everyone's talking about this record. We'll get it up there by next week. Just keep it goin'."

"Keep it going?" answered Arnie. "Who could stop it?"

In less than a week, freshly-minted copies of "Louie Louie" arrived at record stores in New England, where sales soon skyrocketed. At that point, Jerry told the band about his new record deal with Scepter/Wand and said he wanted to get the band in the studio as soon as possible to take advantage of the sales we were now getting in New England.

Not long after that, a couple of Hoosiers attending the University of Alabama headed north to Indiana to spend Christmas vacation at home. There they met up with some high school friends who were attending college in Boston. The conversation between them found its way to cool records and, naturally, "Louie Louie" came up. As fate would have it, the students from Boston just happened to have a copy of the record, and all too quickly the group of college friends found themselves gathered around a 45 RPM record player trying to agree on the words of the obscene lyrics the students from Alabama insisted were contained in the recording.

That evening, when one of the boys returned home, his mother asked him what he'd done with his day.

"I was at Pete's house," he said. "A bunch of us got together over there and spent most of the time trying to decipher the lyrics on a record."

"Oh?" questioned his mom as she continued peeling a potato for that night's dinner.

"Yeah," he replied. "I hear the record on the radio constantly in Boston, but I didn't know it was full of dirty lyrics. They're so garbled, they're really hard to understand."

"It's no wonder," his mother answered, laughing. "The records today all sound the same to me. We had a few like that in my day, too. Popular records contained little messages. We all knew what they were talking about, but our parents didn't. Like '23 skidoo.'"

"No, I'm not talking about code here," he said. "I'm talking about blatant, hard-core profanity."

"You mean indecent obscenities!?" she asked in shock.

"Yeah," he replied, slipping his finger in and out of his relaxed fist. "You know, openly talking about putting you-know-what into you-know-where!"

"WHAT!?" she exclaimed in anger and shock, dropping her potato into the kitchen sink.

"Sure, they even say the *f*-word right on the record."

"What's this record called?" she asked, now in a rage.

"'Louie Louie,'" he replied.

"How did Pete ever get hold of a record like that?" she asked in disgust.

"It's really big in Boston," he said. "I didn't even know it was dirty."

"You mean IT'S ON THE RADIO?" she queried.

"Yeah!" he answered.

"We'll just see about that!" she huffed, wiping her hands on her apron.

In a tizzy, she got on the phone and started calling other parents in her church group to tell them about this obscene record that their children were being exposed to on the radio. The wheels of the gossip mill started turning, sending rumors flying in all directions.

Eventually, a copy of what the students thought were the genuine lyrics made its way into the hands of this outraged, potato-peeling, politically well-connected, Christian mother. She personally called the Governor of Indiana, Matthew E. Welsh and, with the backing of a few additional outraged parents, demanded that he ban "Louie Louie" from being played on the radio in their state—this, despite the fact it wasn't yet on the air in Indiana.

Capitulating to pressure from outraged political contributors, on January 14, 1964 Governor Welsh quickly placed a ban on the record. As news of his action spread like wildfire via the AP and UPI wire services, the amplified sound of an electric piano chord could be heard around the world—*da, duh duh duh*. By the next morning "Louie Louie" was the topic *du jour* on national news. Curious young minds nationwide began wondering what this song was all about, while serious old minds in Washington, DC—in particular in the offices of the FCC and the FBI and J. Edgar Hoover himself—began wondering what could be done to stem this tidal wave of indecency before it was too late.

And so it happened: A record by all rights destined to die an insignificant death now spread across the country like wildfire, fueled by rumors and speculation. It took only a few hours for Boston to learn about the controversy. Did that stop sales? Nooooo. *Au contraire, mon ami*, record stores there sold out of copies of "Louie Louie" as fast as they could get them in. Meanwhile, in Indiana, certain merchants thumbed their noses at the authorities and started selling copies under the counter in brown paper bags by the thousands. The more kids were denied the record, the more they absolutely had to possess this object of their wicked desires.

WLS-Chicago was a federally-licensed, Class IA clear channel station, in 1963–64 beaming 50,000 glorious watts of rock 'n' roll power on its own exclusive frequency across the length of the Midwest corridor with barely a small rolling hill to interrupt their signal. Back during the administration of Herbert Hoover, the federal government had originally authorized a select handful of "clear channel" stations with the idea that their signals would reach isolated listeners in remote rural areas who lacked local stations of their own and thus would otherwise have been denied the opportunity to share in radio's benefits. What would those federal regulators of yore have said had someone told them then that 30 or so years later those same clear channel stations would become the primary mechanisms for spreading the secular gospel of rock 'n' roll and the vulgar lyrics of "Louie Louie?" Surely, this was not what they'd had in mind.

WLS-Chicago could be heard as far south as Mexico, and Indiana to the east was a whole lot closer than that. So, although "Louie Louie" could not be legally broadcast on a radio station operating *within* Indiana's borders, across the state line in Illinois, WLS took up the banner instead and gleefully filled the pristine Indiana air with the unclean, demonic strains of "Louie Louie." Legions of the righteous in Indiana at last had something other than basketball to get excited about, and they were furious about "Louie Louie." Something had to be done.

VERSE 4

FAR removed in place and mind from the growing controversy, at the precise moment Governor Welsh was freaking out, we were in Seattle at the studios of Audio Recording working with Jerry Dennon on the album he'd suggested. We were nearing the end of the session when Jerry suggested a break. He said a reporter from the *Post-Intelligencer*, Seattle's morning newspaper, wanted an interview and was on his way down to the studio. We were excited someone from a newspaper actually wanted to interview us, and Jerry thought it would be a good PR move. When the reporter arrived, we invited him to join us in the studio. As we gathered around him, he began.

"I'm sorry to interrupt your recording session, but we're running a story tomorrow about the ban on your record in Indiana, and I was wondering if I could get a comment from you boys."

We were stunned. We had no idea what he was talking about. We stared at him in disbelief. It sounded like we were in some kind of serious trouble.

"Comment about what?" asked Norm.

"About 'Louie Louie' being banned in Indiana," he answered.

"We don't know anything about it," said Lynn.

"What are you talking about? It's not even on the air in Indiana," added Jerry.

"Well, it's all over the wire that the governor of Indiana has banned your record 'Louie Louie' from being sold in stores or played on the radio in Indiana," responded the reporter.

"Are you kidding me?" said Norm.

"Why would he do that?" asked Mike.

"You mean, you don't know?" questioned the reporter, appearing surprised.

"No!" we all insisted.

"Well," he continued, "according to the wire report, it's all about the lyrical content."

"Yeah, so, what about it?" asked Lynn.

"It's been reported that you guys sing dirty lyrics on the record."

"What!?" we all said in unison and shock.

"You mean you *didn't* sing dirty words on 'Louie Louie?'" he asked.

We looked at each other in wonderment, not knowing what to say. The reporter broke the silence.

"Look, if I can get a comment, maybe we can get this all straightened out. I mean, I can write your comments in the article and we can send it over the wire. What do you think?"

"We've got to find out more about this," said Mike. "That thing has a ton of mistakes on it. I can't believe it's getting this kind of attention."

"Why don't you guys follow me down to the *P-I Building* to read the reports coming in over the wire?" the reporter suggested. "We can take it from there."

We were pretty much finished with the recording session anyway, and who could concentrate on music after hearing news like this? So we called it a night. As we packed up our gear, a *P-I* photographer shot a few pictures of us loading our equipment into the trailer. On the way to the *P-I*'s digs on Fifth Avenue, Norm had the foresight to suggest that we say nothing until we knew more about the situation and could ask our parents for advice.

"Do you guys remember that guy from Alabama that called about dirty lyrics a few weeks ago?" Mike asked.

"Do you think he was for real?" asked Barry.

"I didn't until now," laughed Norm nervously.

"Hey, I wouldn't worry about it," said Lynn, refusing to believe the situation. "We haven't done anything wrong. We'll get it straightened out. There must be some sort of mistake."

We followed the reporter back to his office, trying to figure out how best to extricate ourselves from this mess. Once inside, he brought us the wire reports, one after another after another. We were amazed at how quickly people from all over the United States were responding. The comments came mostly from irate parents and church groups. Every once in a while, a report came in about some radio station somewhere that decided to buck the system and exercise its right to free speech by starting to play the record now that it was banned. Peppered with questions by the press, we made a statement denying all accusations of wrong-doing and responded to all questions with a "no comment."

Loading our U-Haul trailer in Seattle, January 1964

The next morning, completely exhausted, we decided to drive our station wagon and rented U-Haul trailer back to Portland. Through four tension-filled hours on the road, we did our best to project an air of false bravado, constantly breaking out in laughter, telling ourselves this had to be a joke, assuring one another people couldn't really be thinking we'd done what they accused us of and wondering silently to ourselves *How can something like this happen to us?* As each of us arrived home, the same scenario played out: Worried parents met their weary son in the driveway, asking a thousand questions while a noisy phone jangled unanswered in the background. When we reached Norm's house, we learned that the FCC and the city of Boston had joined the list of those banning "Louie Louie."

Banned in Boston! The Kingsmen had arrived, and Scepter/Wand couldn't have been more pleased. Their record presses were in full production and the delivery trucks were rolling. Within a few days, the William Morris Agency offered us a national tour while reporters and talent agents by the dozen continued to pursue us at all hours of the day and night. We plighted our troth to WMA—an easy decision there—and, seemingly overnight, Bob Ehlert in their Chicago office threw together an initial 8-week tour for us. After a week in California, we were to head east to cover the Midwest states and a patch of New England in the remaining seven weeks.

"Too much, too soon" is one way to describe the whirlwind of events now swirling around us. Greenhorns when it came to the ways of the world, we tricked ourselves into believing that our press interview in Seattle with *The Post-Intelligencer* asserting we'd done nothing wrong would solve all of our problems.

An icon like J. Edgar Hoover, a man accustomed to taking down gangsters and kidnappers and spies, was not going to let disclaimers made during a press interview in far-off Seattle deter him from pursuing his particular brand of moral justice at our expense. He declared he was going to personally conduct the investigation into the sordid lyrics of "Louie Louie" and the crass malfeasance of the Kingsmen. He directed his underlings to find out where and when we were performing and ordered local FBI offices to have agents in attendance at every show. He demanded first-hand reports on this group that was brazenly doing so much to corrupt the youth of America. His aim was to use the FBI to build a case against us for the FCC. He figured the commissioners could then use his evidence to ban us nationwide. He no doubt also dreamed of prosecuting us for public indecency. Hoover had no intention whatsoever of sitting still and allowing miscreants like the Kingsmen get away with singing indecent songs. Not in his country, not on his watch, not if he could help it. So much for the illusory power of telling the truth to the press.

70 ♪ LOUIE, LOUIE

```
                Airtel                              3/16/64

         To:   SACs, Indianapolis    (Enclosures 4)
                     Tampa           (Enclosures 4)

         From: Director, FBI

         UNSUB;
         PHONOGRAPH RECORD
         RECORDED BY THE KINGSMEN
         ENTITLED "LOUIE LOUIE"
         ITOM

              Enclosed herewith for information of Indianapolis
         and Tampa are two copies each of a self-explanatory letter
         received at the Bureau from the Department wherein they
         request that ▓▓▓▓▓▓▓▓▓▓▓▓▓▓▓▓▓▓▓▓▓▓▓▓▓▓ be
         interviewed concerning a letter he wrote to the Department
         on 1/30/64 indicating that he had examined a phonograph
         record that had been purchased by his daughter entitled,
         "Louie Louie" and found same to be obscene. Two copies of
         ▓▓▓▓▓▓▓▓ letter to the Department are also enclosed for
         information.

              The Department has requested that they be advised
         of results of current investigation being conducted in
         Florida where a similar record was reported as being obscene
         by ▓▓▓▓▓▓▓▓▓▓▓▓▓▓▓▓▓▓▓▓ at Sarasota, Florida,
         Tampa case entitled "Unsub; Phonograph Record 'Louie Louie'
         Distributed by Limax Music, NYC, ITOM."

              Indianapolis at ▓▓▓▓▓▓▓▓▓▓ interview ▓▓▓▓
         ▓▓▓▓▓▓▓ and obtain any evidence he might have that would
         indicate the record "Louie Louie" to be obscene and thereafter
         present facts to local USA to determine if he would entertain
         prosecution for violation of the ITOM Statute.

              Tampa expedite investigation at Sarasota, Florida,
         concerning the record "Louie Louie" and make extra copy

                                    SEE NOTE PAGE TWO
```

1964 FBI letter referencing irate parents stating "the investigations were dropped." As you will see, they continued for another 18 months.

Airtel to SACs, Indianapolis
              Tampa
Re: UNSUB; PHONOGRAPH RECORD

of your report available to Bureau for dissemination to the Department. For information of Indianapolis, the Department recently received a copy of the record "Louie Louie" from ▓▓▓▓▓▓▓▓▓▓▓▓▓▓▓▓▓▓▓▓ with a request that it be reviewed to determine if it was of an obscene nature. The Department advised that they were unable to interpret any of the wording in the record and, therefore, could not make any decision concerning the matter and were so advising the individual who made the record available to them for review.

For further information, an UPI release dated 2/12/64 indicated that the "Government had dropped investigations it had been conducting into complaints that a popular rock-and-roll record has obscene lyrics.

"The complaints charged that the record "Louie Louie," as recorded on the Wane Label by the Kingsmen, had off-color lyrics which could be detected when the 45 r.p.m. platter was played at 33-1/3 r.p.m.

Investigations of the record were started by the Federal Communications Commission (FCC), the Post Office and Justice Departments after complaints were received from about a half dozen persons, including Indiana Governor Matthew E. Welsh.

"All three Governmental agencies dropped their investigations because they were unable to determine what the lyrics of the song were, even after listening to the records at speeds ranging from 16 rpm to 78 rpm."

NOTE: ▓▓▓▓ Department in receipt of letter from ▓▓▓▓▓▓▓▓ ▓▓▓▓▓▓▓▓▓▓▓▓ complaining that record "Louie Louie" being sold locally and believed to be obscene. Department desires ▓▓▓ interviewed to verify that record lyrics are obscene. Department also requested that they be advised of results of investigation being conducted by the Tampa Office regarding similar record where ▓▓▓▓▓▓▓▓▓▓▓▓▓▓▓▓▓▓▓▓ Sarasota, Florida turned over copy of record to local authorities with obscene lyrics for same. Investigation being conducted by Tampa and Indianapolis Offices to determine if ITOM violation exists.

72 ♪ LOUIE, LOUIE

Mr. Robert F. Kennedy
Attorney General USA
Washington, D.C.

R— January 30, 1964

FEB 7 1964

CRIMINAL DIVISION

Dear Mr. Kennedy:

Who do you turn to when your 'teen age daughter buys and brings home pornographic or obscene materials being sold along with objects directed and aimed at the 'teen age market in every City, Village and Record shop in this Nation?

My daughter brought home a record of "LOUIE LOUIE" and I, after reading that the record had been banned from being played on the air because it was obscene, proceeded to try to decipher the jumble of words,
The lyrics are so filthy that I can-not enclose them in this letter.

This record is on the WAND label # 143-A and recorded by The KINGSMEN "a Jerden Production by Ken Chase and Jerry Dennon" and there is an address 1650 Broadway New York, N.Y.

I would like to see these people, The "artists", the Record company and the promoters prosecuted to the full extent of the law.

We all know there is obscene materials available for those who seek it, but when they start sneaking in this material in the guise of the latest 'teen age rock & roll hit record these morons have gone too far.

This land of ours is headed for an extreme state of moral degradation what with this record, the biggest hit movies and the sex and violence exploited on T.V.

How can we stamp out this menace? ? ? ?

Yours very truly,

ALL
b7C
b7D

145-2961-4

FEB 4 1964

CRIMINAL-GEN. CRIME SEC.

1964 FBI files. Letter to Robert Kennedy from a furious parent. Printed through the Freedom of information/Privacy Act Section 202-324-5520

Second to J. Edgar Hoover and his FBI minions as nemesis, our other bane was an unsympathetic press corps. As the controversy surrounding us continued to boil, negative press coverage abounded, far outweighing anything positive that was being written or said. Nonetheless, at the same time, more and more stations began playing "Louie Louie" more and more often, and all the while record sales soared. We were so out of the loop hanging around in Portland, little did we understand that all those hostile forces lined up against us, and all the negative press they churned out, ultimately proved a blessing not a curse. In the upside-down world of "Louie Louie," bad was good, very good indeed.

In 1961–63, "Louie Louie" became a regional phenomenon in the Northwest. Various local artists, such as Paul Revere & The Raiders, Little Bill & The Blue Notes and The Wailers, tried to take their versions national, and failed. In particular, Pat O'Day at KJR-Seattle loudly tooted the Wailers' horn, to no avail. No one succeeded, until the Kingsmen.

We'd never have gotten the airplay and publicity we did had people said nice things about us. Nor would the William Morris Agency have sent us out on an 8-week national tour. Remaining self-delusional for as long as possible, we continued to tell ourselves that "Louie Louie" was receiving the attention it did out of its intrinsic merits, and that the resultant mass recognition we'd garnered warranted a tour. We deemed ourselves ready for the road and decided to take advantage of all the attention coming our way. Hitting the campaign trail would also boost sales of our new album.

Lynn called a meeting at Norm's house to fill in the band and our parents on our options. He proposed leasing a brand-new Pontiac station wagon and renting a U-Haul trailer and a car top carrier for this tour. He said that once we got to our first stop in California, we'd find a professional show biz photographer in Hollywood to take a new promo picture for us. Now that we had a hit record, we needed a professional picture of the band. That sounded exciting to me.

Norm promised that he'd build a new set of amps in time for the tour. He said we'd need to have the trailer in hand far enough in advance to allow him time to work out a procedure for safely packing the Hammond organ, drums, guitar amps and PA. We decided that, with the five of us riding in one vehicle, we'd each take only one suitcase, one overnight case and one heavy overcoat. Conserving space was made a top priority. We agreed that we'd all stay in the same hotel room with two double beds and a roll-away cot to save money and, hopefully, to keep us out of trouble.

I worked hard to convince my mother and my high school teachers of the wisdom of letting me go on this tour. Despite my tender age and lack of worldly knowledge and experience, my mother said if I could somehow keep up with my schoolwork, I could go. She viewed this tour as a great opportunity for me to earn the money that I'd need to pay for college the following year.

I worked out a deal with my teachers and the school board that allowed me to travel. Truth is, I think they were happy to rid themselves of me. From time to time—that would be from 8 AM to 3 PM every school day—I was known to cause a little trouble. At 17, I was only interested in music and treated most of my teachers with unimaginable disrespect and disinterest. *Good riddance* a few of them no doubt thought as they acceded to my departure.

While on the road, I was to complete all schoolwork as dictated by my teachers, use my textbooks and their handouts for my information sources and mail in my assignments weekly. When I returned home from the tour, I'd make up the tests. As long as I kept up with the daily assignments, whatever grades I received on the year-end final exams would be my final grades.

As things worked out, Barry Curtis proved to be my "Get Out Of Jail Free" card. He was the one guy in the band who'd gone to high school and actually remembered what he'd been taught. In short order, I found that I didn't have to read a thing. I'd just jump to the questions, ask them to Barry and write down his always-correct answers. I retained more information that way than I ever did attending classes.

My orchestra teacher, Mr. Kaza, played violin for the Portland Symphony, and for that I respected him more than any of my other teachers. When he learned of my plans to tour, he said that since I'd be playing music every day, he'd require no additional work from me and my final grade would be an automatic *A*. He smiled, shook my hand and said, "Have a great time, kid!" Mr. Kaza was a cool guy.

When I finally returned from the road and took my tests, I averaged much higher grades than I ever did while attending classes normally. With Barry's help, schoolwork turned out to be a snap. But a few of my teachers proved themselves to be turkeys. In particular, I had an American history teacher that I regularly butted heads with in class. She was always making comments to the class that I considered stupid. Although in general I was socially shy and kept mostly to myself, I was well-known for confronting stupidity in its many forms. While in her class, for example, I found myself regularly disrupting the proceedings and speaking out in disagreement. On a typical day, the teacher would say things like "None of you have the remotest idea of where your life will take you or what you will ultimately have as a career."

Of course, I'd immediately interrupt and strike back.

"Wrong, Julie [I called her by her first name because I knew it drove her crazy], I know exactly what I'll be doing. I'll have a career in music. How can you even say that? Some of these guys will step into their family businesses. You can't make a blanket statement like that."

"That's enough out of you, Mr. Peterson," she'd say in anger. "History is filled with examples of people who thought their lives were cast in iron but who ended up going in entirely different directions."

"Granted!" I'd interject. "But you said *none* of us knew what we'd be doing, not *some* of us."

"Enough!" she'd say, turning a blustery red color. "Okay, *most* of you. Does that meet with your approval, Mr. Peterson? May I continue now with *my* class?"

Trying to maintain control of the moment, I'd calmly yet defiantly answer with something witty like "Can I think about it for 30 minutes?" or "Let me get back to you when the bell rings."

My comments always broke up the class and, once the laughter subsided, Julie would continue arguing her weak point, looking for any opportunity to get back at me or send me to the principal's office.

I think she must've resented the fact that I did better on my tests *without* the benefit of her teaching. Once I finished my testing, she tried to lower my final grade, citing for cause "lack of class participation." I took the issue to the school board, and they overturned her willful act of short-sightedness. After all, she had dictated the terms of the original contract between us and, like it or not, I had fulfilled them. Case closed.

Author in pre-Kingsmen days, Portland

VERSE 5

BOB Eubanks is best known today as the one-time host of the popular television program *The Newlywed Game* and less known, perhaps, for the prominent role he played in the history of radio and rock 'n' roll. On air at KRLA-AM in Los Angeles, Bob was one of Southern California's leading DJs through most of the '60s; meanwhile, off the air, he was one of the region's top concert promoters. He had a string of popular young adult nightclubs, called the Cinnamon Cinder, where he showcased numerous artists, many of them famous, some of them (like Stevie Wonder and the Beach Boys and the Supremes) *very* famous. In 1962–63, a club-inspired dance song made the *Billboard* charts. Sung by local one-hit-wonders The Pastel Six, the song's lyrics included the refrain "Cin, Cin, Cinnamon Cinder/Cin, Cin, Cinnamon Cinder/Cin, Cin, Cinnamon Cinder/It's a very nice dance."

In August 1964, Eubanks brought the Beatles to Southern California for their famous appearance at the Hollywood Bowl. Sandwiched midway in time between those six Angelinos and those four Liverpudlians were five Portlanders just starting to make their own music history. After "Cinnamon Cinder (It's a Very Nice Dance)" and before "She Loves You" came "Louie Louie."

OUR first national tour was scheduled to start in Bob's Southern California nightclubs in late January 1964. Planning to leave Portland at sunrise on a Monday, we spent Sunday evening packing our brand-new station wagon—appropriately, a Pontiac Bonneville *Safari*—with its car-top carrier and trailer. We worked late into the night, making sure we got things packed just right, but the sleep we lost didn't matter. I wouldn't have slept much that night, anyway. We were all so pumped up, knowing we were headed to Southern California, to Hollywood, to the big time.

Crammed full of road necessities—soft drinks, snacks, cartons and cartons of Marlboros, flash light, tire chains, road maps, school books, cameras, sunglasses, a deck of cards—and five musician's bodies, our green gunboat rode about a foot higher at the front bumper than it did at the rear bumper. This tipped the over-stuffed trailer forward, lowering the hitch to a point dangerously close to the pavement. Crushed beneath so much weight, the rear shocks had almost no play, and it took only one or two rude encounters with bumps in the road—*scrape-bounce, scrape-bounce, scrape-bounce*—before we went on 24-hour alert looking for the slightest imperfection in the highway ahead. We were quite a sight as we porpoised our way southward. As the old song goes, "...California, here I come."

As would any carload of red-blooded American teenagers, we had the AM radio blasting the entire trip south. Unbelievably, "Louie Louie" was the topic of conversation on almost every radio station we tuned in. The farther south we drove—maybe *bounced* is a better word to describe our progress—the easier it was to turn the radio dial at any moment and find another station playing "Louie" and talking about the scandal. Honestly, we gave the scandal part little mind, figuring that once everyone read the *P-I* article, the world would calm down.

Our plan was to take two days to drive to LA. We spent the first night in Redding, south of Mount Shasta and about half way to Tinsel Town. We found a motel room, and Norm flipped a coin from his pocket to determine who got the roll-away. I lost, but it was all such an adventure, I really didn't mind. I threw my stuff on the roll-away and opened my suitcase. There on top of my clothes was a letter from my mom. The envelope had "Lil/Dickie" written on it ("Lil" was my mom's name and yes, she called me "Dickie").

Mike quickly grabbed it out of my hands and said, "What do we have here?"

"Hey, give that back," I demanded, grabbing for the letter and missing.

"Lil Dickie!?" he read aloud, laughing.

"Sounds like the kid has a sexual problem!" joked Lynn.

"They call me 'Big Mike!'" bragged our lead guitarist, bringing more laughter.

I reached for the letter in Mike's hand but, playing keep a-way, he threw it to Barry.

"Yep, it says 'Lil Dickie,' clear as can be," said Barry, throwing it to Norm.

Norm held it out in front of him and tauntingly said, "Here, Lil' Dickie, come get your letter from Mommy."

I snatched it from his hand, laughing all the way. I must admit, *it was* pretty funny. Even so, my mother would've served me far better had she simply put the note in my suitcase without addressing it. Her "Lil-Dickie" notation was what attracted Mike's attention, thereby dooming me to years of teasing. The note was just a few words of encouragement, telling me how proud of me she was. I carried it with me the entire eight weeks. It turned out to be a nice piece of home and helped me make it through a few bouts of homesickness.

From that day forward, I was lovingly addressed by my fellow Kingsmen as "Lil' Dickie." Inevitably, the nickname stayed with me for years, and the guys used it to their great amusement and my great embarrassment in many situations, especially those involving mixed company.

We planned another sunrise departure for the next morning, intending to reach LA before dark. To give each of us at least some bathroom time, our wake-up call came early. After a long night of being stabbed in the side by loose springs and trying to conform to the foldable bed's unnatural contours, I finally got my turn in the shower, where I soaked my kinked-up body in the hot water for as long as I could, but not long enough. All too soon it came time to sit once more in the all-too-uncomfortable Pontiac. Half dazed, we continued in our Safari on our safari to the land of surf and sun.

We passed the time talking about ourselves, realizing we shared common teenage experiences — more or less, and I was the less. While my four band mates talked knowingly about girls, I said little, being totally inexperienced in these matters. At 17, I still remained a painfully shy, naïve-in-the-extreme Gig Harbor boy. All I could do was listen and laugh as they chattered endlessly about their many devilish, hormone-driven escapades. Somewhere in the Sacramento Valley, Lynn revealed that he and Karen were married. Although their parents knew, I was sworn to silence because Lynn and Karen wanted to keep their marriage a secret from our classmates until after Karen graduated later that year.

Driving into LA, I felt a little like Buddy Ebsen's character Jed Clampett arriving in Hollywood on *The Beverly Hillbillies* TV show. Jed had struck it rich when, as the show's theme song put it, "one day he was shootin' at some food, and up thru the ground came a bubblin' crude...Oil that is, black gold, Texas tea." We Kingsmen were about to strike our own kind of "black gold"—black vinyl records that sold in the millions and turned to gold we could hang on the wall.

Before we left Portland, Lynn's dad had made a room reservation for us at the Hollywood Center Motel, which advertised itself as being "conveniently located right in the heart of Hollywood." That sounded big time to us, and we could hardly wait to get there. We followed the directions he gave us, which took us down Hollywood Boulevard past Grauman's Chinese Theater and the famous Hollywood Wax Museum a block later. We gaped left and right in awe. Even the slightest thing impressed us. After all, this was Hollywood.

We turned south a few blocks to Sunset Boulevard where, with growing anticipation, we counted down the addresses until we found the Hollywood Center Motel. As we turned in the driveway, scraping the trailer hitch on the pavement, our jaws dropped. The property before us was not just inexpensive, it was a genuine dive. As Lynn drove up to the office, the disappointment could be heard in our silence. We'd just been oohing and aahing over being in Hollywood, feeling on top of the world and quite full of ourselves, and now we were confronted by a place well beneath our newly-acquired lofty stature.

Dry-humored Barry succeeded in breaking the awkwardness.

"Well, *it is* as the brochure promised—it is 'conveniently located right in the heart of Hollywood.'"

That started us laughing.

Looking at the brochure, Mike added, "They must've taken the picture on the front of this brochure 25 years ago."

The laughing turned heartfelt, for he'd firmly planted us back on earth.

As Lynn went in to check us in, Norm commented, "If this place is $25 a night, imagine what the other places in Hollywood go for."

"Before you check in, ask if the plumbing's indoors," Barry joked.

We laughed even harder.

The motel was old, the paint chipped, and the room small and made even smaller with the addition of the old roll-away the manager wheeled into our "deluxe" quarters. We flipped Norm's coin again and again I lost and drew the roll-away. Barry, being his usual optimistic self, said, "Well, look at it this way, Lil' Dickie, you're closer to the TV."

I looked at Barry as I reached for the pillow sitting on the top of the roll-away and said, "Them sounds like fight'n' words to me."

I scored a direct hit with my pillow. He responded by diving on one of the beds and grabbing a pillow of his own. Before a second blow could be struck, all five of us were engaged in a pillow fight with no sides taken. The no-holds-barred free-for-all ended in exhausted laughter with feathers scattered near and far.

The room's aroma grew more intriguing to the olfactory nerves the longer we stayed there. With five junk-food-eating boys living together in close quarters, we badly needed ventilation. Start with the odors that originally came with the room and combine them with Pinesol, farts, cigarettes, bad breath, stale beer and five different brands of after shave. Whew! At times it made your eyes water. With this motel room, we began the tradition of always leaving our door open wherever we lodged. It was either that or suffocate.

The following morning (Wednesday) we hit the streets shopping for souvenirs. We were greatly impressed by every famous name we saw in the stars embedded in the sidewalks of Hollywood. One of our goals was to find new outfits for on stage, and we discovered some "really neat" waistcoats—in two colors, no less, gold and black. With the aid of a salesman who we decided was "fruity," Lynn got the phone number of "a real Hollywood photographer." He was just down the street, so Lynn called him from the haberdashery. He told Lynn that he was free for the next few hours. After we finished our fittings, we journeyed down the boulevard to meet him and check out his studio.

A little bell rang as we opened the door and entered. Scads of pictures of famous stars adorned his walls, all mounted in identical thin black frames. Clark Gable, Rock Hudson, Doris Day, Debbie Reynolds, Errol Flynn—you name the stars, he had their pictures displayed there. We were beyond impressed.

"Look at this picture," exclaimed Norm as he pointed to a photograph hanging on the wall, "Elizabeth Taylor!"

"Here's one of Mickey Rooney," added Barry, "and here's Steve McQueen!"

I was just about to point out Bogie when a short balding man with a see-through comb-over appeared, wearing a white shirt and black slacks. He came from behind a curtain hanging in the doorway that separated the reception area from his studio. In a New Yorkish, east coastish accent he said, "Can I help yooz?"

"Yes," said Lynn, holding out his hand in friendship, "we're The Kingsmen, and I'm Lynn. I talked with you a few minutes ago on the phone."

"Oh, sura," said the man as he shook hands with Lynn. "I'm Delon, photographer to the stars. But you can call me 'Mista D.' Everybody else does. So, yooz boys need some promo pickchas taken, huh?"

I interrupted the pleasantries and asked with an impressed curiosity, "Did you take all of these pictures?"

"I sura did," he answered. "I've shot 'em all."

"That's pretty cool," commented Barry.

"Well, it looks like we've come to the right place," said Lynn.

"And yooz got da right man!" the photographer quickly said. "How many shots ya looking fora, boys?"

"Well," said Lynn, clueless, looking at us for ideas, "probably two, you think?"

"At least two!" helped Mike.

"Two's good," agreed Norm uncertainly.

Mista D spoke again.

"No, ya need tree. Trust me, everybody who's anybody needs tree. I can give yooz a special tree pickcha package."

"Really?" said Lynn, chuckling. "And what's in a 'tree pickcha package?'" he asked mockingly.

"Okay," the photographer said, "ya get tree 8 x 10 glossies in tree different poses wid da name of da act printed on da bottom of one of da pickchas. You got a agent?"

"The William Morris Agency," answered Lynn, name dropping. His effort had the desired effect.

"Hey, you guys must be doin' okay. Dey're da best dere is, ya know. I should trow dere name and contact info on dere, doo. Makes ya look more pafeshenal, ya know?"

"Hey, we've got to have their name on the picture," said Mike enthusiastically as though he'd just had a revelation.

"Oh, yeah, no question," added Norm the PR expert.

"Okay, well, in da tree pickcha package I can give ya five hunderd of each pickcha for doo hunderd twenty fie dallas. How's dat sound? And I'll trow in da 8 x 10 negatives so, if you need mora later, you just take 'em doo a photo duplacata and have 'em run off. Plus, I can re-touch da photos at no extra charge, makin' you look great!"

"How long does it take to get everything?" asked our concerned leader. "We're leavin' next Monday."

"If we do da shoot damorrow, I can have 'em to you by Saturday morning," Mista D answered.

"Let's do it!" declared Lynn. "We pick up our new stage clothes tomorrow at 10 AM, so we can do it anytime after that," he explained.

"I'll be ready for ya at 11," Mista D answered.

Impressed with our find and subsequent negotiations, we enthusiastically messed around Hollywood for the rest of the day. This town offered everything anyone could imagine. We found a place where footprints and handprints of famous movie stars were embedded in cement. You could place your hands and feet in the impressions to compare them with your own. We had a great time doing that. There were so many famous motion picture studios, just seeing their entrances was intoxicating. We drove by Desi-Lu, Warner Brothers, MGM, Paramount and Universal. We even bought a map from some guy by the roadside that he guaranteed would guide us to virtually every movie star's home in the City of Dreams. We soon discovered that the stars' homes were so protected with landscaping, you couldn't see anything except the gates and maybe an occasional roof. However, it was still exciting to us and gave us something to do.

As the day ended, I thought, *This is truly a place where everyone must fall asleep with smiles on their faces.* I fell asleep with one on mine, anticipating that an even greater day awaited us tomorrow. I was eager to finally see Hollywood creativity at work.

After breakfast, we picked up our new outfits, which came in individual hang bags, and arrived at the studio about half an hour before our scheduled time. Mista D had suggested that we bring our instruments to use as props in a few shots. He showed us a few photos and album covers he'd shot of other groups with band members holding their instruments. That was enough to convince us it was a good idea.

He seemed glad to see us and led us through the mysterious curtain draped behind his desk that led to his den of creativity. When I pulled the curtain back to walk in, the first thing I found curious was that the entire room was painted black. In the middle of the room, several cameras sat on tripods. One of them was wooden and much larger than any camera I'd seen before. The other cameras were closer to normal size, but slightly fancier than your everyday, run-of-the-mill camera.

Lights of every size and shape filled the studio, and a few of them were covered with large, hood-like contraptions, while others had some sort of adjustable blinders on them. Other lights sat off to the side of the gloomy room on tripods waiting for Mista D's genius to require their services. The studio had huge rolls of paper, 12, maybe 15 feet wide, hanging from the ceiling. Each roll featured a different scene or color or design, and he could pull them down like portable movie screens to change the background in his photos.

Despite the clutter and equipment, the room seemed asleep. I felt like I had to move quietly in order not to disturb the lifeless surroundings. Then Mista D walked over to a panel on the wall and flipped a breaker, making a loud popping noise. Instantly the studio burst into light, transforming the space, adding life and energy and excitement and electrifying us all. That moment alone seemed to justify the expense.

He showed us around the studio and, as he pointed us to the dressing rooms, he told stories about all the famous people who'd used those sacred rooms and posed in front of his cameras. If you so much as sat on a stool, he'd tell you about all of the stars who'd sat on that same stool before you. He had a mesmerizing tale about each star and what happened during their shoot. So this was showbiz!

We decided to wear our old suit jackets for the first picture so our look wouldn't be the same in all three pictures. We changed into our new waistcoats for the second and third pictures. Mike, Barry, Norm and I put on our new black waistcoats for the second pose, but for some reason Lynn mistakenly put on his gold one. Mista D said he liked the look because it showed who our leader was. That seemed weird, but we let it pass and allowed him to take a few pictures that way. We were a bit intimidated by the whole experience and thought he knew what he was doing. Still, having Lynn dressed in a different look left the rest of us feeling uncomfortable.

During the shoot, Mista D told us that, since we were new to the business, he'd "trow in my photographic genius" and work a little extra hard to get us shots that would become as immortal as any of those he had hanging in his reception area—he was certainly full of himself. By the time he finished, we were convinced we were a big-time band destined for superstardom. As we changed clothes, Lynn filled out a form showing Mista D exactly what we wanted printed on the bottom of the pictures and how it was to be spelled. We left his studio carrying on like children intoxicated on too much candy. We were pumped up, convinced we were on our way to the top and certain the whole world would know it by tomorrow morning, or at least as soon as they saw our pictures.

The following day, we found our way up to the Griffith Observatory and actually stood in the exact same spot where James Dean once stood in *Rebel Without A Cause* (that alone made us cool). We drove down Sunset Strip and took pictures of Dino's Restaurant where Edd "Kookie" Byrnes used to comb his hair every week on the television show *77 Sunset Strip*. I watched that show when I lived in the Harbor and hardly ever missed an episode. Now we were not only cool, we were "ginchy," too. Using our map to the stars' homes, we found still more sights. By merely reading the famous names on the map, we added "groovy" to our list of distinctions. Although we located quite a few of the stars' homes, the only real movie star we saw on the entire trip was Jane Russell. We were stopped at a traffic light when she pulled up next to us driving a white Mercedes. Mike noticed her first.

"Whoa, whoa, whoa you guys. That's Jane Russell, isn't it?"

We stared at her through the windows for about 10 seconds in a collective jaw-dropping drool. When the light turned green, Jane turned right while the Kingsmen just kept on staring. We were thrilled beyond belief. Jane Russell! Who could imagine? After working so hard all day establishing ourselves as cool and ginchy and groovy, we threw it all away in mere seconds transforming once again into goo-goo eyed teenagers! I couldn't wait to tell everyone back home we'd actually seen Jane Russell.

Through all of the excitement of Hollywood, Friday finally arrived. As I mentioned earlier, Bob Eubanks owned several Cinnamon Cinders. He'd contracted with us to play hour-long sets at two different locations each night. Friday night, we played our first set in Pasadena, packed up our gear and, two hours later, played a second set at Bob's Hollywood Cinnamon Cinder. We went through the same drill at two new locations on Saturday. Both nights, Bob had someone pick us up at the motel and ferry us back and forth between his various clubs.

We met Bob for the first time on our first night at the Hollywood show. He was definitely a big deal and chose not to travel back and forth like the hired help. He treated us well and seemed overjoyed to have us play at his clubs. He tried to tell us that the kids were there every weekend in these same numbers; the guy driving us around told a different story. The clubs were usually full, he said, but on these particular nights the kids had turned out in record numbers to see whether any of the rumors were true about us singing dirty lyrics in our show. Bob was elated and accommodating because he was raking it in, because the crowds we drew were incredible.

At each Cinnamon Cinder, we were met with packed houses and lines of people snaking around the block waiting to get in. Bob told us he'd never seen anything like it, but we were so green, we didn't comprehend the scope of people's curiosity about our alleged off-color lyrics. We thought the kids were coming to see our show because we came from a place so far away and our music was so different from the Surf music they were used to hearing. We foolishly kept thinking that by now people surely knew the truth about "Louie Louie," and that we were gaining popularity *despite* the scandal *not because* of it. The evidence displayed before us at the Cinnamon Cinder those nights should have told us otherwise.

As soon as we reached the point in our show where we played "Louie Louie," people started pulling out pieces of paper containing their guesses as to what the lyrics were to the song. They followed along as we bashed out the raucous jungle rhythm and Lynn screamed out the mysterious lyrics, hoping to confirm their version was correct. It was as though no matter what words we sang to "Louie Louie," it didn't matter. In their minds and ears, our listeners could make their own words fit, whatever they might've been. After we finished the song, arguments broke out, with kids on both sides swearing their version was the version we just sang.

In every interview with the press, the first question asked always concerned the lyrics of "Louie Louie" and, in every case, we said the same thing, "We've done nothing wrong." Ignoring our repeated denials, that's all the kids and reporters wanted to talk about. Did they expect that a source inside the band would eventually feed them the *real* story, the story they wanted to hear? Whatever their motives were, they kept on trying.

After the first long day and two exciting shows, the dive on Sunset Boulevard we were calling home looked pretty good to us. In the wee small hours of the morning, I hit the sack exhausted and fell asleep smiling that Hollywood smile, anticipating another great day ahead of us.

First thing Saturday morning, Lynn went with Norm to pick up our new promo shots. I'd never had a professional photo taken before and couldn't wait to see what surely would be works of art. I just knew the pictures were going to be so great, we'd end up hanging in Mista D's gallery. *Just think of it, me joining the elite family of superstars decorating his walls.* Barry, Mike and I hung out at the motel room with great anticipation waiting for the pictures to arrive.

When Norm and Lynn got back, I could tell Norm was upset about something. He said nothing as Lynn took several copies of the first picture out of the box and passed them around. The first shot we saw had no printing on the bottom of it. The picture'd been taken at an angle, which made it look kind of modern, and I liked it. Barry was sitting in front of the four of us, and we were all lined up behind him looking over our left shoulder while holding our band instruments. We all looked pretty good in the picture. I was well pleased.

The second picture was a close-up. Mista D captured us in a pose that made us look like we were all leaning onto the picture. Everyone except me looked fine, and you could clearly tell where

Mista D had re-touched the photo. His attempt at touch-up looked amateurish. I guess my teeth were too long for his taste because he chopped them off with what looked like a black pencil scribble mark. It was greeted with the same general comment from each one of us as it was passed around the room.

"It's okay, but I like the first one better."

Norm was still visibly upset, so much so, he didn't even look at the pictures. He just passed them on without so much as a glance.

I couldn't wait to see the third and final picture. As Lynn unveiled the masterpiece and passed copies around the room, we were all disappointed when we saw our individual images—we were so crazy and weird looking. Mike looked like Frankenstein in make up. Norm decided he looked so bad in his black horn-rimmed glasses, he felt compelled to get contacts and throw his old look away. Barry seemed more like a plant than an animal, while Lynn appeared sinister and my ears stuck out farther than Dumbo's. In every way imaginable, this picture was really, truly bad, and we quickly decided we all hated it. Then something strange happened. The room grew abnormally silent. It took a minute for me to understand why. Finally, as I read the information on the bottom of the picture, I saw it, too. Instead of the band name reading "The Kingsmen," the band name read, "Lynn Easton and The Kingsmen."

In an instant it felt like Lynn had taken something away from the rest of us. Until this awkward moment, he'd been a Kingsmen just like everyone else. He was definitely the leader of the band, and we all looked up to him, but he was still one of us. He was one fifth of a brotherhood, a fraternity, a family of traveling adventurers seeking nothing individually. We were supposed to be Musketeers—"one for all and all for one"—equals in every respect, Kingsmen. Our disappointment came not because he was elevating himself; we'd already accorded him leadership status, not only within our ranks, but also before the press and with our fans as well. The hurt went much deeper than that. Lynn had separated himself from us. Swiftly and without discussion, he'd made a decision that put him on a different team. He'd proclaimed himself "King", and we were now his men. So this was the cause of the anger Norm was carrying. Norm could tell it was now affecting us, too. Stunned and surprised, we were also speechless. None of us wanted a confrontation with Lynn. We loved him as a brother, but hated what he'd just done.

Mike was too nice to say anything, and Barry and I had only been with the band for a few weeks and didn't know how to handle the situation. We all sat in silence for a few minutes, looking at the picture and hoping someone would find a way to break the black spell. I wondered to myself *How could he do that? How could he even want to do that? This seems like a poorly thought out action. Surely Lynn must have considered the possibility that this could be a suicidal act. Surely he wouldn't trade this treasured fellowship for isolation.*

Mike in his wisdom finally broke the silence.

"I don't mind the first picture, but I don't like the other two at all."

"That's pretty much how I feel as well," said Barry quickly.

"Yeah," said Lynn, "I agree, the first one's the best one. We can use it and save the other two until we run out of them or have something else taken."

He said it as though throwing out the picture with the information on it was no big deal to him. For the moment, that eased the tension and offered a good way around the situation.

I could tell we hadn't heard the last of this from Norm. He remained visibly upset. I knew the first time the four of us had the opportunity to talk about this without Lynn being present, we would.

Then, as though nothing were wrong, Lynn said "I talked with the guys in New York at Wand yesterday, and they gave me the phone number of our regional record distributor. We're going to meet for lunch this afternoon. Florence, the head of the label, thought it would be a good PR move. Anybody else want to go?"

"Yeah," said Mike, "I'll go."

"Me too," Barry said.

"Let's all go!" added Norm.

For the time being, we'd managed to run around a hurdle that none of us had enough nerve or desire to try jumping over.

After studying Mista D's poor technique and mediocre sense of style, I realized we'd gotten what we paid for and probably should have looked into a few other studios before entrusting our fate to the first fast-talking dream maker we came across. As far as our big Hollywood photo shoot was concerned, on many levels we were taken to the cleaners on the deal. Over time, that would prove to be nothing unusual for us.

Moreover, the wonderful truth is, today we have a record that was supposed to be a demo, that's full of the original mistakes, that still became one of the biggest hit records of all time.

And those pictures that Mista D took? They've appeared in countless books, ads and articles about the band. That's not to say they're good pictures—we all still hate them. We hate them almost as much as Mike hated his solo on "Louie Louie." To his somewhat shady credit, our favorite Hollywood photographer did keep his promise, for those pictures he shot turned out to be timeless in their own way. We've been stuck with them for 40 years. The unfortunate fact is, we ended up using them for a few years, and the record company even put one of the photos on our third album. And Mista D? He found a place on his wall for us so that any innocent, unsuspecting souls following in our footsteps would know that the Kingsmen, too, had been there.

THE two Saturday night shows at the Cinnamon Cinders went pretty much the same as the Friday night shows—tons of screaming kids cutting loose and having a great time. And again, as the night before, when we started to play "Louie Louie," all we could see was the top of the kids' heads as they read their different versions along with the song. We found it hilarious.

We charged Bob $1,000 a show and thought we were raking it in. That was nearly five times more than what we normally made back home. Even after paying for the motel, our new outfits, the photographer and five hundred copies of the pictures, we were leaving town with just over $3,000 in the bank. I remember thinking, *We made $600 apiece in less than a week and we only played two nights! We've got it made!*

Even with the picture incident, we had a great time in Hollywood on that first trip. It was more than any one teenager from the sheltered Northwest could reasonably have expected. With the euphoria of our success still lingering, we put the USS Pontiac back on the road, pointed her east on Route 66 and headed for the Midwest.

We had five days to make it to Wichita for our next gig. As we drove out of California, no one noticed the date. It was February 2, Groundhog Day. We should've thought to check with Punxsutawney Phil back in Pennsylvania before leaving. If we had, we would've learned that, earlier that morning, "the King of the Groundhogs, Father of all Marmota, Seer of Seers, Prognosticator of Prognosticators" had emerged from his burrow on Gobbler's Knob and seen his shadow. Winter wasn't over yet, as we soon learned. We motored eastward in high spirits, blissfully unaware that a freak, record-setting snow storm was due to hit New Mexico at the same time we were. We were going to miss our Wichita date and almost lose our lives.

The infamous "Lynn Easton and the Kingsmen" photograph

VERSE 6

OUR plan, and admittedly an ambitious one, was to make it well into Arizona by the end of our first day on the road, get a good night's sleep somewhere there, and spend our second night at a motel *nearabout* Amarillo, Texas. For much of the way to Wichita, where our next gig was scheduled the following week, we'd be following Route 66, "the mother road, the road of flight" as John Steinbeck called it in *The Grapes of Wrath*. Unlike the Jode family in Steinbeck's novel, however, the Kingsmen family in this story was headed east, not west on its hopeful trek.

For people living out of suitcases and sporting a life on the road, certain habits develop naturally, evolving out of the circumstances faced and the personalities involved. We'd fallen into a routine whereby each of us navigated as far as a full tank of gas could take us before turning over the USS Pontiac's helm to the next pilot. Mike had finished a leg driving from LA into Arizona, and it was time to gas up the big green gunboat. In those days, gas station attendants filled up your car with gas, checked your water and oil levels, and even washed your windows. That gave us enough time to hit the rest room and grab a snack before the car was ready to tackle another leg of the seemingly endless journey before us.

Once the Pontiac was berthed next to the gas station pump, we all hurriedly got out of the car to stretch our limbs and perform our normal pit stop rituals. With our tasks completed, Norm slid behind the wheel as Barry, Mike and I got in the back seat and started to open our coveted staple, junk food. Lynn opened the passenger's side front door, threw his bounty on the front seat, opened his briefcase, took out the money pouch and went back into the station to pay the truck stop attendant. The four of us were finally alone together someplace where Lynn couldn't hear our conversation.

"So, how do you guys feel about the new band name?" Norm asked.

"It ain't gonna happen," Mike answered. "Just let it go. Why cause problems? We'll just use the other pictures until we can get some new pictures taken. We can have some new ones shot when we get back home."

"I'm telling you, this is just the beginning," Norm said.

"Maybe we should confront him before it gets out of hand," Barry added.

"I think it's over," said Mike. "From now on, we can make sure things like this don't get by us again."

I sat and listened to their discussion, saying nothing, feeling uncomfortable about the discord.

"Are you kidding me? How are you going to do that?" responded Norm. "He's talking with people in Chicago and New York every day. We don't know what he's telling them."

"Norm," said Mike forcefully, "cool it! If it comes up again, I'll deal with it. But why stir things up? I'm telling you, it's over!"

Just then, Lynn opened the door and the conversation stopped.

"Nice guy," he remarked as he began to open his eats. "He said we're going to run into some stormy weather up ahead. But when I told him we were from the Northwest and that we live in stormy weather, he said, 'Well, there you are!'"

We all laughed and started to down our various choices of cuisine as though nothing had happened.

Despite occasional moments like that, traveling across the United States by car was an inspirational experience, the people and the scenery beyond belief, the trip through Arizona filled with awe and wonder. I'd seen Arizona only in pictures and cowboy movies, and that couldn't compare with the majesty and splendor of the land the Navajo call home when seen in person. I'd never been to the desert before, and you must experience the Painted Desert and Monument Valley first hand to fully appreciate the artistic creativity of Our Maker at work there.

On our second morning on the road, a beautiful blue sky greeted us, filled with grand puffy white clouds that turned from one color to another as we sped down Arizona's highways.

By late morning, a light rain began falling. As the day progressed, the rain grew increasingly heavier and the skies turned ever darker. Though we still faced a full day's drive, we felt we could make it through to Texas, even with the heavy rain. Such is the hubris of fledgling teenage rock stars.

By the time we reached New Mexico, the weather had started to turn ugly as snow began to mix in with the rain. Every time we made a pit stop, we asked the truck drivers going west about road conditions and weather to the east. We kept hearing the same thing repeatedly—the rain was mixed with some snow, and it got heavy at times, but the roads were still passable and in good shape. As the light slowly faded and day turned to night, the rain lessened and the snow took over. Somewhere around 8 or 9 o'clock, the snow intensified and began to stick to the highway.

As you travel America's highway system, it doesn't take long to figure out that when you're driving in bad weather, the best thing to do is to hook up with a trucker. The big piece of machinery is easy to keep track of, and you gain a sense of security having an 18-wheeler ahead to clear the way for you. We'd been following this one trucker for quite a few miles and, as we pulled into an Albuquerque truck stop behind him, the weather took a turn for the worse. We questioned the wisdom of going any farther. Inside, we started a conversation with the trucker.

He was a big man—a *huge* man—bearded and soft spoken, wearing a red baseball cap and well-traveled denim overalls. We sat next to him at the counter sharing a strong pot of coffee and discussing the oncoming storm. As the waitress filled his thermos, he told us he'd been on his CB and, as far as he knew, the road east was still passable and he was "going through." We decided if he could do it, we could, too. With Lynn taking the wheel, we left the truck stop following the trucker's lead. It didn't take 30 minutes before we fell behind and he was out of our sight. As we approached Santa Rosa, Norm noticed that we'd not seen any other traffic for some time.

"I don't think we should go any farther than Santa Rosa tonight," he said. "We're the only ones out here, and this is getting pretty bad."

He was right. We hadn't seen another vehicle for some time, and it appeared as though we were the only ones foolish enough to still be out on the highway. It felt like maybe we'd entered Rod Serling's Twilight Zone, only his Twilight Zone wasn't this scary. His was imaginary, ours was real.

The night was extremely black, and the rain had long since given way to heavy snow. All we could see out the front window were big white fluffy snowflakes coming down at an alarming rate. Our headlights illuminated the flakes as they floated down in front of us, and at times the snow was so thick and heavy, it was difficult to see ahead even a few feet through the feathery white curtain. At around 9:30, after slipping all over the road for some time, we wisely stopped to put on our tire chains. By the time we finished struggling with the chains in the deep snow and started on our way again, it had become difficult to keep track of where the road was, for the snow was now coming down in blinding waves. We had no choice but to slow our speed to a crawl in order to keep track of the roadside. Our windshield wipers, though working at full speed, were slowly losing the battle as snow accumulated on the window faster than they could clear it.

Mike rode shotgun and was continually trying to assist the struggling wipers. From time to time, he rolled down his window and stretched out as far as he could to wiped as much snow off of the edge of the front window as he could reach. Even with the heater running full blast, it was growing frightfully cold in the car. By this time, we'd all donned several shirts and our coats in a losing battle to stay warm. None of us had been in this kind of situation before, and I for one was growing terrified.

We'd slowed to near walking speed when, from out of nowhere, like an unexpected cyclone, a semi came flying past us, blowing his horn and furiously throwing snow everywhere. It scared us at first, but once the front window had cleared a bit, Mike, pointing ahead, cried, "Look at that!"

"Whoa!" I said, stunned. "We *are* in the Twilight Zone!"

"Are you kidding me?" Norm added.

"I can't believe it!" shouted Lynn as our hearts pounded out of our chests.

In a flash, as though sent by God, this angel on wheels had carved a path to safety before us and then, just as quickly as he'd appeared, vanished back into the snowy darkness. To our amazement, he left behind tracks that were clearly visible in our headlights. Lynn steered the USS Pontiac's tires straight into those deep furrows, and the going at once became easier. With renewed hope, we pressed on.

We followed his tracks for as long as we could, but as the storm continued to strengthen, the snow between them grew ever deeper. All too soon, it became so deep that once again our front bumper began to hit the snow accumulating there and spray it into the air in front of us. As we plowed ahead, clumps of snow flew over the hood of the car and landed on the windshield with frightening thuds. At first we hit intermittent mounds of snow, but, as we continued traveling down the path the truck had so nicely carved for us, the snow finally grew too deep. The station wagon became a snowplow, and a constant sheet of snow began flying everywhere. We'd lost nearly all control over the elements and our fate, and there was no way out of the mess we were in. Fear gripped us.

Mike noticed that it was getting increasingly difficult to see in the darkness.

"Does it look to you guys like we've lost a headlight?" he asked.

"I don't think so," answered Lynn. "I still have lights hitting the snow on both sides of the car."

"Why don't you stop," Mike suggested, "and I'll hop out and take a look?"

"Where do you suggest I pull over?" Lynn said. "The snow's too deep. I can't get out of these tracks. If I pull over, I'll never get going again."

"No one's going to catch up with us in this mess. Don't pull over, just stop. It'll only take a second for me to see what the trouble is."

"Maybe the snow's shorting out the electrical system," added Norm. "Let's stop and take a look. We don't want to lose power out here, not in this weather."

Lynn stopped the car, and Mike and Norm got out.

"Are you kidding me?" exclaimed Norm as usual.

Raising his hands in front of his chest and separating them about a foot, Mike said, "The snow's about a foot thick on the front of the car. The headlights are buried."

Mike and Norm feverishly started clearing the snow off of the front of the car with their hands. Instantly. the lights turned radically brighter. After they finished freeing the front fender and grill and lights from the clogging snow, the pair cleaned the windshield and jumped back in the car, rubbing their hands together and blowing on them.

"That was amazing!" Norm remarked.

"And how!" added Mike, shaking all over, still nowhere near being warm again. "The snow was a foot thick on the front of the car. It's really comin' down out there."

Shifting into drive, Lynn started rolling down the white highway once again.

"Boy," said Lynn, "I can see so much better. It's incredible!"

Through the nervous laughter and joking, you could tell that clearing the headlights had given us all a renewed sense of optimism and relief.

"We may have to do it several more times before we find a place to stay," said Mike.

We continued cautiously down the highway for some time, following the fading tracks on the snow-covered road until we could see them no longer.

Slowing the car, and with the sound of panic in his voice, Lynn said, "Hey, you guys, I can't see anything out there! It all looks like one big white sheet to me. I can't tell where the road is."

Within a few terrifying seconds, we lost the road in a complete white-out, and Lynn drove the car off the pavement, across the shoulder and down an invisible embankment beside the highway. We all grabbed on to whatever we could reach as the Pontiac, totally out of control, began what seemed like an endless slide down an unseen incline. Our suitcases and junk food containers and everything else loose bounced all over the inside of the panic-filled car. It was weird. In an instant we could no longer see the headlights or anything they once illuminated, as though someone had turned off the outside world. Then, just when it felt like we were about to tip over, the descending Pontiac finally came to a rest. The deep snow completely buried our car, and total blackness surrounded us. The dash lights were still on, and the car was still running, but I couldn't see a thing out the windows.

"Is everybody okay?" asked Mike.

We sat in the blackness for a second, catching our breath, until one by one we answered him.

"I'm fine," I responded, fighting back my terror.

Norm and Barry answered with the same nervous, "I'm okay!"

"I'm sorry," said our nervous and stressed leader. "I lost the road and couldn't see a thing!"

"Hey, I couldn't see anything either," said Mike.

The back seat was pitch black in the leaning car as Norm fumbled around the ceiling, searching for the light switch.

"Here we go," he said as he turned on the overhead courtesy light.

I found the light to be some relief.

Norm rolled his window down. The snow was packed so tightly, it formed a solid wall.

"I think we're completely buried," he said.

Still shaking from having lost control of the car, Lynn took charge.

"Let's just sit here for a while until the snow stops," he proposed. "Then we can dig our way out and get back on the road."

Even in the dim lighting, you could see he was as white as a sheet.

"Let's just take it easy, nobody panic. We're going to be fine," said Mike in a calm and comforting voice.

Reaching in the back for his suitcase, Barry said, "It's going to get cold in here. I think we should put on more clothing or we'll freeze before we're found. We have to retain body heat."

"Jeez," said Lynn. "I'm sweating my eyes out now!"

"You won't be for long," laughed Mike.

"That's a good idea, Bare," Norm said. "As soon as you have what you need, I'll get my suitcase and Dick, you can follow me. And after you get your suitcase, you can change places with Mike, so he can get to his stuff."

One by one, we opened our suitcases in the back of the Pontiac and, shivering from the cold, pulled on layers and layers of clothing.

"I have a flashlight in my suitcase," Lynn said nervously, climbing over the seat. "We'd better use it for light instead of wearing out the car battery."

"I have one, too," I said

"It's not a good idea to keep the car running," offered Mike. "The fumes could gas us to death."

We sat in the still car for an hour or so, saying little until Mike could take it no longer.

"I've had enough!" he announced. "If we keep sitting here, we're going to freeze to death. I say we open a window and dig a tunnel out of here and go for some help."

"I'm with you!" Norm said. "Let's get out of here before we become a headline."

"How will you know which way to go?" asked Lynn.

"Let's dig to the back of the car in the direction we came from," answered Norm, sounding confident. "We'll get to the road that way."

"Let's go for it!" said Mike.

Barry, Lynn and I decided to wait with the car until Mike and Norm came back with help. After they left, we wondered whether they'd come back at all.

Whenever we got too cold to take it any longer, Lynn started the car and ran the heater for a while, reasoning that the hole Mike and Norm had dug in the snow would vent the toxic fumes, but not considering the possibility that the snow was filling their escape route and that perhaps we might still fall victim to carbon monoxide poisoning. The last thing I remember was sitting in fear in the back seat of the dark Pontiac just before I fell asleep to the sound of the car idling in the freezing cold.

TAKING Lynn's flashlight, Mike and Norm managed to dig their way out and find the highway. They walked up the road through the blustery snow for an hour or so until they finally came upon a gas station on the outskirts of Santa Rosa. They'd become cold and worried, and the station was a welcome sight.

Opening the door to the station, almost breathless, Mike said, "Boy are we glad to see you!"

"Where's your car?" asked the attendant. "I didn't see anyone drive up. How did you guys get here?"

"Our car's off the road back that way," Mike said, pointing back down the highway. "We walked."

The station was warm, and the friendly, sympathetic man offered them a cup of coffee and a place to sit.

"Why don't you guys relax for a while? You're okay now. I've got a tow truck with a plow on the front of it. Once it gets light, we can go pull your car out of the ditch and get you going again."

"We left three people buried in the car off the road when we came to get help," Norm informed him.

"I'd love to take you now, boys," the attendant said, "but there's no need to lose us, too. You can't see a thing out there in this darkness. We'll do a lot better if we wait until daylight. I can call the snowplow drivers if you like and ask them to keep an eye out for your car as soon as they start clearing the road."

"Great!" said Norm.

"Any kids in your car?" questioned the concerned stationmaster.

"No," answered Mike.

"I'll call the state troopers," said the attendant, "and see if they can keep an eye out, too."

Mike and Norm sat in the warmth of the station drinking coffee, worrying about us and visiting with the man. They passed the hours telling him about the band and our stormy adventure. The blizzard stopped just before dawn, and when the sun rose at last, it revealed a deep blue sky once more filled with huge puffy white clouds. A few minutes later, the guys saw a snowplow drive past, heading west.

"Let's do it!" the attendant said. "We can get through now."

Mike and Norm threw on their coats and climbed into the cold tow truck. Within seconds, the three of them were on their way to rescue us. The driver got on his CB and asked the snowplow driver whether he'd seen any sign of our car and trailer.

"There's nuthin' out there but snow," said the voice on the CB.

"Keep your eyes open," the attendant answered back on his CB. "They're somewhere around five, maybe seven miles down the highway."

"Ten-four," said the voice on the CB.

As they drove west, scanning the left shoulder, Mike started to worry.

"It's amazing!" he said. "The whole place is one big snow drift."

"I can't remember the last time we were hit with a snowstorm like this!" the driver remarked.

"I think we've passed them," Norm said after they'd driven for a while.

"So do I," said Mike. "I don't think we walked this far."

"We've gone about six, maybe seven miles," said the driver.

"We'd better go back," suggested Mike, "and try to find something that will give us a clue about where they are."

"Let's go a few more miles before we turn back," said the tow truck driver. "I'll get on my CB and ask the sheriff to get some people out here to help us look."

Finally turning around and heading back toward Santa Rosa, the three lookouts canvassed the southern roadside as Mike and Norm tried not to panic.

"It all looks the same," said the attendant, "just one big snowdrift."

"Hold it!" Mike cried just then,

The driver slowed the truck.

"Look at that!" said Mike.

"Look at what?" said Norm.

"That black hole, in the snow, down over there."

"I don't see what you're looking at," said Norm.

"I don't either," said the driver as he pulled his truck over.

"There," Mike said, pointing, "that black ring in the snow with that light smoke coming out of it."

"Oh my God!" said Norm. "Are you kidding me? They left the car running? They can't be alive!"

There in the snow below them was a perfectly round black hole formed by the heat from our exhaust pipe. Mike and Norm jumped out of the truck and frantically started digging through the snow. The driver again called for the Highway Patrol and the snowplow driver to give them our location and buried condition. Then he joined Mike and Norm as they fought through the snow.

They followed the exhaust trail to the back of the wagon and burrowed around to the side of the car. Norm started pounding on the roof of the Pontiac, trying to wake us up as Mike and the driver struggled to free a door. Hearing a faint voice yelling in the distance, Barry opened his eyes. The windows were electric, and he could hear Mike yelling, "Barry! Barry! Roll down the window!"

Barry weakly lifted his arm and pushed down on the window button. The window rolled down and, within seconds, Mike was pulling us out of the buried car and into the fresh air.

"Wake up!" Mike kept saying. "Wake up!"

The first thing I remember was Norm's hand on my cheek and his distant voice saying, "I think he's coming around."

Opening my eyes, I couldn't believe it. It was daylight.

"How did it get to be daylight?" I asked.

"Dick's going to be okay!" Norm cried. "How's Lynn?"

"I'm fine," answered Lynn.

"The sun's already up! What kept you guys?" asked Barry, struggling to regain his senses.

Norm and Mike sat down in the snow and started to laugh, trying to release their pent-up nervous tension.

I was cold beyond belief, but when I fully came to, and Norm and Mike told us how they'd found us, I realized I should be thankful that I was able to feel anything at all. I'd just broken a date with the Grim Reaper. Within a few minutes, the New Mexico Highway Patrol arrived and helped dig out the back of the car. Lynn, Barry and I sat in the warm patrol car while Mike and Norm helped the truck driver hook his cables up to our trailer and pull it out of the ditch.

The patrolman told us we were lucky to be alive.

"I can't believe you made it all the way from Albuquerque!" he said. "The road was closed all night, and I don't think it'll be open again for several days."

"That's crazy," said Barry. "They must've closed the road just after we went through."

I looked at Barry, and we sang in unison, as though we were being conducted by Leonard Bernstein, the eerie theme to *The Twilight Zone—da da da da, da da da da*—and broke into laughter.

Once the wagon was out of the ditch, the patrolman told Mike and Lynn that if Lynn hadn't continually kept starting the car, they would never have found us. Apparently, Pontiac had built the car so well, the toxic fumes mostly found their way out through the tailpipe. The patrolman figured the snow was so tightly packed around us, it isolated us from the deadly vapors. Otherwise, we'd have been goners. Whatever the scenario, we realized how lucky we were to be alive. We'd just lived through a miracle.

Once they'd detached our car and trailer from the tow truck, we followed the driver back to the station where Mike and Norm had spent the night. The patrolman and the station attendant were thrilled to learn we were the Kingsmen. After satisfying their curiosity about "the real words to 'Louie Louie,'" we gave them both autographed pictures to hang on their walls. They were excited to have the pictures and to be forever a part of our tale of rescue. The attendant graciously let us use the station phone to find a motel in Santa Rosa. For the next few days, like Bill Murray and Andie MacDowell and Chris Elliott in *Groundhog Day*, we found ourselves stranded by an unexpected February snowstorm in a small town not of our choosing.

LYNN called Bob Ehlert at the William Morris Agency in Chicago and told him about our escapade. Lynn asked him to inform the promoters in Wichita that we were stuck in this freak storm and weren't going to be able to make their shows. Lynn told him we were probably going to have to proceed to our weekend date in Davenport, Iowa instead.

As soon as we were notified that the road had been reopened, we gassed up and hit the highway. The weather was beautiful and perfectly clear, but the road was filled with people like us that had been stranded by the blizzard. Within a few hours smooth, snowy Route 66 had been transformed by the thousands of chained cars and trucks relentlessly pounding and pressing their way along her length into a bumpy, rutted, rough, pot-holed, washboard-like mess.

We found ourselves barely moving in the endless single line of traffic headed east. The pounding our car took as we traveled down the battered road nearly shook us to death. The good ship USS Pontiac was locked in a rhythm as we moved along at the breakneck speed of 20 miles per hour. *Boom, boom, boom, boom, boom*—the sound was jarring and unceasing. Making matters worse, we continually worried about our musical equipment taking a beating in the trailer.

We decided that once we reached Tucumcari, we'd make a pit stop and check on the gear. As we pulled into town, we noticed that the city streets were in much better shape than the highway we'd been on for the past few hours. Mike saw a Denny's in a shopping center.

"How 'bout we grab a bite to eat there?" he suggested.

We all enthusiastically agreed.

As Mike pulled into the parking lot and clunked to a stop, he suddenly shouted "Hold on!"

BANG! We'd been rear-ended.

"What the hell was that?" yelled Lynn.

"Somebody hit us!" exclaimed Norm.

"No!" Mike said in frustration. "Nobody hit us. *We* hit us."

"What?" asked Lynn.

"I looked in the rearview as I was stopping," explained Mike, "and saw the trailer about 20 feet behind us. It must have come off of the hitch. It was moving on its own. The damn thing smashed us right in the rear."

We all piled out and rushed to the back of the car to check on the trailer. Sure enough, it was off the hitch and the tongue was shoved under the back of the Pontiac. The U-Haul was only a 4' x 6' trailer, so it was easily moved by just a few of us. We pulled it back, and Lynn and Norm crawled under the back of the Pontiac to try to determine what had happened to the hitch.

We had the safety chains on the trailer hooked to the Pontiac, but evidently the constant pounding had dislodged them and they'd become unhooked.

Norm climbed under the back of the car to assess the damage.

"Wow!" said Norm. "Are you kidding me?

"What is it?" asked Mike.

Laughing, Norm answered. "The welds have been ripped from the frame and the whole hitch has been busted off!"

"Boy, are we lucky!" exclaimed Mike.

"That's lucky?" asked Barry. "How do you figure?"

"Whatever last piece of weld was holding the hitch on there must've finally let go right here in the parking lot. Can you imagine what would've happened had that hitch come off somewhere out on the highway? We'd have had equipment everywhere. Our stuff would've been in a thousand pieces. The whole tour would've been over."

"You know, I guess you're right!" Norm said, laughing.

"I guess we'd better find somebody that can fix it," said Mike.

We went into Denny's and, after we ordered, Mike got on the pay phone and found an auto shop not far away. He and Lynn volunteered to take the car to the shop and get it fixed. In order to separate the hitch from the trailer, Norm removed the ball from the tongue so Mike and Lynn could take it with them to the auto shop for repair.

Barry, Norm and I stayed at Denny's in a warm booth by a window where we could keep an eye on the trailer as we waited for Lynn and Mike to return. It took a quite a while for the repair, but we really didn't mind. This particular Denny's featured extraordinary blueberry pie and several attractive waitresses. While waiting, Norm and Barry flirted with the girls and we all stuffed ourselves with hot blueberry pie à la mode and coffee.

Once Mike and Lynn returned, Norm got out his tool kit and re-wired the electrical connections that had been ripped apart when the trailer separated from the car. This gave Lynn and Mike the perfect opportunity to chow down on the aforementioned, delightfully addicting desert and engage with the local action. Although love was in the air—or were those raging hormones I detected?—before too long we were back on the road, well fed and heading for Iowa with yet another memorable road story under our belt.

VERSE 7

ONCE we made it out of New Mexico, road conditions slowly improved, and we steered the USS Pontiac north northeast in the general direction of Iowa without running into further delays. We'd been forced to cancel our Wichita date, and our next scheduled gig was to play for a dance in Davenport, Iowa on the following Saturday night. We arrived in Davenport a day early, checked into the Holiday Inn and headed to a nearby laundromat to wash clothes. So much for doing something thrilling on a treasured day off.

Our room came equipped with the standard-issue two double beds plus a roll-away and, once more, I lost the coin toss (come to think of it, I usually drew the roll-away). That night, we were all sitting around the room in our underwear watching TV and talking about normal everyday stuff. On a nightly basis, the guys reminisced about different sports teams they'd played on, about teachers they'd had, about people they'd met, about different gigs they'd played and more. But always, always, always, all conversations inevitably returned to their favorite subject of all, girls. On this particular evening, the guys were trading stories about girls they'd met at our shows, girls they'd known back home and boy/girl antics they'd gone through in high school. And I was feeling left out.

Although I was satisfied with my life up to that point, listening to them made me feel as though I'd been living in isolation, like in a sound-proof room where I was unaware of the full-blown party going on just outside my door. Normally, I could listen to them talk like this for hours, laughing on cue, with no ill effects on my psyche. But now, I must admit, envy was starting to creep up on me.

As we lay on our beds watching Ben and Adam and Hoss and Little Joe on *Bonanza*, Norm looked over at Mike and, with the look of a fraternity brother about to toy with a prospective pledge, asked me, "Hey, Lil' Dickie, have you ever had a girl?"

I could feel my face turning red with embarrassment.

"What?" I answered awkwardly as all eyes in the room focused on me.

"Have you ever had a girl?" he reiterated.

"Sure," I said, a bit hesitantly.

"Really?" said Norm, again locking eyes with Mike, that bad boy look still on his face.

"Yeah," I said with enthusiasm, "in fifth grade I liked this girl named Penny Harper and…"

"Fifth grade?" interrupted a smiling Barry, drawing closer to the end of his bed. "This ought to be good."

I could feel a giggle about to erupt in the room. It was all they could do to hold it back.

"What?" I asked.

"No, no, no," said Norm, nudging Barry with his elbow. "I mean, have you had a girl since you've been a man? You know, been with a woman?"

"What do you mean?" I asked.

Mike joined in.

"Have you ever even kissed a girl?" he asked indignantly.

"Well, sure," I said with confidence.

"Oh?" questioned Mike. "Now you're talking!"

"And just where exactly did you do this kissing?" said Lynn.

"Right here," I answered, pointing to my cheek.

That set them howling.

"Hey, hey, guys, get a hold of yourselves," said "professor" Norm, looking at the others and continuing to torment me with his teasing. "Lynn meant *where*? Like in the back of a car? Or in her bedroom? You know."

"Oh, I see," I said with a little laugh. "In her dad's house. In the basement, actually."

"Oooo, darling!" cooed Lynn.

"Cool," added Barry.

"Tell us more," begged Norm.

Mike interrupted.

"I had a girl friend in high school I used to feel up in her living room while we were watching TV..."

All eyes turned Mike's way.

"...with her parents sitting right across the room!" he finished.

Everyone broke up.

Once the room calmed down, the focus returned to me.

"Did you ever get caught?" Lynn asked. "Was her dad home?"

"No, he wasn't home when I got there," I said, "but he came home while we were in the basement, and I had to sneak out of the house through the basement window because she wasn't allowed to have anyone in her house when her dad wasn't home. I was lucky. It was kind of an accidental sort of kiss."

I tried to make my story sound as interesting as their many escapades. Lacking substance, however, my tale was unworthy of their attention.

"We were playing checkers and had the basement kind of dark so her dad couldn't tell we were down there. When he came home, we panicked and kind of bumped into each other. She was right in front of me. Then she whispered, 'Thanks for coming over. I'll see you tomorrow at school.' And then she put her hand on my shoulder and kissed me right here."

I pointed to my cheek and added, "But she definitely got a little of my lip."

The guys doubled over with laughter.

"Did you get any tit?" asked Mike, intensifying the merriment.

"Hey, don't push Lil' Dickie, let him tell us the story," said Norm, like a gossip trying to extract a hidden secret. "He's just getting to the good stuff. Besides, I have a feeling he's not the kind to kiss and tell, are you, Lil' Dickie?"

"You mean *feel and tell*, don't you?" said Mike.

That cracked everyone up, and they were again rolling with laughter.

Once a semblance of order was restored, Norm continued his interrogation.

"When did all of this happen?"

"In seventh grade," I answered.

Upon hearing this, the guys hit the floor in uncontrollable laughter.

"SEVENTH GRADE?" shouted Mike through his laughter.

Hysteria reigned.

"Hold on, you guys," said Norm, trying to regain control of himself and the rolling teens. "You *have had* a girlfriend since seventh grade, haven't you?"

"No," I answered, my discomfort growing, "not really. There's this girl at school I more or less like, but she doesn't really give me the time of day. I've invested most of my time in music."

Slowly the room calmed down.

"Well, let me ask you this…," Norm said,

"Yeah, what?" I answered.

Norm looked over at Barry and then slowly turned to Mike as though he was about to reveal a deep dark secret.

"What?" I said again.

"Are you a man yet?" he said, poking Barry slightly with his elbow.

I paused.

"What do you mean?" I finally said.

"You know, *are you a man* yet? Have you gotten your period yet?"

The room fell silent. I couldn't tell whether the other guys, like me, were wondering what the hell Norm was talking about or whether they were breathlessly anticipating my answer, curious about what it would be. I was clearly shocked; the other guys waited like a jury sitting in judgment of my response.

"What?" I asked yet again.

"Have you gotten your period yet?" Norm reiterated.

"What are you talking about?" I said in disbelief. In an effort to show these guys I wasn't completely sheltered from the world, I added, "Girls get periods, not boys!"

"Oh, boy, he's not a man yet!" exclaimed Mike as he threw up his hands in disbelief.

"We have a child on the road with us!" said Barry.

"He doesn't know about the birds and the bees!" Added Lynn.

Realizing I was as gullible as gullible gets, Norm raised his arms to silence the rowdy teens once again.

"Take it easy, you guys," he ordered. Turning back to me, he said, "No, no, I'm serious. Have you gotten your period yet?"

I just looked at him. No one spoke. *How come I don't know what they're talking about?* I asked myself.

"I've had mine!" Norm announced.

"Me, too," Lynn quickly added.

"Yeah, man, I had mine when I was 16," Barry said, slightly smirking.

They were all giggling like this news was going to be a great source for future teasing.

Then, like a show-off, Mike said, "I got mine when I was 14."

They all threw their pillows at the braggart guitarist.

"What are you talking about?" I insisted, my innocence continuing to show.

Kindly and fatherly, Norm went on.

"Well," he said, "women have periods every month, right?"

"Right," I agreed hesitantly.

"Well, guys just get one in their life, and before they get it, they can't perform…" he paused for effect and then finished, "…the sexual act."

"Yeah, you know, *do the deed*!" added Mike.

"What?" I questioned again. "Are you nuts?"

"No," they all insisted in unison. "It's true. It is!"

"Hey, man, until you get your period, you can't have sex," Norm insisted. "Well, you can try, but you won't be able to perform."

"Yeah," said Lynn, right on cue. "That's what turns you into a man—when you get your period."

"What?" I questioned for the umpteenth time.

"Oh yeah," Norm said, "have you ever had like a hot flash and then ended up with a little blood in you underwear?"

"No," I said, still disbelieving.

"Clearly you're not a man yet," said Mike.

"One of these days you will, you'll find blood in your underwear," Norm said. "and let me warn you, you'd better not try to have sex with a girl until you get your period. Otherwise you'll just embarrass yourself."

"Yeah, man, you won't be able to do it," added Barry.

"Girls learn all about this stuff in their sex ed courses," Lynn pointed out, "but they leave it to our dads to tell us boys about sex."

"You guys are pulling my leg," I said—me, without a father at home.

"No!" they insisted, again unanimously.

"Really? Are you sure? I never heard of such a thing."

"Well, not ever having had a girlfriend, I'm not surprised," said Barry.

"Hey, man," said Norm. "I'm just trying to save you a great deal of embarrassment."

"It's true," Norm went on. "Believe me. For your own good, stay away from girls until you get your period or you'll do nothing but piss them off."

"He's right," counseled Mike.

"We're just lookin' out for you, Lil' Dickie," said Barry.

"Hey, you can ask anybody. Don't take our word for it," Lynn said.

"Oh, sure, like I'd ask someone something like that!" I exclaimed.

"What did you think," asked Norm, "that you slowly turn into a man? Think about it. It's logical. Women can't have babies until they get their first period. Until they get it, they're still children. But once they get their period, they turn into women. Boys become men with just one period. Are you kidding me? I can't believe you didn't know this."

"Never heard of it," I said, concerned.

"Yeah, well, that doesn't mean it isn't so," said Barry.

"I'm not really that great around girls, anyway," I admitted reluctantly.

"That's probably why," said Mike. "Once you get your period, that will all change."

"Your hormones haven't been released yet."

"Yeah, when you finally get your period," Barry said, "that's the signal that your hormones have been released and you're a man."

"Really?"

"Would we lead you down the wrong path?" questioned Mike.

"I'm glad you told me this," I said.

"That's good stuff to know, man," added Barry.

"I wish I would've known about it before I got mine," Mike said. "When it happened, I told my dad about the blood in my underwear. I was afraid I had something wrong with me."

"What'd he say?" I asked.

"He just laughed and explained the whole thing to me."

"I had no idea!" I said. "I'd never heard any of this before."

"It's good we had this little talk before you started partying out there," counseled Norm.

"Oh, yeah," agreed Barry. "Glad we had this talk."

"Okay, that's enough for tonight," Lynn said. "We'd better get some shut-eye. Lights out!"

Before falling asleep, I heard Lynn whisper to Mike, "I'm sure glad we caught him in time."

"Yeah," snickered Mike. "I'm sure there's a lot of stuff we can help Lil' Dickie with."

"Oh, yeah," agreed Norm.

As I lay in the dark, I thought to myself, *Gee, I'm really lucky to be on the road with these guys. They're so open and caring. They've had so much more experience than I have.* I went to sleep feeling a little more secure knowing I was with a truly great bunch of guys who were all looking out for me.

THE following night, we played a three-hour dance in Davenport for a ton of kids, and a good number of them followed us back to the Holiday Inn to party with the band. We only had the one room, so there were people everywhere. I was sitting on the roll-away watching the guys talking with different groups of people when my eye caught this really cute girl looking at me. She had short dark hair and deep blue eyes that seemed to be looking right through me. Locking eyes with me, she walked my way.

"What's your name?" she said.

"Dick," I replied nervously.

"Ooooh, I love dick," she slowly whispered.

"Really?" I said.

"Oh, yeah," she said softly, "dick is a real favorite of mine. I'm hungry. How about you?"

"I could eat," I said.

"Do you like pizza?" she asked.

"Sure," I answered.

She took my hand and with a gentle tug said, "Let's go."

As I stood up, I thought *Imagine that! Finding a girl all the way in Davenport, Iowa whose favorite name is Dick!*

"Hey, you guys," she said to the room. "I'm taking your friend for a while. We'll be back."

Norm jumped up and took me aside.

"You're not going to get yourself in trouble, are you?" he asked.

"What?" I said. "Oh, you mean…"

"Yeah, I mean…"

"No," I laughed. "We're just going to get some pizza."

"That's good," he said, sounding relieved. "Here, take some money. Bring a few pizzas back with you. We're all hungry."

"Cool," I answered, trying to sound like one of the boys.

Still holding my hand, my new friend led me out the door into the parking lot. I could feel my heart pounding as I tried to think of something clever to say. She walked up to a new dark brown Jeep, and I said, "Nice ride." I'd heard Barry say it many times, and I thought I was being pretty cool.

"Thanks," she answered. "I got it for graduation last year."

She had a blue graduation tassel hanging from her rearview mirror. "Is that yours?" I asked.

"Yep!" she answered. "Good ol' Central High."

She took off like a maniac. I held on for dear life as her driving threw me from one side of the seat to the other. She must've found every chuckhole in the state. There were no seat belts required in those days and so, in an effort to stay in the car, both of my hands were locked in death grips. My right hand was denting the black metal roll bar above my head while the fingers on my left hand were penetrating the leather on the back of her seat.

She drove out of town and up into the hills and pulled out on a plateau where she brought the car to an icy, sliding stop. I swallowed in relief, trying to get my heart out of my throat. Looking through the windshield, I could see the entire city from our high vantage point.

"How's that for a view?" she said.

"Incredible!" I answered nervously. "Really cool."

"There's a handle on the side of your seat," she instructed.

"Oh?"

"Yeah, it lays the seat down."

"Well, I can see better with it up."

"I didn't bring you up here for the view," she said with a grin on her face.

"Oh?" I questioned.

"Oh!" I got it.

"Oh no!" I exclaimed.

"Is there something wrong?" She asked.

I looked at her and slowly said, "I'm so sorry."

"What's the matter?" she asked.

"I can't do it," I said clumsily.

"Why not?" she asked with a hint of frustration in her voice.

"Well," I said, my embarassment growing, "I just can't yet."

"YET? We don't have a lot of time!" she said, now becoming a little annoyed.

"Well..." I started.

"What's the problem?" she interrupted.

"Oh, gee," I stumbled. Giving in to reality, I fumbled with embarrassment. "I'm not a man yet."

"What?" she said in disbelief.

"I'm not a man yet," I repeated, my face starting to flush.

"NOT A MAN YET?" she asked. "You're kidding me, right?"

"No," I answered, "I'm still waiting."

"What the hell are you talking about?" she said, backing away from me.

"I'm not a man yet. You know..."

"Oh, my God, you're a homo!" she loudly concluded. "Why did you let me bring you up here, then?"

"No, I'm not a homo," I insisted.

"What, then, DICK?" she asked.

"Well," I said, swallowing again, "I haven't had my period yet."

"YOU HAVEN'T HAD YOUR PERIOD YET?" she said, looking at me like I was a perverted serial killer. "Are you a girl, you sicko?" she said in shock.

"What? - No," I insisted.

"You're kidding me with this, right?"

"No, I know I look old enough, but I'm sorry. I'm not a man yet."

"You're not a man yet?" she repeated.

"No, but we can still get a pizza!"

"Okay, that's it, I'm out of here."

She started the Jeep and slammed the gearshift into reverse. The wheels spun in the dirt as she floored it and sped back onto the highway. At the time, I thought she was pissed because we couldn't do it. But now I know that wasn't it at all. She thought I was nuts.

She didn't say a word to me all the way back to the motel. She turned her radio up as loud as it would go. I could tell she was pissed, but it wasn't my fault. It was just Mother Nature. As we sped and bounced into the parking lot, I tried to lighten the air,

"Hey, we forgot to get pizza."

She skidded to a stop, turned down the radio and looked at me.

"Get out," she whispered.

"No pizza?" I asked.

"Get out!" she repeated, outwardly calm but inside a pressure cooker ready to explode.

As I stepped from the Jeep, she took off in anger without saying another word.

When I entered the room, the party was over. It was just the guys layin' around watching TV again. Lynn must've cut it short and kicked everyone out because we had to get up early the next morning.

Norm looked at me and said, "Where's the pizza?"

"No pizza," I answered.

"No pizza?" he repeated.

"No," I said.

"Oh," he said. "What took you so long? Was the place closed?"

"No," I said. "We didn't even go to get pizza."

"Where *have* you been?" Barry asked.

"Well, she drove up to the local make-out spot and asked to have sex."

That got their attention. They all sat up. Barry turned down the TV.

"What did you do?" asked Norm.

"Nothing," I said shyly, wanting to keep the embarrassing experience to myself.

"Well, what happened?" Asked Mike, curious to know the particulars.

"Nothing," I repeated, not wanting to share any more details.

"Yeah? What'd you do?" pressured Barry.

"Well," I said, reluctantly giving in, "we got up to the make-out place and I told her I couldn't have sex because I wasn't a man yet."

First came silence, then big smiles began to break out on their faces.

Barry stuck out his hand for me to shake it.

"Wow!" he said. "You're my hero."

"Goooood maaan!" added Norm.

"Oh, yeah, you're the coolest," said Mike, patting me on the back.

"Good for you!" said Lynn. "Good boy!"

"Did you get her number?" asked Mike.

"What for?" I questioned. "She was pissed."

"We'll be back, you know, and you might be a man when we come back."

"Oh, yeah, I didn't think about that," I said.

"Hey," said Norm as the guys headed back to bed, patting each other on the back, "I'm really proud of you. You did the right thing. You'll get your period pretty soon and things'll be a lot different. You'll see."

"I guess," I said, laying down on my roll-away. "But I'm really not worried about it. Besides, she kind of scared me. I'm just glad that we didn't start messing around before I told her. Imagine how mad she would've been if we'd gotten to the moment of truth and I couldn't, you know, do it."

"You're a thoughtful guy," said Norm, smiling.

They all laughed.

"That would've pissed her off good!" said Mike through his laughter.

"Yeah, that would've been something, alright," said Lynn, laughing, too.

I could hear them whispering and giggling in the dark. As I started to fall asleep, I thought to myself, *I'd better be a little more careful to not put myself in embarrassing situations like that any more. Boy, the road is sure going to be a lot different than high school. That was scary.*

VERSE 8

WHOEVER said, "I don't care what they say about me as long as they spell my name right!" was wise, oh so wise. Positive or negative, notoriety is a powerful force, and if you're lucky and prepared, you'll take advantage of the opportunities that arise when your moment in the sun comes. In our case, the PR surrounding us courtesy of "Louie Louie" was overwhelmingly negative and spanned the world. It made us famous and infamous and brought us our fair share of monetary rewards. But at the same time, it also created challenges that took many years to overcome. Some of those challenges were large and intimidating, others were modest and immediate. One of them, happening early in the game, was very personal and involved the quality of sound—or lack thereof—emanating from my vocal cords. Using the term loosely, I'm talking here about my singing.

Beginning in the '50s, the recording industry was transformed by an endless succession of advancements in technology. With the introduction of electrified guitars, basses and keyboards, rock music took off. Through its early years, rock 'n' roll was characterized by lead singers performing with backup groups, evidenced by male teen idols like Elvis Presley, Ricky Nelson and Roy Orbison. In the late '50s and early '60s, girl groups like the Crystals and the Shirelles used several lead singers. By 1963, a new trend had emerged, with groups featuring artists singing three- and four-part harmony and sharing the lead singing throughout the records. The Beatles, the Beach Boys and the Four Seasons exemplify this genre. Straight-from-the-gut garage rock was the Kingsmen's forté, and we had a strong heritage as an instrumental group, but as we traveled down the highways of America, we occasionally fancied ourselves as harmonizers. All it took for the guys to break into song and attempt a semblance of harmony was for someone to sing a phrase from a classic hit like "All I Have to Do Is Dream" by the Everly Brothers or "Lonesome Town" by Ricky Nelson. With that, the Kingsmen gunboat was instantly transformed from a rolling hotbed of musical anarchy into a three- or four-part harmony wagon.

Although we didn't sing harmonies much on stage, it was a favorite pastime for us off stage. Our dauntless attempts to reach harmonic perfection were usually experiments in terror at best. Once in a while, however, when the forces of the music universe were aligned just right, the guys happened on to vocal parts that could move angels to smile.

We were a few weeks into the tour, driving through Governor Welsh's Indiana—the Land of the Ban—when just such an inspired, heavenly moment hit. The song being covered was an Everly Brothers tune, and Lynn, Norm, Barry and Mike were doing the honors. Noticing I wasn't joining in—I never did—Mike asked, "Hey, Lil' Dickie, with your musical background, why don't you ever join in and harmonize with us?"

"I can hear the harmony parts," I answered with a giggle, "but I don't sing. Trust me, my singing voice is nothing you want to hear. Plus, I don't really know the lyrics to any of the songs you sing."

"Hey, none of us can sing, either, but we're not proud," joked Barry.

"You know the lyrics to 'Walkin' In A Winter Wonderland,' don't you?" Lynn asked.

"I suppose so," I answered somewhat reluctantly.

"Well, then, let's try it."

He immediately started singing the famous carol, leaving no room for me to refuse.

"Sleigh bells ring, are you listening," he sang."

Everyone joined in with the harmony parts they'd learned in high school choir.

"In the lane, snow is glistening/A beautiful sight,/we're happy tonight..."

At that point, I joined in with a well-placed, badly executed harmony.

"Walking in a winter wonderland."

The sound I made and alleged to be singing brought tears of laughter to the eyes of my kind, compassionate, loving fellow Musketeers.

"Oh, you sound awful!" teased Mike, wincing from the pain I'd just inflicted on his ears.

"Was that singing, or were you giving birth?" joked Barry.

"I told you I couldn't sing," I laughingly responded, trying to salvage what little pride I had left.

"Are you kidding me?" said Norm. "You sound as bad as Jack did on the vocal to 'Louie!'"

"Hey, there's an idea!" exclaimed Lynn.

"What is?" queried Mike.

"I played drums on the record," Lynn said. "Why doesn't Lil' Dickie come out front when we do 'Louie' and I'll go back to the drums? We'll sound even more like the record."

What I hoped was his joking produced a near riot of laughter.

"Do you know the words to 'Louie?'" Mike asked.

"Are there words to 'Louie Louie?'" I parried.

"Seriously," said Norm, "sing the chorus to 'Louie.'"

"Really?" I questioned.

"Yeah, let's hear it!" answered Mike.

Figuring Why not? I broke into the chorus.

"Louie Lou-eye, Oh no, me gotta go!"

Astonished shrieks echoed inside the Pontiac.

"You sound as bad as the record!" screamed Mike.

"Yeah," added Lynn through his laughter. "That was horrible!"

"No, wait!" interrupted Norm. "I think it's a great idea."

"What's a great idea?" said Mike.

"Having Lil' Dickie come out front and sing 'Louie' and having Lynn go back on drums."

"Oh, I don't know," I reacted, hoping to dissuade him.

"No, that'd be great!" said Lynn.

"I love it!" added Mike.

"Are you kidding me?" I questioned, stealing Norm's patented line.

"Let's do it tonight!" suggested Mike.

"Yeah!" agreed Lynn. "I've been wanting to play drums in the show. It adds to our Chinese fire drill."

"I don't even know the words!" I argued.

"All the better," said Mike. "You don't have to know the words. Just make the sound of words. The kids'll fill in the rest."

"You can't be serious!" I complained, terrified.

Ignoring me, the boys started working out the choreography as we sped along Back Road USA. They decided that, when it came time for "Louie" in that evening's performance—the scheduled venue was the Armory in Evansville, Indiana—without notice, Barry would start the keyboard intro. Meanwhile, Lynn and I would switch places and the surprise would be on. The guys loved the idea; I was petrified. While I was comfortable sitting behind the drums, I'd never been a front man before. What, me sing? I couldn't sing a lick, and I was worried. Knowing I was getting the job because I couldn't sing only made it worse.

Thoughts of me out front warbling in front of thousands of screaming teens, making up words as I went along to a song I didn't even know, consumed every second of my existence for the rest of that day. I was convinced I was going to explode into a thousand embarrassed pieces on stage. As zero hour approached, my shirt struggled to restrain my nervous, pounding heart from popping out of my skin. As we ended "Twist and Shout" and the kids were going wild, Barry started those distinctive chords on the keyboard, and Lynn came back to relieve me of my drumsticks. Strangely, few people in the crowd noticed the switch. As Barry started his *da, da da da* riff, they were far too busy getting out their words to confirm their versions to realize what we were up to. Grabbing the mic and breaking out in song, I mostly saw the tops of people's heads as they followed along, and my nervousness gave way to relief. All I had to do was sing the chorus, whose words I knew, and make sounds in the rhythm of the vocal through the rest of the song, and the kids bought it, hook, line and sinker. In a two-and-a-half-minute metamorphosis, I went from fearing for my life to loving the experience. By the time I reached the last chorus, I was rockin' 'n' rollin' with the best of them.

Louie Lou-eye, oh no
Me gotta go
Yeah, yeah, yeah, yeah, yeah, yeah
Louie Lou-eye, oh baby
Me gotta go

I couldn't believe the commotion unfolding before me. The crowd was on its feet, screaming at the top of their lungs and clapping their hands and waving their arms. Many in the audience were singing along, and they were all looking at me in wild anticipation as I reached the penultimate line, "Let's hustle on outa here." It was all so incredible and amazing, unbelievably thrilling—a total turn on for Lil' Dickie.

I shouted "Louie"'s famous last words, "Let's go!" and we ran off stage as wave after wave of thunderous applause surged over us. At that moment, who was more excited, the guys or me? They were all laughing and slapping my back and throwing me around like a newborn baby. It was a toss-up.

"That was great!' said Mike, rubbing my head like one would a small child's.

"That's the way it will be from now on!" exclaimed Lynn. "Playing the drums again was too much fun."

"What words did you sing in the verses?" asked Norm through his laughter.

"Nothing," I answered. "I just made up a bunch of things and tried to make them sound as slurred and crazy as the record."

As I write these words—41 years almost to the day after that fateful night in Evansville—I've sung "Louie Louie" at every Kingsmen performance since, in other words, thousands of times. Exceptions were lip-synced TV appearances on shows like *Shindig* and *Hullabaloo* when we didn't have to reproduce the sound of the record. On those occasions, Lynn wanted to act as front man for our signature song.

LET'S not forget, the year I'm writing about here was 1964, during an era when societal standards declared it a no-no for news reporters to say a word as harmless as "pregnant" during their broadcasts. Swear words of any kind, even mild cuss words like "damn," were totally *verboten* on radio and television. Married couples on TV shows like *Ozzie and Harriet* still slept in separate beds and, in mixed company, adults—and especially gentlemen—said "PG" instead of "pregnant," as though "PG" were code for something sinful, something that if called by its proper name might offend the delicate sensibilities of what many still referred to as "the weaker sex." And, just in case some miscreant dared to flaunt society's moral standards and stretch or break one of its rules on air, squads of network censors hovered nearby, ready to pounce on and punish any and all transgressors. If judged by the standards current then, more than any other Kingsman I was a child of the time—or maybe of the time before—the offspring of an age that was soon to pass.

Now that I was performing "Louie Louie" one, two, sometimes three or more shows a night, every time I turned around, I found myself confronted by an embarrassing situation involving girls demanding to know the details of the obscene lyrics I sang. A perfect stranger to the ways of women and the world, I felt clumsy at such moments—uncomfortable, inelegant and graceless. Indeed, you couldn't find a less-likely, less-qualified, less-prepared candidate for dealing with the issues surrounding "Louie Louie" than Lil' Dickie. And here I was, being accused morning, noon and night of singing words I found impossible to hear or read or speak without turning bright red. The point is, my sheltered childhood life, spent mostly in Gig Harbor, was devoid of obscene ideas and mostly untainted by off-color language. The one exception was Herb Cook, town mailman. Following the flashback format of *The Wonder Years*, I'd like to tell you about Herb Cook, another life-shaping influence I was blessed with.

THOUGH kind of heart, Herb had a reputation for communicating in a most colorful, salty way. Compared to what's commonly heard and seen today, his language was soft; even back then, his choice of words was not considered obscene, technically speaking (I don't recall ever hearing an out-and-out sexual obscenity spoken in the Harbor). Instead, Herb brandished what was known in local parlance as "a sailor's tongue." Offsetting—or perhaps stemming—from that fact, he also had a true gift for communicating with the local kids, one of whom was me. A highlight of my summer days was meeting him at the mailbox, where he'd always inquire as to my plans for the afternoon and more often than not hand me a Baby Tootsie Roll.

Although childless, when Herb heard that a bevy of Harbor kids had gone unpicked for an area Little League team, he couldn't stand it. So he gathered together the disappointed, rag-tag bunch of rejects and, with our parents' reluctant permission, helped us form a team of our own which he called "the Damn Leftover Bunch." He believed that every kid should have the experience of playing in Little League—he called it "the American Way" as though it were the right and obligation for every young boy to love his country and play baseball. Although pleased that we'd all get to play on a baseball team, with uniforms and everything, our parents harbored great misgivings about having Herb serve as our coach. Given that he was the only person in town willing to step up to the plate on our behalf, the village had but one choice if it wanted to see its sons play ball, and that choice was Herb Cook.

The Leftovers met every day after school to practice. Parents who showed up to watch cringed as Coach Cook yelled things like, "Damn it, get in front of the damn ball!" or "How the hell did you miss that ball?" It didn't matter to him that the infield we played on was a miniature rock garden, making it almost impossible to accurately predict the bounce of a ball; Herb expected you to catch every ball hit or thrown your way—or at least to "stop the damn thing!" During games, umpires often issued him warnings about his choice of words, and heaven forbid he should disagree with a close call. Umpires and players, spectators and attending stray dogs all got an earful of his colorful language on such occasions. Herb used "hell" and "damn" frequently, and was not above taking the Lord's name in vain; he elevated those mild forms of profanity to an art form, stringing them together in an impressive progression of colorful images. For all that, Herb Cook *never* used sexual obscenities, especially not the *f*-word or any of its variations. Woe be to me had I ever said anything around Herb as a baseball player like what I was now being accused of singing as a Kingsman.

In my Harbor days, people didn't use or need swear words to communicate and, as far as the opposite sex was concerned, it was beyond my comprehension that a girl could know there were such things as obscene language and dirty words. Throughout high school, I thought that swearing was something kept between guys.

The strongest language I'd ever heard a girl use up to that point was "Darn it!" On those counts, my attitudes would've fit in easily with some of the mannered civilities of the Antebellum South as described in *Gone With The Wind*. And that's very nearly how far removed in time and place I sometimes felt while on that first tour as a Kingsmen.

I knew that girls had naughty little secrets they only shared with each other, and that girls used "never talk-never tell" hush-hush pacts amongst themselves to keep the boys guessing and off balance. But for me to use bad language in front of a girl was simply not possible. Not only would I have been too embarrassed, I would've lived in mortal fear that my parents would somehow find out about it. Had that happened, I would've been in more trouble than a fly in a spider's web. More than a matter of parental fear, for me it was, and is still, an issue of respect.

Guided by Coach Cook's firm hand, the Leftovers went undefeated that year, the ultimate "na na na na na!" to the teams that had rejected all of us. Although Coach Cook was constantly in our faces and on our backs, we loved and respected him. He believed in us and taught us to be winners and there are few better ways to affect another's life than those. The trophy I received for playing a part in that Cinderella/underdog story is still one of my prize possessions.

You've heard about some of my most embarrassing moments as a Kingsman; it's time to reveal the most embarrassing moment of my childhood—a true life story dating from my brief career as a Leftover. I think true stories are the grandest, anyway.

THE baseball uniforms we Leftovers wore were made of wool, and I was extremely allergic to wool. Thankfully, we only had to wear the uniforms for games, not for practice. On game days, I wore long cotton underwear beneath the wool pants, and on hot days I chose to suffer through the heat rather than put up with a rash for several subsequent days. I also wore a long-sleeved T-shirt under my uniform top, but the wool collar still rubbed against my neck. My mother fixed the problem by wrapping one of my brother's diapers around my neck to safeguard the tender skin. This seemed an ideal solution until it came to the bottom of the ninth inning of the District Little League championship game when the Leftovers came to bat, down by two runs.

Steve Wilkerson, Lester Frye, Jack Finholm and Dennis Colby were all due up before me. With this crew, I was positive I'd never get to the nerve-racking plate. Steve, our clean up hitter, began our final at bat with a shot down the third base line that left him standing on second base as his teammates in the dugout and our parents in the stands screamed and jumped with excitement. Coaching third base as he had all year, Herb clapped his hands together and shouted, "Yeah! Good job! Here we go!"

Looking back at Lester, the next batter, he yelled, "There's one sittin' there for ya, son."

Lester was a short, skinny kid who reminded me of one of the Seven Dwarves. He wore the smallest size uniform we had, and still it looked several sizes too big for him. That didn't keep him from being as fast as greased lighting on the base paths. He stood in the batter's box as the pitcher delivered a ball in the dirt.

"BALL ONE!" cried the ump.

With tension building, the pitcher delivered his next pitch.

"BALL TWO!" came the call.

Pitcher and opposing fans alike squirmed as the pressure mounted.

"Come on, you can do it!" shouted their fans to the pitcher. "This guy can't hit. Just throw it across the plate."

Again clapping his hands together as the crowd noise grew in intensity, coach Cook yelled encouragement.

"Get picky now, son," he instructed Lester. "Hitter's pitch right here. Make sure it's in there and give it a ride!"

As the pitcher readied for his next delivery, I could hear the team on the field yelling, "Hey, batta, batta, batta! Swing, batta, batta, batta!" trying to unnerve the normally cool Lester. The screaming and yelling rose to a feverish pitch as the pitcher threw the ball to the plate. As Lester tried to jump out of the way of the errant pitch, it hit him square in the back with an ugly-sounding thud.

He fell to the ground in pain as Coach Cook ran to his aid. Ignoring his injury, the tough little guy rose to his feet and trotted to first base, teary eyed and clutching his side.

Jack Finholm batted next, and I prayed that he'd get a hit to drive in Steve and Lester and tie the game. That way, we'd go into extra innings were Dennis and I to make outs.

"STRIKE ONE!"
"STRIKE TWO!"
"STRIKE THREE!"

Three pitches, three strikes, and Jack was called out.

How could this be? I thought. *Jack's one of our best hitters!*

As I assumed my place in the on deck circle, I felt more pressure than I'd ever known before in my life, on the field or off. The game, the season, the championship might come down to whether or not I could get on base and avoid being the third and final out. I crossed my fingers, hoping against hope that Dennis, our number seven hitter and batting next, one spot before me, would save the day for the Leftovers, and me from being the goat.

Sweating Den's at bat pitch by pitch, I stood in the on deck circle trying to appear unshaken. I limbered up by swinging my bat to and fro exactly like I'd seen my hero, Milwaukee Braves third baseman Eddie Matthews, do so many times on the *Game of the Week* on TV.

Dennis swung at the first pitch and missed by a country mile.

"STRIKE ONE!" shouted the umpire.

Oh no! I thought. *Well, that's okay! He'll get the next one.*

I stood in the on deck circle praying, "Please God! Please God! Please God! Please God! Please God!" as Dennis readied for the next pitch.

After checking for a sign from Coach Cook, he stood confidently in the batter's box and waited.

"BALL ONE!" yelled the umpire.

Dennis took a deep breath of relief, gathered himself as supporters in the crowd shouted their encouragement and stood in for another pitch.

"STEE..RIKE TWO!" declared the umpire.

Deafening screams rose from the other side of the field as opposing fans anticipated the doomed fate of the nervous batter.

"Come on, Den," I shouted anxiously, "you can do it!"

Dennis and I were batting at the bottom of the lineup that day for one good reason: We hadn't hit the ball that well all year long. Those who'd followed our club closely were praying for a miracle as much as they were yelling for a hit. The sounds coming from the bleachers told the tale; spectators were living and dying with each pitch.

The pitcher delivered another tension-filled offering to the plate as the opposing team continued to yell, trying to unnerve Dennis.

"Hey, batta, batta, batta! Swing, batta, batta, batta!"

I was still chanting in prayer, "Please God! Please God! Please God! Please God! Please God!" when Dennis swung from his heels. He hit the ball high in the air and far, and my teammates and I and our fans screamed with joy—until Mr. Spalding landed foul just outside the third base line, a short distance from the left field fence.

"FOUL BALL!" yelled the umpire.

"Ooooh!" shouted the Harbor crowd in unison, making one of the most famous sounds in baseball. I felt myself dying. I couldn't take any more.

"Come on, Den!" I called out hopefully. "Straighten it out! Give it a ride!"

I swear I could feel the wind from Dennis' bat as he swung with all of his might at the final pitch.

"STEE..RIKE THREE!" shouted the umpire as Dennis went down swinging.

"Oh, no!" I cried out in panic.

The other team and their parents went crazy as Herb instantly yelled, "Time out!" My fellow teammates and our parents sat silently, breathlessly as the coach called me over to him.

"You going to pinch hit for me, coach?" I asked hopefully.

"Look me square in the eyes, son," he said, bending over.

I looked up in his eyes in fear.

"Listen," he said, "this is a tough spot. Not many guys get to be in this situation in their lives."

"Get to be?" I thought. *There's that 'get to be' again. "Stuck," you mean.*

Then with great insight, Coach Herb spoke words I've never forgotten.

"No matter what you do in that batter's box right now," he said with a firm, calming voice, "I'm going to guarantee you somethin'. You won't forget this moment for the rest of your life. Safe or out, you're my last batter. Do you understand?"

"Unless he walks me, then Terry's up," I answered.

"Oh, no you don't!" he said to me firmly. "Don't let moments in life like this get away from you, son. They don't come along every day. Damn it, I don't want a walk! I want you to hit the damn ball and hit it as hard and far as you can. Nobody ever expected us to get this far. Win or loose, hold your head up. There's a thousand other guys sitting at home just wishin' they were in this championship game. I don't care if you're out! Just go for it. Hit the damn thing and make yourself a memory!"

Drawing me closer to him and clinching his teeth, he spoke in almost a whisper.

"Well, hell," he said, "look at it this way, damn it. Look at that pitcher."

I looked over at their pitcher and saw him shaking his head up and down at his coach in the dugout, assuring him I was as good as out.

"Think about this," Herb continued. "What kind of a memory are you going to give that stupid little idiot on the mound?"

With that, he slapped me on the rear.

"Now, get the hell out there," he said, "and show me what you've got!"

I turned and walked to the plate. What came over me, I can't explain, but the jitters were all gone. I took a few practice swings and stepped into the batter's box. It was the first time I understood it was okay if I was out. Nobody expected me to get a hit, not the other team, not even my team if the truth be known. I could see the other team yelling, but I couldn't really hear them. Instead, I focused on the ball in the pitcher's hand.

As the ball approached the plate, the whole world passed in slow motion, and the ball just sat there, waiting for me to smash it. I swung as hard as I could and crushed it.

So many times in the past, when I hit the ball the bat would sting my hands with a sharp fiery pain. But this time, I barely felt a tick on the bat. As the ball flew off, high in the air and far over the center fielder's head, the crowd erupted in a roar. Steve and Lester took off, heading for home. The crowd went wild as, one after the other, my teammates crossed the plate, tying the game. Rounding second, I noticed the center fielder picking up the ball. Looking over at Herb, I saw he was waving me on, sending me home to try to win the game. I was running so fast, my hat flew off my head and my brother's diaper came loose from my neck and sailed into the air behind me. I felt like I was going to run out of my legs.

With one final, joyous leap I jumped on home plate and raised my arms high in the air in triumph. Home run! Game over! We'd won! My teammates mobbed me in utter joy.

Reaching into the pile of triumphant, out-of-control, celebrating Leftovers, Herb grabbed me and lifted me into the air, shouting, "You did it, dammit, you did it!"

As the commotion peaked, a sound filled the air that could be heard as far away as Tacoma, a sound that echoed in barber shops and restaurants and homes in Gig Harbor for weeks to come as celebrating citizens relived again and again this glorious day.

"Dickie, Dickie!"

It was my mother. Hearing her excited, piercing voice repeating my name again and again, I searched the bleachers for her, thinking I was about to receive her well-earned adulation.

As our eyes caught each other's, she pointed toward the field and hollered above all of creation the immortal words, "Dickie! Dickie! You dropped your diaper!"

The color of the redness cooking my skin revealing my embarrassment was only eclipsed by the jaw dropping look of mortification on my face.

"Good one, Lil!" I heard one parent say.

"Oh, good Lord, Lil!" said another.

My mother's words provided great ammunition for taunting shots from the ill-mannered bad sports on the opposing team. We gathered at home plate and lined up, preparing to pass each other, shaking hands and exchanging good sportsman-type greetings. Normally in such a line, all you hear is "Good game!" "Good game!" "Good game!" On this occasion, in contrast, I was the target of "Good game! Now don't forget your diaper, Dickie!" Chuckle, chuckle. "Good game! Don't worry, Dickie, you'll wear the big boy pants soon!" Giggle, giggle. "Good game! Nice diaper, Dickie!" Snicker, snicker. I greeted each congratulatory remark with a friendly elbow to the chest.

Hearing the rude comments from the losers, my elder loving sister Nancy decided to come to my defense—as usual—only to add to the unforgettable memory. Standing in front of the backstop as the teams ended the line ceremony, Nancy punished the "bad boy losers" with her sharp-edged, clever tongue.

"Yeah, well," she yelled, "Dickie only wears a diaper because he has to."

That brought the house down once again, putting the perfect capper on the moment.

As I ran back past home plate with my teammates still hitting me on the back and jumping for joy, I felt a certain kinship to the Mighty Casey and his humiliation in Muddville. Shaking my head and smiling in disbelief, I said to my defender-and-champion older sister, "Thanks a lot, Nancy."

That night, as I tried to fall asleep, I started to laugh. Finally, I saw humor in the day, and it hit my funny bone. Hearing me laughing from his bed across the room from mine, my little brother Karly asked, "What's so funny, Dickie?"

"I just realized I'm not like Casey," I said. "Casey lost the game, but we won."

"Who's Casey?" he asked.

"Never mind," I said. "Time to go to sleep."

As fast as the indignity came, it was gone and forgotten, with one exception. In the following years, at various community get-togethers, as people sat around trading "remember when" stories, the memory of that day all too often returned. Those affairs usually ended with me getting my head affectionately rubbed and my hair lovingly messed up by one of the obnoxious grownups.

VERSE 9

MY fifth grade year was special in so many ways. Not only did the Leftovers win the whole shooting match, but I also developed a huge crush on Penny Harper. It seemed like every girl in the Harbor knew about it before I did. They were always passing notes and whispering private things between themselves that made me feel like they were watching and waiting for me to do something so they could report it to Penny through their secret girlfriend network. Believe me, such things exist.

What is it with girls? I still don't know how they do it. Every time one of them enters a room, within a matter of minutes every other girl there knows everything good and bad about her current relationship. Personally, I think they must have a secret nationwide information line hooked up to every girl's restroom in the country. That would explain why they all disappear in there together—never alone—and spend so much time. Guys don't do that. For example, never once have I tapped Mike or Barry on the shoulder and suggested that we go to the men's room together. It's definitely a girl thing.

Now that I think about it, I bet that's where the Internet started—in a girl's restroom somewhere, not in Tim Berners-Lee's lab in Geneva, Switzerland or in Al Gore's office in Washington, DC. The girls have been plugging in all along, and we boys just couldn't figure it out for the longest time. Think about it, it's amazing. Anything any boy does, anywhere in the country, if any girl has an interest in him, within seconds all of the other girls know about it and soon after that the interested party has a complete file on the matter covering every detail of the incident, long before the poor guy can think up a good excuse for his actions. It's even worse if the boy's sin has something to do with their relationship. In that case, every girl in the loop instantly becomes a counselor and hours are spent in rest rooms plotting retribution against the enemy.

Getting back to Penny Harper, she was the first girl I ever took an interest in. A beautiful young lady of 12, she had it all, including flaxen blonde hair and blue eyes to die for. Penny was kind and well liked, with a sense of humor that was unsurpassed. She lived on a farm about a mile or two from me, an easy bike ride over mostly flat roads. The Harbor was small enough then, you only had to ride a couple of blocks until you were out of town and peddling down the kind of two-lane, tree-lined country road that inspires poets and painters to great works.

Penny owned her own horse, a black and white pinto she called "Scout." Most of the time, she rode the gentle boy bareback, and I can still see, in vivid detail, her ponytail dancing in the wind behind her as she rhythmically pushed the big gelding, lungs heaving, down dusty trails at a gallop. Every day after school, come rain or come shine, Penny rode the endless power line trails that cut across the driveway leading to her house. Some days after school, I'd make my way to the top of the hill across from her place and sit in the brush and secretly watch as she rode the tractor-mowed fields behind her house — she was poetry in motion. Once in a while, we'd "accidentally" run into each other on the wide trail under the power lines and talk small talk for a while before one of us had to be home for dinner. Those were exciting moments for me, and all of that was just a prelude to the most thrilling thing that ever happened to me in all the years I lived in the Harbor.

Weekends found most of us local kids gathered at the movie house, a quaint old theatre that everyone joked had been built by settlers in the 1800s. It had wood-framed seats covered in a fuzzy, maroon-colored cut-velvet material. As you walked through the front door, the smell of freshly-popped popcorn always filled the air. But you couldn't buy anything at the candy counter until Mrs. Fuqua had finished selling tickets out front and made her way from the ticket booth to the concession stand in the lobby. Mrs. Fuqua's movie house was definitely a one-woman operation.

We didn't mind. We were all patient, for we knew she never started the movie until after everyone had filled up with all of the junk food they could carry and was seated. You could have any cold drink you wanted, as long as you wanted bottled Coke. As for candy bars, you had three and sometimes four choices: a Hershey's Chocolate, a Baby Ruth, a Snickers or, on special occasions, a Butterfinger. Butterfingers were divine, a real favorite of mine with their unique taste. For those who preferred boxed candy, you had Good and Plenty and Dots to choose between.

Mrs. Fuqua always showed the latest movies. After the feature was over, when the lights came up, she'd stand down front and poll the crowd on their choice for next week's feature. I didn't realize it at the time, but she was outsmarting all of her clueless patrons. By having the crowd pick the next movie, she wouldn't have to advertise. We'd all know in advance what film was playing the following week. And we'd all be lined up buying tickets the next weekend, knowing for certain we wanted to see the film being featured. By having us choose, she took the gamble out of her business. All in all, she was a sweet lady. Giving her the benefit of the doubt, I'll allow that her primary motive was trying to please the good folks of Gig Harbor. And please us, she did. Her establishment was a favorite haunt for local residents of all ages.

Normally, we kids descended on the theatre in a pack and sat where we could. Occasionally, through clever maneuvering, you magically got to sit next to the person you really wanted to sit next to, all the better if the opposite sex was involved. On this one momentous night, I had my dreams fulfilled. For the first time, I got to sit next to Penny Harper.

The movie was a real thriller, *The Fly* starring Vincent Price. It's about a scientist who invents a transporter machine. As promo, the studio produced a waiver that moviegoers viewing the film by themselves were supposed to sign before entering the theatre.

The waiver read:

> **YOU CAN'T SEE**
> **The Fly**
> **ALONE**
> **UNLESS YOU**
> **SIGN THIS**
> **WAIVER**
>
> In consideration of my being allowed to see **The Fly** alone, I hereby agree to enter this theatre at my own risk, blaming no one but myself for whatever startling, shocking effects this picture may have upon me. In witness whereof, I hereby set my hand and seal.

As I sat down and looked up, the skin on my entire body turned flush and my heart began pounding out of my shirt. There stood Penny Harper, turning around and about to sit down in the seat next to mine. I had my hands on my thighs and, as she sat down, her full, freshly ironed, soft cotton dress spilled over onto my seat, touching my hand that was at rest on my leg. I was so thrilled, I didn't move a muscle for over half the movie for fear of losing contact with that electrifying two-inch piece of material. With one hand immobilized by the touch of her dress, I found it impossible to open my candy bar with my other hand. I was not about to move the hand at rest in heaven for a stupid candy bar, and my Butterfinger went uneaten throughout the first feature.

As the movie played on, I occasionally looked around to see whether anyone had detected my impropriety. Several times, I elbowed my friend David sitting on the other side of me, trying to get him to notice my lucky hand, but he was too enthralled by the movie to understand the reason for my subtle poking. I kept my hand perfectly still, not daring to move a muscle, watching the movie as my system spat out adrenalin and my tell-tale heart pumped furiously, charging every cell in my body.

Then came the scene where the unfortunate scientist/inventor, who just minutes before had successfully transported several items from one side of his lab to the other, decides to try out the disintegrator on himself. Putting the machine on automatic, he climbs in the cubical expecting to arrive unscathed in a similar cubical on the other side of his lab. However, as he opens the door to climb in, he fails to notice that a fly has accidentally entered the cubical with him. When the machine re-assembles their molecules, this stupidity results in the scientist exchanging parts of his body with those of the uninvited fly. The scientist covers his head with a sheet and buries his hand in his pocket so his wife can come into his lab without having to see what's happened to him. He writes a message to her, stating he's had an accident and asking her to find a fly that is half white. The scientist accidentally removes his hand from his pocket, revealing it's a fly's hand, and his wife screams and leaves the room. From that point on, the movie grew ever more terrifying. We were all on the edge of our seats when the sheet fell off the scientist's head in a later scene, revealing a giant fly head with bulging compound eyes and a gross hypopharynx tongue. The entire theatre joined the horrified wife and erupted in terrified screams.

    I don't know exactly where the sound came from that emerged from my mouth at that moment, but it was from some dark place I'd never visited before. I was so frightened, I forgot about touching Penny's dress and grabbed the armrest in hopes it would keep me from jumping through the roof. Just as I did, the most wonderful and miraculous of events took place. Penny, jumping out of her skin as well, grabbed the armrest, too. Our hands were locked in fear. Instinctively, bravely, I intertwined my fingers in hers as though I were heroically going to save her from a fate worse than death that at any moment might jump out of the screen and destroy us. For the rest of the movie, we squeezed hands through every scary scene. Neither one of us wanted the movie to finish or the night to come to an end. It was thrilling.

UNTIL 1964, my evening spent watching *The Fly* with Penny in 1958 was, without question, the closest thing to a sexual experience I'd had. Knowing that, try imagining my reaction when a beautiful

136 ♪ LOUIE, LOUIE

young girl, sweet and innocent in appearance, tapped me on the shoulder as I signed autographs after a show. Thinking I was the voice on the unintelligible recording, and without so much as a hint of embarrassment, she said to me, the boy still waiting to get his period, "I have all of the words to 'Louie Louie' worked out except in the last verse."

Unfolding a piece of lined notebook paper, the blonde-haired, blue-eyed, well-fashioned girl moved in close to me to share her version of the lyrics to "Louie Louie."

"I think I have it," she continued. "Could you help me out? My girlfriends and I have listened to it at every speed, and I'm pretty positive this is it."

I would've agreed to anything this perfect creature wanted.

"Sure," I said, unsuspecting.

"Right here," she began, pointing to the last verse on her piece of paper, "do you say 'lay her again' or 'eat her again' in the last verse?"

I was shocked beyond belief.

"Did she actually say, 'Lay her again?'" I asked myself.

I knew what "lay her again" meant, and I didn't know how to answer that half of her question. So I focused instead on the "eat her again" quote, not knowing what she really meant. With a condescending chuckle, I said, "I think you've been watching too many Tarzan movies."

"What!?" she said, a puzzled look on her face.

"I can guarantee you it has nothing to do with any kind of cannibalism," I explained. "The song is Jamaican, not African. How did you ever come up with an idea like that? 'Eat her again?' Now that's a new one! Wait until I tell the guys that one. What will you people think of next?"

She looked at me as though I were out of my mind.

"Ooooo-kay," she said, slowly returning to her paper, "so, it's 'lay her again?'"

In my wildest dreams, I'd never imagined being in this kind of predicament. I'd been brought up lacking the ability to swear, or even to insinuate anything off color—least of all in front of a girl. Trying to stay cool and respectful while yet retaining the bad boy image I was a part of, I took the paper from her hand and stared at it, uncertain what to do next. By pretending to read her version of the lyrics, I thought I might win myself enough time to gather my thoughts and exit from this situation gracefully.

Then I made the mistake of reading her carefully-deciphered version. It was filled with words I recognized but would never have dared use. The obscenities mortified me, and I felt embarrassed just standing beside a girl, knowing she knew I was reading such things in her presence. The more dirty words I read, the redder my face turned. Still trying to hold it together, I refolded her paper and handed it back to her.

"You're close, but not there yet," I masterfully informed her, my face on fire.

"Well, show me the parts I have wrong," she begged, refusing to let me off the hook.

"I'm not allowed to do that," I said, trying to muster a laugh. "It's illegal. That could get me in a lot of trouble. The FBI is watching us, and they're everywhere. I can only tell you if you're right or not."

"Please," she whined, "I really want to know!"

"Why?" I asked, turning to walk away.

"Are you kidding?" she answered, smiling. "Everybody wants to know, and nobody can figure it out."

"I'm sorry," I said, "I can't help you, but you're really close."

I started jogging away as though I were late for something. Behind me, I could hear the girl giggling to her friends.

"Well," she said, "he says I'm close. Do you think he was for real about that cannibal-Tarzan line?"

"Oh," said her friend, "he was telling you in a nice way it definitely is not 'eat her again.' I think he's funny."

What did she mean by that? I wondered. For the first time, I found myself wondering whether "Louie Louie" *really was* corrupting the youth of America. A girl like that should never have known what words like that meant. And I thought, *Why the cannibal line?*

In the dressing room afterward, I told the guys about the girl and her belief that "Louie Louie" had lyrics in it about cannibalism.

"What do you mean, cannibalism?" asked Mike.

"She asked me if there was something about eating someone in the lyrics."

Mike looked over at Barry as they both broke up.

"What did you tell her?" Mike asked.

"Oh," I said innocently, "I straightened her out and told her, no, the song has nothing to do with cannibalism or anything African. It's Jamaican."

That raised quite a laugh with the boys. They told me next time to send those inquisitive girls to them and they'd take over from there. Fortunately, it didn't take long for me to become skilled at avoiding lyrics seekers and sending them along to the other guys. They were right: It *did* make things a lot easier for me. Unlike me, however, they seemed to enjoy the encounters.

Author on the drums

VERSE 10

WE'D been having a great time on the road, setting attendance records everywhere we played—mostly dance halls and rowdy college campuses in the Midwest. Those college dates were scenes straight out of *Animal House*. Typically, we played for three or four hours at a frat house or at the local college hangout to a group of drunken party animals. By morning, we'd become honorary members of their frats—or, in some cases, sororities—and our newly-minted brothers and sisters would be begging us to stay another night. We gained countless new "best friends" at every such stop. The great difference between the one type of date and the other was, instead of myriad versions of "Louie Louie" circulating among the crowd like what invariably happened at our public performances, each individual school settled in advance on its own unique version, with students agreeing to what was being said on the record. Then, when it came time to play "Louie Louie," instead of reading along with the band, the kids *sang* along with great inebriated prowess, belting out their own lyrics with a roar that could be heard for miles.

The dance halls were relics from the Big Band era, most of them still operated by their original owners. We would arrive a few hours early and visit with the proprietors before unloading and setting up. We got a kick out of talking with these people and listening to their stories about the various artists—many of them legends even to teenage rockers like us—who'd played their halls in years past. Without exception, everyone who hired us and everyone who saw us play thought we were the loudest band they'd ever heard, hands down. We loved hearing that. To a Kingsman, loud was good, louder was better and loudest was the best of all.

The dance halls were created for music and dancing and were

fabulous. Their sprung wooden floors enabled patrons to dance the night away without wearing out their legs. Their stages were built in the shape of a shell, and the on-stage acoustics were so well engineered, the enhanced sound we heard was an added inspiration as we played. Those stages reflected the sound more evenly to the crowd, heightening their enjoyment as well. Dance halls, what incredibly wonderful places to perform!

The dance hall owners formed a circuit that famous bands had been working for decades. For months at a time, a troupe would travel cross country from one dance hall to another to another in a historically-perfected route, with hops between cities averaging two to three hundred miles each. In the Big Band era, the connecting roads were largely two lane state affairs, poorly paved if at all, and it could take all day and sometimes two, weather permitting, to get from one gig to the next. By 1964, in contrast, when five Kingsmen first visited themselves upon unsuspecting Midwesterners, the US Highway System was already long in place. The majority of the roads designated as part of that system were still only two lanes for most of their length, but their lanes and shoulders were much wider and better paved and their routing was much less circuitous than what the traveling troubadours of the '30s and '40s had endured. Ike's pet project, the Interstate Highway System, was just then being developed, and occasionally we lucked out and ran into a stretch of four-lane Interstate that cut our travel time to almost nothing.

As a result, musical barnstorming '60s style wasn't nearly the hardship that touring the circuit had been for the big bands that blazed the trail before us. The biggest difference between their schedules and ours was, we could easily make the jump between one venue and the next in a single day with room to spare, our daily travel time averaging between four and six hours. Instead of playing one or two halls a week like the bands of old once did, on this tour we played a different hall every night for nearly eight weeks straight without repeating a venue. Though always fun, it became hard work. And subsequent tours were to prove even more challenging, stretching out 12 to 15 weeks.

THE more the guys perfected their pick-up lines, the less of a challenge the girls became, resulting in a two-fold benefit. Needing less time to score left my four band mates with more time for much-needed sleep, which gave them added energy to face the following night's challenges.

Early one particular morning—I think we were in Nebraska, or maybe Iowa—we were rudely awakened by someone pounding on our motel room door. Outside, an irate mother was screaming at the top of her lungs, "Open up, you perverts! I know you're in there! I want the guy who broke my little girl's cherry to come out here right now!"

"What've you done this time, Norm?" asked Lynn, still half asleep.

"It wasn't me!" asserted the squinting, whispering youth. "Mike and Barry were the only ones that went out last night."

Climbing out of bed, Mike defended himself.

"Hey, she just brought me back here," he insisted. "We sat in the restaurant for a while talking, and then she left."

"BARRY!" Lynn whispered. "What the hell did *you* do last night?"

Throwing back the covers, Barry quietly professed, "I didn't touch her."

I started to turn on the light, but Lynn stopped me.

"Don't turn that on!" he warned. "She'll know we're in here. Besides, the sun's up. It's bright enough to see in here already."

As Barry stood up, dried blood could clearly be seen on the front of his T-shirt and underwear. I briefly wondered whether he'd had his period, but quickly realized it had to be something else. Mike was the first to speak.

"Aw, Barry," he whispered, "what the hell were you thinking?"

The commotion outside grew louder.

"Well, um...," winced Barry as he looked down at the tell-tale evidence. "...Well, um, I only screwed her a little bit."

"A little bit?" laughed Mike.

"Well... we didn't go all the way".

"Far enough!" answered Mike.

"Hey, she said she was 18!" Barry said, trying to defend himself.

"Crap! Everybody get your stuff packed," Lynn ordered. "We've got to be ready to beat feet out of here the second she leaves."

We hurriedly packed as the woman continued to pace the sidewalk, pound the door, scream obscenities and demand we turn over the guilty party. Norm snuck a peek through the side of the curtain and noticed the woman's daughter sitting in the front seat of a running car parked right outside our door. When we checked in the previous afternoon, the motel manager wouldn't allow us to dock the USS Pontiac with car-top carrier and trailer in front of our room. Fortunately for us this morning, that meant our gunboat was moored at the far end of the lot some ways away, where it took up several parking spaces without impeding motel traffic.

Lynn whispered our instructions.

"Okay, everybody, listen up! I'll climb through the bathroom window, and you guys pass the suitcases to me. Then you climb through while I sneak out front and grab the car. I'll drive it to the back of the room. When I pull up, throw the stuff in the back and we'll get the hell out of here. And for God's sake, Barry, change your damn clothes!"

As quietly and as swiftly as we could, we followed Lynn's orders, clambering out the bathroom window after him while the enraged mother intensified her attacks on the front door, threatening to inflict an escalating array of physical punishments on the S.O.B. bastard who'd deflowered her daughter. (A particularly painful form of castration was now among the options being suggested.) *Bang! #$@&!?%#! Boom! #$@&!?%#! Crash! #$@&!?%#! Screech! #$@&!?%#!* The lady was so determined, so busy concentrating on breaking down the door and choosing just the right shade of purple for her vocabulary, she failed to notice events unfolding to her left. Half a football field away, our fearless leader was creeping up on the far side of the station wagon.

Once there, he gently cracked open the door, squeezed in behind the wheel, switched on the ignition, shifted into gear and slunk around the side of the motel and along the rear to where his anxious crew was awaiting rescue. With hearts pounding, we tossed our luggage in the back and flung ourselves into the big green lifeboat. With all aboard, Lynn set sail, steering a course along our back alley escape route and through the adjacent filling station. It looked like our getaway was a success.

"I can't believe she didn't see you," said Norm.

"Nah, she was too busy and way too angry to notice me," replied Lynn. "But her daughter saw me."

"Do you think they're coming after us?" asked a worried Barry.

"Nah!" responded Lynn. "When her daughter saw me, she just smiled and gave me a slight wave with her fingers as I started the car. It didn't look to me like she was going to rat on us."

All the way to our next gig, Barry kept a constant eye on the side-view mirrors, checking again and again to make sure no one was trying to track him down. He needn't have worried. Our getaway was clean, and we never heard from the girl or her mother again.

ALTHOUGH we enjoyed the advantage of youth, playing four-hour shows every night for a month exacted a toll, and at last the grind began to wear us down. Blisters turned to calluses and soreness became strength, but that wasn't enough. For the most stressful part of life on the road proved to be not having any time to ourselves. We were always together: riding in the tilting Pontiac together, sleeping in the motel room together, playing on stage together. We even ate and did laundry together. And naturally, as is the case with most families, we laughed and cried and sometimes quarreled together.

One side effect was, without consciously realizing it, we all became extremely possessive of our suitcases. They held all our personal possessions, and more and more we came to treat them as treasure chests, as our hands-off, exclusive, inviolate private property.

I started collecting newspaper ads and articles and interviews for a Kingsmen scrapbook my mother wanted to keep. At every motel check-in, I'd locate a copy of the local paper and cut out the ad for the show that night. Mornings following shows, I routinely checked to see whether anything had been written about us that might be worth saving. The concert ads usually read, "THE KINGSMEN TONIGHT —at such and such place at such and such time at such and such admission price—PERFORMING THEIR NUMBER ONE HIT, LOUIE LOUIE." The morning-after articles usually read something like this:

> Last night The Kingsmen, known for their controversial hit "Louie Louie," appeared at the "local ballroom" [or college] to a packed house of wild and raucous dancing teenagers. The band was playing through custom-made equipment that was so loud, at times the vibration would cause pictures to fall off the walls and tables to creep across the room.

Sometimes, sometimes not, a quote followed from one of the guys or a fan and perhaps a quote from the promoter as well. These articles all sounded the same, except for once in a while when an interested reporter essayed an in-depth article covering our music, where we were from, our likes and dislikes and, of course, the "true" lyrics to "Louie Louie" and the story behind the recent banning of the song by the governor of Indiana. Over the course of a tour, I collected as many of these articles as I could, repetitious though they were, and stashed them in my suitcase.

We'd been working the Midwest circuit for a few weeks when we found ourselves in Wichita, Kansas. Bob Ehlert, our agent, usually scheduled an interview in advance with a jock at the local Top-40 radio station. Upon arriving in any new town, we'd drive straight to the radio station for our on-air interview. Only after meeting with the jocks and station managers would we find the motel and check in before heading to the venue late in the afternoon to set up. Wichita was no different.

Once at the motel, I followed my normal routine and tracked down a copy of the local paper. To my pleasant surprise, I saw that the concert ad included a picture of the band—a breakthrough for us. My sunny mood soon darkened, however, when I noticed it was the picture we'd decided not to use, the one where Lynn wore a different jacket than the rest of us. Even worse, for the first time the ad copy read, "LYNN EASTON AND THE KINGSMEN TONIGHT AT THE COTILLION BALLROOM."

I was stunned and shocked and hurt, all at the same time. That familiar gut-wrenching feeling of separation I'd felt at the Hollywood Center Motel returned. Once more, the Musketeers were on the verge of losing their leader and becoming his subjects. It felt like, against our will, with no voice in the process, we were silently being handed over to a self-proclaimed ruler.

I didn't know how to handle the situation, so many questions were going through my mind: *How did the newspaper get that picture? Why do they have that picture? What will Norm do? Does Lynn know about this? What will Mike say? What will this do to the band?*

I cut out the ad and took it to our room, hoping no one would ask to see it. Luckily, my clippings ritual had become such an everyday non-event by now, no one asked to look at the latest ad before I slipped it into an envelope with the others in my collection and snapped my suitcase shut.

Having arrived in Wichita early, we used the extra time to iron our stage shirts and call home. After lying around the room watching TV for a while, we packed up our gear and headed for the venue.

Lynn had the directions to the Cotillion Ballroom, so he drove. About a mile or two from our destination, a couple of girls pulled up alongside the Pontiac. The driver motioned for Mike to roll down his window.

"Are you guys The Kingsmen?" she yelled.

"Yeah!" Mike yelled back as Lynn tried to match their speed.

"We're going to the Dome to see you tonight," she yelled. "Do you know where it is?"

"No," answered Mike, "but we have directions."

"Follow me!" she ordered. "I'll show you how to get there."

She pulled her Mustang forward, and Lynn maneuvered the Pontiac in behind her.

"Wow, she's cool looking!" said Mike.

"Her friend is kind of cute, too," added Norm.

Ahead, a traffic light turned red as we approached, and our prey was forced to stop. As Lynn pulled up behind her, Norm said, "I have an idea. When they stop, let's jump out and climb in with them."

"Let's go!" Mike said.

Within seconds, he and Norm had jumped out of the station wagon and climbed into the back seat of the girls' car. The latter seemed thrilled.

"Wow!" said Barry. "I hope all of the chicks in Wichita are this friendly."

"Well," said Lynn as he pulled into the parking lot, "these ladies must have friends."

Then I saw it. The ballroom had a big marquee by the side of the road, and it read, in foot high letters,

"TONIGHT LYNN EASTON & THE KINGSMEN."

Trying to distract Barry, I said, "Wow! Look at this place. It's a dome!" Silence. I knew then that Barry and Lynn had both seen the sign. If they saw it, then there was a good chance that Mike and Norm saw it, too. Uncomfortable but trying to act normal, the three of us got out of the car just as Mike and Norm walked over, beaming with excitement. I was now sure they had been too busy flirting with the girls to notice the sign.

We were all amazed at the shape of the place. Domes were just coming into fashion around that time, and none of us had ever been in one before. That added to the excitement of the newly-acquired girl friends.

"Hey guys," said Mike with his arm around the driver of the Mustang. "this is Jeanie."

As she stuck out her hand, Mike continued, "Jeanie, this is Barry, Lynn and Dick."

We shook hands with her as Norm introduced his new companion.

"They're going to stay with us while we set up," Mike explained. "Then we're going to grab a bite to eat. Afterward, they're going to go to the show with us tonight."

Giggling and full of energy, the girls jabbered non-stop as we started for the front door.

Walking into the Cotillion Ballroom, we ran smack dab into a poster advertising that evening's show. The poster was the standard-issue 18 x 24 inch size that promoters posted throughout their towns to advertise their shows. It featured the same picture as the newspaper ad and, like that ad, also read, "TONIGHT LYNN EASTON & THE KINGSMEN." Having the girls there was a godsend and helped avert an unpleasant confrontation. Clearly no one was comfortable with this latest development, not even Lynn.

Not wanting to spoil their fun with the girls, the guys outwardly treated the poster incident lightly, but I knew eventually we were going to have to deal with the situation.

As was standard operating procedure, one of the disc jockeys from the station we visited earlier came to the show to introduce the band. Also SOP was to invite the DJ back stage to the dressing room to hang out with us before the show. This gave us a chance to do a little PR and fill him in on the details he needed to cover in our introduction. It also gave the jock a chance to ask us about the lyrics to "Louie Louie."

It was an unpleasant surprise for everyone except Lynn when the

DJ took the mic and said,

> Ladies and gentlemen, it's time to let it all hang out. I've had the honor of spending some time today with these boys and let me tell you, it's been a real pleasure. I've met a lot of entertainers, but I've never met a better bunch of guys. I know you're going to love 'em as much as I do. So, without further ado, I give you [the crowd stirred] all the way from Portland, Oregon [the clapping grew louder] the Louie Louie boys, [the crowd started screaming] Lynn Easton and The Kingsmen!

The crowd went nuts, completely oblivious to the looks of disgust and frustration being exchanged on stage between Mike, Barry, Norm and me as we nailed the opening number, "You Can't Sit Down." Despite that awkward beginning, we made it through the performance in good fashion and had a blast inciting mass euphoria amongst yet another house packed full of wild teenagers. Everyone shared in the fun, with two exceptions. Standing in the far back, wearing suits and ties, a pair of older men stuck out like sore thumbs from the teenage horde before them. Periodically, they took notes and talked amongst themselves, neglecting to applaud and cheer. We couldn't help but notice them and talked about them during breaks. They didn't look like the usual bouncers, so we figured they were chaperones or something like that. In idle conversation during our last break, the promoter corrected us. "They're FBI agents," he said.

The mere sound of the letters f, b and i gave me chills and sparked an unsettling curiosity in the group. At the end of the night, when we played "Louie," the agents did what the crowd did at every show: they followed along reading their version(s) of the lyrics. We found it unnerving but comical, and remained oblivious to the sort of big-time trouble we were about to endure courtesy of a frustrated J. Edgar Hoover.

After signing autographs and spending time with lingering fans, Mike and Norm returned to the dressing room and asked, "Can you guys load up the trailer without us? Our stuff is all packed up and in their cases. We want to take off with the girls for a while. They'll give us a ride back to the motel."

"Yeah, sure," said Lynn. "We've got it handled. Go have some fun."

About that time, the promoter walked in looking for Lynn to settle accounts. Off they went, leaving just Barry and me to load the trailer. As soon as Lynn was gone, Barry asked, "What do you think of that 'Lynn Easton and The Kingsmen' thing?"

"I don't like it one bit!"

"Me either."

"I guess it'll come up in the car tomorrow," I predicted.

"Yeah, I hope it doesn't get ugly," Barry responded.

"I know Norm's really mad about it," I replied, very worried.

"I am, too." Barry admitted. "I don't think it's right. How did this happen? It can't be a mistake."

Concerned though we were about this latest complication, nothing more was said about it that night. And in the morning, when we drove down to Tulsa, Oklahoma to our next gig, Norm and Mike were so busy telling us about their night on the town, the issue was skirted then, too. That night in Tulsa, the same "Lynn Easton and The Kingsmen" thing happened again, and again the following night in Stillwater, and again and again and again at show after show after show. It became increasingly obvious that the materials being sent out by the William Morris Agency were promoting Lynn Easton and The Kingsmen and that the agency had been given their directions by Lynn.

It got so that every time Lynn wasn't around, the rest of us talked about him behind his back. He was assuming more and more control over our day-to-day business and interviews and sharing less and less of the details with us. When the tour began, we'd been so unified, not five individuals but one team. Now, with each passing day, the distance between us grew—at least the distance between the four of us and the one of him did. For the time being, Mike and Barry and I played ostrich, avoiding the situation by burying our heads in the sand. We were having a good time and figured we'd fix things once we got home by taking some new pictures. To Norm's credit, he continually sought support for a confrontation. He was the only one of us four who accurately foresaw the effects Lynn's actions would have on the band's image and on our ability to regain control of the situation.

THE silent war took its toll on Lynn as well, and he started drinking after shows. At first it was "just a few beers with the guys," then it became "just a shot before I turn in," and eventually it turned into drinking too much and drinking alone, an unhappy combination, guaranteed. By the end of the first tour, he was getting a bit more than tipsy several nights a week.

One evening after a performance, I happened upon him in the lounge at the Holiday Inn where we were staying. Thinking I'd join a friend for a Coke, I sat down beside Lynn and couldn't help but notice he was a few steps beyond happy.

"Hey, are you okay?" I asked.

"Sure, happy as a lark," he smiled in a woozy manner. "Why wouldn't I be? Everybody loves me. My folks love me, Karen loves me, the fans love me, you guys love me. I'm even going to be a daddy."

"Really?" I said excitedly, relieved to think his drinking was a celebration of good news and not a reflection of a state of depression. "Did you just find out?"

"No," he answered in a slurred vice. "No, I've known about it for some time."

"Why didn't you tell us sooner?" I questioned. "That's exciting news!"

Lifting his drink and tipping his head back, he drained the ice-filled glass and continued.

"Karen doesn't want anyone to know yet, not until after graduation. Hell, we aren't even supposed to be married, let alone Karen pregnant."

I sensed he was about to get angry or was on the verge of becoming a crying drunk. Not wanting to deal with either, I quickly changed the subject.

"Oh, yeah. Hey, man, it's getting pretty late. We'd better call it a night and get daddy some shut-eye. We have a long trip ahead of us tomorrow."

Trying to stand up, Lynn lost his balance and fell back in his chair.

"I suppose you're right, Lil' Dickie."

Holding on to the table, he stood and put his arm around me like a long-lost pal.

"You won't tell anybody about this, will you, Lil' Dickie?"

"About what?" I answered, thinking he was referring to his condition. "All you need is a little sleep. You'll be okay by morning."

"About the baby," he answered. "I don't want the other guys to find out yet."

"No problem, I won't say a thing," I promised. That was the first time I'd ever been in such a situation without one of the other guys present.

I managed to half walk-half drag Lynn back to the room and lay him on his bed, where he fell asleep with his clothes on. The next morning at breakfast, he apologized to me at length for his intoxicated condition the night before.

"No big deal," I assured him, but it was an act.

AN hour or so later, we were back on the road when, out of the blue, Lynn asked, "Have you guys ever taken a look at Mike's autograph?"

"What are you talking about?" wondered Barry.

"He signs his name '*Nube*'!" Lynn answered with a laugh.

"Nube?" asked Norm.

"What?" said Mike. "No I don't. I always sign 'Mike Mitchell.'"

"Hey," answered Lynn, "I'll prove it. Get a piece of paper and sign your autograph on it."

We were all curious to see evidence of Lynn's Nube claim. Eager to discredit his accuser, Mike rustled through the jumbled potpourri of on-the-road junk spread across the wagon's dash—candy bars, packs of gum, assorted scraps of paper, maps, a pack or two of cigarettes and whatever else we'd tossed there in our carelessness. Finally, he managed to unearth a pen and a suitably unmarked envelope.

"Now write it like you do when you sign your autograph," instructed Lynn.

With a quick studied flurry of strokes, Mike scribbled his name on the paper the same way he signed autographs for fans.

"Here, let me see it!" said Norm, tearing the paper out of Mike's hand. "Hey, you're right!" he exclaimed. "It *does* look like Nube."

"Let me see!" demanded Barry.

"Me, too!" I added.

Norm handed the paper to Barry and Barry and I looked at it together while Mike sat in the front seat, slightly embarrassed and laughing in disbelief.

"Wow!" I said.

"Look at that!" said Barry. "It sure looks like Nube to me."

"Let me see that!" said Mike with diffidence, snatching the evidence from Barry's hand.

"Take it easy, Nube," cautioned Barry, "you'll tear the thing."

Looking at the autograph, laughing at his own scribbling, Mike good-naturedly conceded.

"I never noticed it before, but it *really does* look like Nube."

We had quite a laugh over Mike's new nickname, and he didn't dare object. How could he? He'd penned it himself.

Barry started in with the razzing.

"Hey, Nube, pass me a piece of gum, would you?"

"Sure!" Mike agreed, seeing the humor and smiling, trying to look unaffected by the teasing.

Norm was next.

"Hey, Nube, would you hand me a candy bar?"

Refusing to let the rub get to him, Mike responded with another cheery "Sure!"

Poking Barry in the side, I said, "Hey, Nube, let me see the map."

"Well, at least I'm grateful for one thing," declared the grinning Mike as he reached for the map on the dash in front of him. "Being called 'Nube' isn't half as bad as being called 'Lil' Dickie." That broke everyone up, including me.

"Oooo, he got you!" said Lynn.

Mike was right. I would much rather have had Nube as a nickname than Lil' Dickie, especially when in mixed company. But there's nothing one can do about a nickname save live with it or fight it.

At first we tried to tease Mike about his new handle, but he accepted it with such grace and affection, he seemed to actually like it. He viewed it as a harmless term of endearment, one that didn't mean anything. Nube thus proved itself a poor source for teasing. It took but a few days before it seemed natural to call Mike "Nube."

THE fun and thrills of life on the road were not enough to make the issues regarding Lynn go away. We still had to deal with them. Every time Lynn was out of ear shot, Norm started in about the picture and all of the promo stuff that was being circulated with Lynn as the focal point.

"Can't you guys see what's happening here?" he'd ask us. "He's making a name for himself so he won't need any of us. He's diminishing the name The Kingsmen and replacing it with his own. You just wait. Pretty soon it'll be 'The Louie Louie boy, Lynn Easton.' He doesn't care about us."

One day at a truck stop, while Lynn was inside paying for the gas, Mike announced that he'd come up with a solution he thought might solve the problem without creating an argument.

"I'm not going to let this thing fall apart," he told us. "When we get back on the road, you guys follow my lead."

We'd been on the highway about an hour, working our way north, when one of our infrequent quiet spells set in. Mike broke the silence with a suggestion.

"We need to change the picture that everyone seems to be using. I really don't like it, and I thought we decided we weren't going to use it."

"I sent them to Bob," Lynn quickly answered, "because he said he needed something from us that looked professional and had the agency's name on it. He said it would help him get us work, and it's all the PR we have. I kept the other pictures for us to use on the road ourselves. We can change it when we get home."

I was afraid Norm was going to start an argument by saying something about Lynn using his name on the pictures, but Mike jumped in before he could and said, "Okay, I understand the need for PR, but I think we can fix the problem while we're in Chicago."

"What do you have in mind, Nube?" asked Barry.

"Well, we've got the negative of the picture we like, don't we? I think as long as we're going to be in Chicago for a few days, we might as well find the time to take it to a duplicator. We can have them run off a few hundred copies with the info across the bottom for WMA. We're going to see Bob while we're in Chicago, anyway. We can trade the photos while we're there. At least then it'll be something we all like. We can get a new photo when we get home and send those on to Bob, too."

"It'll cut into the budget," said Lynn. "He'll need more like 500 pictures."

"Maybe so," answered Norm, "but if it's our responsibility to provide WMA with promo stuff, then we need to spend the money if we want to hand out something that we like. Look at it this way, it's one of the costs of doing business."

Jumping on this opportunity to resolve our dilemma, Barry said, "That's a good idea, Nube. When we get to Chicago, why don't you and I look into it?"

"Why don't I call Bob and see if he knows a place in Chicago where we can get it done?" answered the quick-thinking Lynn.

"Okay," said Norm, "but I know we'd all feel a lot better about it if we had a picture and PR out there that we all liked instead of feeling embarrassed every time we see that horrible thing we're using now."

"I'll call Bob tomorrow," Lynn promised.

That put us back on track, at least temporarily, and printing new pictures didn't appear to be that big of a deal to Lynn. With everyone feeling much better about our situation, the atmosphere in the car returned to its former state of non-stop levity and fun-loving banter.

As promised, Lynn called Bob the next day, and Bob gave him the phone numbers of a few Chicago-area labs WMA used. Lynn passed those phone numbers along to Mike, and Mike talked with the labs. We were only going to be in Chicago for four days, and none of the labs could schedule the work in time for us to get the new pictures to Bob before we were supposed to leave. As a solution, Bob suggested we bring the negative with us when we came to visit him. He'd have someone on his staff handle it for us. Bob said when the pictures were ready, he'd have the lab ship them to him at WMA. We told him we didn't care what it was going to cost or how he got them. No price was too great to have us be The Kingsmen once again.

After playing a few days in the Chicago area, we took the negative to the WMA office. At last, face to face, we were going to meet colorful, famous, industry legend Bob Ehlert and the other men and women behind the voices on the phone. Over the past few months, Lynn had described Bob's manner and personality to us many times, and nearly every promoter, DJ, secretary and artist we'd met who'd ever dealt with him had done likewise. Everyone everywhere had colorful Bob Ehlert stories to share. As a result, when we walked through WMA-Chicago's doors, we felt like we already knew our agent well.

In person, Bob equaled or surpassed the image of him we'd all created in our minds. Entering his office, we saw before us a cigar-chomping, white-haired little man sitting coatless behind an expansive desk, his crisp white business shirt open at the collar and his sleeves rolled up. Piles of papers and contracts and correspondence nearly obscured the head and shoulders of the world's premier booking agent.

Most of Bob's co-workers in the WMA office spoke in a thick Chicago accent we Portlanders found hilarious. [For the uninitiated, here's a typical sample of Chicago-ese: "So da udder day Frankie goes, 'Yo, Richie, where's uze goin'? Didjaeetyet? Waja do wit dose tree sassage sammiches I asked fer? Howmy supposta eat lunch wit no brahts wit kraut? Dere's dese guys waitin' fer me down at da Mare's office, so's I gotta hurry. So's git me instead summa dose sliders and pop from dat White Castle acrosta street over by dere. Whutteva ya kin find, jus go. Getotta here or I'm gonna bust yur butt!'"] We jokingly imitated their accents, and they were good sports about it. Outsiders like me may think Chicagoans speak with a funny accent, but citizens of the Windy City are among this nation's warmest, most fun-loving people. No one at WMA took themselves too seriously, and laughter came easily to them.

While we were hanging out with Bob in his office, the phone rang. He listened for a few minutes and then, covering the mouthpiece with his hand and speaking in a less-grating dialect, said, "I got Waaally Amos on the line [yes, the Famous Amos cookie man; he was a WMA agent back then]. He waaants to know if you guys wanna play a Murray The K show in Brooklyn."

"When is it?" asked Lynn

"What's a 'Murray the K show'?" asked Barry.

Bob spoke with Wally a while longer before telling him he'd talk it over with us and call him back.

Bob hung up the phone, took a long puff on his cigar and addressed this novice band of newcomers parked in front of his desk.

"You dunno who Murray The K is!? Murray The K issa big deal disc jahckey on WINS in NEW YORK CITY!"

Squinting his eyes to see through the head-saturating smoke, he continued.

"Murray's da numba one jock on da numba one station in da country. If Murray plays it, da nation plays it. You get dis guy behinja and you get hits. Murray's the guy who took over for da father of rock-'n'-roll, Alan Freed himself! This could be a big break for you guys."

"Really?" questioned Mike.

Bob went on.

"Heez got these big holiday shows at da Brooklyn Fox Theater. Tonssa acts! Tonssa press! Murray's got one coming up in March over Easter vacation and he wants you boys to be on da show."

"But that's the 17 days of R & R we were taking off before we hit the road for our next tour!" complained Norm.

"Cool!" said Barry. "It would be cool to play the Big Apple."

The last date on our current tour was scheduled for Missoula, Montana, and we were planning to drive home after that for a few weeks' break.

"What're you suggesting, Bob," Lynn asked, "that we drive straight to New York from Montana for one show and forget about going home? That won't be a popular idea back in Oregon."

"No, Murray's show is a 10-day engagement. Look, here's da deal. You play four shows a day for 10 days straight, to a packed house every show, 500 bucks a show, flat. Twenty grand for 10 dayssa work. And dat ain't chopped liva!"

"Are you kidding me?" exclaimed Norm. "That's a lot of money!"

"Well," said a troubled Lynn, "this tour ends in Montana, and that would mean we'd have to drive straight to New York instead of going home at all."

"Nah," answered Bob, "ya go home for a few days, ya fly ta New York, do da shows, then ya fly home for a few more days before ya hit da road for Idaho. Now dat's routing. You can make it ta Boise in one day, done deal."

Lynn answered with a slight laugh.

"Easy for you to say, you're not the one on the road."

Sliding to the edge of his chair and pointing at Lynn, cigar in hand, Bob condescendingly said, "Hey, I put my time in on da road.

I been doin' dis for 40 years. Don't try ta hassle me about gigs! You guys waaanna work or not?"

Smiling back at Bob, Lynn exhaled cigarette smoke and said, "Well, we'll have to figure out the expenses before we can give you an answer."

"Let's do it right now!" said Bob, reverting back to his role as agent. "Wally needs dat ansa taday."

Excited, Bob called in his secretary and asked her to price five round-trip airfares from Portland to New York. Next, he called Wally back and asked him to price hotel rooms close to the venue. Before long, he had everyone working on the logistics and costs associated with the date.

While information was being gathered, we visited with Bob, exchanging a few road stories. Leaning back in his overstuffed chair, he dropped his bombshell.

"So, howzzit goin' wit da FBI?"

"How's *what* going with the FBI?" Lynn shot back.

"What? You dunno aboud it? Dey're da ones dat's doing da investigation for da FCC."

"What investigation?" asked Mike.

"About da lyrics to 'Louie Louie' and you guys!" he answered.

"Are you kidding me?" exclaimed Norm. "The FBI? What did they get involved for? I thought the whole thing was just about over."

"Nah, nah," said Bob, "it's just gettin' started. You boys gotta lotta people upset with you."

"Hey, we've got those guys in the grey flannel suits at almost all of our shows," said Lynn.

"You got FBI guys comin' ta your shows?" asked Bob, a bit surprised.

"Yeah, there are these older gentleman in grey flannel suits that show up at all of our shows," said Barry. "All they do is watch the show. Then they disappear."

"I'm just glad they don't stick around afterward. That's when we do the stuff with the girls that should get us arrested!" joked Mike, lightening up the room as usual, breaking us up with his simple yet truthful comment.

"Are dey da same guys every night?" asked Bob.

"I don't think so," answered Lynn. "They're different guys every night. But they're all FBI. What the hell do they want from us?"

Laughing as he sat back in his chair, Bob said, "You know, dey came in here ta ask me about you guys."

A chorus of startled responses followed.

"What?"

"Are you kidding me?"

"Why?"

"Holy crap!"

"Oh, my God!"

"They wanted ta know if I'd eva seen your show and whuddid I know about you, and did I know about da lyrics ta 'Louie Louie.' You know, stuff like daaat. Oh, yeah, you wanna hear sumpin' funny? Dey asked me if I knew if you guys ever performed wearin' nothin' but jock straps! Dat cracked me up."

"Jock straps?" questioned Lynn. We all started laughing.

"Yeah, dey said dey had dese reports dat you guys played some college show in gold lamé jock straps."

"There's a new one!" I exclaimed as I continued to laugh. "Tell him about the girl that thought we sang songs about cannibals in Africa eating people."

"What?" said Bob as the guys collapsed in laughter. "Nuthin' surprises me any more."

"Well, what did you tell the FBI guys?" asked Mike, bringing us back on point.

"I told 'em da same ding I tell da promoters whuze concerned about you guys and your show."

"Promoters, too?" questioned Lynn.

"Sure. Nobody knows whaaat ta expect from you guys. I mean, all dey hear is dat you sing dirty songs and perform haaalf nude. Whuddaya expect?"

"Well, what do you tell 'em?" asked Mike.

"I tell 'em, I don't create da act, I just book what people waaanna see, and as far as I know, you seem ta be a good bunch of kids ta me. Hell, da promoters seem ta love ya, and I've never heard anything but positive reports from anybody about your show. They're all booking you guys back on da next run. Dat's gotta say somethin'."

"What else did the FBI want to know?" asked Norm.

"Nothin', really. Dey wanted a copy of your itinerary and your promo, so I gave it to 'em and dey left."

"That explains how they know where we're performing every night," observed Barry.

"All you can do is all you can do," said Lynn. "We live with the controversy every day. No matter what we say, they never believe us."

"Yeah, but now the rumors have escalated to include lewd acts and jock straps?" complained Norm. "We have to do something about it."

"I wouldn't worry about it," Bob advised. "Yer workin', ain't ya? And besides, what caaan dey do about anything? I mean, da record is already banned and it's sellin' like hot cakes. Ban it worldwide? Hell, dat'd be da best ding dat could happen ta ya. If dey do dat, we raise your price and I'll never let ya get home."

We got a kick out of Bob's stereotypical agent personality. It wasn't long before Wally called back and said he'd found us a place to stay in Brooklyn, the St. George Hotel. It was a short, direct subway ride between there and the Brooklyn Fox, and the price was right. Bob's secretary had quotes for airfares from United.

Norm was keeping track of the numbers, and I could sense that, with the exception of Bob, we were all sort of hoping the numbers wouldn't work out and we could go home for a few weeks.

"Okay," said Norm, "after WMA's commission, and figuring food, transportation, laundry and hotel and incidentals, it looks like we're going to net around 28 hundred dollars apiece."

"That's almost a new Chevy Impala!" said Barry.

"Are you sure about the numbers, Norm?" asked an anxious Lynn.

"Yeah," answered Norm, "they're right. I'm sure."

"That's a lot a money for only 10 days work," Mike observed. "I say we do it. We'll still have a few days at home. That should to be enough time to break a few hearts."

Lynn hated to make the call home and break the news to Karen, but the money proved to be a great motivator for everyone, expectant Karen included. Lynn and Karen needed to buy a house and prepare for a new baby and could use all the bread they could get. And, after all, we'd still be able to go home for a few days. The upside was too tempting to resist: we'd get in with Murray the K, and that would be good for sales; we'd get to see the Big Apple, and that sounded exciting; we'd get to hang out with some of the stars we admired, and that would be fun; plus we'd walk away from New York with some serious coin, and that was just plain smart. The only downside was being home for only a few days.

While Bob had Wally on the phone, Barry asked Bob to ask Wally who all was on the show. The list of artists Wally gave us blew our collective minds: Ben E. King, The Tymes, Chuck Jackson, The Shirelles, Dick & Dee Dee, Bobby Goldsboro, Johnny Tillotson, Little Anthony & The Imperials, Dionne Warwick...

"Dionne Warwick!" I said. "That's it, we do the show. She's incredible. Have you heard 'Anyone Who Has a Heart"? I've got to see her sing that song."

"Are you serious?" asked Mike. "Ben E. King? I'm in."

On the spot, we decided to take the New York date. As we were leaving his office, Bob said, "Wait 'til ya meet Wally. He's a great guy. He'll show you guys a fantastic time in da Big City. Whatever ya want, he'll know how ta get it for ya. I hope you boys like cookies."

"Why, are the cookies that good in New York City?" asked Lynn.

"No, 'cause when you meet Wally, he'll hava batcha home made cookies for eachaya. It's what he does. He loves ta make cookies and give 'em ta everybody he meets."

"Next time you talk to Wally," Barry said, "tell him I like chocolate chip."

It was fun meeting Bob and his people. Getting to see him in person made our relationship much more personal. Driving back to the Holiday Inn, Norm asked, "What about the FBI? Are we getting into some kind of trouble here?"

"What more can we do?" responded Lynn. "No one ever believes us."

"They don't want to believe us," added Barry. "Everybody wants 'Louie Louie' to be dirty."

"Why don't the FBI guys ever come talk to us?" I said. "They just stand in the back of the halls and watch."

"Hey, whatever, I think it's cool," said Mike.

Trying to imitate Bob and his accent, holding his fingers to his mouth as though he were knocking the ashes off a cigar, Mike broke us all up when he said, "Hey, you're workin', and da record is sellin' like hot cakes. What more do ya want?"

Mike was right. Record stores couldn't get enough product, and everyone either wanted to see us perform or interview us. The controversy was heating up daily, and no matter what we said or did, it didn't seem to matter to either side. What more *could* we want?

Kingsmen in concert, powered by Sunn amps

VERSE 11

WE were loud, oh so loud, and audiences loved it. Much of the credit for our decibel-laden performances must go to Norm, whose passion for the technical side of his art led him to develop the awesome custom-built amplifiers that drove our sound. At the end of every show, ears still ringing, we all signed autographs, but serious guitar players mostly ignored the rest of us and gravitated straight to techno-wizard Norm, seeking information about the black magic he worked with our equipment. Following our final set in Chicagoland, Norm was talking to a curious young guitar player named Milo who was trying to convince Norm to build him an amp just like the one Mike had. Milo's parents wouldn't let him come to the show by himself, so at their insistence he'd dragged his sister along with him. Sis apparently preferred keyboard players over guitarists and was locked in an animated conversation with Barry. When it came time to leave, Milo couldn't tear the two of them apart. The impasse was quickly resolved when invitations were made to Barry and Norm to spend the night at home with their family. They lived about an hour south of town via the El [elevated train], and our plan was to head that direction the following day to our next gig. Brother and sister gave us directions to their house, and Lynn and Mike and I agreed we'd pick up Norm and Barry on our way out of town.

When we arrived, the two of them couldn't stop talking about the wonderful time they'd just been shown. Home cooking had become a rarity for us, and Milo's mother spoiled Barry with hers, filling the famished lad beyond the point of gluttony. Norm, on the other hand, came away from the evening not only gorged, but seriously considering making Milo an amp and shipping it back to him in

Chicago from Portland. Norm planned to do a little research into costs and shipping and was inspired about the possibilities that suddenly appeared before him. A spark had kindled his imagination, and great things would soon result.

Continuing south, again a full quintet, we pulled into a station for the customary pit stop. As soon as Lynn left the car, a worried Norm asked, "Did anybody give the new copy for the picture to Bob?"

We all just looked at each other for a second, not saying a word, then delivered three answers in the negative: "No!" (Mike), "Not me!" (Barry) and "I didn't even think about it!" (yours truly).

"Nube," Norm said, "do you still have Bob's phone number?"

"Yeah, I think so," answered Mike.

"Good. When we get to Kansas City, why don't you give Bob a call and tell him that we want Lynn's name taken off the bottom of the picture? We've got to get this done."

"Okay," said Mike as we climbed out of the car. "I'll talk to Bob the first chance I get."

Before leaving Chicago, Norm had called his brother Conrad back in Portland to tell him about the phenomenal attention the amps were getting. He saw the possibility of a successful future business designing and manufacturing electronic equipment for the music industry, and asked Conrad to look into costs, shipping and whatever other possible set-up requirements they might face. When we reached Kansas City, Norm took the car and trailer down to a local music store and held a demonstration with his amps for the store owner. When he got back to the Holiday Inn, he was pumped. He had taken orders for five amps from the store and invited the store owner to the show that night. After seeing the response from musicians in the crowd, the merchant asked to become Norm's regional distributor. The next morning, as we left Kansas, Norm was understandably excited.

"Do you guys realize," he asked, "that I can go to music stores in every city we play in and demonstrate my amps to generate sales?"

"Well," said Barry, "there's nothing out there on the market that can even come close to your stuff, that's for sure."

"How're you going to run a company from the road?" asked Lynn.

"My dad and brother will handle the day-to-day stuff back home," Norm replied, "and I'll be in charge of sales on the road. We have a ton of ideas we've been playing with. We'll see how it goes when I get home, but if that many people want this kind of equipment, I'll be happy to make it for them. We can start out small and see where it takes us."

"Once we're home, you won't have time to do much of anything, let alone start a company, not if we're going to New York," said Lynn, sounding a discouraging word—something we often heard from him in the weeks ahead.

"They'll have a lot figured out by the time I get home," responded Norm, "and I'll do the rest from here."

Feeling the conversation turning into a joust, Barry jumped in.

"I think it's a great idea," he said. "Rock 'n' roll needs to be played like we play it, loud, and what better piece of equipment to do it on than a Sun amp?"

"*Sun amps*?" responded Norm. "I like the name. I'll run it by Con and Dad when we get in."

"Sun—I like it!" added Mike. "It's catchy."

"Me, too," said Barry—no surprise there since it was his idea.

The next morning, we were all sitting at a table at the Holiday Inn—where else?—having breakfast when Norm said, "Hey, Bare, I ran your name by Dad and Con this morning."

"What did they think?" asked Barry, chewing on a pancake.

"They love it!" he exclaimed. "But we're going to spell it with two *n*'s—S-u-n-n."

"That's a great name!" Mike said.

"But instead of Sunn Amps, we're going to call it 'Sunn Musical Equipment,'" Norm informed us.

"Good work, Barry," said Mike.

"Hey, does that mean I get a royalty?" joked Barry.

"No, but you get all the amps you need for free," laughed Norm.

"I think you should have a Mike Mitchell model," Mike suggested playfully. "You can use my name and give me free amps for my endorsement."

"You still haven't paid me for the parts for the amp you're already using," Norm poked back at Mike.

"I don't have to pay you now," Mike retorted with a snicker.

"What!" said Norm. "How do you figure?"

"My amp's a prototype," Mike quipped. "It's R & D for Sunn Musical

Equipment. Besides, you're using it as a demo. I'm not paying for any demo model."

"Ah, well, don't worry about it," provoked Norm. "I knew you were going to stiff me, so I got your dad to pay me for the amp before we left."

Nothing ever excited Mike to anger—normally. He was so mild-mannered and easy-going, his sleeping temper (assuming he had a temper, sleeping or otherwise) was never awakened. On this occasion, however, Norm hit an unexpectedly sensitive nerve.

"What!" cried Mike, slightly miffed at the least. "You really went to my dad for money?"

"Just kidding!" Norm devilishly confessed, laughing like a Japanese humorist. "But I got to you, didn't I?"

Having found an unsuspected path to getting under Mike's skin, we all lowered our guns and started razzing and taunting our normally cool and carefree colleague.

"Oooo, Daddy's boy got miffed!"

"Hey, Mikey, don't worry about the ten you owe me. I'll get it from your daddy."

"Yo, Mikey, think if I call your daddy he'll buy me a guitar, too?"

And those were three of our kinder comments.

Mike took the razzing well, and it was fun to see the unflappable Mike Mitchell get riled for a change. Before long, as we cruised down the highway in our over-packed, junk food-filled, big green Pontiac wagon with the radio blasting away, conversation turned back to the normal topics of interest: music and girls.

VERSE 12

KANSAS City fans, promoters and members of the press proved no different from their counterparts in other cities: they all asked embarrassing questions about the lyrics to "Louie Louie." It was almost as though our concert performances were an afterthought, however wonderful and fun they might be (and, by all accounts, wonderful and fun they always were). The boys in the grey flannel suits ran true to form as well, ever present and conspicuously inconspicuous.

After the show, we returned to the Holiday Inn to hose off and grab a bite to eat before calling it a night. Mike jumped in the shower first while the rest of us hit the restaurant before it closed for the night. Nube was going out with a few kids he'd met and wasn't interested in eating. Our showers could wait; our growling stomachs demanded nourishment.

Earlier in the day, Norm had phoned a couple of local music store owners and invited them to the gig to experience his amps in action. Anyone who heard the roaring monsters up close always came away more than impressed, and Norm was meeting with a few of the awe-struck prospective buyers that night at the hotel to discuss a purchase order for Sunn. Once Barry and Lynn and I had filled ourselves to the brim with local culinary favorites—steaks and other barbecue delights—Barry and I retired to our room to call home and watch a little tube before giving in to some much-needed shut-eye. Lynn said he was going to grab a beer in the lounge and would join us "in a bit."

We'd been in the room for about an hour when Barry commented, "I wonder what happened to Lynn. Don't you think he should've been here by now?"

Notice the attire worn by the audience

"Maybe he ran into Norm and those music store guys in the lounge and he's hanging out with them."

Just then the door opened. It was Norm.

"Was Lynn with you guys?" asked Barry.

"No," answered Norm. "He's in the lounge having a beer, isn't he?"

"Weren't you guys in the lounge?" I asked.

"No," Norm responded, showing concern. "We went down to the music store to check out their place and talk about my amps."

Barry hopped out of bed and started pulling on his trousers.

"I'd better go down to the lounge and see if he's alright," he offered.

"I'll go down with you," Norm proposed. "If Lynn's had a few too many, you'll need some help getting him back here."

While Norm waited for Barry to dress, I asked them, "Does it seem to you guys like he's drinking more and more lately? I mean, what's the deal, anyway?"

"I think he's under a lot of pressure from home," Norm answered.

"Couple that with running things on the road and I think it's just his way of unwinding. I also think he's aware of how much the new band name bugs us and he's feeling a little guilty about that whole mess, too."

"Lynn'll keep it under control," Barry said, slipping on his shoes. "It'll be okay. I think sometimes he gets into visiting mode and doesn't realize how much he's had to drink."

"Don't worry," added Norm. "If it gets out of hand, we'll ask Mike to talk with him. Mike and Lynn have been best friends forever. Lynn will listen to Mike."

Twenty minutes later, Barry and Norm reappeared with Lynn in tow. He was soused, and his two rescuers laughed long and hard at his slurred proclamations of loving appreciation as they put him to bed.

Mike slid in a few hours later and by morning "situation normal" had returned: fight for the shower; pack the green beast; grab some breakfast; hit the road; listen to Mike's inventive, outlandish account of his latest conquest; watch Mike fall asleep a few minutes later; watch as a sleeping Mike presses his head against the window of the Pontiac; look for a filling station to fuel the rolling party wagon. Like I said, situation normal. Lynn seemed fine as he climbed behind the wheel and steered our trusty ship toward the next town, a full tank of gas to burn.

We were working our way east toward Indiana and scheduled to play four or five venues en route. While loading the trailer after one of those gigs, we were approached by a semi-plain young girl who walked up to us and asked smilingly for our autographs. She wore an extremely sexy pair of white hip-huggers and a loose-fitting, blue-striped, boat-neck cotton top. We accommodated the diminutive teen but, in a change of pace, the guys paid her no mind, which seemed odd to me because I was thinking at least her attire made her somewhat attractive.

I noticed she was the only person left in the parking lot and asked if anyone was with her.

"No, I came by myself," she answered.

I asked if she was on foot or if maybe someone was picking her up. I didn't want to leave this innocent (though somewhat sexy-looking) young teen alone and in danger in the dark parking lot as we simply drove off.

She said she was parked on the far side of the building. She wasn't cute enough for any of my fellow Muskeeters to come to her rescue, so, being polite and concerned for her well-being, I volunteered to walk her to her car. The guys promised they'd drive around and pick me up as soon as they'd finished loading the trailer.

Walking through the darkness, we exchanged small talk, with me asking most of the questions—"Where do you live?"..."Where'd you go to school?"..."How'd you like the show?—you know, small talk. The longer we walked, with each new step, the more the diabolical moonlight transformed the rather plain looking lass into an exquisite young vision of beauty and desire.

We turned the corner of the sleeping old brick dance hall, and I could see her car sitting by itself a good distance away. She curled her hands around my arm, and I thought she was frightened and that doing this was a source of comfort to her. I felt her hands rubbing up and down my arm as we approached her car. Thinking it was a friendly parting gesture, I gave it no further mind, though it was stimulating my teenage testosterone levels. We arrived at her white Chevy Impala none too soon for me.

The now beautiful (to my aroused eyes) teen caught me totally off guard when she opened the back door of her car, climbed in, laid back on the seat and invited me to join her, devilishly pointing out we had some time before my friends arrived.

My mind froze. In shock, I stuttered as I delivered those embarrassing, familiar words: "Th-th-thanks, I j-j-just c-c-can't. S-s-sorry, b-b-but I'm n-n-not a m-m-m-man y-y-yet."

Not knowing what to do next and seeing the confused look on her face—barely visible in the glow from the car dome light—I panicked and slammed the car door shut. Leaving her untouched and stunned on the inviting back seat, I turned and sprinted as fast as I could through the darkness to rejoin the boys. They'd just closed the trailer doors and were about to drive over to pick me up when I reached the Pontiac, all out of breath.

"Afraid of the dark, are we, Lil' Dickie?" teased Mike.

"No!" I exclaimed, panting heavily as I collapsed into the back seat of the wagon. "You won't believe what just happened. You know that sweet, innocent little girl I walked to her car?"

"Yeah, so what?" they responded as one, their curiosity piqued.

"Well," I sputtered, "when we got to her car, she opened the back door and laid on the back seat and asked me to have sex with her."

"What did you do?" asked the shocked Barry, his interest now becoming more aroused.

"I told her I couldn't, that I wasn't a man yet. Then I closed the door on her and ran back here as fast as I could."

In a wink, everyone jumped in the car with me, Mike taking the helm. He started the engine and gunned it, spinning his wheels in the gravel and all the while begging to know where I'd left the disappointed teen. By the time we arrived at her last known address, she'd disappeared—vanished without a trace. Disappointed by an opportunity wasted, the guys all laughed at me and went overboard with their teasing. They made me promise that if something like this ever happened to me again, I'd keep the girl warm until they arrived or, as an alternative, bring the needy female to them. They were such thoughtful friends, volunteering like this to help me deal with these awkward situations. For a long time after, I couldn't get it out of my mind how this young girl's transformation had amazed and affected me, how attractive she'd turned in such a short distance. A few years later, a line from a popular country song captured perfectly the lesson I learned that night: "Oh, the girls all get prettier at closing time."

THE longer we toured, the more structured and unvaried our daily travel routines became. We soon learned that getting from one city to the next as fast as possible was imperative if we wanted enough time to drop by the local radio station, check in the motel, set up, eat, shower, change and still relax a little before we performed. By the second month, we'd motor for four or five hours and then start looking for an "acceptable" place to get some gas, grab some grub and hit the head. Wherever we stopped, we executed our tasks with the speed and polish and precision of a NASCAR pit crew. By the time we used the rest room and loaded up on enough junk food and soda pop to get us to the next pit stop, the gas tank was full, the water and oil and tires were checked, and the Pontiac was ready to tackle yet another stretch of highway.

For the first half hour back on the road, our big green overloaded rolling snack shack was devoid of conversation while five sets of jaws occupied themselves with chomping down fat-infused, sugar-filled gourmet goodies with the enthusiasm and manners of a litter of starving puppies. We easily fell into fixations for certain foods that became automatic purchases for days and weeks at a time. With health and nutrition always foremost in my mind, my preferred choices for road fare included a Hostess Berry Pie, a box of powdered sugar doughnuts, a bag of chips and a couple of bottles of Coke.

Aluminum cans were rarities in 1964, and Cokes and Pepsis and Dr. Peppers and Ne-his and their carbonated kin were sold primarily in cumbersome glass bottles. In those days, if you were fortunate enough to find Coke in a can, you needed a "church key" to punch a pair of holes in the can in order to enjoy the sugar/caffeine fix inside. On rare occasions, the aluminum can came with a "pop top" that left you with an inconvenient tab to dispose of.

Good citizens that we were, we littered not our treasured American highways, confining our trash to the car. Our irreverent methods for dealing with garbage and leftover junk food packaging would've scandalized the editors of *Good Housekeeping*, but we didn't care. We read *Playboy*. Mile after mile, bottles and wrappers were carelessly, thoughtlessly tossed on the floor, front seat and back. Five thirsty guys each guzzling five or six bottles of pop a day generated prodigious numbers of glass empties in no time at all, and they all ended up on the floor of the wagon. Every morning before embarking on our next Discover America adventure, a couple of us would glean all paper materials from off the floorboards and toss them in the motel's trash bin. Every few days, we gathered together the mountain of bottles piled up on the floor and turned them in for their cash deposit value, usually a penny or two apiece. The trick was to keep them from cascading out of the car when one of us opened a door. Luckily, no one told our mothers.

LATE one night, somewhere on a highway in the middle of Missouri, the fun gods breathed inspiration into Norm, and

Norm's brainchild jolted the rest of us into action. It was like when Dr. Frankenstein threw the power switch that sent that bolt of electricity surging through the inanimate body of Boris Karloff, sparking the monster to life. Norm's brainstorm, like Frank's, far transcended the ordinary. Indeed, it was a defining moment in his life, a stroke of pure genius, a fine example of the old adage "Success is achieved when opportunity meets preparation."

Sitting shotgun side in the back seat, Norm calmly rolled down his window and selected a bottle from the pile of empties under his feet. As we approached a large green road sign sporting white reflective letters reading, "ST. LOUIS 71 MILES," he gracefully tossed the glass projectile into the air. Much like when a satellite released from the Space Shuttle continues to shadow the mother ship, the missile tumbled forward in an arching, slow-motion trajectory alongside the car, perfectly matching our 65-mile-an-hour speed for several seconds. Wondering what Norm was up to, we watched awestruck as suddenly, with a thunderclap that stirred our primal need for kicks, the hourglass-shaped Coke bottle collided with the sign with the force of a flying cannonball and the sound of a thousand sledge hammers pounding an empty oil drum, shattering into a million tiny pieces and gouging a pronounced impact crater in the target.

"Whoa!" exclaimed Barry, rising up in his seat. "That was outstanding!"

"Great shot!" blurted a stunned Mike.

Norm had that comic book caricature Japanese look on his face and was tee-heeing with pride.

"I gotta try some of that action!" Mike said, rolling down the front passenger-side window and reaching for his own bottle.

At first, the noise startled me, but momentary trauma quickly turned into adrenalin-induced amazement and overwhelming astonishment.

"Isn't this littering?" I asked.

"No, this is fun," answered Mike with a mischievous grin.

"Just one more thing to add to the list of crimes they're going to charge us with when they finally haul us into court," joked Barry.

Heavily armed and dangerous, possessed by this new challenge, Norm and Mike eagerly readied a fresh pair of glass weapons for attacking the next target.

172 ♪ LOUIE, LOUIE

"Ahoy!" shouted Captain Easton. "Here comes a Route 40 sign, straight dead ahead off starboard bow."

Barry and I were sitting in the back seat, I on the driver's side behind Lynn, he in the middle between Norm and me. Hearing Lynn's warning, we jockeyed for position to better catch the approaching target meet its doom. Barry won, and I peered around him as best I could.

Much smaller than the last target, this new sign presented a formidable challenge to our adrenalin-filled sharpshooters. As we came within range, Mike launched his Pepsi, missing everything. Norm proved the better shot when his Seven-Up glanced low off the sign post. The force of the impact broke his bottle with a cracking thud. Norm's shot was no bulls-eye, perhaps, and it's muted sound no loud explosion, but his effort was worthy of praise. After all, he'd actually hit something.

"Yeah!" we all cheered, filling the war wagon with new life and joy.

"Nube, you suck!" teased Barry.

Schooling Mike in the newly-discovered art form of bottle tossing, Norm advised, "Don't throw the bottle at the sign, Nube. Just gently toss the thing out and up so the path of the bottle intersects with the approaching sign. Let the sign hit the floating bottle. Don't throw the bottle at the sign."

"Trade places with me, Norm," begged Barry. "I want to try one."

As Barry climbed over Norm, the clinking of bottles beneath his feet was no longer the noise of a penny-ante inconvenience; it was now the jingling sound of treasured ammunition.

"Oh, man," cried Lynn, "look at this monster up ahead!"

He pointed to a sign twice the size of Norm's first score, a multi-city mileage marker requiring two—count 'em, two—posts to hold it upright.

"Gentlemen, ready your weapons!" commanded Captain Easton.

Barry and Mike sat at the ready, anticipating the moment of release.

"Now!"

They floated their glass torpedoes with grace and accuracy.

Pow! Boom!

Two perfect hits accompanied by one record-setting volume

of noise, five delighted Kingsmen erupting in cheers—a new and thrilling indulgence had been invented.

"Hey, I want to try one!" pleaded Lynn as he drove down the road.

"This'll be great!" said Mike, handing Lynn a bottle. "You've got to toss that baby over the car and time it just right if you want to hit a sign while sitting in the driver's seat."

As the USS Pontiac closed in on the next sitting duck, four able-bodied seamen wore ear-to-ear grins, anticipating their captain's first shot as a gunnery officer. Gripping a Coke bottle, Lynn hung his left arm out the window. Standing at the ready, his arm eagerly cocked, Lynn took a deep breath and waited as we approached ground zero.

"Five, four, three!"

We counted down, intoxicated with excitement.

"Two, one!"

All eyes focused on the approaching road sign.

"Fire!"

With all his might, Lynn looped the bottle over the top of the car. CRASH!

We'd completely forgotten about the car-top carrier attached to the roof. Instead of reaching its intended target, Lynn's missile struck the metal box full force, strewing shards of glass everywhere. Most hit our U-Haul trailer with a sound like gravel striking a thin sheet of metal. We all ducked for cover.

Once the shrapnel had passed, we raised our heads again and broke into laughter as we realized Lynn's mistake.

"Oh, yeah, I get it," he said. "I hit us! This sport will have to be confined to a passenger-side-of-the car activity."

We'd exhausted eastern Missouri's supply of road signs and were across the Mississippi River and well into Illinois by the time our ammunition ran out. We spent most of our time in the car; it was our home more than any motel ever could be. Sometimes, we needed to add something fresh and new to our tedious routine. Bottle-tossing provided a spark of welcome energy to life aboard the USS Pontiac. For days to come, we shared the story of our latest comical escapade with anyone who'd listen. Having had so much fun, we were doomed to increase our intake of pop for some time to come.

From that day on, bottle tossing remained a real favorite. Eventually, we developed a system for rating signs by size and distance from the road. We scored the signs from one to ten and kept track of points to make the game more interesting. Although Lynn's toss into the car-top carrier preceded the rating system, it was easily the single most memorable toss of them all.

It's funny how glass bottles we once considered hassles in an instant turned into valuable weaponry. We became quite possessive of our empties and made sure everyone knew exactly which bottles were whose. Stealing a fellow bombardier's ammo could be extremely hazardous to one's health. A miraculous side effect of the bottle wars was, we started putting our garbage in a bag and throwing it away every time we pitted. We wanted to make sure we didn't mix our garbage with the coveted ammunition. Bottle tossing was sinfully fun and boosted and sustained morale among the troops. Plus, it helped keep the green beast significantly cleaner.

THAT same night, once the initial excitement over our discovery of the joys of bottle tossing had subsided a bit, Lynn brought us to attention and said, "Financially, we're doing pretty well. So how would you guys feel about making road life easier and changing our transportation into a convoy?"

"What do you mean?" questioned Mike.

"Well, I've been thinking. We're so cramped in here. If we got rid of the trailer and car-top carrier and bought a van, it wouldn't cost us that much more money than we're spending now, and we'd pick up a ton of extra room. The van could carry the equipment and get two guys out of here, opening up the back of the wagon for our personal stuff and giving one of us a place to stretch out."

"What kind of van?" asked Norm.

"Like a Ford Econoline," answered Lynn.

"Hey, that would be cool for me," said Norm. "I could use it to go to the music stores for my amp demos, and you guys would still have a way to get around."

"Well," added Mike, "what do you guys think about getting a

roadie, too?"

"What's a roadie?" I asked, eternally naïve.

"A band guy," answered Mike. "You know, a guy that sets up our gear and loads up the equipment while we sign autographs and do interviews and settle accounts with the promoters."

"It would certainly make things a lot easier for us," Lynn observed. "We might not be so worn out all the time."

"How much would someone like that cost?" questioned Barry.

"I don't know, maybe a hundred-and-fifty a week," answered Lynn.

"That's not bad," Norm remarked, "and the roadie could drive the van. That'd put four in here and two in the van."

"That'd be great!" I said. "How do we find somebody like that?"

"Well," Mike answered, "I was thinking my cousin Jim would be a perfect fit with us. He's a great guy."

"He sure is," interrupted Lynn. "It would be too much fun having Cousin Jim on the road."

"We could teach him how to set up and tear down the gear," Mike continued, "and he can drive anything. He was a half-track driver in the Marines."

"Marines?" remarked Barry. "*A jarhead?* Sounds like he could act as a body-guard, too. Not that I want anyone protecting my body from the chicks."

"What about rooming?" questioned Norm.

"Well," said Lynn, "we could get two rooms instead of one and put three in each room."

"I like it!" encouraged Barry. "Three guys to a bathroom? We could get on the road at least half an hour sooner. It wouldn't hurt us to spend a few bucks on our own comfort."

"Can we afford all of this?" questioned Norm.

"I don't think it'll cost us more than three or four hundred a week for the added expense," Lynn answered. "If we add a room, that's about $175 more a week, and Jim would be $150. The van is about $200 a month, and $200 divided by four is $50. Added together, that makes $375 a week plus the extra gas. We're in there!"

"Really? Are you kidding me?" asked Norm. "That would be worth it."

"Mike, why don't you call Cousin Jim," Lynn suggested, "and see if he wants a job?"

"I know he'd love to go out with us," Mike answered. "He's living at his mom's, and he'd kill to get out of there and be with us."

"See if he can start right after the New York shows," suggested Barry.

"Ok, I'll call him when we get in," answered Mike.

"Did we just have our first band meeting?" asked Barry.

"Probably as close to one as we're ever going to get," responded the laughing Lynn.

"Gee, after an intense business meeting like that, I could use some grits," said Barry.

"I agree, let's look for a place to stop for some eats," added Mike. "We need to load up on some of that glass ammo, too."

Mike's new found love for the pop bottle was showing.

At the next pit stop, once Lynn was inside the station, Norm asked Mike, "Did you call Bob?"

"No, there wasn't enough time. I'll phone him in the morning."

"Do it when you call Jim. We need to get this 'Lynn Easton and The Kingsmen' bullshit nipped in the bud or it'll get out of hand."

Mike agreed, and we all piled out of the car to load up on candy and Coke—I mean ammo.

VERSE 13

A few days later, Mike, Barry, Norm and I were sitting around our hotel room somewhere in Illinois. Lynn had gone to a radio station to do an interview for that evening's show.

"Hey, Nube," Norm began, "have you called Bob yet?"

"No," answered Mike, "and I haven't reached Jim yet, either. I'll try them again right now."

Mike rummaged through his suitcase searching for his address book. Finding it (what a trove of beauties' numbers were entered in *that* little black book), he sat himself down on the edge of the bed and dialed Bob. We listened as WMA's top dog explained that Lynn had instructed Bob to leave the pictures as they were for the time being, that we'd try to get WMA some new promo sometime after New York. We were disappointed by the news—in particular Norm, who was visibly agitated by this latest maneuver by Lynn.

Bob asked Mike what the big concern was over the picture. He said he didn't think the photo was all that bad. Mike told him that the print on the bottom was in error, that we weren't "Lynn Easton and The Kingsmen," but rather just "The Kingsmen." He explained that it was something Lynn had done inappropriately on his own, and that the rest of us were now trying to fix it, quietly and without argument.

Mike asked Bob not to mention their conversation to Lynn and to let it go for the moment. When Bob expressed concern that we might be having problems, Mike assured him everything was fine, that we were working our way through the situation. He also requested that henceforth, when Bob sent out promo, would he please instruct promoters and buyers to bill the band as simply "The Kingsmen?" Bob agreed and promised to make sure that Wally in

New York saw to it that the correct billing was used for the Murray the K shows in Brooklyn.

As soon as Mike hung up the phone, Norm started venting.

"You know why Lynn doesn't want the other picture used, don't you?"

"I guess it's because he wants to keep his name out front like it is now," Mike answered, "and he's afraid it won't be on the new picture."

"It's more than that," responded Norm. "It's because Barry's featured in the photo, and we're all standing together behind him. Plus we're all wearing the same outfits. There's nothing in the photo to distinguish Lynn from the rest of us, and he's trying to make a name for himself. This wasn't an innocent mistake. Lynn did this on purpose."

"I hadn't thought of that," said Barry.

Trying to calm the situation, Mike said, "Look, it's only a couple of weeks until this tour ends. I say we ride it out and fix it while we're in New York. We can get the WMA office there to work with us on this. Let's get through this tour and change the photo after we're finished."

"Just remember, Mike," said Norm, "if we wait, Bob will already have sent out the promo for the next tour. We can't wait any longer."

Barry saw Lynn pulling up to the motel door.

"Let's talk about this later, okay?" he cautioned. "Lynn's back from the interview."

"I'd better call Jim," said Mike, thumbing through his address book again. Just then, Lynn walked through the always-open door.

"That was an interesting interview," he remarked before changing subjects when he noticed that Mike was on the phone. "Who's Nube talking to?"

"He's talking to Jim," answered Barry.

"Cool!"

Returning to his original subject, Lynn continued.

"Wait until you hear what this jock was telling me. Have you guys ever heard of a gospel group called "The King's Men?""

"They have the same name as us?" questioned Barry.

"No, not exactly," Lynn said. "It sounds like our name, but it's not quite the same. The spelling's different. They call themselves The

King's Men—two words. The 'King' is God, and they're God's men. Thus, King's Men. Get it?"

"Are you kidding me?" asked Norm. "Pretty close."

"No kidding, it's true," Lynn went on, "They had their records down at the radio station and the jock showed me some of them. He told me the group's been around for years and wondered if we added 'Lynn Easton' to our name in order to distinguish ourselves from them."

"What did you tell him?" asked a distrustful Norm.

Laughing as though he found it funny, Lynn said, "I told him originally it was a mistake, but it looks like it might've turned out to be a blessing in disguise 'cause it does set us apart." Still laughing, he added, "I told him we were named after a bottle of aftershave lotion, not a gospel group."

Lynn was trying to make light of it, but we knew where he was headed. Things turned awkward for a moment, then Mike hung up the phone.

"Jim's in!" he announced.

"Cool!" "Yeah!" "Neat!" "Great!" Reaction to the news was unanimous and positive. The subject quickly changed from Lynn's agenda to Jim, easing the tension in the room just when it appeared that something might break. Mike went on, telling us how excited Jim was and how he couldn't wait to start working for us. Mike was just as jazzed as Jim about having his cousin join us. They were close, like blood brothers who were also best friends. Mike shared a few hilarious stories from their childhood together as we readied for that evening's gig.

"What're we wearing tonight?" Barry interrupted.

"How about black?" Norm volunteered.

"Sounds good to me," responded Mike, and, with that, we loaded up the green gunboat with our hang bags and headed for the venue.

As soon as we arrived, Lynn went off in search of the promoter. The second he was gone, Norm started in again.

"So *now* do you guys see the positioning that's going on here? Now he's going to try to sell us on the idea we need to keep his name out front to distinguish us from some gospel group no one's ever heard of."

"I guess you're right," Barry said. "We'd better stop it before it goes any farther."

"Agreed!" Norm said. "We' better have it out with him, no delays, no excuses. I'm sick and tired of his sneaky tricks and I, for one, am not going to put up with his crap any more! This isn't his band; this is *our* band."

"Hey!" said Mike emphatically. "We're smarter than that. Why argue? It'll only drive a wedge between us. That's no way to do things."

"What do you mean, Mike?" asked Norm. "The only way to stop him is to call him on it straight to his face."

"Let's think of a way to fix the problem with alternative suggestions," returned Mike.

"Like…?" questioned Norm.

"I'm open," added Barry.

"Well, let's suggest something like putting 'The Louie Louie Boys' on the new pictures or something else that would help us market ourselves as The Kingsmen and separate us from any other group. He'll get the picture that we're removing his name."

"Good idea!" I said. "I think Nube's right. If there's a way, we should try to avoid a divisive confrontation. We don't need that."

"Okay," said Norm, "I'm not trying to pick a fight. I just want this to be set right and for things to feel equal again. It's this kind of stuff that's always caused us headaches in the past. Why do it to ourselves?"

Trying to create peace and solidarity, Barry said, "Tomorrow in the car, let's work the conversation around to the new picture and promo."

"Okay," answered Mike. "I'll open it up, and you guys jump in."

With that tactic agreed to, things seemed to be back on course.

WE returned to our normal pre-concert routine and began setting up equipment, flirting with the girls from the dance hall staff and grabbing bites of food in between. Judging by their prowess at attracting accommodating female company, the guys would've gone far had they made the Navy their career. For if sailors at sea have a girl in every port, the Kingsmen on land did their best to have a girl in every town. Playing a new city every night and meeting so many different girls along the way, the guys developed an uncanny sense of what moves and lines would best capture the hearts and minds of teenage girls across America. As the tour progressed, I noticed them falling into pick-up patterns past experience had proven would work and rejecting techniques that had failed or taken too long to succeed. Call it speed dating Kingsmen style.

Norm favored "I could really fall in love with you" lines, which in many cases resulted in someone's heart being broken (never his). Mike always let it be known he was out for nothing more than fun ("I'm here for a good time not a long time" could have been his mantra), and there was definitely an element hanging around our concerts that found his devil-may-care party attitude to their liking. Barry usually hung back until he met someone he could "relate to on a deeper level." He also enjoyed the challenge of breaking down a conservative conviction, were that the only option available. Lynn tried to suppress his urge to merge with a can of beer or a drink of some sort, but on occasion he'd strike up a conversation with a fellow lounge lizard (female) who sympathized with his situation and was well versed in the art of discretion. As for me, I was shy beyond human reason. Not being a man yet, I mostly served as platonic friend/amateur relationship counselor to a growing list of casualties.

Once the guys finished marking their evening's prey, we'd retire to the dressing room and change into our performance wear. Open-minded fellows that they were, they always kept their social commitments flexible in case something better came along later in the course of our daily activities.

Milling around backstage awaiting our introduction on this particular night, we were all dressed in our black waistcoats—all of us, that is, except Lynn. He had on his black slacks and white shirt, but for some reason he was holding off donning his jacket until just before we went on stage. When the moment arrived, he opened his hang bag and said with mock surprise, "Oh, no, I brought the wrong jacket! How stupid of me. What was I thinking? I brought my gold coat."

Skeptics one and all, we believed nary a word of what Lynn said. Avoiding direct eye contact with any of us, he hurriedly put on his gold coat.

"Oh, well," he said, laughing at his "mistake," "we'll just have to look like our picture tonight."

Backstage, we were painfully unhappy — totally stressed out — by this unexpected charade, but what could we do? We were entertainers, and an expectant crowd awaited us. The jock from the local radio station was already at the mic delivering his shtick, and in a few moments he'd be calling us up. We had no choice, and Lynn knew it. The show must go on. So we put on our game faces and decided on the spot to let his convenient bout of forgetfulness pass. Like Scarlett O'Hara, we vowed to "think of it all tomorrow." We'd figure out then how to put an end to this nonsense. There was no way we were going to accept this "new look" to go along with our "new name." This was insult added to injury. Lynn was daring us to challenge him, and the longer we did nothing, the more liberties he'd take. We knew all that, but we also knew that backstage before a concert was neither the time nor the place for a showdown. That would come in the morning, in the car, on the road. We already had it planned. Lynn's gold waistcoat was just one more wrinkle to be smoothed out. "After all, tomorrow will be another day."

On stage, a few minutes into the show, Lynn removed his coat and finished the performance in his shirtsleeves. Afterward, testosterone took over as it always did, and no one was willing to trade an evening's female companionship for a dog-eat-dog confrontation. Giving Lynn a provisional benefit of the doubt, we said nothing about his jacket. Unilaterally, silently, truce was declared. For one more night, we let the sleeping dog lie.

The following morning, once we were back on the highway, Mike found an opportunity to bring up the new picture and his idea of putting "The Louie Louie Boys" on our photos and promotional materials.

"I was thinking..." Mike began.

"Did it hurt?" Lynn said, laughing at his own witticism.

Knowing as we did where Mike was about to go, our laughing

responses were semi-forced. Undeterred, Mike continued.

"No, really, when we get this new picture done, I think we do need something printed on it that sets us apart from this King's Men gospel group and anyone else out there with a similar-sounding name."

No doubt thinking Mike was going to suggest keeping it "Lynn Easton and The Kingsmen," Lynn responded with excitement.

"I agree!"

"Got any suggestions for how we do that, Nube?" Barry asked, on cue.

Before Lynn could say anything, Mike jumped back in.

"Yes! I think it's a good idea to put 'The Kingsmen' under the picture and somewhere also add 'The Louie Louie Boys' or something like that, something that refers to our band."

"That's an interesting idea," observed Lynn cautiously, starting to squirm behind the wheel.

"That's a great idea, Mike!" exclaimed Barry.

Ready to confront Lynn if necessary, Norm said nothing. He was waiting to see if this ploy was going to work before pouncing.

"Yeah!" I added with enthusiasm. "It certainly would solve a few problems and give the promoters another angle to advertise."

Hoping to bust Lynn, Norm added his piece.

"Nube, can you call Bob and see if we're not too late to add 'The Louie Louie Boys' to the picture he's duplicating?"

"We won't be too late," said Lynn with confidence. "I told him to hold off on the picture. I thought that since we'll be going to New York in a couple of weeks, we could take a few new shots there. I mean, WMA in New York must know who to contact in order to get something that looks a lot better than the stuff we had taken in LA. Let's call that Wally guy and ask him to set it up."

Barry cut in and added, "New York is the fashion capital of the world. With all of the big-time photographers there, we ought to look like we just stepped out of the pages of *Esquire*."

"Sounds good to me!" said Norm. "But let's make sure we get it done this time, not like Chicago. We've got to do something to look classier and worth the money we're asking. I *hate* that picture."

"Okay," volunteered Lynn, "I'll call Bob on Monday and get Wally's number."

No one spoke for the longest time as we each contemplated the artful sparring that had just gone on. As usual, it was Mike who got things going again with one of his classic lines.

"Anybody want to smell what I had for dinner last night?"

Mike always had a way of livening things up and getting us back into our more typical carefree mood. I loved that about him, but this time his magic didn't last for long. That next night, Barry asked which outfit we should wear. When Mike called "gold," Lynn said that since he'd worn gold the night before and got it all sweaty, he'd have to wear black this time and catch up with us at the next gig. After that, wearing a different colored jacket became a habit with him. The rest of us hated it, but no one said anything. We always managed to rationalize that everything would change for the better in a few weeks. Maybe in New York a tomorrow would finally come that was truly another day.

Over the next few weeks, Lynn started feeling the pressure from Norm and realized something was going on. In response, he began running Norm down whenever Norm wasn't around. In various subtle and not-so-subtle ways, he tried to separate Norm from the rest of us.

Lynn advised the three of us to notice the look on Norm's face whenever he backed up the car. Admittedly it *was* funny—what we called his "Japanese" expression—and one we'd all seen a thousand times before. Lynn started making fun of this idiosyncrasy every chance he got, even referring to Norm as "Jap" without Norm ever knowing it. Lynn also didn't like the "I think I love you" line Norm used on girls to get them in the sack. Norm rarely bent his fingers when he used his hands, keeping them basically straight and sort of stiff. Lynn began mocking that trait by imitating the way Norm moved his fingers whenever he was fixing something or smoking a cigarette. He also took to referring to Norm as "Ox"—only behind his back, of course—trying to sell him to us as some sort of big clumsy Swede. We listened, but we weren't buying whatever he was selling.

Lynn clearly was trying to drive a wedge between Norm and everyone else. To his credit, Barry spoke up during one of Lynn's derogatory tirades.

"Hey man," he told Lynn, "I like Norm, and I'd appreciate it if you wouldn't say things about him behind his back that you wouldn't say in front of him. I really expect all of us to give each other that much common respect."

Another one of those uncomfortable pauses followed, and then Lynn laughingly said, "You're right, Bare. But he's so easy to make fun of."

"I don't care if you make fun of any of us, man. You can pick on me all you want. That's okay. Just don't do it unless the person you're making fun of is present, and that goes for all of us. Cutting each other down is the best way to break up a brotherhood like ours."

"I'm all for that!" added Mike. "It's hard enough being with each other so much of the time. We don't need to say or do things that might potentially divide us."

Lynn managed the kind of condescending, forced smile one wears after losing an embarrassing confrontation.

"Well, it gives us all something to work on, doesn't it?"

"You're right, Lynn," said Barry. "We all have to do whatever it takes to maintain mutual respect or we'll start driving each other crazy and the next thing you know, we'll all be stuck with boring 9-to-5 jobs like everybody else and this'll all be over."

"Point well taken," said the admonished Lynn.

"We're a family," Mike said, "and this is just the kind of thing families go through that brings them closer together."

At that precise moment, Norm walked in. Overhearing Mike's comment, he sensed that something was going on, but wasn't sure exactly what. A lost air of optimism and vitality seemed to have returned to the group. Dark clouds had parted, and a shining ray of sunlight had suddenly burst through the gloom. He wondered why.

"What's going on in here?" he asked. "You guys look like the cat that swallowed the canary."

"We've just now reaffirmed our commitment to each other," Barry explained, "and decided to rid ourselves of all the needless BS that's been creeping into our relationships."

"I'll drink to that!" said Norm. "We should never lose sight of the fact that it's us against the world. We can't let things get to us. We're having too much fun to let the little stuff come between us."

"Everybody hug!" Mike half suggested-half ordered.

Drawing close together in a circle, we held out our hands in a "one for all, all for one" gesture. With that, everything appeared to be back on track.

For the moment, all was forgiven and forgotten, and keeping the Kingsmen's party carefree and happy and fun once more became our single-minded mission. With attitudes adjusted and minds cleared, we plowed through the next few weeks with relative ease, at least when compared to what we'd just been through. There was one raw exception, however: four out of five of the Louie Louie Boys continued to cringe every time they saw that hated picture or heard another DJ introduce the group as "Lynn Easton and the Kingsmen." Our concert-a-day schedule meant we saw and heard such things far too often to hope we could maintain our fragile peace of mind for long. Bucking the odds, we soldiered on, crossing our fingers while doing our best to keep our end of the bargain.

Despite taking part in the same mutual vow of renewal as the rest of us, Lynn never stopped feeding jocks the wrong information for our concert introductions or trying to elevate himself above the rest of us at every turn. Nube knew it, Norm knew it, Barry knew it and Lil' Dickie knew it, and we all felt hurt. Lynn must've known it as well—how could he not have?—but, judging by his drinking, he felt guilt not hurt.

Discretely, the four of us did what we could to thwart his moves. During interviews, for example, we made sure our questioners knew that the band's name was "The Kingsmen," pure and simple, and that the "Lynn Easton and the Kingsmen" caption was an error we meant to fix. Prior to every concert, one of us would try to catch the person announcing the show that evening before Lynn got to him first and make sure he introduced us as "The Kingsmen" and nothing more. Other than making those subtle efforts, we tried our best to ignore and go on. Time, we hoped, was on our side.

AT some stop along the way, Lynn was out shopping and found a unique suede cap he thought not only enhanced his look, but gave him an identifiable trademark as well. He bought the hat in several colors and thereafter wore one or another of them during every performance. Before too long, the hat was having the effect he'd hoped for, giving him added confidence and earning the audience's attention. I thought it was cool.

FOR most of the eight weeks of our maiden voyage, we stuck to the Midwest, with the notable exception of a frantic, whirlwind 10-day dash we made from Michigan to the Eastern Seaboard. After a show in Detroit, we hurried on to Buffalo and Syracuse and Albany in New York, to Brookline and the Boston area and Lowell in Massachusetts, to the Hampton Casino in New Hampshire and to Old Orchard Beach in Maine.

Ban-everything-fun New England proved to be the hottest of hot spots for unleashing the Kingsmen's unique brand of mayhem. From his broadcast booth at WMEX radio in Boston, Woo Woo, aka Arnie Ginsburg, had worked the area into a frenzy promoting "Louie Louie," and we found ourselves playing in the land of the Pilgrims for at least a few weeks on every subsequent tour. On this, our first hop-skip-and-jump through Robert Frost/Grandma Moses territory, we played a limited number of gigs. All were notable, with our shows in the Boston area verging on the incredible. Those dates fell toward the end of the tour, and "Louie Louie" remained at the center of a prolonged and animated public debate. The song had officially been banned for weeks, but Beantown teens still loved it and maybe loved it even more now that this most chaotic of records with its garbled, mysterious lyrics had been declared a forbidden fruit by the powers that be. What better way to rage against the status quo and indulge in a little vicarious sexual fantasy than attending a Kingsmen concert? So what if the parents didn't approve? All the better. "Let's give it to 'em right now!" was their clarion call to rebel.

WE were booked for a date at the Surf Ballroom in Nantasket Beach. In those days, just like "Louie Louie," rock 'n' roll shows were banned in Boston. With some serious bucks to be made, ingenious promoters rose to the occasion by inventing creative ways to skirt the ban. One typical ruse was to label an event a "fashion show" with "live entertainment." Via creative semantics like this, in mid-March 1964, promoters successfully gutted the intent of local statutes and brought to town reputedly the baddest rockers of them all, five by-now-homesick teenagers from far away Portland, Oregon.

Bill Spence, an honest, fair and well-respected businessman in the southern district, owned the Surf. When we arrived hours before the show, there were kids milling about everywhere. Bill explained that the show had been sold out for days and offered us the door if we agreed to play a second show. We quickly accepted his generous offer and were overjoyed with our popularity in the Bay State. After the first show, Bill appeared at our dressing room, nervously seeking permission to announce *a third* show. He took us upstairs to a top floor window where he pointed to a massive crowd gathered on the beach. Apparently, when word got out we were adding a second show, eager teens had started lining up six wide in a line that now stretched a quarter of a mile through the sand. Bill was concerned problems might develop if some in the waiting crowd were turned away. He hoped a third show would be enough to accommodate everyone in the long line of curious fans.

We agreed without giving his request a second thought. For us, doing a third show would be no problem. We were use to playing three or four sets a night anyway and, besides, the money was unbelievable. As we looked out the window, we were amazed by the sight of so many kids from Boston waiting on an Atlantic beach for a chance to hear a band from Portland, a city not so far upriver from the Pacific's waters. Though east is east and west is west, the twain did meet that night.

Following the second set, we were sitting in Bill's office devouring a platter of badly-needed sandwiches he'd ordered in for us when the local fire marshal whose job it was to count patrons burst in the room, talking loudly and gesturing frantically. He was excited about crowd control and gripped with fear of the growing masses outside. He said some no-good radio station was broadcasting live reports of the craziness going on at the Surf (sounded to me like Woo Woo's doing) and that George Washington Boulevard was jammed bumper to bumper with carloads of eager and rowdy kids trying to join the party. Bill assured him things would not get unruly as long as the fire marshal and his men remained calm and let the shows go on (as all shows must).

Instead, the man wanted to call out his entire department, and legions of state troopers as well, to keep the crowd under control. He and Bill argued about tactics, and the fire marshal told him it was his, the marshal's job to make sure the situation didn't get out of hand. Having established—in his own mind—his position of superior authority, the officious public servant exited as abruptly as he'd entered.

Midway through the third show, things started to turn ugly outside between the kids and the police. When we came off the stage after our "Louie Louie" encore, Bill asked if we had a fourth show left in us. We told him we'd do whatever was necessary to help the situation. He said as soon as the Surf was emptied, it would only take 20 minutes or so to get the final group of curious teens in place. He also told us we had to finish our show before curfew.

Curfew? What curfew? We couldn't fathom the idea. Out west, we could rock all night long and no one ever complained. Curfew? We'd never heard of such a thing. So we shrugged our shoulders, nodded our heads, grabbed our guitars and drumsticks and went back to work. Bill managed to pack the ballroom a fourth time and hooked up a sound system outside so the kids left on the beach could dance and blow off a little steam, toll free.

So much for the best laid plans of mice (callow rock stars) and men (enterprising promoters). Within minutes, while five charged up Kingsmen were happily rocking before a delighted crowd inside, a squad of panicked policemen were gingerly dodging rocks being thrown by an unruly crowd outside. To our great shock, a full-scale beach riot was underway.

We watched appalled from top floor windows as out-of-control firemen turned their hoses on the crowd, trying to disburse the sea of partying teens. Hours of pandemonium passed before calm was restored and it was finally safe to load our equipment in the trailer and attempt an escape from the Surf. A helpful policeman warned us that the highway out of town was grid-locked and that we'd never make it to Boston that night going that way—or any other way, for that matter. We were stuck, and it was well past curfew.

Coming to our rescue, Bill offered us his nearby summer house as a place to crash for the night. The next morning, with the road out finally cleared, we meandered back to our Boston lodgings with an ungodly pile of money stuffed into a large bag on the front seat—our wages for an unforgettable night's work.

Beach riots must sell concert tickets, at least out Down East way. For years to come, we played to packed houses all across New England.

Our next stop after Nantasket Beach was Cambridge for a grad party at Massachusetts Institute of Technology—MIT—finishing school for some of the world's foremost minds. The college kids helping us unload that day were far more interested in the equipment we carried than in the music we played. The foreign language of electronic circuitry that Norm found so stimulating was far beyond the ken of the mere oxygen-breathing, food seeking mortals who were his fellow Kingsmen. Not so with the brainiacs populating the labs and classrooms of MIT. That day in Cambridge, Norm happened upon a university chock full of kindred spirits, of his own kind.

It was not your normal Kingsmen booking. To this day, I remain uncertain where those budding Einsteins learned to dance. Their floor moves drew inspiration from moment-to-moment rhythms with no discernible foundation in the popular dances of the day. Improvised, inspired, random, unpredictable, jarring—the MIT Shuffle was all this and more. Picture in your mind several thousand nerds and nerdettes dancing wildly, heedless of social norms, cutting loose and having a blast, and you have a general idea of what the scene was like that night.

As the boisterous party drew to a close, the kids didn't want us to stop playing. One of the student organizers jumped up on the stage and asked how much money it would take for us continue to play. Lynn looked at the rest of us and asked what we thought. No one knew.

"Wait!" the young man interrupted. " I have an idea."

He grabbed Lynn's mic and asked for a garbage can. A pair of quick-acting students grabbed one sitting next to one of the stage exits, emptied its contents on the floor and passed it to the party animal controlling the mic. The latter then announced that if they could fill the garbage can with donations, we would continue to play. The can sped across the room, passed over, under, around and through the excited crowd. By the time it re-approached the stage, it was overflowing with greenbacks. The students had to keep compressing the loot down into the can to accommodate the endless stream of cash being collected for the band waiting with anticipation on stage.

"How's that?" asked the ringleader, handing over a minor fortune in small unmarked bills.

Most pleased, we were about to pick up our instruments and resume playing when our host informed us it would be a few more minutes before we could continue. Like seemingly all of Massachusetts, Cambridge had a curfew which MIT students were expected to observe, and curfew time was fast approaching. Undeterred, these student geniuses weren't about to let some trifling legal technicality like a curfew stop them from having a good time. They were well prepared for this moment in the evening, as was proved by the series of scripted events that quickly unfolded with the precision of a Swiss watch. Within a few seconds, all chaperones and adult types were cleverly escorted out of the gym, kegs of beer were shuttled in and all doors were chained from inside, locking outside all members of the Establishment world. Free from prying eyes and authority figures, the real party began, and the primitive acts of the uninhibited studentry that followed were astonishing even to us, America's Party Band.

Campus police and college administrators and faculty members tried everything they could think of to breach the fortress walls, to no avail. The prodigies within had anticipated their every move. Even the electricity could only be turned on or off from inside the gym.

The band played on until sunrise and through those late night and early morning hours, every form of nude and drunken and lascivious behavior known to humanity was acted out before our astonished eyes. MIT's finest minds held nothing back at this orgy, this party to end all parties, this toga party without togas and for some without clothes of any kind. Anyone searching for proof that "Louie Louie" was "corrupting the moral fiber of the youth of America" needed to look no further that night than the banks of the Charles River and the confines of the MIT gym. Fortunately for all parties present, the FBI sent no agents that time, missing the best opportunity it would ever have to dig up legitimate dirt on us. Perfect timing for us, not-so-perfect timing for J. Edgar Hoover and his troops.

The following morning, once the doors were unlocked and authorities had finished sifting through all the craziness of the previous evening, we were released from custody with the firm understanding that the Kingsmen would never again be allowed to play at MIT. As we loaded our equipment into the trailer, we noticed that all of the tubes in Norm's amps were missing—the students had taken them. To this day, I wonder how many of those high-powered beauties made it aboard a space capsule or were instrumental in some great scientific breakthrough.

FIFTY-SIX days. Eight weeks. Nearly two months. Take your pick. By any measure, our first tour amounted to a very long time for five teenage boys—four of them barely out of high school and one of them still in—to be on the road, on their own, far away from home, zigzagging madly across their nation's highways and byways. On our final, longest of zags, we worked our way back to Portland (Oregon, not Maine) from Boston, performing gigs here and there along the way. We arrived home exhausted from our trip, excited about the upcoming shows in New York and optimistic about putting past troubles behind us.

From West Coast to East Coast and back, we'd coped with challenges large and small with little or no time in between to pause and reflect on what we'd just been through or what we might encounter next. Lacking experience, we'd invented solutions on the spot as needed, surviving at times on blind luck and wits. Just one week out, we nearly met our demise courtesy of a once-in-a-lifetime blizzard in New Mexico. Thanks largely to the quick thinking and grit of Norm and Mike, we survived, and I'm alive today to tell our story.

From Davenport, Iowa on, we performed every night in a different town to another packed house with only four days off along the way. At tour's end, controversy over the lyrical content of "Louie Louie" corrupting the moral fiber of the youth of America was at an all-time high, a key element in determining our bank account's balance. Generally, we played for the guaranteed sum of $500 against a percentage of the gate. Owing to the brouhaha surrounding song and band, kids everywhere became morbidly fascinated with both, and flocked to our performances if by chance we showed up in their neighborhood. As a result, we broke into percentages without fail, sometimes grossing five or six times our guarantee. We were having a ball, we were on top of the rock world and we were hauling in the loot—making out like the bandits we were, our critics might say.

We deposited all proceeds in a single account run by Lynn's father. As leader of the Kingsmen pack, Lynn collected the money due us after each show. As a rule, in order to secure a date, promoters were required to send a 50 percent deposit to the William Morris Agency in Chicago. After taking their 10 percent booking commission, WMA forwarded the remainder to Mr. Easton. Whenever one of us needed money for personal expenses, we'd take a draw out of the money Lynn collected on the road. Lynn paid for gas, motel rooms, food and all other road and operating expenses out of these funds as well. Not wanting to carry large sums of cash with him, a few times a week he wired what money we didn't need to the bank in Portland. Once the tour was over and the accounting completed, we divided the spoils five ways. Until that moment, none of us had a clear idea of exactly how much we'd net from our labors. It really didn't matter. We were having much too much fun to care.

I have zero recollection of what the actual figure was on my check when it finally was written, but I vividly recall that with my bounty I was able to give my mother enough money to buy a new house and have more than enough left over to buy myself a Hammond B3 organ and a Steinway grand piano and pay cash for my first car. That was a tad bit more than the 20 bucks a weekend Shannon had mentioned to me in study hall that fateful day five months before when she told me her boyfriend's band was looking for a new drummer. And to think I gave up playing timpani in the Portland Junior Symphony for this.

E V E R Y O N E should have at least one favorite relative—an aunt or uncle, perhaps, or maybe a cousin or a grandparent—one special family member you always love being with and can't wait to see again. On this count, I was doubly blessed with two such kinfolk, my biological father's brother, Uncle Art, and sister-in-law, Aunt Ernestine. They truly have no equal.

Dad started driving buses for Greyhound long before the company was known by that name. That translated into seniority, and seniority gave him a lock hold on the coveted Seattle–Spokane run. Federal guidelines dictated the maximum number of hours and miles a driver could work. All freeway with very few stops, this route across Washington state offered both. Maximum allowable hours plus maximum allowable miles times serious seniority equaled maximum possible wages, making the Seattle–Spokane run primo all the way. For eleven months of the year, Dad's work schedule was perfect as well: six days on and three days off, six days on and three days off, six days on and…and you get the idea.

When my parents divorced, their agreement stated that my sisters and I could spend one month each summer with my father. Dad lived by himself in an apartment, and his work schedule during our one summer month together meant that for much of that time he was on the road and we were apart. We couldn't travel with him, much as we all would've liked to, nor could we stay home alone in his apartment in his absence, intriguing though that prospect was to us young'in's. As a result, in order not to lose visitation privileges, Dad had us stay with Uncle Art and Aunt Ernestine during those months and joined us there on his days off. Dad and his brothers were extremely close, and they loved to sing and play the guitar and make music together. From the moment my father appeared until the time he left for work, for three precious days it was one continuous country music jam session at Uncle Art's, with an occasional time-out thrown in for food and sleep.

My father and his siblings were raised on a farm in North Dakota and were no strangers to hard work. In calendar years, Art was the youngest of the lot; by general acclaim, he was the brightest; in my eyes, he was always the first to enjoy a good laugh; and in his own eyes, he was without a doubt the best looking lad in the Nicklaus clan. These qualities caught the attention of another pair of eyes, those of Ernestine Crane, the belle of Shelton, Washington, the prize catch of the Olympics' eastern approaches. Art and Ernie were a perfect match, everyone's favorite couple, well-suited to one another in every respect. Spending a month—sometimes two—with them every summer was always a fun-filled, positive experience. I loved them both like parents, and their sons, my cousins, like brothers.

Uncle Art always had one car or another in his garage that he was fixing up, and his love for cars matched any other in this auto-crazed country of ours. He took great pride in building his jalopies from the ground up—it was a special joy for him—and from his constant tinkering he'd learned every trick in the book to make a car go fast. From an early age, I knew that when it came time for me to start looking at cars, he'd be the one to help me find "a ride to die for." He even sold cars for a living and ultimately became a partner in Mel's Chevrolet and Oldsmobile in Shelton. Naturally, when I was at long last ready to buy my first car, Art Nicklaus, my favorite uncle, was my first and only choice for guidance. Whatever make and model he helped me choose, I knew it would be fast and cherry, a ride worthy of a Kingsmen.

The same day I received my first tour payout, I phoned Unc and told him I was ready to roll. He was pumped about selling me my first car and proposed that we meet at his dealership the next day. He had several models to recommend, and we quickly settled on a brand new red 1965 Chevy Chevelle "Malibu" Super Sport with a 350 HP 327 Corvette V-8 nestled under its hood, bucket seats and a four-on-the-floor. It was a teenage boy's ultimate dream machine, with a 'Vette engine to boot. Another option was of course a Corvette, but Norm already had one of those, and I wanted to be different. My Malibu was a special order from the factory, not due on showroom floors until late summer. Back then, the wheels of industry turned substantially slower than they do today, and when you special-ordered a car, it took a few months for GM or Ford or Chrysler to actually make it and ship it. That was fine with me—we were going to be touring for most of the summer anyway, and the car would just be sitting in my absence.

Uncle Art explained to me all of the things he'd do to trick out a car like mine were it his, and I told him to go ahead and do whatever he wanted to do to it once it arrived. "I'll spring for the modifications," I told him, patting my newly-fattened wallet. That got him more excited than a kid set free in the candy store. I could see him running through in his mind all the possible ways a car like my new SS could be beefed up to maximum performance levels. He vowed he'd have the best of everything waiting for me when I returned.

With my first set of wheels safely ordered, I was ready for New York. The Big Apple. Metropolis.

The Kingsmen backstage
Left to Right: Norm Lynn, Mike, Barry, author

VERSE 14

BOB Ehlert put together an expanded, ambitious 13-week tour, kicking off with Murray the K's musical extravaganza at the Brooklyn Fox Theatre. With our first show scheduled for Friday, March 27, Wally Amos booked us seats for the 25th on United. At that time, the airline offered New York-bound jet service out of Portland only once a day, with an afternoon departure time that didn't meet our needs. So instead, Wednesday morning early we were to fly a turbo-prop, Douglas DC-7 to Chicago's O'Hare Field, where we'd transfer to a New York-bound Boeing 727 jet airliner for the second leg of our trip. We were to arrive in New York that same evening, giving us all day on Thursday and most of Friday to acclimate ourselves to the area and our accommodations and prepare for our performance.

None of us had ever flown before, and nervous excitement was the rule as we and our small army of well-wishers gathered at the United counter to get our tickets and check our instruments and luggage. From there, we led a parade of parents, girlfriends and siblings to the departure gate for the big send-off. Spotting a life insurance vending machine in the terminal, I stopped and bought a million-dollar policy, a real bargain for a buck. If the plane went down, my mother and sisters would be set for life.

At the gate, we noisily traded hugs and kisses and tears. With bon voyages completed, braving the chill air on that typically cloudy Portland morning, we exited the terminal on foot, walked a short distance across the tarmac and climbed a wheeled stairway to where a smiling stewardess awaited us. (This being 1964, covered jet-ways and the term "flight attendant" were still things of the future.) Pausing at the top, Lynn, Norm, Nube, Barry and Lil' Dickie turned and waved to the assembled multitude à la what John, Paul,

George and Ringo were to do many times at airports across America that year.

In late January, on the eve of our first tour, "Louie Louie" had topped the charts (a true number one on *Cash Box*, a questionable number two to "Dominique" on *Billboard*). On February 1, the day before our chilling visit to that snow drift in New Mexico, the Beatles and "I Want to Hold Your Hand" officially deposed the Kingsmen, Bobby Vinton, the Singing Nun and all other pretenders to the throne of number one, and the British Invasion was officially on. Oblivious to the lasting threat those British mop-tops and their ilk posed to clean-cut, short-haired, well-groomed all-American boys like the Kingsmen, the entire hoard of our supporters planted themselves at the gate and vowed not to move an inch until our plane was safely in the heavens and out of view. They had a long wait.

As the pilot started the engines, Lynn was the supreme definition of a white knuckle flyer, gripping his armrests so hard it caused his hands to shake. A passing stew asked if this were his first flight. Hoping to win her favor and perhaps a phone number, we chirped in that it was the first flight for all of us. Untouched by the words of encouragement she offered, Lynn became so frightened, his nervousness began to spread among the other four of us. As we sat in that rickety old aircraft at the end of the runway, the pilot revved the engines to maximum as the brakes held the roaring bucket of bolts in place. Just when it seemed the vibrations would surely bounce us out of our seats, he released the brakes and the aircraft jolted forward, speeding down the runway. Half-way to the end, at the very moment the nose of the plane started to lift off of the pavement, the pilot reversed engines and hit the brakes, aborting the takeoff.

"We're going to die!" Lynn roared as his hands fought to alter the shape of the armrests on his seat.

Scared to death, we now shared fully in his fear.

The pilot spoke over the intercom, explaining that a warning light and alarm had come on just as we were about to go airborne, causing him to abort our take-off. He informed us that it was a false alarm, that the light and the alarm had been reset and that he was going back to the head of the runway to try it again. His words, meant to calm, only further jangled our already-frazzled nerves.

As we sat again at the end of the runway, engines revving a second time, I squeezed the armrests with a vise-like grip like Lynn's and planted my head firmly against the headrest. I glanced over at Mike and noticed he had similarly braced himself for our second brush with death. Again, the pilot released the brakes, and the plane sped down the runway. Once more, the nose rose fitfully, this time reaching the desired angle of attack. Grunting and groaning in protest, the fuselage, wings and tail of the plane followed the nose's lead, and slowly the aircraft struggled skyward. We could see our throng glued to the terminal windows, standing there and watching, but no one dared to spare a hand and wave to the curious bunch. As the plane reached an altitude of a few hundred feet, the pilot suddenly banked steeply to the right, catching us off guard and sending personal belongings flying from the overhead racks.

"Whoa!" terrified passengers cried as one.

The pilot returned to the intercom, announcing that the light and alarm had once again come on, this time right after liftoff, and that he was circling back to land the aircraft so that mechanics could check it out. Just then, a smoke-like cloud started billowing out of an overhead vent at the front of the passenger cabin. As we were being jostled about in the unstable air, one of us asked the stewardess sitting in the crew seat facing us whether she'd noticed the smoke, and did it alarm her.

"Oh, that!" she yelled, her calm voice rising over the strident noise. "That's only condensation, nothing to worry about. It's normal for this aircraft."

As we landed, we could see our curious gang still watching from the gate. We were going to have to de-plane until the problem—whatever it was—was fixed. Lynn was white as a sheet, scared out of his wits, and I was doubtful that anyone without a crowbar could pry him loose from his seat. Sighing deeply, he emerged from his semi-catatonic state, rose from his seat and staggered off the plane, the rest of us following behind. On our way out, the stewardess told us that as soon as they were ready to go again, they'd make an announcement at the gate.

As we re-entered the terminal—I was beginning to understand why they called it a "terminal"—our entourage surged forward and embraced us, excitedly sharing their fears and concerns for our safety, which did nothing to calm our jittery nerves and only made them worse. Trying to make light of the trauma, I reached in my pocket and pulled out a fiver. Intending to announce to one and all that I was going to use it to increase my life insurance policy, I stopped, speechless, and stared at my feet. Lo and behold, when I removed my hand from my pocket, my mother's set of keys fell on the carpet in front of me. Car keys. House keys. Garage door keys. Keys to the store where she worked. Keys to padlocks. Keys to anything and everything you can think of. They all were on that key ring, and I'd taken it with me on my attempted flight to New York. This was the only set of keys she had, and the plane's system malfunctions proved to be good fortune. Otherwise, my mom would've been left keyless in Portland and Lil' Dickie would've flown to New York with a useless pocketful of them.

United's mechanics finally managed to fix whatever was wrong with our plane, and our third takeoff attempt came off without a hitch. Our pilot flew eastward past the snow-covered cone of Mount Hood without having to beat another retreat. Over Idaho and on into Montana's not-so-friendly big skies, Lynn sat motionless, staring blankly ahead, watching his life pass before him, jerking to attention with every new bump. By the time we landed safely six hours later at O'Hare, his complexion had changed in color from a ghostly shade of white to a nauseous tint of green. An hour later, we flew on to New York's Kennedy airport on a Boeing 727 jet that rode like a feather bed on wings compared to the turbulent, rough and bumpy ride of the DC-7 turbo-prop. All hail the Jet Age! Lynn would gladly have kissed the ground once we landed at JFK had he been able to find it. But all we saw was concrete everywhere. Plus, he was still too scared to recognize terra firma had any been accessible.

We'd all heard stories about the cabbies in New York and their shenanigans, about how sometimes they'd take rookies like us on circuitous routes to their destinations, traveling twice as far as necessary in order to run up their meters. We'd been told how New York cabbies loved to act friendly, but that their apparent good nature was just a device used to lower a passenger's defenses determine whether their fare was a mark from out of town or someone with Big Apple experience. Oh, yes, we'd been told, and we were ready to prove to the New York world that we hadn't just fallen off the turnip truck.

With our gear rounded up, we hailed a taxi. We had a ton of stuff, and our hard-edged cabbie told us he could only take four of us in his car. Two cabs had not been figured into Norm's budget, so Lynn, leaving his recent fear-of-flying episode behind and returning to his normal king-of-the-road self, defiantly told him that in that case, we'd wait for a larger cab with a more accommodating driver. After some heated dickering, the cabbie gave in and loaded—no, forced—our gear into the trunk of his beat-up yellow Checker. Burdened with so much stuff, the trunk refused to close, and the cabbie produced several tie-down straps he used to keep from losing his load when dealing with situations like ours. Even with that, we still had to stuff items under our feet and hold a piece of luggage in our laps. It was either that or leave something behind.

The cramped and crowded ride in from the airport was an exercise in perseverance over roads riddled with potholes. In what we assumed was true New Yorker fashion, the cabbie made no effort to avoid a single one of the craters, heedless to possible damage to property and posteriors. Thoroughly shaken and stirred, the Kingsmen arrived at the St. George Hotel five disheveled, uneasy pieces.

At the hotel, an alert bellman unloaded our belongings and, to our amazement, disappeared with our stuff, saying that once we'd checked in, he'd deliver everything to our room. We weren't in Kansas anymore, and this wasn't a Holiday Inn; this was Brooklyn and the St. George, and things were already proving different.

Thinking he was being generous, Lynn paid the cabbie his fare and added five bucks as a tip for his efforts.

In a thick New York accent, the aggressive little man screamed, "What da hell is dis?"

"It's a tip," replied Lynn, wondering why this strange man was refusing to recognize his generosity.

"And for your kindness, you can keep the change," he added with a smile.

Overweight, balding, rude and now enraged, the cabbie thrust his jaw at Lynn's face and said in a loud, curdling voice, "I drive all yoos guys all da way in from da airport and ya lay a lousy five spot on me? Dat ain't a tip, dat's an insult. I can get a betta tip from a handycapa!"

"Hey, five bucks is a lot of money," answered the tired and embarrassed Lynn, standing up for his gift.

"Say bud, dis is da city. If yoos boys tink a fiver is a tip, yoos gotta big dose of reality comin' to ya."

Standing his ground, Lynn retorted, "I've been warned about guys like you trying to cheat guys like me, and that's all you get!"

"I don't need to drive five guys and a house full of junk to get aggravation!" yelled his irate adversary.

Standing up for Lynn, Mike curtly added, "You can buy a half a tank a gas with five bucks."

Hearing that, the angry New Yorker spun around and stormed back to his cab. Slamming his door, he flipped Lynn off and yelled, "Screw yoos guys!" before speeding off, furiously swearing to himself.

We laughed in disbelief as we entered the hotel.

"Can you imagine scoffing at a five buck tip?"

We checked into the hotel, found our room and, as usual, I drew the roll-away. The St. George was old and well worn, but you could tell that it must have been considered a luxury property in its day. Our room was much larger than any of the Holiday Inn rooms we were used to and gave us plenty of space to spread out. As promised, our belongings were soon delivered and, after we helped the bellhop deposit our stuff in the room, Lynn handed him a dollar.

"That's it?" asked the bellman in shock.

"You know," responded Lynn, "I'm not some stupid guy from Oregon you New Yorkers can take advantage of. In the movies, they usually flip you guys a quarter and the bellman's always more than thankful!"

"This ain't the movies," argued the bellhop. "This is New York!"

"Bye!" said Lynn as he slowly closed the door in the bellman's face.

"I've heard stories about these guys," Lynn said, laughing, "and I'm not going to let them take advantage us. We're on a budget."

I was grateful that Lynn was in charge and *wisely* looking out for us.

VERSE 15

FIRST thing next morning, Lynn telephoned Marvin Schlackter, VP at Scepter/Wand, our New York-based record company, to let him know we'd arrived safely. Marvin was excited to hear from Lynn and told him the controversy surrounding "Louie Louie" now verged on insanity. He said his company was offering a $10,000 reward to anyone who could prove the record contained dirty lyrics, figuring that would surely put an end to the rumors. Reward or no reward, the feverish debate continued to rage unabated. Lynn and Marvin agreed upon a time early the following week for us to visit their offices. We'd meet then with his staff and discuss plans for our future direction. Lynn phoned Wally Amos next. Wally said he'd come down to the theatre later that week to catch the show and promised to take us out afterward and expose us to a side of New York that most visitors didn't get to see, a slice of the Big Apple he thought we'd find tasty.

With Lynn finally off the phone, we set about making our way on foot and by train to the Brooklyn Fox Theatre where we and the other acts had an 11 AM production meeting scheduled with Murray the K and his people. Loaded down with guitars and hang bags, we walked the streets of Brooklyn in search of the train station. Everything about the city—every sight, every sound, every smell, every person—was strange and new to our experience. We spent the entire time pointing things out to one another with a constant stream of comments and exclamations. Sometimes two or more of us would simultaneously point to the same thing, in particular the Brooklyn Bridge looming over the East River just a few blocks away. Passers-by no doubt thought we were nuts, and who could argue with them? We were from Oregon. Following exactly the directions

Wally'd given Lynn—like the good Boy Scouts that we were—we boarded precisely the right train and exited at the appropriate station, a short walk from our final destination.

From a block away, the Brooklyn Fox Theatre with its brightly-lit marquee beckoned to us. This was one of the true meccas of American rock 'n' roll, one of the ornate entertainment palaces where Alan Freed once staged his legendary extravaganzas—a tradition now being carried on four times a year by Murray the K. Every rocker worth his salt from Chuck Berry on had played here, and we were about to join that exclusive club. As we drew closer, we saw before us our name in bright lights: "THE KINGSMEN" sandwiched between "LITTLE ANTHONY & THE IMPERIALS" and "JOHNNY TILLOTSON." We were so impressed with ourselves, our heads swelled an extra hat size.

The police had set up hundreds of feet of wooden barriers along the curb to hold back crowds of young fans and autograph seekers often 20 or 30 sets of screaming lungs deep. Several dozen of New York's finest stood watch over the barricades, tapping their truncheons and looking bored. We threaded our way through the constabulary to the metal backstage door, off on a side street. There, a gruff-speaking sergeant was posted, checking artist passes and taking care of general entrance-door business: clearing stagehands, caterers and radio station personalities and determining who else among the many supplicants was or was not deserving of admittance into the *sanctum sanctorum*.

Once inside, we were taken upstairs to our dressing room by a stagehand. As we climbed the dark wooden stairs, we could hear the musicians on stage running through the charts for the acts they'd be backing in the show. Violinists and bassists, clarinetists and flautists, trombonists and trumpeters, percussionists and harpists—they were all there, nearly a full symphony orchestra. I strained my ears, seeking the familiar, resounding boom of a timpani (old habits die hard).

Everywhere, people were scurrying about, toting ironing boards, electrical cables, costumes, props, food, refreshments, even bouquets of flowers. It was all so show biz, and love at first sight for the five of us. The energy and colors and sights and sounds—the entire atmosphere— was intoxicating. Non-stop, we traded funny little glances and excited smiles as we made our way to our dressing room.

The dressing rooms were lined up one after another along the upstairs corridor, like in a college dorm. Star-shaped plaques hung on each door, with the name of an artist or group neatly printed on each one. "Ben E. King." We whispered and poked each other like giddy little children. "Little Anthony." More whispers. "Dionne Warwick." *I love Dionne Warwick!* I thought to myself, starting to feel intimidated. "The Shirelles." "Johnny Tillotson." "Bobby Goldsboro." "The Tymes." Love 'em or not, it just didn't seem real.

Finally, the stagehand stopped before a door hung with a star reading "The Kingsmen." I noticed that the dressing room on the left was assigned to the Tymes, the one on the right to Dick & Dee Dee. Fumbling with his key ring for a moment, the stagehand unlocked the door and handed Lynn the key.

"Here yaz are, boys," he said as he left. "Let me know if yaz need anyding. I'm always at da desk by da stairs."

We set our stuff down, hung our hang bags up and soaked in our newly exalted status in the entertainment world.

"I can't believe we're here!" said Mike, smiling from ear to ear.

"We've hit the big time now, brother!" Barry said, jokingly pushing Norm on the shoulder.

I ran over to the window, and the guys crowded around behind me.

"This is perfect!" Lynn exclaimed. "We're right above the fans."

A can of Ajax couldn't scrub the smiles off our faces. We ran around the room like lunatics on the loose from the asylum, feeling for the first time like we were really in show business. In the midst of our impromptu celebration, we heard a knock on the door jam.

"Hi, I'm Dick St. John," said the voice at the door.

We scrambled to introduce ourselves to the famous rocker, one half of the boy/girl duo that recorded "Mountain's High." He wore an ear-to-ear grin that put Mike's to shame and was so out-going and friendly, I figured he couldn't possibly be a typical example of the recording stars we were about to meet. Introductions completed, Dick told us that everyone performing in the show was to meet downstairs in five minutes for a briefing. He said he was on his way down and we could follow him if we were ready. We were.

Trailing Dick backstage and through the side curtains, we couldn't suppress our giddiness. We carried on like debutantes attending their first ball—giggling, trading secret glances, nervously awaiting our introduction to society. Just think, behavior like this from the arch-fiends behind the "Louie Louie" conspiracy. Our true colors were showing—hicks from the sticks.

Wearing his trademark hat, Murray Kaufman, aka "Murray the K," aka "the Fifth Beatle" introduced himself and handed out sheets of paper listing the show order, schedules and rules for the next 10 days. Once Murray and his stage manager were finished covering the logistics, we hung out on the stage visiting with the other acts. Everyone questioned us about the lyrics to "Louie Louie," even Murray, and wanted to know about our experiences with the FBI and the FCC. We were thrilled to meet so many famous rock stars all at one time and pleasantly surprised at how friendly and special everyone seemed.

THERE were two types of dressing rooms at the Brooklyn Fox Theatre—outboard and inboard. Outboard dressing rooms had windows overlooking the backstage door side of the theatre. Across the hall, inboard dressing rooms were slightly larger, but lacked windows and light and were not nearly as nice. Dick and Dee Dee's outboard dressing room was located directly above the backstage door entrance. Dick seemed overly excited with his window's location.

Dick St. John, who died in a fall from a ladder at his home in December 2003, was one of the most energetic and warm and gutsy persons ever to walk the face of this earth; in her own special way, Dee Dee Lee was every bit Dick's equal, but different. From the second these two lovable characters arrived in our lives, it was as though we'd all known one another since birth. Meeting Dee Dee was like finding another sister; meeting Dick was like discovering you had a living, breathing not-so-evil twin ready and willing to try all the crazy things you never dared to consider doing by yourself. A prankster without equal, Dick was always up to something—and planning in the back of his mind what he'd do next after his current prank had run its course. Just when the shows would start to get boring, Dick would come up with something fresh and exciting to re-energize all of us and turn us back into the laughing bunch of little children we really were.

THE shows ran back to back all day long, with only an hour or so in between. That allowed just enough time to empty the house and fill the seats again. These programs were reviews made up of a string of acts, each called out to perform one or two of their hit songs before turning stage and mics over to the next act. Because each show ran about an hour in length, you had a little over 90 minutes between your performance calls.

The street outside the theatre was filled with kids breathlessly waiting for one of the stars to open a window and say something. Sometimes when doing so, we'd drop souvenirs, like autographed pictures or guitar picks, down to them, and they'd go crazy. If you were eating an apple, they'd die for the core; if you were wiping off the sweat from your last performance, they'd kill for the used towel.

Our first show was unforgettable. Instructed to report backstage, guitars in hand, ready to plug in and play before the preceding act finished, we stood in the wings watching nervously as the Younger Brothers performed. Once they were through, Murray the K grabbed the mic, delivered a theatrical introduction and called us out. As we walked onto the stage, deafening screams shook the Fox. Whatever the decibel level of a Beatles crowd was, this had to be close. The noise actually hurt my ears.

Of course, we played "Louie Louie." But, in an effort to take advantage of the heavy airplay "Louie" was getting, Scepter/Wand had recently released our second single, "Money," and it was streaking up the charts on the coattails of "Louie." Knowing this, Murray asked us to play both "Money" and "Louie" in his show.

Poster for Murray the K's Easter Holidays Extravaganza—March 1964

From the second he introduced us until the moment we ran off of the stage, the fans didn't stop screaming long enough to take a breath. It was exhilarating. Who in their right mind would ever want something like this to end? It was the same for every show: fans endlessly screaming and jumping around to the music. The smiles on our faces turned permanent.

On the third day of this hysteria, we were sitting in our dressing room marveling at the sound the Tymes were making as they rehearsed next door. Their harmonies were perfect—flawless and beautiful—exactly like on their hit records "So Much In Love" and "Wonderful Wonderful." We loved it, and we didn't have to pay admission or stand in line to hear it.

Interrupting our concentration, Dick, minus Dee Dee, barged into our dressing room shouting, "Look, I found some balloons! You guys wanna have some fun?"

Norm answered first.

"What're you going to do with those?" he asked.

"Fill them with water and drop them out the window on the kids," Dick said, wearing a devilish grin. "What else?"

He spun around and ran out of the room and down the hall to the bathroom. We all hurried after him, he being our Pied Piper, we being his wonder-struck children. We knew for certain that with Dick behind it, whatever he was proposing was going to be fun.

We watched in the bathroom as he filled a balloon with water from the tap and tied the end in a knot, transforming an innocent, uninflated balloon into a menacing, filled-to-bursting water bomb. Pitching in, we each grabbed a few balloons and quickly loaded them with liquid ammo.

Two doors down from the Tymes, Johnny Tillotson was sitting in his dressing room with the door wide open, playing his guitar and minding his own business.

"Hey guys," Johnny said in greeting, "what's going on?"

"We want to use your window," answered Dick as he slid the wooden sash up. "You don't mind, do you?"

"No," answered the curious, somewhat apprehensive singer.

Dick opened Johnny's window, and the fans started screaming. He yelled down to the crowd as he showed them the red balloon he was holding in his hand.

"Anybody want a balloon?" he cried.

Cheering, the kids begged him to throw it down to them. Obligingly, Dick raised his hand in the air and tossed the first balloon at the crowd. As one, they all reached up for the souvenir, and all you could see from our perch was a sea of outstretched hands. As the red missile struck those reaching hands it broke, showering a circle of fans. Wet or dry, the crowd cheered with excitement.

"Hand me another one!" ordered the laughing jokester, not bothering to look around as he held his hand out behind him, waiting for a reload. Dick showed the fans his next balloon, this time a green one, and again they went crazy. He teased the crowd with the projectile until they begged him to release it, and only then he'd fling it earthward. Once again, the balloon popped, soaking more screaming fans. Now the rest of us each took a turn dispensing holy water on our worshipers.

Retaking the window, Dick commanded his troops to "Watch this!"

To our astonishment, he fired a bright yellow balloon straight at the cop guarding the backstage door. We all held our breath as the water-filled blob exploded at the officer's feet, missing the unsuspecting target by inches.

"Hey!" the cop yelled, turning around and looking up at the windows. "That's enough for tonight, boys! That one was a little too close."

Laughing uncontrollably, Dick waited until he was sure the cop thought that his stern warning had worked. Then he slowly stuck his head out of the window and launched a new attack. Again, maybe because it was orange, the balloon missed its target and hit the nearby sidewalk with a splat.

"Hey, you little idiot, that's enough! Don't make me come up there."

By now, the other cops had joined him in searching the windows above, trying to identify the felon that was throwing balloons at him. Of course, after each throw, we all backed away from the window and hid from the angered flatfoot's view. Johnny started worrying aloud that he was going to be the one to get in trouble—after all, we were using his window. But, driven and tenacious, Dick was bound and determined to finish the job he'd started.

```
              PERMANENT RUNDOWN
                ─────────────

1. CHIFFONS ─────────────── A. "HE'S SO FINE"
2. BOBBY GOLSBORO ────────── A. "A FUNNY CLOWN"
3. DICK & DEE DEE ────────── A. "MOUNTAINS HIGH"
                              B. "TURNAROUND"
4. MURRAY BK intro ─────────
5. THE TYMES ─────────────── A. "SECRET LOVE"
                              B. "Somewhere" or "So"
6. YOUNGER BROS. ─────────── A. "I WANNA Nod..."
                              B. "IT WON'T BE LONG"
7. LITTLE ANTHONY + IMPERIALS ─ A. "TEARS ON...."
                                B. "I'M ALRIGHT"
8. DIONNE WARWICK ────────── A. "ANYONE WHO...."
9. JOHNNY TILLOTSON ──────── A. "TALK BACK"...
10. KINGSMEN ─────────────── A. "LOUIE, LOUIE"
11. BEN E. KING ──────────── A. "DON'T PLAY..."
                              B. "I"..
                              C. "ALL MY LOVIN"
12. SHIRELLES ────────────── A. "TWIST & SHOUT
                              B. "EVERYBODY....."
13. CHUCK JACKSON ────────── A. "STUBBORN FELLA
                              B. "ANY DAY NOW"
                              C. "I DON'T WANT
                                   TO CRY."

         FINALE ─── BEN E. KING
```

Actual schedule hand written by Murray on the back of the poster above. It was posted backstage for Easter Extravaganza, March 1964

"Okay," he said, "hand me an empty balloon, and you guys go back to your room and sit around like you have no idea what's been going on."

We watched as Dick returned to the bathroom and filled another balloon with water. Except this time he didn't tie off the end of it. Instead, he purposely dripped water from the bathroom, leaving a fresh wet trail that led down the hall and directly to the closed door of the unsuspecting Tymes, who as always were practicing harmonies in their dressing room. Once finished, Dick surveyed his handiwork and pronounced it a success. "Perfect!" He'd just created a water path that made it look as though the Tymes were the guilty parties.

We all crept into Dick's room, where he issued new orders.

"When I hit this cop," he said, "he's going to come up here loaded for bear and mad as a hornet. When he does, start talking and acting like you have no idea what's happening. Trust me, this is going to work. This is going to be fun."

We nervously watched as he carefully held the water-filled balloon out the window and centered it directly over the cop's head, adjusting his aim a few times before he let go.

BOMBS AWAY!

Quickly but coolly, Dick ran toward the door and sat on a table, pretending like he'd been parked there all along, visiting with his musician pals and passing time.

We heard the sound of the angry cop rushing up the stairs.

"Just wait 'til I get my hands on the slimeball that dropped that balloon on me!" he shouted.

Through the open door we saw the officer stomp down the hall toward us. His soaked hat dripped with water as it drooped down around his ears. He was so drenched, it was so comical, we could barely keep from laughing. Dick didn't bat an eyelash, didn't flinch, didn't blink.

"What happened to you?" he asked the cop.

"It's what's about to happen that should worry the reprobate that threw that water balloon on me," came the angry reply.

Looking down at the hall floor, the cop spied the water trail leading from the bathroom to the Tymes' door. Seven strong, we leaned out our door, jostling for position, trying to get a good view of whatever happened next.

The drenched cop, now a raging bull, stormed over to the Tymes' door and threw it open, surprising the innocents within.

"Which one of you deadbeat canaries threw the water balloon?" he demanded.

Shocked at first by the cop's sudden intrusion, the vocalists responded in what I thought was convincing fashion.

"What?"

"Hey man, what's your problem?"

"What're you talkin' about?"

"Don't play innocent with me!" the angry officer shouted back. "I see the trail of water leading from the bathroom to your door."

Looking down at the evidence, the Tymes nodded their heads in perfect unison.

"Yeah," one of them said, "funny how it stops at the door, ain't it, man?"

"Hey, we don't know nothin' 'bout this!" said another of the accused.

"It must've been those guys that ran out of the bathroom and down the hall just before you showed up," Dick, unruffled, calmly suggested.

"Yeah," Barry chimed in, "I heard a commotion and saw a bunch of stagehands out here a few minutes ago."

The cop pointed a fleshy finger at Dick.

"If I catch the guy responsible," he warned, "it'll be the last balloon he ever throws out of any window!"

With that, he turned around and sloshed back down the stairs, resuming his post as our protector.

"See, wasn't that fun?" Dick said as the rest of us collapsed in laughter. Even the Tymes were grinning, although they weren't exactly sure yet about what. Lynn summed things up best.

"He looked like a drowned rat!"

We sat for quite a while, reviewing the comedic episode we'd just performed in and critiquing one another's performance. In a landslide, Dick won the Oscar for best actor.

Like I said before, you never knew what to expect next from Dick St. John. One minute he'd be calm, cool and collected and the next minute he'd be the Devil incarnate. Invariably, his inspired schemes put someone else in the hot seat, at risk, but never Dick himself. First and foremost, Dick was an instigator; the rest of us were but pawns in his grand schemes.

MURRAY'S shows started in the afternoon and ended late at night. Doing four shows a day meant we had three long breaks to fill. Usually after the first show, most people went to lunch. Acts formed into groups and headed off in several directions in search of different types of cuisine. Usually after the second show, most of us visited dressing rooms and generally hung out. Usually after the third show, most of the performers filtered in and out of a bar just around the corner from the theatre.

I didn't drink—and still don't—so at that point in the day, I usually stood in the wings and watched the show. I made it a point to always catch Dionne Warwick singing "Anyone Who Had A Heart." Her voice was spectacular, and the song was a perfect match for her unique style. Four times a day, she'd walk on by as she walked off stage after a performance and I'd say, "You sounded fabulous!" and she'd say, "Thanks!" and that would be the full extent of our conversation.

On one such occasion, the boys decided to play a little trick on Lil' Dickie. They went to Dionne beforehand and told her I had a crush on her, but was too shy to do anything about it. They also told her I'd never had a drink before and had never been with a woman, either. They even told her the comic tale of my not being a man yet. "Count me in!" Dionne told them, whereupon she and my loving brothers put their heads together, concocting a scheme to get me tipsy.

After the third show, just when I thought she was going to walk on by one more time with just a "thanks," Dionne stopped when she heard my "You sounded fabulous!" looked me straight in the face and said, "I'm going down to the corner for a drink between shows. Would you like to join me?"

I felt my face flush as somehow I managed the word, "Sure!"

"I'll change and be down in a minute," she answered.

As I turned around, there stood the guys.

"Oooooooo, you're so cool, man!"

"No, he's suave and debonair!"

The razzing was endless, and the crowd of my admirers was growing.

Bobby Goldsboro showed up, then came Dick and Dee Dee, and then Johnny Tillotson just happened to wander by. The numbers kept on growing until Dionne reappeared.

"Ready?" she asked.

"Yes," I answered, and out the door we walked, chaperones in tow.

As soon as the backstage door opened, the crowd outside started screaming. Our friend the sergeant was back, and he cocked an eyebrow when he saw who I was with. We all stopped at the barricades and signed autographs and visited with fans.

"Hey, we gotta go!" someone finally said.

Tongue-tied, I walked down the street with Dionne on my arm.

"Where are you from?" she questioned, taking over the lead.

"Portland, Oregon," I sputtered. "Where are you from?"

"I started out in New Jersey, but now I live here in New York."

My date was acting so nice and friendly and seemed so easy to talk to about anything and nothing. She even remained patient as I stumbled through my nervous, single word, mostly monosyllabic answers. By the time we reached the bar, I could almost breathe again.

The drinking age in New York then was 18, and I was 17 going on 18. Maybe that explains why the bartender didn't seem to notice anything amiss as we entered his establishment. Still, I'd never been in a bar before, and the protocol was all new to me. I watched open-mouthed as the group pulled several tables together and deposited me in the back with Dionne on one side of me and Mike on the other. If the police came by checking IDs, maybe they'd miss me. With the drinking age being 18, my band mates were safe on that issue.

"What's your pleasure?" Dionne asked, playing me like a fiddle.

"What?"

"What are you drinking?"

"Oh! Um…I don't know. I, um…I don't drink."

"Oh! Then you should try the lemonade."

Mike distracted me with small talk while Dionne ordered drinks. As the waitress left the table with our orders, Dionne got up and followed her to the bar. Unbeknownst to her male companion, she instructed the bartender to mix me a weak Vodka Collins—"lemonade" New York style—and to slowly increase the amount of hooch with each new order. With that critical element of the plot covered, she returned to the table.

Sitting around in a smoky bar just shooting the breeze with so many celebrities had my head spinning well before our drinks arrived.

So this is what they do down here every day, I thought to myself. *Not bad. No, not bad at all.*

Our nurse arrived with the medicine and, at first sip, I thought the lemonade tasted a little strange, to say the least. Like in the Havana bar scene in *Guys and Dolls*, I was playing Sister Sara Brown to Dionne's Sky Masterson. This lemonade was my *dolce de leche*. Would luck be a lady tonight? I dared not think it. What exactly happened anyway when men and women went to bars together? I was about to find out.

Dionne asked how I liked my lemonade, and I told her it was the worst I'd ever had, which brought quite a laugh from the conspirators. Not missing a beat, she explained that the funny taste I detected was the result of old pipes and hard water. They treated the water in New York, she said, and tried to remove some of the bad taste, but this foul brew was mostly what you got. Like boys having a period before becoming men, that sounded logical to me. Frankly, I didn't give a hoot what the lemonade in New York tasted like. I was with Dionne Warwick!

I soon found myself engaged in a toasting-fest and getting used to the strange taste of the lemonade. My fellow celebrants insisted on raising glasses to everything under the sun and moon: the bartender, the waitress, Murray, all the acts in the show, Louie, J. Edgar, the drenched policeman and on and on and on—the toasts were endless. After five or six rounds, I felt like I hadn't a care in the world and began thinking the room was moving. How many more lemonades it would've taken to fully quench my thirst, I'll never know. Time was up. We had another show to perform.

Heads are supposed to spin when you're drunk, but when I stood to go back to the theatre for the final show, my head more like bounced up and down as though it were on a trampoline. Beyond that, I remember nothing of the rest of the night. People told me later that I pranced about all over the stage during our performance, and that my drumming was equally dramatic. The good news was, my vocal to "Louie Louie" never sounded more authentic. Upstairs, I was told, I held my arms out like the wings of a jet fighter and buzzed dressing rooms, stagehands and acts, providing my own sound effects. According to the guys, I continued my act all way the back to the hotel, on the subway and in the streets of Brooklyn. The next morning, Mike told me that I was so far gone by the time we reached the hotel, I actually thought I could fly and at one point attempted to launch myself out of our hotel room window à la Peter Pan. With none of Tinkerbell's fairy dust to help, I wouldn't have flown very far had I made that leap. Thankfully, the guys stopped me in time.

Outside of a slightly sickish feeling that quickly disappeared, I was fine the next day. After hearing my so-called buddies describe my behavior from the previous night, I was embarrassed and dreaded returning to the theatre, knowing I had a lot of apologies to make but uncertain as to whom to make them to or for what. Fortunately for me, everyone had had a good laugh at my expense and was more than kind and forgiving. That was the only time in my life I've ever been drunk. I'd seen enough. That morning I decided that getting soused served no useful purpose and that alcohol had a flavor I had no interest in acquiring a taste for.

WALLY Amos came down one afternoon as promised and took us all to lunch, bearing bags of cookies as gifts. He filled us in on plans he was working on for an East Coast tour. Over lunch at one of his favorite haunts, we began what has turned out to be a life-long friendship.

ONE afternoon, between shows, Mike and I were sitting in the dressing room with Norm when he brought up his concern that nothing seemed to be happening to fix our situation with Lynn.

"We've been here five or six days now and still we have no photo shoot scheduled," he said. "Nothing's going to be done unless we do it, or the first thing you know, we'll be back on the concert tour again as 'the Lynn Easton show.'"

Just then, Dick came walking up to the open door. Peeking in, he asked, "Whatcha doin'?"

"We're trying to decide what to do about our group situation," answered Mike.

"Oooo, serious!" joked Dick. "Sounds like I should come back at another time."

"No, don't go," Norm said. "Come in. Maybe you can help us."

"What's the problem?"

"Well," Mike began, "we started this band as a group of equals, kind of a Five Musketeers sort of deal. Lynn always handled the business end of things. You know, booking the band, paying the bills, disbursing the money. And now he's…"

"He's taking over?" interrupted Dick.

"More than that," said Norm. "Without talking it over with any of us, he put 'Lynn Easton and The Kingsmen' on the bottom of our PR pictures and told our agents at WMA to sell us that way."

"Really?"

"Really!" I answered. "And he's telling the DJS at the gigs to introduce us as 'Lynn Easton and The Kingsmen.'"

"Plus," added Mike, "on the last tour, he started dressing in different stage dress than the rest of us."

Walking in the room in the middle of the conversation, Barry quickly offered his views.

"It's like he's not only tried to put himself above the band," Barry explained, "but sadly, in doing so, he's separating himself from us as well."

"Why don't you tell your manager to talk to him about it?" asked Dick.

"Lynn is acting as our manager, too," answered Norm. "He's even taking 10 percent off the top for the service."

"What?" exclaimed Barry.

"I didn't know that!" I said in shock.

"Sure," said Norm. "Didn't you guys read your statements after the tour?"

"I thought 'management commission' was WMA," said Barry.

"No, the agency commission wasn't even on the statement," explained Norm. "WMA takes their commissions before they send us the money from the deposits."

"That was a lot of money!" complained Barry.

Tension filled the room, more so than in any previous crisis we'd faced.

"If you want to put things on an even keel again," Dick began carefully, "you need to hire professional management. Have whoever it is you choose handle the PR decisions. You guys can dictate who you are. Besides, now that you're a national act, you need national management. You need someone to build your career, not just talk to booking agents."

About that time, Lynn walked in the room.

"What's this about building a career?" he asked, curious.

"I was just saying, I think you guys need to consider getting a professional manager to go to work for you," Dick said smoothly, as though this was his lead.

The pained look on Lynn's face clearly betrayed his displeasure. He tried to disguise it with a simple question.

"Oh?"

Dick continued.

"A good manager would get you on television and in a few movies," he pointed out, moving his argument to solid ground, "you know, do things that will create mass media exposure for the band. You guys should be doing *Bandstand*, Beach Party movies, TV teen shows. You should have articles about the band in teen magazines and national publications. That's the kind of stuff a good manager gets for you. You need to hop on it now while you're hot. You'll increase your revenue and longevity by increasing your popularity."

"Do you know anyone we could talk to about national management?" asked Mike.

"If you're interested, I can talk to our manager, Bill Lee, Dee Dee's husband. He handles us, and he'd fit right in with your down-to-earth personalities. He's been in the business for quite a while and has a ton of industry contacts. Bill's a great guy. He could do wonders for a band with your notoriety."

"Where's he located?" asked Norm.

"LA," answered Dick. "Couldn't hurt to talk to him."

"What do you think, Lynn?" asked Mike, trying to include him in the process.

"Couldn't hurt," replied Lynn sullenly as he rummaged through his hang bag.

"He's coming out to see Dee Dee either tomorrow or the day after," Dick informed us. "I'll call him and tell him about you guys. If you want, I'll introduce you to him when he gets here. But right now, I've got to go get a bite to eat. Anybody want to come?"

We all agreed to go, except Lynn. He'd just been to the deli and decided to stay behind and eat his sandwich alone in the dressing room.

Once we were outside, the rest of us started laughing.

"Wow, did that work out or what?" said Norm.

"The timing was perfect!" I added.

"Yeah!" said Mike. "And Dick, you handled it with such smoothness. Thanks!"

"It's going to be important to let Bill know your goals and how you want this band to work," advised Dick. "You need to talk with him before Lynn does."

"Just in case we don't have the chance to get him alone," Mike said, "when you talk to him, let him know our problem. Tell him that by hiring a manager, we not only want to further our career—we want to right the ship as well. Lynn's not the enemy here. We just want to be The Kingsmen again."

"I'll handle it!" said Dick. "I'll even have a few upbeat conversations with Lynn about management before Bill gets here."

VERSE 16

As the day wore on, the more we talked to Dick without Lynn around, the more convinced we became that finding a manager was the ultimate answer to our problems. We needed someone to represent all of our interests and realized at last we couldn't do it for ourselves. Plus, we needed to get rid of all of the guilt we'd been feeling—four of us for the things we were saying and thinking about Lynn, and Lynn for the things he was doing behind our backs. (We assumed that guilt and pressure were two of the reasons why he drank so heavily.) Above all else, having a professional manager would help build our long-term careers. Until now, we'd contented ourselves with just playing gigs and enjoying the short-term fruits of our unexpected popularity. There was a whole lot more out there just waiting to be had, and we decided that a manager was exactly what we needed to help us take better advantage of the opportunities.

The key was meeting Bill Lee, and all of us—Lynn included, thanks to Dick's skillful sales job—looked forward to that moment with great anticipation and high, high hopes. We crossed our collective fingers, hoping he'd take the job.

One morning, Dick announced that Bill was coming to the third show that afternoon and promised to bring him up to our dressing room afterward to get acquainted. That news had us all pumped, and we hit the stage with a renewed sense of life in the present and hope for the future. The Kingsmen rocked louder, the fans screamed louder, too, and electricity filled the Brooklyn Fox Theatre that day.

After the third show, we merrily rolled along to the dressing room to change and prepare for Bill's arrival. The place buzzed with laughter and conversation as Mike and Norm debated the merits of the outstanding girls sitting down front, while Barry and Lynn likened the odds of either one of them scoring with one of those beauties to the chances of that famous snowball making it through a sunny day in hell.

Just then, our guru walked through our always-open door with the object of our professional affection following close behind.

"Gentlemen," Dick announced, "say hello to Bill Lee."

We rushed to stand and shake his hand and introduce ourselves.

Bill came dressed in a well-tailored suit of silver-grey material with money and class written all over it. Dark hair, medium height, medium build, polite manner, obvious intelligence—this handsome young man won our immediate approval as a suitable husband for our newly adopted little sister, Dee Dee.

Lynn suggested that, since it was dinner time and we were on an extended break, perhaps we should all grab a bite to eat somewhere and get to know each other better over platefuls of grub. Dick graciously bowed out, pleading a prior commitment. We'd miss him, of course, but were confident he'd already done his job briefing Bill about our many concerns. Dick had also spelled out for us in large block letters what sort of commitment Bill was expecting from us in return. So Dick left, Bill stayed, and six of us hit the sidewalks of Brooklyn in search of a suitable place to dine and talk.

It took only that one break between sets for us to fill our stomachs and realize that we liked Bill and wanted to move forward with plans to make him our manager. With a dazzling display of knowledge and preparation, he won our trust and confidence. *Bandstand*, *Sullivan*, *Shindig*, *Hullabaloo*—these were just some of the TV shows he mentioned. Then there were the teen publications, the trade rags, the movies and so much more. Bill presented many good ideas and made them all sound sensible and achievable. He pointed out how vitally important it was for us to take advantage of the incredible publicity being generated by the lyrics controversy *right now today*—and sooner if possible. Time was a-wastin'.

Had we been free that moment to act on our impulses, chances are the five of us would've signed up with Bill on the spot, but a minor detail killed that idea: we were all still underage. As such, we needed our parents' signatures on any contract to make it legally binding. Acknowledging reality—not always easy for teenage boys then or now or at anytime to do—we mutually decided to take our time and ease into the relationship. We asked Bill to visit Portland as soon as possible to meet our parents and spend more time getting acquainted with us individually. If all went well, then we could proceed with negotiating the details and signing a contract. Bill proved more than sensitive to our need and desire to act sensibly for a change. If we didn't delay too long, time might still be on our side.

Bill stayed for the last show and joined us upstairs afterward for a second, shorter visit. With our mutual admiration well established, all sides exchanged "thank yous" and "you're welcomes," said their "good-byes" and filtered off to their respective hotels for the night. We fell asleep feeling good about Bill and the promising future that lay before us working together as a team. The next day, we eagerly listened as Dick related what Bill had to say about us and emphasized how anxious Bill was to get started working on our future. Dick was great at educating us in matters of business and the inner workings of Hollywood. In less than a week, he'd become the closest thing to a mentor we'd ever had, save for Ken Chase. Already, we loved and trusted the guy. In time, he changed our lives.

THE next day, Mike, Lynn and I were sitting in the dressing room when Dick surprised us.

"I think we should celebrate," he said, "and do something outrageous."

"I got it!" he continued, acting as though an idea had just popped into his head. "Lunch is on me. You guys can pick any place you like."

As Dick finished his invitation, Bobby Goldsboro walked in to see if Mike and I wanted to go to lunch with him.

"Why not join us?" Dick suggested. "I'm taking care of lunch today."

Walking by and hearing the clarion call of a free lunch sounding, Johnny Tillotson poked his nose into the conversation and said, "Did I hear you're buying lunch today, Mr. St. John?"

"Thanks, I'd love to!" Johnny added with a twinkle in his eye.

"You're more than welcome," answered Dick.

"Oooo. Hey, big spender!" said Lynn.

"How about Italian?" suggested Mike.

"Good idea, Mr. Mitchell!" Dick responded. "I know the perfect place. If everybody's ready, you can follow me."

Like in Robert Browning's tale of the children of Hamelin being led into captivity by a Pied Piper who hadn't been paid, we followed our master down the stairs and out the stage door, straight into the midst of a mob of screaming fans. There we stopped and signed autographs until our fearless leader summoned his flock and we resumed our adventure.

The sun shone bright that lovely April day (April Fool's Day, in fact, which should've been a warning to us)—springtime in New York at its best. Old Sol's warmth embraced and emboldened us, and we were all feeling our oats, joking and bantering and trading jibes as we paraded down the back streets of the Borough of Brooklyn. Dick led us in a bee-line to an Italian restaurant we'd passed by many times before, always commenting on the divine aromas emanating from its kitchen.

"Here we are, gentleman," said the Pied Piper. "This will be one culinary experience you'll never forget."

Like children under the Piper's spell, we obediently followed him inside, where it took a moment or two for our eyes to adjust to the muted lighting. Dark wood-paneled booths with high backs for privacy ringed the large, dimly-lit space. Elaborately set tables covered in fine white linen filled the center of the room. The maitre'd led us to a vast round table way in the back and seated us there. Before our bottoms could meet the seat cushions, an attendant appeared with water, and a waiter with an armload of menus. I was reaching for the elaborately folded napkin sitting atop my plate when the maitre'd plucked it from my grasp and, in a graceful sweeping motion, snapped it open and laid it in my lap—the first time anyone had ever done that for me. Sounding and looking like he'd just stepped off the plane from Rome, our waiter told us about the specials of the day.

Immediately when the waiter had finished, Dick asked him to bring the manager over to our table. We all wondered what he wanted with the manager. We'd just been seated. What possible trouble could Dick have had with the place already? Moments later, a short little man, roundish and well-dressed, approached us. Dick rose to greet him.

"Are you the manager?" he asked, extending his hand.

"Yes-a sir, I-a am-a," the man replied, clasping Dick's right hand between his two and bowing.

"What-a can I help-a you with, sir?" he asked, raising his head.

The man's accent brought a smile to Dick's face. Dick toyed with the manager like a cat playing with its prey.

"Are you from Italy?" he asked. We all laughed.

"Yes-a sir, I-a am-a," answered the dark-haired man. "And-a what-a can I-a do for-a you."

Lighting the room with his smile, Dick said, "I just wanted you to know who you are about to serve in your fine establishment. Sir, seated before you are some of the biggest rock 'n' roll stars in the world!"

"Really?" responded the manager, clearly pleased and impressed.

"Oh, yes, really," assured Dick.

With rhetorical flourishes meant to impress his listener still further, he introduced Johnny and Bobby and the three of us to the wide-eyed man. When he got around to mentioning "The Kingsmen" and "Louie Louie," the manager just kept nodding his head, while several young members of his more-than-curious staff reacted with a start. It looked to me like one of them was singing the chorus.

"If you have a photographer," Dick said with emphasis, "I suggest you have him take pictures. Opportunities like this don't come along every day, you know."

"What's he doing?" I whispered to Lynn out of the side of my mouth.

"I don't know," he whispered back. "I think he's just being Dick and having a little fun."

"He may be acting like his normal unpredictable self," Mike said, smiling awkwardly, "but this is kind of embarrassing."

Talking above the noise in the room, Dick continued.

"These guys are the most visible stars in the press today," he said, "and I want them treated to a meal they'll never forget. Before morning, everyone will know who dined at your establishment.

You'll be famous!"

Grateful, overwhelmed and inspired, the little gentleman thanked Dick profusely, retreating backwards a few steps and bowing several times before turning around and barking orders to his staff in Italian, which set bodies scurrying in all directions. With that task out of the way, Dick sat down and focused on playing the gracious host, a role he was a natural at.

For the remainder of the afternoon, we were treated like royalty. The food came from heaven itself, with stops along the way in Milano and Parma and Napoli and Roma: mounds of pastas, a pool of minestrone soup, a sea of colorful vegetables, a pyramid of meatballs, a pile of sausages, a green field of salad, buttery logs of warm Italian bread and everywhere the smell of garlic, garlic and more garlic. Forgetting for a moment my recent pledge never to drink again—made the morning after my date with Dionne Warwick—I even ventured a sip or two of genuine Italian chianti, poured from large wicker-protected bottles.

The spumoni was being served when Johnny turned to Dick and said, "Boy, Dick, this is going to cost you a small fortune."

The expression that crossed Dick's face was that of a cat burglar interrupted half-way through an attempted burgle.

"I didn't say I was buying lunch," he countered.

"What!" cried Lynn, feeling his pocket squeeze.

"You did so!" insisted Mike. "You're not getting out of this, St. John!"

"No way!" added Johnny, laughing along with the rest of us, still not exactly sure what Dick was up to.

Dick got a very serious look on his face and spoke in a soft voice.

"I didn't say 'I'm buying lunch,'" he whispered, "I said 'Lunch is on me.'"

"What are you talking about?" I asked the jokester.

Leaning forward in his chair, Dick spoke in a hushed voice.

"Nobody's going to pay a thing for this meal," he announced.

"What are you saying?" probed Mike

"Here's how it works," Dick said, licking his chops. "In a few minutes, I'm going to scream and fake a heart attack."

"You're what?" cried Lynn. "Are you kidding?"

Lynn was laughing, but deep inside he feared Dick wasn't kidding.

"No, "I'm not kidding , Lynn." Dick answered emphatically,

"I'm not kidding anyone. In a few minutes, I'm going to hit the floor. When I go down, you guys start yelling for an ambulance and a doctor, anything to create chaos. Bobby, you're the one with the cojones. You get frantic and tell the manager you have to get these guys out of here without creating a scene. Everybody else, just act really upset."

"No," protested Lynn, "You can't do this!"

"Oh, I'm going to do it, alright," said Dick. "You guys get ready."

"How's that going to get us out of paying the check?" asked Mike.

"Once I'm in the ambulance and everybody has escorted me out of the restaurant on the stretcher, there's no way the manager will give you a bill."

Laughing like a demon possessed, Dick continued.

"The manager will feel awful," he said, "and he'll do anything to avoid the bad publicity of a lawsuit from 'superstars' like you guys."

"Don't do it!" pleaded Mike.

"I'm going to," smiled Dick.

"Please don't!" I begged. "It won't work! You're going to get us in a lot of trouble."

"Oh, I feel it coming on," said Dick, grabbing at his heart.

"Don't do it!" groaned Johnny in a final call to reason.

"I'm going down!" the Pied Piper announced, winking at Bobby.

Committing to the crime, Bobby stood up.

"Help!" he cried. "This man is having a heart attack. Help! Somebody call an ambulance."

Standing up with a shudder, his face twisted as though in agony, Dick clutched his chest and slumped forward, dragging the tablecloth and several dishes with him to the floor. In the chaos and commotion that followed, we played perfectly into our master's grand plan. The frantic, worried looks on our faces were genuine. Onlookers might've thought we were concerned about our stricken comrade's condition, but, in truth, we were scared spitless by the prospect of going to jail once Dick's ruse was discovered. Not knowing what to do, we just stood around, totally useless, while the manager and waiters yelled, patrons crowded around the faker on the floor and pandemonium set in. At that moment, Mr. "Funny Little Clown" took control.

"Stand back!" Bobby yelled, elbowing his way through the crowd and bending over that certifiable lunatic, Dick St. John. "Stand back, I said! Give him some air."

"Please!" yelled the manager as he made his way through the crowd. "Everybody, please, calm-a down, the ambulance is-a on its-a way."

Bobby looked up at the manager.

"Maybe you'd better get these guys outta here," he said. "There's going to be a lot of people out front when that ambulance pulls up. Do you have a rear entrance? If the press finds out about this, it could be bad for your place, and bad for them."

"Sure-a, yeah, whatever you say!" agreed the nervous man. "Come, I-a will show-a you boys out-a the back."

"You guys get back to the show!" Bobby said with a wink. "I'll ride with Dick to the hospital and meet up with you later at the theatre."

Four of us followed the manager out the back entrance. With tears in his eyes, he actually apologized. Accepting his apologies, we said goodbye using the only Italian word we knew, "Arrivederci!" and quickly retreated down the alley toward the street and safety. We emerged on the sidewalk just as an ambulance pulled up to the front door, siren blaring. Certain we'd be busted if we hung around, we abandoned Dick and Bobby to their fate and hightailed it back to the theatre, looking back over our shoulders every few seconds the entire way.

In the safety of our dressing room, we reviewed the spectacle we'd just witnessed. None of us had taken part in such an elaborate charade before, and all of us worried about the possible consequences we faced. Even so, we couldn't stop laughing and telling every stagehand and performer we saw about our experience.

No more than 20 minutes had passed before Dick and Bobby came sauntering down the hall. Dick had his arm draped over Bobby's shoulder, and the two of them shook with laughter as they walked.

"Good work, Kingsmen!" exclaimed Dick. "April Fools!"

It was one of those slap-your-forehead moments. Of course! Today was the first of April—April Fool's Day—and the joke was definitely on us.

Once we recovered from the realization that we'd been snookered, we had a million questions to ask, and we asked them all at once: "What happened?" "Did you actually go to the hospital?" "What happened when the paramedics showed up?" and so on.

Finally, Dick cut us off.

"Hey, slow down, one question at a time!" he pleaded. Between laughs, he filled in a few of the details.

"They put me on the stretcher," he said, "hooked me up to the oxygen and carried me out to their ambulance."

Bobby took it from there.

"Once we were in the ambulance," he said, "Dick woke up and told the paramedics that he was diabetic and just needed a little candy to raise his blood sugar."

"Did they buy it?" questioned Lynn.

"Not only did they buy it," Bobby answered, "as soon as Dick said he was feeling fine, he talked them into dropping us off here on their way back to the station. They dropped us off right in front of the theatre."

Devil's horns sprouted from Dick's head as he spoke again.

"I told you I was going to treat you to a meal you'd never forget," he said. "Well, I don't think you'll soon forget that lunch."

"If you ever do that to me again," Mike said, still slightly nervous, "you won't need an ambulance, you'll need a coroner 'cause I'll kill you!"

"Stand in line!" Lynn added.

From that moment on, we were all a little more cautious about agreeing to do anything suggested by Dick. During the next show, I was standing in the wings listening to Dionne when Dick walked up and stood beside me.

"I've got to admit it, man," I whispered under my breath, "that deal at the restaurant was pretty gutsy."

"Nah," he said, "that was just a little fun."

"I thought I was going to die," I giggled. "You scared me to death!"

He paused and then countered.

"Nah," he said, "I scared you to life."

I thought about his statement and decided he was right.

"Let's pay for the ride," he whispered.

"What?" I answered, startled.

"Give me 15 bucks," he requested.

"What for?" I demanded.

"I'm charging everyone 15 bucks apiece for this afternoon's fun," he explained. "Think of it as buying one of those E-tickets at Disneyland. The only difference is, you're paying for the fun afterward instead of before."

"You're going to *charge* me for this afternoon?" I asked, amazed.

"I'll take the money back to the manager of the restaurant," he elaborated, "and thank him profusely for his quick thinking and pay him for the lunch. It's only fair, dontcha think?"

He delivered this same speech to everyone who'd been there, and we all chipped in our $15, happy to relieve the guilt we felt and still not quite certain that the police weren't out there looking for us at that very moment.

With a hundred or so dollars thus collected, Dick and Bobby returned to the crime scene to finish the gag. They pretended they were grateful to the manager, who on his part was greatly relieved to learn that Dick had completely recovered. He was no less relieved to be paid.

Paying up like that left everyone feeling better about the situation—at least until someone did the numbers. We shook our heads in disbelief when we realized Dick had collected more money from us than the dinner had actually cost. The Pied Piper, Dick St. John, ended up paying nothing for his lunch.

In Robert Browning's famous poem, the Piper lured the children from their homes after the town's elders refused to pay him for ridding Hamelin of rats. In Dick St. John's famous caper, the Piper lured the musicians from their dressing rooms before he refused to pay the restaurant for feeding his friends with food. April Fools, indeed!

EARLY the following morning, we left for our meeting at Scepter/Wand, wearing black slacks, white shirts with black ties and our famous black Kingsmen sweaters. We saved these sweaters for special occasions like this when we wanted to dress as a group without wearing our stage clothes. They were thick, heavy, warm bulk-knit sweaters with "The Kingsmen" and our individual names embroidered in a king's crown located on the left chest. Individually, they read, "The Kingsmen Mike," "The Kingsmen Norm," "The Kingsmen Lynn," "The Kingsmen Barry" and, of course, the always-noticed-if-not-already-pointed-out, endlessly embarrassing "The Kingsmen Dick." I treasure the memory of the day we removed those loathsome garments from our wardrobe.

Scepter/Wand was located in downtown Manhattan at 1650 Broadway at the corner of West 51st, six blocks north of Times Square. It took us a little more than half an hour to get there on the subway. The action on the street awed and amazed us and seemed like something out of a movie or a Damon Runyon short story. We elbowed our way to the record company's office and bounded through the front doors, exploding with energy.

"Hi," Lynn said, addressing the attractive young black woman sitting behind the reception desk. "We're the Kingsmen, and we have an appointment with Marvin."

A smile slowly grew on her face.

"Oh?" was all she said.

She measured Lynn with the strangest of looks as she picked up her phone, dialed an extension and announced our arrival.

"Could you tell Mr. Schlackter that I have the Kingsmen out here?" she spoke into the receiver, wearing an enigmatic smile. "Thank you."

Snickering, she hung up the phone.

"He ain't gonna be ready for you guys, honey," she said to Lynn.

Sitting on a couch in the lobby of a fancy New York office made me feel special, like I was someone important, but it did nothing to settle my nerves. I was about to reach for the copy of *Billboard* lying on the table in front of us when a well-dressed man walked through the double doors that led to the offices, paused for a moment and asked, somewhat awkwardly, "*You're* the Kingsmen?"

Lynn stood and extended his hand.

"I'm Lynn Easton."

The man's jaw dropped to the floor, a look of amazement on his face.

"You're all white!" he exclaimed.

"Yes, we are," Lynn replied. "I can't help it. I was born that way. I notice you are, too."

Everyone laughed. Gathering himself together, the man continued.

"No, I'm sorry. No — I mean yes, yes I'm white, but no, I'm Marvin."

"I can't wait until Florence meets you," he said, shaking hands with each of us.

Florence Greenburg was the owner and head of Scepter/Wand. She had a reputation for being very aggressive and for speaking her mind. It was widely known that Florence didn't take guff from anyone, man or woman.

Marvin led the way into their main offices.

As we walked past occupied desks and open office doors, Marvin stopped several times and announced to all within earshot, "These are the Kingsmen, everyone." Stunned looks and quiet applause followed each introduction.

He led us to Florence's secretary, who slowly looked us over.

"I'll tell her you're here," she said.

Marvin stopped her.

"Never mind," he said. "She's expecting us, but she's in for a surprise."

Bursting into Florence's office unannounced, Marvin turned slightly toward us, raised both arms in our direction and swept them forward toward Florence.

"Florence," he dramatically announced, "I'd like you to meet the Kingsmen."

"Oh, damn, you're white!" she said in disbelief, half standing up before collapsing back into her chair with a grunt.

"Yes, they are," Marvin agreed, "and doesn't that throw an interesting twist into the mix?"

Mike proved himself again the master of any awkward situation.

"Hi, I'm Mike," he said, walking over to Florence's desk and holding out his hand, "and I see that you're white, too."

Momentarily unable to speak, Florence began to shake with laughter. Marvin and the rest of us shared in her mirth, but we Kingsmen still had no explanation for all the fuss.

Finally regaining a semblance of self-control, Florence apologized and tried her best with Marvin to make us feel comfortable and welcome in their offices. They offered us soft drinks and snacks and explained their reaction to our skin color.

"Jerry didn't tell us you were white," explained Marvin.

"We just assumed you were black," added Florence.

"Why would you do that?" asked Norm.

"Don't get me wrong," said Florence. "I don't care what color you are. You can be polka-dot for all I care, but we're an all-black label."

"What do you mean?" asked Barry.

"Every one of our artists is black," answered Florence.

"Except for now, with you guys," corrected Marvin,

"Is that a problem?" asked Lynn.

"No, it's not," replied Florence. "We've never sold so many records. It's just that, since we're an all-black label, everyone assumes that you're black."

"Hell, I did!" laughed Marvin.

"Who didn't?" added Florence. "All of the radio stations we deal with on the East Coast and in the south, our distributors, the press back here, they all think you guys are a bunch of rebellious black ghetto kids challenging the white establishment for control of the already corrupt white rock 'n' roll fan. And here you are, showing up at all-black Scepter/Wand, a bunch of clean-cut white boys dressed in Ivy League clothes! That oughtta frost J. Edgar."

"Maybe not," said Mike. "The FBI already knows we're white. They show up at our concerts almost every day."

"You're kidding!" said Florence. "Well, our phones are constantly ringing off the hook with complaints from church groups and individuals who think we're selling pornographic records by black artists."

"You're right, Florence," added Marvin, "but they're also ringing off the hook with orders for 'Louie Louie!' Isn't life wonderful?"

As we were laughing at Marvin's comment, Stanley, Florence's brother and Scepter/Wand's resident record producer, walked in the room. Stanley was blind and used a white cane, but he knew the place so well he could navigate the offices as easily as any person with sight.

"What's all of the commotion about?" he asked.

"The Kingsmen are here, and they've surprised us by being white."

Hearing that didn't phase Stanley one bit.

"Black, white, you all look the same to me!" he joked, a beaming smile on his face.

We introduced ourselves to Stanley, who volunteered to show us around their facility while Florence and Marvin tended to lunch.

Stanley led us to a fully equipped, state-of-the-art (circa 1964) stereo recording studio ("Louie Louie" was recorded in mono), a mastering room and editing suites. Impressive!

"This is where I added the crowd noise to the new album," said Stanley, stopping in the mastering room.

"What crowd noise?" asked Norm.

"Haven't you heard it?" smiled Stanley.

"No, we havent," replied Lynn. "Why would you want to add crowd noise to our album?"

"To make it sound like a party," answered Stanley. "Your sound exemplifies the very meaning of the word 'party.' I lifted the crowd noise from your live recordings at the Chase."

We were none too thrilled to hear about the added crowd noise. Mike spoke for us all.

"Next time we record, we want to have a say in what we're recording. We need new stuff, not just the same old stuff we've been doing for years. Stanley, we need to find some new material and actually record in stereo instead of this simulation thing."

"I agree," said Stanley. "I'll talk to Jerry about it and see if we can't come up with some new stuff you'll like."

We were encouraged to hear Stanley say that.

He took us to the conference room where Florence and Marvin had lunch spread out on the table.

"Help yourselves, boys," said Florence.

As we grazed and joked, we discussed ways to keep the "Louie Louie" controversy in the headlines. Florence and Marvin were concerned about the FBI investigation. They thought that if the bans were lifted, demand for the record would wane. We all agreed a new strategy was needed, one that would continue to drive record sales. Halfway through lunch, several reporters and a few photographers entered the room.

"I have a surprise for you, boys," Florence said, rising to her feet. "'Louie Louie' has just passed the million mark in sales. We invited you here not just for lunch, but also to present to you your first in what we hope will be a long line of gold records."

As she finished her announcement, the room was flooded with record company staff, five of them carrying beautifully-framed gold records. The others were applauding. Stunned and elated, we couldn't believe this was happening. Marvin started orchestrating people and positions for the photographers and reporters attending the presentation. The UPI and AP wire services, *Billboard*, *Variety* and *Record World* all covered the event. Scepter/Wand used the occasion to create quite a buzz. Our unexpected skin color helped.

Once the ceremony was over and things had returned to normal, we explained to Florence and Marvin about our intention to work with Bill, sharing some of his ideas regarding TV shows and movies. The remainder of our time together was spent clarifying our responsibilities to Scepter/Wand. Before we left, we gave them a stack of the promo pictures with Barry sitting in the front. We also autographed a box of records for them to use for promo.

Our gold records created an immense stir among our fellow entertainers. Murray insisted on showing the crowd our milestone rewards when he introduced us for the last two shows. It was a funny thing, though. When we told our friends back at the theatre about the record company thinking we were black, they all confessed to thinking the same thing themselves. They, too, were surprised to discover the Kingsmen were, in Dick's words, "just a bunch of clean-cut, average white guys singing dirty songs."

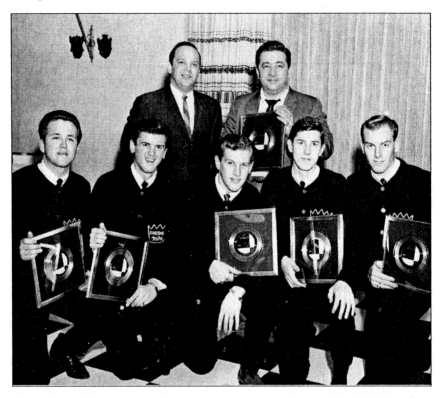

"Louie Louie" gold record ceremony, New York— April 1964
Standing, rear, left to right: *Bob Levinson (Scepter/Wand distributor), Pete Garris (Scepter/Wand National Promotion Director)*
Kneeling, front, left to right: *Norm, Mike, Lynn, Dick, Barry*

VERSE 17

WE'D left Portland for New York near the end of March confident we understood how certain things worked in the world at large. By the end of our first night in town, we'd proven to a cabbie and a bellman, if not to ourselves, that our understanding had its limits. Over the next two weeks, our perspectives began to change as one person after another, one event after another, one experience after another opened our eyes ever wider to the complex challenges we faced. Still, for the most part, learning life's lessons as a Kingsman remained immense fun—and our favorite teacher was Dick St. John.

Under his guidance, we started squeezing field trips into our breaks between sets. With Dick in the lead, we walked Times Square, toured the Statue of Liberty, visited the Empire State Building, rode the Staten Island Ferry and even found time to catch a few jazz players in the Village. For a taste of what it was like to play tourist in New York City with Dick St. John as our guide, I have one favorite story to tell. Our adventure takes us to the United Nations headquarters hard by the East River.

WHEN Dick proposed a trip to the UN, only Barry and I accepted his offer. Taking us aside beforehand, he asked me whether I spoke French.

"Not a word," I answered.

"Fine, don't say anything when we get there," he instructed. "Just remember, your name's Pierre."

"Pierre?" I asked, suspicious. "What's going on?"

"Don't worry," Dick assured me. "Just be quiet and pretend you're a Frenchie named Pierre.'"

"Hey, Barry," Dick went on, "do you speak any German?"

"Sure do," Bare answered. "I took German in high school."

"Excellent!" Dick declared. "You can say a few things in German. And remember, *your* name's Hans."

"Hans?'"

"Yes, Hans," Dick confirmed. "Now, when we get there, you two just follow my lead."

Like lambs being led to slaughter, we obeyed and followed the leader.

Arriving at the UN complex by cab, Dick led us to the imposing main entrance. Stopping before the reception desk, he began his tale.

"Good morning!" he said, smiling. "My name's Dick Rockefeller. My father donated the land your building sits on. I'm here for my guided tour."

My God! I thought to myself. *What's he up to this time?* I was worried already, and the game had barely begun. I smelled trouble.

"Good morning, Mr. Rockefeller," the receptionist replied with a smile. "Welcome to the United Nations. Please give me a minute while I check on arrangements."

The woman picked up a phone and dialed a number. While she made her inquiries, Dick wiggled his finger at us behind his back, indicating silence. The woman put down the receiver and addressed him.

"I'm sorry, Mr. Rockefeller," she said, "but we don't seem to have you on the schedule. Are you sure your appointment's today?"

"Yes, of course, I'm *positive* it's today," he shot back, raising his voice. Turning toward us, he went on.

"I have Pierre and Hans with me," he said. "They're the sons of ambassadors, and I promised their fathers I'd personally arrange a tour of the UN for them. Now you're saying you have no record of it. I think you'd better do something quick, or you're going to have an international incident on your hands."

He pounded his fist on the desk and stared down his opponent.

Keeping her composure and excusing herself for a minute, the woman turned to the side, picked up another phone and dialed someone—I suppose her supervisor. After a few minutes of hushed exchanges, she put down the receiver, swung around in her chair, stood up and smiled.

"We've taken care of the problem, Mr. Rockefeller," she said warmly. "Your personal guide will be here shortly. If you don't mind, would you please wait over there. It won't be but a few minutes."

"Thank you, Mam," Dick said, flashing an incandescent smile. I appreciate your prompt handling of the problem. We'll wait right over here just like you asked. *Ici, Pierre, s'il vous plaît. Merci beaucoup. Hier, Hans, bitte. Danke.* She says to wait over here. It won't be long."

My first instinct was to head for the hills, but instead, I followed Dick's and Barry's example and stood and waited, outwardly calm, inwardly wondering how long it would be before someone got wise to our act and had us arrested as spies.

A few minutes later, an attentive, immaculately groomed young woman appeared, speaking the Queen's English with an accent I couldn't quite place. (It wasn't Brooklynese or Chicagoese—two dialects I'd recently mastered—but something more refined, more foreign, maybe something European.) Introducing herself as our guide for what she promised would be a special VIP tour, she began our excursion by pointing out the impressive Foucault Pendulum dangling nearby.

Under her guidance, over the next 45 minutes we saw just about everything there was to see, including the rooms where banks of interpreters labored simultaneously in five different languages and even (from the outside) the offices of Secretary General U Thant. With all sights seen and all questions asked answered, our guide returned us to the main entrance. She looked like she was about to break into that famous line from the song the von Trapp children sing in *The Sound of Music*—"So long, farewell, *auf Wiedersehen, adieu*"—when Dick interrupted her.

"Excuse me, miss," he said with emphasis, "what about our lunch?"

"Lunch?" she reacted, sounding confused. "I'm not sure I understand."

"Lunch, you know, that midday meal some people call dinner?" Dick said, raising his voice, feigning anger. "I promised these boys' fathers they'd have lunch here today, and we're not leaving until they're fed."

Flustered, our guide excused herself, promising to be right back.

"Don't worry, boys," Dick reassured us, "this is going to work just fine."

Five minutes later, our guide returned, smiling broadly.

"Mr. Rockefeller," she said, "I'm pleased to inform you, we've organized a lunch for you and your two guests. Unfortunately, however, our main dining room is not presently available. But we can bring you some hamburgers and hot dogs and soft drinks. Will that be satisfactory?"

"American food, perfect!" Dick beamed. "I'm sure Pierre and Hans will be quite pleased."

The guide led us into a small conference room where standard American picnic fare was served up in fine fashion. We gobbled down the offerings, wasting no time on conversation. Barry and I were determined to get out of there as quickly as possible.

Our repast finished, Dick had one more trick up his sleeve.

Stopping again at the reception desk, he picked a fight with the woman there when she informed us that we wouldn't be able to visit the hall where the General Assembly met. As the volume and intensity of the argument rose, I grew increasingly more uncomfortable and worried. Dick's big argument on all points was that he was a Rockefeller, that his father had donated the land the UN building stood on and that they'd damn well better see that his demands were met—or else.

Finally, his patience appearing to run out, he marched over to the Foucault Pendulum, grabbed its shiny metal orb and heaved it against the metal stanchion with a loud, ringing crash.

"Run!" Dick shouted to Barry and me as he fled out the main entrance, doing his best imitation of an Olympic sprinter.

Overcoming our shock in an instant, we raced after him, with UN guards in hot pursuit.

We tore out the front entrance and down to where a long line of yellow taxis sat waiting to carry diplomatic luminaries to city destinations. Grabbing the first cab in line, Dick shouted orders to the surprised driver.

"Step on it!" he orderd. "Let's get the hell out of here."

Barry and I barely made it into the taxi before the cabby sped off.

Looking out the rear window, I saw several UN personnel come to a screeching halt at curbside, shaking their fists at us as we escaped into the crowded streets of the city. hey, we had the FBI and FCC wanting our heads, we might as well add UN Security, Interpol, and CIA to the list.

Laughing and slapping one another on the back, we excitedly celebrated our adventure all the way back to Brooklyn. Only in bed that night did my nerves calm down to near normal levels, allowing me to consider rationally this latest Dick St. John escapade. There was no doubting the fact any more: *This man is nuts!*

I've often wondered what the Rockefeller family's response was when UN officials contacted them to discuss the carryings-on of their wayward son, Dick.

IMPULSIVE and unpredictable, Dick made every excursion, every moment spent with him memorable. Saying goodbye to him, to Dee Dee, to Johnny, to Bobby, and to so many others when our two-week stay ended was difficult.

Unlike our flights east to New York, our flights west to Portland were as smooth as glass—and jet-propelled all the way. None of that mattered to white-knuckled Lynn, who steadfastly held on for dear life all the way from New York to Portland, leaving a lasting impression on his armrests.

WITH only a few days to spend at home before we hit the road again, we had little time to do anything more than eat, sleep and prepare for the next trip. Our stage clothes demanded cleaning, and certain pieces of equipment cried for repair. Teaching Mike's cousin Jim how to set up and tear down our equipment was a priority. And, with a new van, we needed to work out a revamped packing procedure with him.

Norm the budding entrepreneur was swamped, working with his dad and brother to solidify plans for Sunn Musical Equipment and discussing ways to maximize his own marketing efforts with music stores while out on the next tour. Barry, meanwhile, lived in Yakima, Washington, a four-hour drive northeast from Portland. The next time we saw him was the day before we left. Slow to change his ways, Lynn talked to Bob Ehlert in Chicago and Bill Lee in LA almost every day, discussing Kingsmen business while trying to promote his own agenda and cement his place as the sole conduit between them and us. Knowing our feelings and pre-warned about Lynn's separatist tendencies, Bill handled the situation with great sensitivity and the smoothness of a politician.

Mike called me, and we agreed on a time for a meeting at Norm's garage to teach Cousin Jim how to set up my drums and to work out the packing of the van. Our goal was to make absolutely sure Jim knew how to arrange the drums in the exact same positions I normally set them in so all I'd have to do when the music started was sit down and play. With Jim on our team, all of the meticulous pre-performance fiddling I'd been doing with the drums—so tedious and demanding—would be a thing of the past for me. I was all for that.

Meeting Jim for the first time, it was easy to see why his nickname in the Marines was "Smiley."

He had a permanent smile etched into his face not even boot camp at Quantico could erase. He had dark hair, a perfect uni-brow and buck teeth that stuck straight out. They were so bucked, in fact, he couldn't close his lips around the protrusions to properly pronounce any word beginning with the letter "m." He'd mastered the challenge, though, and, as needed, he could pronounce a "v" so that it sounded like either a "v" or an "m." Like when he referred to himself as a Marine, it came out sounding more like "Varine" than "Marine," yet somehow you could always tell he was saying "Marine." Body-wise he was Charles Atlas compared to the rock star weaklings he served and could easily heft twice the weight that any of us ever dreamed of lifting. It took two of us to handle any one of Norm's formidable speaker cabinets while Jim, with one hand on each side, could hoist one of the black monsters, swing it around and slide it into the van without apparent effort. What shoulders! What biceps! No bully at the beach ever dared to kick sand in Smiley's face.

All those muscles came with a fantastic attitude. Always agreeable, Jim accepted any and all chores we gave him with one of his unique enamel grins. Nothing was beneath him or too painstaking or too hard. He spent hours measuring distances, determining angles and finding visual keys that would help him set my drums up precisely to my liking. From that first meeting on, I embraced him as a friend and one of us. Adopting Cousin Jim into the Kingsmen family proved the perfect move.

As we left Portland for Idaho, I volunteered to ride shotgun in the van with Jim. He was a newcomer, and I was fairly new to the band myself, and that was one reason I felt comfortable around him. He didn't know that I wasn't a man yet, and maybe that explains why I was able to open up to him more easily than with the other guys. Certainly, less teasing aimed my way came from his direction. Traveling together in the van, mostly just talking, rarely bragging or exaggerating, we soon found ourselves becoming best friends. Now that our troupe was sleeping two to a room, we agreed to be roomies. Jim had this unusual way of looking at the world and was, about certain things, even more gullible than I—a statistical improbability, I know, a near impossibility, yes, but true nonetheless. I'd describe Jim as "Marine wise"—he knew the Corps handbook inside and out, while math, English and quantum mechanics never made it into his core curriculum. One of us needs to write a book someday about the many comical road adventures we experienced together. Believe me, that would be quite a read.

WE opened our second tour with a show in Boise, Idaho to more of the same insanity that had marked our first tour and our just-completed 10-day/40-performance marathon in New York. The venue overflowed with screaming fans, and afterward, as always, everyone wanted to know the real words to "Louie Louie." By then, we were beginning to master the nuances of teasing the curious masses about those lyrics. Our inquisitors usually believed whatever we chose to tell them (as long as they weren't with the FBI or FCC, that is). Everyone thought that since "Louie Louie" was recorded by the Kingsmen, the Kingsmen wrote the masterpiece as well. None of them thought to check out Richard Berry's original lyrics, which were available if you knew where to look—and assuming you thought of looking for them in the first place. But most people had no idea who Richard Berry was, and they had no internet for googling, so they asked us stale, repetitive questions instead, *ad nauseam*. What made the situation even more humorous was, previous recordings by other groups with clearly audible lyrics were out there, but none of them had made as much as a ripple outside select pockets in the Pacific Northwest. People in the Seattle and Portland areas never asked about the lyrics—they had other points of reference. People in Boise and Los Angeles and Davenport and New York *always* asked. Plus, whatever the words might've been that Berry originally intended, the noises captured on the Kingsmen's "Louie Louie" record that passed for lyrics didn't sound anything like Berry's words anyway. They sounded then, and continue to sound today, like whatever a listener imagines or wants.

In Idaho, the men in the grey flannel suits returned, watching and listening and taking copious notes. By now, their presence had become so commonplace, they were little more than stick figures to us, stage props, minor irritants. They had no effect on our live performances—we knew we had nothing to hide, so we just rocked and rolled and rocked some more. Why worry? The more agents in attendance, the bigger the gate. Off stage, away from the noisy arenas and dance halls and theatres and crowds, in quieter times and places, people began whispering to us that the imperious J. Edgar Hoover himself was now personally directing his agents in the field in his determined quest to nail our nasty little hides to the wall. As quiet whisperings turned to talk, and talk grew louder, we began to wonder whether maybe we shouldn't take this matter more seriously.

The following morning, on the road again, we decided to pull over at Little America, a famous truck stop in Wyoming in the middle of nowhere that was more like a small city than a place to gas up and pig out. There in a clothing store, Barry found a green sweatshirt he became quite fond of. He particularly loved the way the inside of the garment felt against his skin. Barry'd had sweatshirts before that he'd loved, that he'd deified, but had lost them all to the murderous clutches of a washing machine. Remembering past love affairs thus thwarted, he vowed to preserve this new article's virgin softness in pristine condition, forever, by never washing it. He swore that its soft, smooth-textured fabric would never know the defiling touch of a Maytag or a Kenmore. If there's such a thing as a fabric fetish—and the textbooks say there is—Barry's sensory connection with his sweatshirts must surely have been the manifestation of one. Sigmund Freud would know.

Our star keyboardist began wearing his new shirt daily, refusing to wash her for fear she'd be changed forever into something rough and unwearable. A few days later, while exploring the delights of an amusement park, Barry found a name tag in the souvenir shop that read "Irma." For reasons he kept to himself, Barry liked the name. [I speculated at the time that he took it from Shirley Maclaine's character in the previous year's flick, *Irma La Douce*—"Irma the Sweet."] Whatever his reason, he purchased the name tag and pinned it to his sweatshirt. Henceforth, "it" was no longer an "it" but a "she," and "she" had a name, and that name was "Irma," and Irma and Barry became inseparable companions. Day and night, rain or shine, nothing could tear them apart. It was this same closeness that eventually drove us to intervene.

It's said that "Beauty is in the eyes of the beholder," and when Barry beheld Irma, he saw great beauty. It's also said that "Love is blind," and Barry's love for Irma blinded him indeed to the fatal flaw in their relationship: a unique, penetrating ripeness that grew ever stronger with each passing day, offending everyone's nose save his. And finally, it's said that "Love conquers all"—but that's a myth for fairy tales and romance novels, not an argument that plays well in a story about rock 'n' roll. Here, the formula's been reversed: We *all* became desperate to *conquer* Barry's *love* for Irma. Each of us asked ourselves the same fateful question: "Who will rid me of this turbulent fleece?" We knew the answer—every morning we saw the would-be assassin staring back at us in the mirror when we shaved—and so did Barry, and the game was on.

While plotting and scheming to do away with Irma once and for all, we made the mistake of first asking Barry—and eventually *pleading* with Barry—to launder his love, *or else*. Or else what? Or else we were going to kidnap Irma and do despicable, untoward things to her. Our threat put Barry on full alert, and he strengthened his defenses and vowed to guard his love with his life. It was now four Musketeers against one, with a foul maiden at the center of the feud, a role traditionally left to *fair* maidens. One more platitude applies—"All is fair in love and war"—for this would be a war fought over love. The fairness rules of chivalry were forgotten as the battle intensified.

We coordinated our efforts and stood constant watch, waiting for an opening, waiting for Barry to lower his guard, to leave his beloved unattended for even a moment. We enlisted Jim to rifle through Barry's things while we were on stage, only to discover that Barry, fearing for Irma's life, had taken to wearing her under his stage clothes during every performance. That may have protected Irma for the moment, but it only strengthened our resolve to find a way to win the war. Irma's bouquet, already unique, turned more unique, if such is possible. Irma and Barry even slept together—imagine, a Kingsman on the road in bed with the same woman for more than one night in a row. Scandalous! When Barry took showers, he'd lock Her Royal Ripeness in the bathroom with him. Starting to lose hope, we turned to Jim and asked the impossible. He accepted the mission with the patience and tenacity of a good Marine.

One evening after a show, Barry was invited to attend a party by a lovely young dark-haired temptress. In his haste to be unfaithful to Irma, Barry faltered in his concentration (why is it that there always seems to be a woman behind the fall of every great man?). Hiding in the shadows, Jim observed Barry rush into his room, shower, change clothes and rush out again. The four of us were sitting by the pool when Jim emerged from his hiding place to alert Norm, Barry's roommate, to the results of his clandestine surveillance. Seizing the moment, we all jumped to our feet and raced pell-mell to Norm and Barry's room. We looked under the beds, we searched the bathroom, we dumped out the contents of the dresser drawers on one of the beds, we peeked in his suitcase—we turned the room upside down—and still Irma eluded our grasp.

"Stop!" yelled Norm, freezing us in our tracks. "Barry's been too clever. We can *look* for Irma no longer. We must *sniff out* the creature!"

Everyone broke into laughter, everyone, that is, except Jim. He immediately fell to the floor and started sniffing like a dog.

Seeing the human bloodhound at work, Mike yelled, "Don't anybody move! You might disturb the scent! Let the Marine track his prey!"

We stood still and watched in awed admiration as GI Joe/

Huckleberry Hound crawled around the room on all fours, methodically working left to right and right to left, trying to pick up Irma's exotic stench. His search led him to sniff around the bathroom, and then to the front door area where he stopped, retreated a foot or two, raised his nose in the air and began sniffing the curtain. Rising on his hind legs, Jim the Human Bloodhound carefully pulled back the curtain with his right paw, revealing, to our great joy, the well-seasoned jewel.

The cry that rose from the mob was instantaneous.

"Burn it!, Burn it! Burn it! Burn it! Burn it!" we chanted. "Burn it!'

With two fingers, Lynn carefully picked up the heretic Irma as Norm removed her name-tag. We walked her out to the parking lot as the mob's cries continued to ring out, "Burn it!, Burn it! Burn it! Burn it! Burn it! Burn it!"

Mike doused the odorous bacteria factory with lighter fluid and administered last rights.

The mob continued to chant: "Burn it!, Burn it! Burn it! Burn it! Burn it! Burn it!"

Lynn raised his hand to stop the chant, admonishing us to show Her Majesty some respect in these, her final moments on earth. And in the silence of the parking lot, beneath the light of a full moon, he held out his Zippo, flipped open the top and snapped his thumb against the flint wheel. A flamed erupted, and with it he lit the fragrant beauty, sending her up in flames to meet her Maker.

We erupted in cheers and gleefully watched as flames devoured the enemy. Once she was reduced to nothing but ashes, we danced on her last remains in wild celebration.

"Hey, what do we tell Barry?" Norm asked.

"Don't tell him anything," Mike answered. "Let's just put the name tag back on the floor behind the curtain and act as though we know nothing of her whereabouts."

We liked the idea.

The following morning we were standing outside Barry's room when he went to his hiding place only to find Irma's name-tag and nothing more. Instantly he knew we'd taken her.

"Alright, where's Irma?" he demanded to know, slightly smiling. "You didn't wash her, did you?"

"No, we didn't wash her." answered Norm. "In truth, she died a reverent Nordic death."

"You burned Irma!?" he cried in obvious distress. "Nooooooooo, not Irma!"

Mike pointed to a black spot on the pavement, and Barry went over to view her final resting place. For the first time it crossed our minds that our actions might upset him and that he might never forgive our act of *lese majeste*. We'd had too much fun ridding ourselves of his evil companion. We'd thought only of the welfare of our olfactory nerves. We never considered his sensitive feelings. What kind of friends were we?

"She was a good sweatshirt," he said sadly. Then, with a beaming smile, he turned to us and said, "Well, I did get laid, and nothing lasts forever! What do you guys think about blue this time? I mean, I still have the name tag."

"Oh, no, not another sweatshirt!"

We laughed and ruffled him up, relieved to see that he'd taken his defeat so well. As sad as he was to loose his beloved Irma, Barry never had a chance of winning the Great Sweatshirt War. After all, we had a Marine.

MARINES make diligent, hard-working citizens once they re-enter civilian life, if Jim was a typical example of the breed. Having him there at concert venues, sweating and slaving without complaint until everything was in place, made life for the five of us much, much easier and far less stressful. Once his set-up work was completed, Jim would change into his Nehru-style sport coat and slacks and take on a new set of tasks. During performances, he'd walk out on stage several times a set, bringing us glasses of water and towels. In between, he'd hover in the wings on the side apron to the stage, awaiting a signal from one of us that something was needed.

The tour was barely underway before Jim's attentiveness became an excuse for Lynn to introduce him to the audience as the sixth member of our team. He'd use these moments to harmlessly embarrass our fledgling roadie and add some humor to the show. After a few weeks of playing along with Lynn's joking, Jim shed his inhibitions and started adding dance moves to his stylish routine. Eventually, he was able to summon enough courage during his time in the spotlight to flirt with the girls, and occasionally he'd attract some interesting-looking dates. On one occasion, as Lynn introduced Jim, several girls hovering nearby seemed to be especially taken with the muscular Marine. After the show, as we signed autographs, they inquired as to his whereabouts. When Lynn asked what they needed with our traveling comrade, they responded "We want Jimmy-John's autograph, too!"

Jimmy-John? Autograph? Following standard Kingsmen procedure, we teased him unmercifully for days afterward about his adoring fans and new identity. "Jimmy-John" became his affectionate handle forevermore. *Semper fi*!

WE'D been out for several weeks when out of the clear blue sky, Bob Ehlert asked Lynn to call Bill Lee. We had no inkling before then that Bill and Bob were even communicating. The tour had been booked to run 13 weeks, but Bob told us that Bill needed to talk to us *immediately* regarding "a golden opportunity" that we needed to consider. If we didn't call him that same day—or the next morning at the latest—we might lose the opportunity, whatever it was.

"What do you think Bill wants?" asked Norm.

"If you ask me," answered Lynn, "I think he's just trying to keep us from booking dates that he isn't making any commission on."

"Oooo, that sounds a little negative," said Mike, "I thought you liked Bill!"

"Are you having second thoughts about him being our manager?" asked Barry.

"No, not really," responded Lynn. "I just don't know how much we really need a manager."

We all felt Bill was our way out of this unwelcome Easton dictatorship. The room was uncomfortably silent for a few seconds, and then Mike said, "Well, let's call him and find out what he wants."

Lynn wanted to call Bill without us around, but we were all in his room, and we pressed the issue.

Skeptically, reluctantly, Lynn dialed Bill's number.

After exchanging the usual pleasantries, Lynn asked Bill what was on his mind. We listened as Bill told Lynn that he had an opportunity for us that no matter what, sign with him or not, we couldn't pass up. He told Lynn that he'd been talking to the Beach Boys about us going on tour with them for that entire summer. We were getting so much PR from the "Louie Louie" controversy, he explained, the Beach Boys thought we'd help the draw for their tour. Bill said that the exposure would be huge, and that the Beach Boys wanted us to join them for all 40 dates they'd booked for the tour. He further told Lynn that he didn't mean to hurry our decision, but the Beach Boys needed an answer ASAP. It was crunch time, and they were trying to get out tour publicity. They needed to print their programs yesterday, and they wanted an answer from us before they went to press.

The money mentioned was great, and even though we hadn't yet signed a contract with Bill, he rightly asked to commission the tour. He assumed that we'd pretty much decided to sign with him, and he was right. He proposed to meet us in Portland after the end of the tour to wrap up a management contract. With that task accomplished, he could finally start helping us take advantage of all the press we were getting.

And that wasn't all. Bill laid another gem on us: the Beach Boy tour was scheduled to begin in Hawaii! Almost instantly we decided to accept their offer. None of us had ever been to Hawaii, and the prospect of traveling there became a favorite topic of conversation for days.

Bill was thrilled about us going out with the Beach Boys and said at least two times he couldn't emphasize enough how big this could be for us. We normally played for three or four or five thousand curious fans a night. On this tour we'd be playing to 15-to-20 thousand screaming teens every night. And instead of playing in dance halls, we'd be playing in ballparks and coliseums. Bill also told us it was going to be a bus tour, that the Beach Boys were hiring a Greyhound for their company of players and that there'd be four or five acts on the show that would be traveling on the bus with them.

We had Lynn ask who the other acts were. Bill told him Ray Peterson ("Tell Laura I Love Her"), Eddie Hodges (winner on the

Sixty-Four Thousand Dollar Question game show and co-star with Frank Sinatra in the movie *Hole In The Head*) and Jimmy Griffin (a singer and actor who starred in the movies *None But the Brave* and *For Those Who Think Young*). [Jimmy would later become a member of the band Bread.]

Four of us were totally jazzed, but Lynn hung up the phone with mixed emotions. On the one hand, it was going to be tough for him to give up managing the band, that extra 10 percent and all the self-promoting. On the other hand, a tour like this would mean a lot to us. I think when he got home from New York, Lynn was met with a lot of pressure from his parents to keep the management of the group in their hands and squash the Bill Lee movement. With this new development, that was no longer possible or practical. We were in huge demand thanks to the "Louie Louie" controversy and the FBI investigation, and even Lynn had to admit we needed to take the best advantage of it we could. Plus, who could turn down the Beach Boys and Hawaii?

Now that we knew in what direction our future was headed, our current tour couldn't end soon enough for us. Millions of kids would've traded places with us in a heartbeat, but being on the road had become routine for us, almost too common to endure. In so many ways, we were still just a bunch of young kids winging it. We'd gone about as far as we could go relying on our own resources. It was time to move on, to see what was next, to enter a new stage in our development. Our lives were changing, as individuals and as a group. We were growing up and, biology tells us, with growth come growing pains.

As the tour went on, Lynn's après-show drinking became more and more of an issue. Norm was now openly pushing for the proposed change in management direction, and the harder he pushed, the more Lynn tried to drive a wedge between Norm and the band. Lynn constantly made fun of Norm behind his back in an obvious effort to undermine the dissenter. Although they'd not yet had an open confrontation, the negative energy they generated between them continued to grow daily.

Hating the way he looked in our photos, Norm's simple cure was to get contacts. Having thereby done away with his Buddy Holly-style black horn rim glasses, he noticed a definite increase in his sex appeal. And the funny mad scientist/Japanese look he once made trying to see through thick lenses as his glasses slipped down his nose was gone forever. Newly confident, Norm developed a stage presence and wink that, coupled with his dimples, was attracting a host of female fans from which he could pick a companion most every night.

During a concert in Syracuse, on stage, while playing his bass, Norm winked one too many times at a potential victim. Enraged, her boyfriend leaped on the stage and jumped on Norm, sending him flying backwards into his five-foot-high Sunn amplifier, knocking both to the floor. We pulled the heated lad off Norm and threw him back into the crowd. With order restored, we gathered around the amplifier, praying it wasn't damaged, ignoring altogether our bloodied and beaten comrade.

As the focus of female attention shifted from Lynn and Mike to Mike and Norm, a touch of jealousy began to creep into the band's delicate inner-dynamics. It also kept our young leader, Lynn, company as he drank, often alone, in one of the endless number of bars that lined this parade route known as a concert tour.

Just after Norm got his contacts, Lynn announced to the rest of us with a laugh bordering on a sneer that he was changing Norm's nickname from "Jap" to "Ox" because Norm was such a big, dumb, clumsy Swede. Norm may have been Swedish and a bit clumsy at times, but we were all well aware that on the intelligence scale he was further from dumb than any of us.

One evening, as Norm was driving off with his latest new female friend, Lynn said, "Have you guys heard the line Norm lays on these unsuspecting girls to get them in the sack?"

"What're you talking about?" questioned Mike.

"He lies to them and tells them 'You're the girl I've been looking for my entire life!' I've heard him! How can they buy into it?"

Imitating a big dummy and speaking with a half-southern red neck accent, Lynn did his unflattering impersonation of Norm:

"Hey, honey, ya know yer kind of cute? I luv yuuu! Wanna get married?"

"Yeah," laughed Mike. "I can't believe it works so well for him. Girls are so gullible."

"It's like they want to believe him so badly that no matter what crap he lays on them, they go for it!" said Lynn. "He doesn't care who he hurts, not even Shannon, as long as he gets what he wants from them, and it's starting to piss me off."

"Maybe I should try that!" Barry speculated. "I could use a little more action."

Barry's comment was genuinely funny, and we all did laugh, while Lynn's comments had an element of truth to them, but were not so funny. We were well aware of what Lynn was trying to do. It ate at him to have Norm subtly buck his rule. Instead of winning us over to his side with his snide comments and innuendos, however, Lynn continued to lose ground with Mike, Barry and me with every new put down of Norm. Lynn was no slouch—he was sensitive and talented—and he could feel his authority slipping away, even as he struggled to maintain it. I'm sure that was part of why he drank like he did. Above all else, he resented Norm for questioning his authority, and for doing so well with his amps and the girls.

Ah, the mysterious workings of the male ego. When Lynn talked about Mike and Barry and their conquests, they were "studs" who "did the deed" with foxy chicks. When Lynn talked about Norm and his conquests, he was a "jerk" who "screwed" young innocents. When Lynn talked about me and my lack of conquests, I was "Lil' Dickie" who hadn't a clue what to do. Each viewpoint, in a different way, had that element of truth so essential to enabling us to believe what we say and ignore the obvious contradictions.

The longer I was a Kingsmen, the more complicated my world became. Being young and on the road touring with a hit record had its obvious joys and rewards. But they came with a price tag few recognize and most can't pay. It's difficult for people outside the entertainment industry to fathom how a performer can feel all-powerful and elated in front of thousands of people one minute and feel powerless and insecure when left alone a few minutes later. I've seen no study of the cumulative effect that years of adrenaline rushes can have on the human body and mind. I can only look within and around me for answers. The expectations people impose on you are to always be on time, to always smile, to always live up to your image, to always perform at your best. For that you're applauded or ignored or booed. Afterward, after the crowd has gone and the stage has emptied, people assume you simply flip a switch that turns off the charged-up state you were just in. In truth, there is no switch, and you're left alone to deal with coming down off that giddy adrenaline high you just were on, and your emotions at moments like that can tear at you and confuse you. For all of its joys and rewards, it's one exhausting elevator ride.

I've lost count of how many of those elevator rides I've taken over the past 40 years. I know the number's in the thousands—how many G's doesn't really matter. Enough to tell you from first-hand experience that performing for a big crowd is an adrenaline rush of the first magnitude. It's an unmatched high. The problem is, 30 minutes after the show, security has rushed you to the safety of your hotel room where you find yourself still pumped up while climbing the walls. That's when some guys party, others turn to drugs, most find sex and many raise the bottle. And then there are those special cases who indulge in all of the above.

As for me, I partied after a fashion, but was too earnest and young and naïve to ever wear a lamp shade on my head or dance on a table. Drugs I never considered an option, especially in later years when I saw what they were doing to so many of my friends in show biz. Because I wasn't a man yet, sex was out, although there were countless opportunities. That left alcohol, and I didn't like the taste or the after-effects. So, instead of losing myself in any of the options traditionally available in the rock music world, I succumbed to my passion and became a symphonic music junky. For a while I even carried a reel-to-reel tape recorder with me on the road so I could enjoy the masters in my room.

The PR surrounding a band as famous/infamous as the Kingsmen created a great deal of our public image, so much so that finding people to accept us as individuals separate from the band became increasingly difficult. We were always introduced as being "one of the Kingsmen" as though it were our last name. You know, like this:

"Mr. Hoover, this is Dick Peterson, *one of the Kingsmen*. They're the band that sings "Louie Louie," the song that Governor Welsh of Indiana banned. You know, the one with the dirty lyrics."

Having "one of the Kingsmen" as a second last name didn't bother Barry or Norm or me nearly as much as it bothered Lynn, whom it bothered mightily. He found trying to live up to his public image while being secretly married nearly impossible. He needed an escape, and the bottle was fast becoming his exit of choice.

Mike was the only one of us who loved having "one of the Kingsmen" for a last name. Out of all the past Kingsmen, Mike has been the only one of us to live as a Kingsmen 24/7. From his first gig in '59 to our latest in '05, Mike has lived and loved being a Kingsmen.

Not yet an everyday drinker, Lynn enjoyed a shot or two whenever he felt undo pressure from home or had to deal with unpleasant band business. Warning signs were starting to appear, however, and it was becoming a more regular occurrence to find him in a pickled state or crocked as we traveled the roads of America. The tragedy was, Lynn was a master entertainer on stage. He didn't play the sax well, and his voice wasn't anything special. He was, however, as quick and funny as Jonathan Winters and could run a show with the timing of Bill Cosby. Lynn always left the stage as a crowd favorite, and it was tough watching such a talented friend hurt himself with our success. The truth was, he wore too many hats for a 19-year-old to have thrust on his head: manager, accountant, travel agent, band leader, PR man, babysitter. He was doing a job none of us appreciated or wanted or were capable of handling. The weight he carried on his shoulders allowed the rest of us to do little more than have fun on and off stage. We'd chased girls, attended parties and gone bowling, while Lynn balanced the books, book hotel rooms and organized PR campaigns in the next town. Our popularity never allowed Lynn to be a carefree kid like the rest of us. Lynn took 10 percent, and churches call that a tithe. To this day, I wonder whether the 10 percent we paid to him was enough. It bought us our freedom; it cost Lynn his.

MUCH as we wanted our upcoming tour kicking off in the 49th state of Hawaii to start, and our current swing across the Lower 48 to end, we couldn't help but savor in wide-eyed fashion some of the spectacular new places marking our travels and marvel at the down-to-earth hospitality of the people we met along the way, the same people, I concluded, that shaped this country and made it such a great place to live. For me, those extended 13-week tours were great lessons in history and geography and all of the social sciences. If only that could have lightened my load in terms of my high-school obligations. I was still a month away from graduation, and while the guys were out on the town enjoying the extra-curricular activities that so livened up life on the road (and this story), I was still parking my posterior in my room most nights doing homework. Some big-time rock 'n' roll star I was.

Norm, meanwhile, spent much of his free time demo-ing his amps for music store dealers. Hardly a day went by that he didn't blow the ears off another new covey of unsuspecting store owners with demonstrations of his earth-shaking equipment. [I can't do justice in these pages to the contributions Norm later made to rock music through the innovations he introduced via his Sunn line of amps and equipment, now owned by Fender.] Those demonstrations consistently led to multiple orders, as Norm made history with his technical expertise as well as his music.

When not hawking amps or strumming his guitar, Norm joined forces with Mike as they made it their highest priority to service the needs of America's teenage female population. Barry did his level best to help out the cause, capturing the hearts of girls passed over either accidentally or on purpose by Norm and Mike. When not listening to Beethoven or Brahms or Bach, or doing my homework, I spent what time I could spare watching and learning the ways of the world from my fellow traveling Musketeers. Secretly, I was awaiting the arrival of manhood, picking up tips from the masters about how to handle my virility when it finally came.

Lynn was spending an ever-increasing amount of time trying to suppress his inner demons with demon rum and its cousins. And, when the opportunities presented themselves, he would attempt to work his persuasive political magic on us in a failing effort to convince us to continue following his direction and stifle all notions of bringing in outside management. Lynn had his rare sexual indiscretions, which he did his best to disguise, but we always saw through his comical song-and-dances. We knew his youthful hormones demanded action and we never faulted him for that. Because we loved him, we laughed and turned our heads the other way, raising eyebrows to each other and pretending for Lynn's sake that his prevarications were believable, thinly-disguised lies though they were.

We were the true living definition of an American family of brothers. We each had our faults and we each had our strengths. Together we argued and laughed and cursed. We each had our idiosyncrasies that alternately drove the others crazy or provided fodder for the endless cycle of teasing and ridicule that marked our fellowship.

When we hit the stage, no matter what positive or negative behavior had been going on beforehand, we united as one and had more fun playing rock 'n' roll than any band I've ever heard of or seen, before or since. We were and still are America's Party Band. Unless you were one of the five of us on stage in Tuscaloosa or Toledo or Louisville or Laramie back then in '64, it's impossible to fully relate the feeling to you of what it was like. Those out-of-control parties we threw on stage and called performances were worth any price we had to pay, without question.

WE ended our second tour of '64 feeling hope and optimism and excitement for the changes before us. Bill was coming up to Portland to meet our parents and sign on as our manager, and we were going to get Lynn back. The four of us knew that, kept telling ourselves that. Plus, we would soon be taking our good-time party juggernaut to the beaches of Hawaii. Life was good.

VERSE 18

WITHOUT Lynn present, we called Bill several times from the road to discuss our mounting concerns regarding Lynn's leadership and maneuverings. Initially, we just wanted to put a stop to his self-promoting and the awkwardness it brought and reestablish a feeling of equality among us. As the end of the tour neared, however, we sensed the distance between us was growing larger every day and worried the elevator ride Lynn was on was affecting his health. We wanted changes made, and quickly, and we wanted Bill to know. We feared the end of the world as we knew it, the end of the Kingsmen, perhaps even the end of Lynn. We struggled with adult problems, still clinging to our youth a while longer.

Lynn and Karen had recently purchased an attractive new split-level in the fast-expanding community of Gresham on the eastern outskirts of Portland. It was good-sized, with a two-car garage and plenty of room into which the family they planned to raise could grow (their first child was expected to arrive soon). Proud of their new home, they invited Bill to stay in the guest room during his visit. He told us he was going to accept the Eastons' invitation because he wanted to spend as much time with Lynn as necessary to make him feel comfortable with Bill as our new manager. There'd be time as well to discuss career-building moves Bill hoped to pursue for us.

Bill arrived in Portland the day after we returned home. We decided it would be a good idea for the five of us to greet him at the airport and spend a few hours together before meeting the parents. He was smooth and likable and skilled in the art of winning people over to his way of thinking—something he'd have to be if he were to have any chance of convincing Lynn and Karen. Things in Gresham got off to a good start, and Bill proved himself right to spend so much time together with them. In just a few short days, the three developed mutual respect and trust for each other. By the time Bill left, Lynn and Karen were as convinced as any of us that he could have a major positive impact on our career. They encouraged us to sign a management contract and we, of course, agreed.

During his three days in Portland, Bill devoted as much time as possible to each family. He started his mornings at Lynn and Karen's, then around 10 o'clock Lynn dropped him off at another home. There, Bill spent five or six hours getting to know that individual and his family, their interests and their goals. Around 4 o'clock, the Musketeer he was visiting drove him to another home where the ritual was repeated. At around 10 PM or so, Lynn arrived to take Bill back to Gresham for the remainder of the evening. In those five or six hours at each stop, he was able to get to know our families, and we in turn had a chance to give him the once-over.

Bill was open and forthcoming with everyone, sharing enough of himself and his dreams that by the end of his visit each of us felt like we'd personally begun a relationship with him that would endure, like we'd made a friend for life. After my family's visit with him, I phoned Dick St. John to say thanks for helping us and for connecting us with Bill. He was thrilled to learn things were going so well and said he couldn't wait for us to become official members of "the Bill Lee Family of Entertainers." Bill's other acts were doing well at the time, but none of them were getting the press we were—no one was, if you exclude invaders from the UK. He was champing at the bit to join in the fray.

A few hours before Bill was scheduled to fly back to LA, we all met at the airport for the official signing of our management contract. Moms and dads, brothers and sisters, wife and baby-to-be, girlfriends—all came to see our newly-adopted relative safely on the plane. My mother called him "Mr. Hollywood Bill," and he accepted the name with the same warmth and grace with which it was given. She told Bill she liked him so much, she was sad to see him leave, and that he'd always be welcomed in her home. "The next time you come to Portland, you make sure you bring Dee Dee with you!" were her parting words to him.

There must have been 20 of us at the airport to see Bill off. As he boarded the plane, tears were shed. In a week, we'd see Bill again when we flew into LA to meet the Beach Boys, practice and prepare a bit and hop a plane with them for Hawaii.

WE arrived at LAX just before sundown and were surprised and thrilled to find Carl and Brian Wilson waiting for us at the gate. I'd expected to be met by someone from their staff or maybe by a limo driver sent to deliver us to our hotel. The last thing any of us expected to see as we walked off the plane was Carl and Brian standing there smiling at our stunned reactions. Instantly, they made us feel like we were going to be part of a special family and not just hired hands for their Endless Summer Tour of '64.

The famous brothers helped carry our mountain of guitars and suitcases from the baggage claim area to a van they had waiting at the curb. It took us a few minutes to stuff everything inside.

"I'm driving the van," Brian announced. Who wants to ride with me?"

"I do!" Norm immediately volunteered.

He climbed in the passenger's side opposite Brian while the rest of us followed Carl to his car. As we were piling in, Carl turned to Lynn with the look of an innocent-yet-curious child and asked, "So, what did you guys sing on 'Louie Louie'?"

"Now that's funny!" giggled Mike.

"What?" laughed Carl. "Hey, everybody wants to know, including me."

"Exactly!" chimed in Barry.

"Did you guys know we added 'Louie Louie' to our *Shut Down* album?" said Carl.

"I saw that," smiled Lynn.

"Yeah, *Billboard* called it a 'white bread' version of your record," he joked. "We thought it might boost our sales."

We liked Carl instantly. He was just like us, a '60s-era teenager.

"So, are you going to tell me or not?" asked Carl, shutting his door.

"I asked Bill, but he said he had no idea. He promised that you guys would tell me."

All of us laughed, none of us volunteering a thing.

"You are going to tell me, right?"

We kept laughing as he looked around the car with a "I want to be one of the 'in' guys" look on his face.

"What'd you sing on your version?" asked Mike.

"We got the words from the publisher, but that's not what's on your record, is it?"

We just sat smiling at each other as he started his car.

"Right? Come on, give," he begged like a hurting teen.

As Carl drove us to the hotel, we gave in and shared with him the comical story behind "the Growing Legend of 'Louie Louie,'" finishing the bizarre tale just as we pulled up at the main entrance.

"That's crazy!" he said, pausing. "So, what *are* the words on your record?"

Again, we all just laughed.

"They're whatever you want them to be, my friend," Lynn teased.

"Okay, so don't tell me!" laughed Carl. "I'll find out on my own. I'll be listening to you guys all summer."

Carl was the social Wilson brother: friendly, funny and well grounded; he seemed to thoroughly enjoy the life he was living. Brian was the reserved Wilson brother: quieter and more matter of fact; he mostly wanted to know how we got a certain sound, what kind of recording equipment was used to get the bass effect on "Louie Louie"—that kind of stuff. Technophiles at heart, he and Norm hit it off right away.

"Say, did anyone tell you," Carl said as we were checking in, "we've added a couple of other acts to the Island shows? Jan and Dean are going to play. They're two of our best friends. And Screamin' Jay Hawkins is going to be there, too. Just wait 'til you see *him* perform!"

Noticing that Mike and Lynn wore their hair in pompadours, much like they did, Carl proposed that he fix them up with his friend, Jay Sebring, the famous Hollywood *coiffeur* who crafted all of the Beach Boys' hairstyles. He offered to pick them up the following morning and drive them over to meet Jay and have him cut their hair. Touched by Carl's hospitality and generosity, they gladly accepted his offer.

For several days, we ran through the Hawaii show with the other acts, artfully dodging their determined efforts to have us reveal what they called "the real words to 'Louie Louie.'" Working sessions like those quickly tell you how well you're going to get along with your fellow performers, and in the persons of Eddie Hodges, Ray Peterson and Jimmy Griffin we found three great new friends wonderful to work with, closely plugged in to the local scene and possessed with a hip style of Hollywood humor we found strange and amusing. Every night they hauled us off to another chic hot spot in Tinsel Town. Like Dobie Gray, we were "in with the in-crowd" already, and the serious good times were still ahead.

FLYING into Honolulu for the first time for me was like entering into another world. Viewed from the air, the gleaming white of the beaches, the lustrous blue of the sea, the lush green of the islands together were more vivid than any picture I'd ever seen. As we slowed to a stop before the arrival gate, a stairway down to heaven was rolled up to the door for us to deplane. At the bottom, lovely Hawaiian angels dressed in native attire greeted each of us by placing a flower lei around our necks. Mike, our resident humorist, noted that he'd been in Hawaii for only a few minutes and already he'd been lei-d. Aloha! Welcome to Hawaii, paradise on earth.

The Beach Boys were true egalitarians and not prima donnas. They treated the other acts exactly the same way they treated themselves. They put all of us up in our own individual bungalows at the Hilton Hawaiian Village (Dennis Wilson was my next door neighbor) with the beach a 30 foot walk from our sliding glass doors. Perfect sunsets every night, warm ocean breezes in the day, bikinis and sun tans as far as the eye could see—given the chance, I would gladly have stayed in Hawaii 'til the end of time.

They called themselves "The Beach Boys"—upper case *B*s—but Dennis was the only true surfer in the band. Whenever I saw him, he was either "goin' surfin'" or just getting back from a "totally gnarly ride." For our entire time together in Hawaii, Dennis lived a true beach boy—lower case *b*s—life off stage.

We played several concerts on Oahu, the first at Pearl Harbor. Jan and Dean were on the program and reminded me of Dick

St. John—always at the ready with a prank of some sort, usually involving shaving cream.

An armed forces bus served as our transportation. On the way to the Naval Base, insisting he had to relieve himself, Dennis talked our driver into stopping along the side of the road. Only when he stepped off the bus did his real motive became clear. Without warning, Dennis dashed into the adjacent field, copped a pineapple growing there and jumped back on the bus—neglecting to relieve himself. The driver went bananas (pineapples?).

"That's illegal!" he shouted at Dennis. "The fine's $500! I could do time in the brig if we get caught stealing a pineapple."

No one spoke as we all sat motionless, astonished by the crime we'd just witnessed. Meanwhile, unperturbed, the contented thief carved the purloined fruit with his Swiss army knife, shaking off the driver's disapproval like it was no big thing.

"I know it's illegal," Dennis calmly answered the driver, "but you wouldn't have stopped had you known I wanted a pineapple."

Looking up from his task and holding out a freshly-cut slice, juice dripping on his fingers, he addressed his fellow passengers: "Hey, who wants a bite of some fresh Hawaiian pineapple?"

"Oh, what the hell!" said the driver, smiling and closing the door. "I've gone this far, I might as well go all the way and eat some of the damn thing before they lock me up!"

The entire bus erupted in cheers as Dennis passed around chunks of the forbidden fruit. He was just that kind of guy—a fun-loving, devil-may-care, swim-against-the-current, go-for-the-biggest-wave-in-the-ocean, semi-crazy personality. We all had a secret wish to be like Dennis, but none of us were brave enough—or perhaps crazy enough—to perpetually challenge the universe with the same impudence and careless disregard for mortality that he did.

WE also did a show at the HIC Arena in Honolulu in front of 15,000 screaming fans. That was indisputably the smelliest concert the Kingsmen ever played in their history—smelly good. Many of the locals brought flower leis to give to their favorite artists. During our set, fans randomly ran up to the stage and placed bright-hued garlands around our necks. By the time we'd finished our half-hour performance, we had so many of the fragrant wreaths on our shoulders, we could barely see over the sweet-smelling mass—floral tokens of our fans' appreciation.

Until Carl Wilson mentioned his name in the lobby of our hotel in LA, I'd never heard of—let alone seen or met—"Screamin'" Jay Hawkins. At the Hawaiian Village, just before we left for the HIC, someone told me he was the most outrageous performer ever to hit the concert stage. That was hard for me to imagine. Tonight, I'd let my own eyes be the judge.

Moments before Jay was scheduled to go on as the first act of the night, I was sitting in the dressing room with the guys sipping a Coke and looking at a magazine when Carl rushed in and shouted, "Come on, let's go, follow me! Jay's about to start. Forget about the Coke, Dickie, you can finish it later. Come on, let's go, hurry up, you've got to see this!"

Dropping everything, we rushed after Carl, joining him backstage where we took up positions in the wings and watched with curious anticipation as the house lights dimmed, plunging the arena into almost total darkness. On the stage before us, amp lights hovered like fireflies on a moonless summer night as an invisible band started to vamp loud, scratchy, crazy surf music. From high above in the rafters, spotlights snapped on, focusing their narrow beams on four caricature figures standing at the back of the arena. They were pallbearers from some exotic, faraway jungle, and above their heads they bore a flaming coffin. With slow, exaggerated strides, they solemnly proceeded down the main aisle through the spellbound crowd, the music swelling and moaning as though calling forth the dead. Reaching the stage apron, the bearers came to a halt and stood silent and still as the music crescendoed, then abruptly stopped.

A creaking sound filled the arena as the lid slowly opened and a spectral figure emerged from within. Dressed like a voodoo witch doctor, made up like a zombie, draped with rubber snakes, crowned by a headdress of feathers, wrapped in a swirling animal-skin cape, a savage shape leaped to the stage, holding high a stick with a flaming skull on top. Grabbing the mic, he screamed and screeched:

I put a spell on you
Because you're mine.
I can't stand the things that you do.
No, no, no, I ain't lyin'. No....

[Dick Peterson, one of the Kingsmen, meet Jalacy "Screamin' Jay" Hawkins, one of the legendary performers in rock 'n' roll history. And this is Henry, his flaming skull.]

The crowd went berserk, and we weren't far behind. I turned to Carl, who spoke before I could say anything.

"See," he said, slapping my back, "didn't I tell you? Isn't he something?"

"Unbelievable!" I answered. "He's fantastic! I wouldn't have missed this for the world. Thanks for coming and getting us."

According to legend, Jay Hawkins first performed his flaming coffin routine at the urging of Alan Freed, who supposedly paid him $300 to overcome his reluctance and do it. The act debuted in 1956 at one of Freed's holiday extravaganzas at a theatre in Brooklyn. Small world. Or, as Screamin' Jay Hawkins used to say, "Ugu-ugu!"

EXCEPT for the shaving cream fights in the dressing rooms, which Jan and Dean always seemed to start, and the deafening screams of the fans, which our music always seemed to inspire, our stay in Hawaii was mostly a relaxing, laid back, pleasure-filled first encounter with paradise. When the time came for us to fly back to the mainland, I gave silent thanks to the Beach Boys for bringing me there and vowed to one day return to that Pacific island Garden of Eden.

The "Louie Louie" controversy and ongoing FBI investigation remained the source of 90 percent of our fame and notoriety and helped drive our second single, "Money," up the charts to #16 on *Billboard*. Hoping to take advantage of our Beach Boy tour exposure, Scepter/Wand decided to release a third Kingsmen single, "Little Latin Lupe Lu." The move paid handsome dividends as "Lupe" became a Top-10/Top-20 hit in many of the regional markets we played and charted nationally on *Billboard*. Figuring if "Louie

Louie" could be a hit once, it could be one twice, Scepter/Wand re-released it in 1964, and sales continued to mount on the Jamaican sea chanty front. On the LP side, our second album, *Kingsmen Volume II*, recorded the same day we first learned that "Louie" had been banned by the governor of Indiana, reached #15 nationally on *Billboard*. By such measures, we were on a roll.

For all its beauty and pleasures and diversions, Hawaii had been a side trip, a turn off the main highway leading to our primary destination—$uccess. It was time to hit the road in the Lower 48, for we had concert dates to keep and record sales we hoped to reap.

UPON our arrival back at LAX, 21 brave souls boarded the Greyhound bus that was to be our sanctuary on wheels for the remainder of the summer. Really wanting to use his Sunn amps on this tour, Norm hired Jimmy-John to drive the van with its precious cargo down to LA from Portland and meet us at the airport. There, directly outside baggage claim, Kingsmen roadie Jim reluctantly handed the black-clad earth shakers over to the care of Beach Boys roadie Brian [I'm sorry, but I don't recall Brian's last name], who would be handling set-ups and tear-downs on this particular crisscrossing of the US of A. With his mission accomplished, Jim turned right around and drove back up I-5 to Oregon to await the completion or our summer tour and the beginning of our next.

Norm was delighted to see Jim, and even more delighted to wrap his arms again around a full set of his precious darlings. Out of convenience, we'd used another brand of amps in Hawaii, equipment lacking the power and drive we were accustomed to. With Sunn amps once more driving our music, we could return to our normal battle plan: assaulting audiences head on with wave after wave of overwhelming sound, no quarter given. Norm figured exposure on a Beach Boys tour would be the ideal selling tool for Sunn. He figured right.

Our first stop was Phoenix. Dennis Wilson played drums for the Beach Boys, and he liked his kit set up differently than what I preferred. That meant that everything had to be repositioned during intermission. Added to that, the Beach Boys used Fender

Showman amps, not Sunns. As a result, during the set change, between tweaking the drums and switching the amplifiers, Brian had a lot of work to do. Hoping to make his job easier, we pooled our collective genius during sound check and tried to work out a stage plot that would place the amps and instruments in such a way that all Brian would have to do was change over the drums. The result only partly solved the problem. Something better was needed.

Eager to get back to playing on our own gear—Norm's amps were such a vital part of our sound—we hit that Arizona stage already on an adrenalin high, ready to flex our musical muscles and show the world once more our real stuff. From the very first note, it felt like we were home again, home again, jiggedy jig. It was like putting on your favorite pairs of old shoes and socks; it just felt comfortable. The musical gear we'd used in Hawaii had been good, but it couldn't hold a candle to Norm's stuff. We pounded out our set, bashing and crashing and whipping the crowd into a frenzy. In the summer of '64, no one knew better than The Kingsmen the power of loud.

Anyone who went to a Beatles concert that season heard little more than the screaming of teenage girls. The Fab Four's equipment couldn't produce enough decibels of clear sound to overcome the shrieking of ten thousand-plus sets of teeny-bopper lungs. Those English blokes would've had a better shot at making themselves heard had they used Sunn amps. The screams of our fans told us bad boys from Portland we were into something good—and loud. Above the screaming, we were heard.

When the Beach Boys took over the spotlight from us that night, the drop in volume level as they played their opening number was dramatic, almost shocking. It sounded as though there'd been a major malfunction with their sound equipment, or maybe someone had forgotten to plug in their amps. As perfectly as the Beach Boys sang their harmonies, as precisely as they performed their music, their Fender-backed sound was wimpish compared to the raucous, animalistic, deafening roar of our Sunn-powered thunder. The girls may have screamed every time Dennis waved his long surfer hair in the air, and they may have yawned every time yours truly flashed his drumsticks for all to admire, but as an ensemble, if measured by volume and quality and clarity of sound, The Kingsmen blew the Beach Boys right off the stage—and those surfer dudes knew it.

After the show, we returned to the hotel, cleaned up and headed to the restaurant for a bite to eat before hitting the sack. No sooner had we sat down than Carl and Brian Wilson appeared and asked to join us.

With little more than a "how you guys doin'?" Carl cut straight to the chase.

"Norm," he said, "what would it take for you to make us some amps like what you guys have?"

Norm smiled and took a puff of his cigarette.

"They sound pretty good, don't they?" he said with a giggle.

"You guys sounded incredible!" said Brian. "We need to sound that loud. How do you do it? I've never heard anything like it!"

"I'll call my brother Con tomorrow," Norm replied, laughing, "and have him get started on some equipment for you guys right away."

"How long will it take?" asked Carl.

Before Norm could answer, Mike stepped in.

"Why don't you guys use our stuff for the rest of the tour?" he suggested.

"Would you let us do that?" asked Carl in amazement.

"Well, of course!" answered Mike. "Why wouldn't we?"

"Well," smiled Brian, "most bands would want to keep a competitive edge and wouldn't want to help another band on the same show."

"Hey," said Norm, "you guys have treated us so well, we'd be wrong not to share our stuff with you."

"We're not competing with you guys," Mike added. "Besides, our music is a totally different style than yours. We don't have a problem with sharing equipment. We're happy to do it."

Norm was next up with an idea.

"Why don't you guys buy the amps we have with us?" he suggested. "I can make new gear for our next tour, and that would save me from having to ship these amps back to Portland when this tour's over."

"Would you be up for that?" asked Brian.

"Sure," answered Norm, "but only if you let us use your 'new equipment' for the rest of the tour."

We all laughed at the switch and spent the rest of the evening talking about music and the tour and recording techniques used on different hits. In Hawaii, we'd become acquainted with one another. There at that restaurant in Phoenix, we became true and lasting friends. It helped establish the relaxed and comfortable atmosphere that prevailed throughout the rest of that endless summer of touring.

HALFWAY through the tour, Lynn called the four of us into his room.

"I just talked with Bill," he began soberly. Rising enthusiasm entered his voice as he added, "He just got the word. Plans have changed. When we get back to LA, we're going to be on *American Bandstand*!"

We erupted in joyous cheers. *American Bandstand*! The show every teenager watched, the national showcase every band dreamed of playing, the home of The Man himself, Dick Clark, the next step up the ladder to success for The Kingsmen—the news seemed too good to be true, except for the undeniable fact that it was. Bill Lee had delivered as promised. Even Lynn was pleased. Who wouldn't be? *American Bandstand*. At last!

A rock musician on a bus tour playing cards is like a sailor on shore leave chasing girls: both are addicted to games of chance and lust for the prize; both play to win and consider victory their right; and both have short memories in defeat, believing, always believing the next card dealt, the next line delivered will bring victory. Maybe that explains why some lovers love to gamble and some gamblers love to love.

In *Guys and Dolls*, the ne'er-do-well nogoodniks pursue "the oldest established permanent floating crap game in New York" in the back room of a gospel mission and in the sewers beneath Broadway. On the *Endless Summer* tour, preferring cards over dice, members of the Beach Boy entourage established a permanent floating *poker* game in the back of the bus as we bounced from town to town across America. On one occasion, the game carried over into the hotel room of one of the tour members. I was paired with Mike, and it was around two in the morning when he came into the room and woke me up with his noise.

"What time is it?" I asked sleepily.

"I don't know!" he answered impatiently as he rummaged through his suitcase.

"What are you looking for?" I asked.

"I only have about 10 minutes and then I have to be back in John Hodges' room or I'm out of the game. We're just on a break."

"Go to bed!" I advised.

"I've lost all my money and I need some more or I'm out!" said the desperate young mark—er, I mean, astute young sport. "I thought I had a hundred left in here."

"Didn't you use it at the clothing store in Chicago?" I asked.

"Oh, no, you're right! Shoot, I would've won all my money back and taken those guys to the cleaners if only I could've stayed in the game."

I sat up in bed, scratched my head and laughed.

"How do you figure that?"

"The cards were just starting to turn. I could feel it."

Leaving the game had been frustrating, obviously a major disappointment to Mike.

"Sounds like the famous last words of every loser," I said as I threw back the covers on my bed. I walked over to my suitcase and pulled out a hundred dollars I kept stashed for spending money.

"Here, I'll stake you," I said, handing over the cash.

"Really!?" he said in surprise.

"This isn't a loan," I said as Mike reached for the money. "This is a stake. If you lose it, I lose it. You're already down too much. But, if you lose it, learn from it! Gambling's a losing proposition. Never chase your losses."

With a big smile on his face, he gave me an appreciative hug.

"Lose?" he said. "I can't lose. I'm not playin' with my money anymore."

With that, he dashed out of the room as I shook my head in disbelief and went back to sleep.

Exhausted but excited, Mike burst into the room around 8 o'clock the next morning, waking me up once more.

"I won 750 bucks!" he crowed.

"You're joking!" I said, yawning happily, surprised to be the unexpected recipient of a $375 windfall.

"Breakfast is on me!" I offered.

"Thanks," Mike answered, "but I'm too wiped. I just want to go to sleep."

Here's your hundred back," he said as he fell on his bed. "Thanks!"

"Hey man," I laughed in amazement. "That wasn't a loan."

"I know," he said as he fell asleep, "but I want to pay you back anyway."

"Nube?" I said in an effort to keep him awake and collect my half of the riches. "Nube!?"

But the prognosticator of chance was already asleep. Shaking my head again, I showered, dressed and called Lynn to meet him for breakfast.

That afternoon, Mike and I were loading up to go to the concert venue. As he picked up his winnings and stuffed the stack of loot in his pocket, I said, "You'll find you're a few bucks short."

"Oh?" questioned the cool Maverick wannabe, a puzzled look on his face.

"Yeah!" I said. "As I was leaving the room, I saw the pile of moolah you left sitting on the dresser and helped myself to a ten spot. I figured you owed me breakfast at least."

"Cool!" Mike said, grinning. "I was going to buy you dinner tonight, but breakfast works for me. Costs me less, and I didn't have to be there."

I picked up a pillow and threw it, hitting him in the back of the head.

"Hey, watch the hair now, Lil' Dickie!" he called back as he ran out the door, laughing.

I was laughing, too, because the joke was really on him. I was more than confident he'd lose it all before the tour was over, while I'd gotten back my hundred bucks.

OUR concerts proved an incredible forum for Norm to demonstrate his wares. First there were the musical equipment buyers he personally invited to attend, who ordered Sunn amps in massive numbers. Then there were the musicians in the audience, their hair blown back by the force of the sound thrown at them by his black behemoths. Every rocker there wanted to be the first kid on his block to own a Sunn. Surging demand forced Norm and Con to move production out of their dad's garage and into a dedicated manufacturing facility. They struggled to keep up with orders for current designs while developing new product lines that would produce more orders still.

For a few weeks, Lynn's old self returned, along with his sense of humor, and he started spending more time with the rest of us. Having Bill Lee on board handling much of our business relieved some of the tension between Lynn and Norm and much of the burden from Lynn; having 20 other people to interact with on tour instead of just four helped each of us individually. Lynn's love affair with the bottle noticeably waned. Although he still enjoyed his evening libations, he rarely drank solo anymore, usually tippling in the company of fellow spirit-seekers traveling with the show.

Late one evening, Barry and I were sitting in the room he shared with Lynn, playing our acoustic guitars, when Lynn wobbled in, fairly soaked. It'd been many weeks since we'd seen him in that condition, and Barry and I were instantly transported back to the awkward days preceding our management change.

"I warned everybody!" slurred Lynn, "but, would you guys believe me? Nooooo!"

He waved a finger in the air. Barry put his guitar down and helped Lynn over to his bed.

"Why don't you get some sleep, and we'll talk about it in the morning?" Barry said.

"Nothin' to talk about!" he murmured. "Bill sold us out!"

Bill sold us out? Neither Barry nor I had the foggiest idea what Lynn was talking about.

"I know, I know," said Barry, trying to comfort and agree with Lynn in an effort to pacify him, "but let's deal with it tomorrow, okay? Right now, it's time to bag some z's."

"No, no!" said the staggering, exasperated Mr. Easton. "I talked to him tonight after the show. Here, look at this!"

Lynn woozily pulled a piece of paper from his pocket.

"There's the phone number of our new managers in New York City. Bill, our trusted friend Bill, sold our management contract to them!"

As Lynn plopped down on his bed, just before he passed out, I snatched the piece of white scratch paper from his hand and read it. Written there was the name, "Scandore and Shayne, Management Company." Also scribbled on the paper was a phone number with a New York area code.

"What do you make of this?" I asked Barry, handing him the crumpled piece of paper and shrugging my shoulders.

"Beats me!" replied my equally confused friend. "You don't suppose Bill really would've sold our contract to someone, do you?"

"I don't get it! Why would he sell our contract?"

"*Can* he sell our contract? is what I want to know!" answered Barry.

"Me, too!" I agreed.

"Let's go see if Mike's in your room," Barry suggested, moving toward the open door. "Maybe he knows something about this."

Good idea! I thought to myself, grabbing my guitar and following him out into the hallway.

We walked a few doors down to my room and found Mike and Norm watching TV and shooting the breeze. When told this latest news, neither one of them could offer a clue to help solve the mystery.

"Should we call Bill and ask him what this is all about?" asked Norm.

"Maybe we shouldn't," I speculated. "I mean, what if there's no truth to this? I don't know that we need to tell Bill that we heard this from Lynn, especially when he was in one of his 'less-than-ideal' conditions."

"Maybe we should wait until tomorrow," said Mike, "and see if Lynn still knows anything about this then?"

Barry offered an idea we all agreed to at once.

"Why don't we call Dick St. John?" he proposed, "Maybe he knows something about this."

Barely saying a word, I retrieved Dick's home phone number from my suitcase and checked my watch. It was just going on 10 o'clock in the evening on the West Coast. Dick would still be up. I sat down on Mike's bed and picked up the black phone from the night stand. After a brief hesitation, I began using the rotary dial and called the hotel operator.

"Front desk, may I help you?" a man's voice greeted me.

"Yes, I hope so!" I said. "This is Dick Peterson in room 310. I wish to place a person-to-person call to Mr. Richard St. John in Los Angeles, California. Can you help me? This is important."

"Certainly, Mr. Peterson. I'd be glad to connect you to a long-distance operator. What's Mr. St. John's number?"

I gave him Dick's number and sat down impatiently on the bed, crossing my right leg over my left and shaking my right foot furiously. Barry and Nube and Norm stood nearby, watching and waiting. After a short while I heard the operator ask for "Mr. Richard St. John."

"Yeah, that's me," I heard Dick reply, sounding weary and perturbed at the same time.

"Mr. St. John," the operator said. "I have a long distance call for you from a Mr. Peterson in Detroit. Please hold the line while I connect you."

"Mr. Peterson, I have Mr. St. John on the line for you."

"Thank you!" I said. "I appreciate your help."

"Hello, Dick!" I said, "This is Dick Peterson."

"Oh, hello, Lil' Dickie!" Dick said. "What's the weather like in Michigan?"

Dick was trying to sound upbeat, but I could tell he wasn't his normal fun-loving self.

"Oh, the weather here's hot and humid," I answered. "Thank goodness for air conditioning! Sorry, Dick, but I'm not calling to talk about the weather. I have a question about Bill Lee."

"Yes, what is it?" Dick asked, sighing deeply. I could tell something was wrong.

"Have you heard anything about Bill selling our contract to some management firm in New York?"

A long pause followed.

"Dick," I said, "Dick, are you there?"

"Yeah," he finally said, "I'm here. I guess you haven't heard the news yet about Bill."

"Heard *what* news about Bill?"

"He's been diagnosed with cancer. The doctors just told him."

"Oh, my god, no!" I cried. The guys all jumped, hearing my words and seeing the shocked look on my face.

"Is it…" I began to ask before Dick interrupted me.

"It's terminal," he said in a flat voice. "They give him a few weeks, maybe a month, maybe two, no more."

I held my hand over the mouthpiece and whispered the news to the guys. They stood motionless for a moment, looking at each other, bewildered, grief-stricken. As one, they sat on the bed.

"How's Bill handling it?" "How's Dee Dee taking it?" "What can we do to help?" I peppered Dick with these questions and more.

"Bill's a brave man, a braver man than I. He's working non-stop trying to finish his business and take care of his clients. He wants to set you guys up with a new management firm. That's probably what you heard about."

"What about Dee Dee, how's she taking it?" I repeated.

"She's shaken up by the news, of course. You can understand that. But she's doing her best to support Bill and help him through all this."

Dick's voice was starting to break up. He and Bill were great friends, and I could tell he needed someone to talk to, and badly. I listened for a while as he tried to talk through his many confused feelings—about the effect this was having on him, on Dee Dee, on Bill, on their circle of friends, on their fellow artists, on everyone and everything. After a few minutes of this, Barry and Norm left the room, saying they'd talk to me in the morning. Mike stood by, and I passed the phone over to him, and together we did our best for the next half hour to help Dick through his emotional turmoil, passing the phone back and forth every few minutes. It was confusing for us all, and talking seemed to help.

The conversation worked its way around to Dick telling me that Bill did indeed have someone in mind for us as our new manager, a man named Shelly Berger. He said Shelly was a well-respected man about the industry, well-connected and a good friend of Bill's. He said Shelly was the West Coast partner of some New York-based firm. He didn't know anything about the guys in New York, but he did know Shelly personally and felt he would be a perfect fit for us. Before hanging up, Dick suggested we phone Bill the following day and discuss the situation with him. In the meantime, he said he'd call Bill himself to let him know that we'd talked, that one of us would be calling him and that we were aware of his condition. We agreed with Dick that it would make it easier on Bill if he knew we'd already been told of his unfortunate situation. Because of my relationship with Dick, I suggested that maybe I should be the one to talk to Bill, and Dick agreed. With that, we said good night. For the balance of the time it took for us to fall asleep, Mike and I lay in the darkened room on our beds, talking, trying to make sense of things that continue to this day to make no real sense to me. I remembered Fawnie and thought to myself, *Oh, no! Not again!*

WE respected Bill and admired the way he was trying to find the best situation for us while dealing with his own, far greater problems. We felt like those forlorn creatures the Whiffenpoofs at Yale sing about (in a song dedicated to someone named "Louie," by the way):

We're poor little lambs who have lost our way
Baa! Baa! Baa!
We're little black sheep who have gone astray
Baa! Baa! Baa!

Gentleman songsters off on a spree
Damned from here to eternity
God have mercy on such as we
Baa! Baa! Baa!

We were about to lose our shepherd, and without his guidance, we feared we'd once more lose our way; we'd been on the right path for a short while, but now we sensed ourselves about to go astray again. Teenage songsters, we needed to gather together and devise a plan.

The next morning, however, without bothering to discuss strategy with the rest of us first, Lynn called the offices of the mysterious "Scandore and Shayne, Management Company" in New York and spoke with Mel Shayne himself. Mel, Lynn reported afterward, told him we were under no legal obligation to sign with Scandore and Shayne. Based on Bill's recommendation, however, Mel wanted a chance to meet with us to discuss having his firm take over our management. He told Lynn he was willing to fly to LA and proposed to meet with us while we were taping *American Bandstand* and personally introduce us to Shelly.

As Lynn told us about his conversation with Mel, he intimated that perhaps we should postpone replacing Bill until we had a chance to "look into all of our options." Four of us knew what he really meant: a return to power of King Lynn I, and we didn't want that. We pushed instead for the meeting with Mel and Shelly, rationalizing that we didn't have to commit to Mel, and convincing Lynn that it couldn't hurt to listen to what he had to say. We wanted to keep Lynn in the fold with us and, besides, Mel's proposal might prove to be a good opportunity for us, something worth exploring. Reluctantly, Lynn agreed to call Mel back and accept his offer. Everyone agreed that I should be the one to call Bill.

BACK in my room, uncertain about what to say to Bill, I picked up the phone then put it down, picked it up then put it down again, picked it up a third time and finally dialed the number. I wanted to talk with him, and I wanted to say the right things, but what are the right things to say at a moment like this? I decided to just be a friend, to keep things as positive as possible and to be a good listener.

Bill picked up on the first ring, answering with a cheery and upbeat "Hello!" and sounding the same as he always did.

"Hello, Bill," I said, "this is Dick Peterson."

"Lil' Dickie! It's good to hear your voice. Dick said you might be calling."

"How are you doing? We heard about your situation."

"I'm doing alright, I guess," Bill answered, the tone of his voice losing some of its brightness. "It's Dee Dee and you guys I'm worried about."

"Don't worry about us! How's Dee Dee? We're all thinking about her. What can we do to help? Whatever you need, just ask. We love you both."

We talked for the longest time about Dee Dee, about life in general and about Shelly Berger. Bill liked him really well and assured me

Shelly was more than capable and had a style completely suitable to our personalities. He said he'd see us when we got into town for the *Bandstand* show and promised to spend more time then talking with us about Shelly

Lacking magical words that could change his hardship, the best I could do was offer words of comfort and my prayers.

"See you in LA, Bill. Give my love to Dee Dee."

"See you then, Dick. Say 'hi' to everyone for me. Good luck!"

It was the last time we ever spoke.

THERE are hundreds of other stories I could tell about things that happened during our tour with the Beach Boys; I'll make do with telling just one. Several times already I've referred to shaving cream fights as a regular featured event. Those contests usually ended with all of us ganging up on the poor soul who ran out of ammo first. On this one occasion, Barry became the target of the biggest Burma Shave-Barbasol battle ever.

Rumors of a skirmish had circulated the night before. In anticipation, we all boarded the bus that morning surreptitiously wearing our swimsuits under our clothing. You could feel the tension building as everyone sat in their seats and engaged in small talk, waiting for the opening salvo to be fired. Somewhere in the middle of Nowhere, USA, the cry to arms trumpeted through the speeding Greyhound.

The volume of laughing and screaming and shouting was eclipsed only by the amount of shaving cream filling the air as 19 rockers ran amok. The vicious attacks and ruthless counter attacks were brutal and unmerciful. We were having a blast as the combat zone swayed back and forth in rhythm with the desolate highway. We all held our ground, defending our territories until Barry's last can ran out of propellant. The entire bus load of lawless, boisterous teens seized the moment and unloaded the full measure of their remaining ammo on the unarmed keyboardist. By the time the last shot was fired, Barry was covered head to toe in a foot-thick mountain of white foamy mush. He looked like a cross between the Michelin Man, the Pillsbury Dough Boy and a tub of Gillette

Foamy. The story doesn't end there.

Barry was so completely covered with goo, we told him "You can't sit down!" and banished him to the front of the bus to stand in the stair well until Bill, our driver, found a gas station where we could hose off the casualty of war. When at last we drove into a station, we passed a sign reading "Last Chance for Fifty Miles to Fill with Gas." The bus rolled to a stop not 10 feet from the attendant, who was visiting with a state patrolman while fueling the officer's prowl car. We were in the heart of red neck territory, and the last thing this cop wanted to see on his watch was a bus load of unruly, shady-looking, defiant delinquents messing with his world.

Getting out his new toy—an eight millimeter home movie camera—Brian Wilson slid back a window and started filming Barry as he approached the two astonished locals. We were all hanging out of the windows watching as the walking pile of shaving cream, followed by a leprous-looking Lynn, stopped before the two annoyed red necks. Clever Barry jokingly said to the scowling patrolman, "Got a blade?" and the bus rocked with laughter. The officer didn't find Barry's comment much to his liking.

"I'm going to need to see some ID, young man," he curtly announced.

"Yes, sir," Barry answered, "but I haven't any clothes on under the shaving cream, so after I shave I'll go back to the bus and get my pants."

We were all in stitches as Lynn chimed in.

"I'm Doctor Easton," he said. "I was taking this bus load of mentally disturbed people back to the asylum when they got slightly out of control with some shaving cream."

Ignoring the officer's macho attitude, Lynn picked up the water hose used for filling radiators and began hosing off Barry.

Aboard the bus, we continued our defiant joking around as the officer showed signs of increasing frustration. Sensing danger was close, Lynn attempted to lighten the atmosphere and rescue Barry—as well as the our bus load of rock 'n' rollers—from the patrolman's wrath.

"Do you guys ever watch *Candid Camera*?" he asked.

"Yeah," said the attendant, growing curious.

"Well, do you see that cameraman in the window of the bus up there?" Lynn asked, pointing to Brian who was still filming through the window.

"No!" cried the cop. "Are you kidding me? I can't believe it! Wait until my wife and the boys at the station hear about this! I was ready to run you all in!"

Giddiness overcame the officer as he did a great imitation of Gomer Pyle. All that was missing was a "Golly" or two and maybe an "Aw, shucks!" for good measure. The gas station attendant fumbled right along with his buddy as the two of them asked Lynn a million questions—"When will the episode be on the air?" "Is Allen Funt on the bus?" "Can we have his autograph?"—stuff like that. All the while, Lynn continued to hose off Barry and we on the bus continued to howl.

Once Lynn finished with Barry, one by one the rest of us hosed ourselves off as the patrolman and his sidekick looked on, their mouths agape. As though waking from a trance, the stage-struck targets of Lynn's quick wit eventually stirred to action and ended up actually helping with the clean-up. Standing in a sea of white foam, still holding the hose, they waved good-bye as the *Candid Camera* troupe re-boarded the bus, pulled out on the highway and faded into the sunset. Alan Funt never did give them his autograph.

THE other stories, however worthy, will just have to wait for a second book or, lacking that, remain untold. Stories like how I got to play drums with the Beach Boys for several shows when Dennis failed to show up on time, or the countless insane, almost-nightly episodes involving wild young females, or the wonderful moments we all lived for, when Brian Wilson would get an inspiration and have everyone on the bus singing his experimental and inventive vocal parts that, when performed, sounded like a rock 'n' roll celebration, or when thousands of teenage fans mobbed the bus and held us in fear—the list goes on and on. It was only a two-month tour, but because of the many egos and diverse personalities and unique circumstances, we packed a year's worth of action into 60 days.

To a man, we all loved and respected Carl Wilson. His warmth, grace, talent and consistency were rarities in this business. Over the years, we've played on at least 50 other occasions with the Beach Boys and, without exception, Carl always was genuinely happy to see us, always went out of his way to make us feel comfortable, always welcomed us as though we were family. He treated the world with respect and, through his actions, made it easy to love him. Carl Wilson's gone now, and we all deeply miss him.

BEACH BOYS ENTOURAGE (JULY 1964)

Standing in rear, left to right: *Carl Wilson, Jimmy Griffin, Mike Mitchell, Lil' Dickie, Connie Wright, John Hodges, Eddie Hodges, Brian (the tech guy), Security Guard Brian the cop (with wife), Barry Curtis* Kneeling in middle, left to right: *Mike Love and wife, unknown couple;* Lying down in front, left to right: *Dennis Wilson, Lynn Easton*

SAYING our good-byes to the other members of the Endless Summer tour was an emotional test. According to show biz tradition, acts always trash each other on the last show of a tour. Our last show, held in San Diego, was no exception, and fans simply had to put up with our antics as we all pulled tricks on one another throughout the evening. An abundance of toilet paper and, of course, shaving cream flew around the stage all night. Nearly all of the artists in the show were from the LA area, and many had family and friends in attendance. Afterward, most of them hitched rides home with whoever had come to see them, leaving the five of us nearly alone as we rode the bus back to LA. Absent our friends, absent the mayhem, absent the camaraderie, the atmosphere aboard the Greyhound was ghostly, almost funereal—perfect for sleeping, which we did.

WE were excited about meeting the legendary Dick Clark and appearing on *American Bandstand*, but unsure about how things would turn out for us with Shelly and Mel. We worried as well about Bill. I badly wanted to visit him, but Dick St. John said Bill was dealing with his condition and probably wouldn't be able to see us while we were in town.

The location was convenient, the digs were familiar and the price was right, so naturally, we had the bus drop us off at our "home away from home", the beloved Hollywood Center Motel with its sumptuous accommodations—nothing but the best for famous rock stars like us. We had a day to kill before taping *American Bandstand*, so we agreed to meet with Shelly and Mel on our day off. Shelly came to the motel to pick us up and take us to the hotel where Mel was staying.

Shelly Berger quickly showed himself to be one of the funniest people we'd ever met. He kept us laughing throughout the entire ride to Mel's hotel with a style of humor not unlike that of Don Rickles. He found flaws in everything and everyone and dissected those imperfections with the precision of a surgeon. He sliced and diced and cut apart his victims with sidesplittingly funny insults.

Mel, on the other hand, turned out to be a fun-loving former Air Force pilot who fancied fine cigars and dressed in high-dollar, custom-tailored suits. He projected the air of a "big deal guy" and had no problem trying to impress us by dropping names or making big promises, delivering it all in a smooth and inoffensive manner. Mel could've taught our designated Romeo Mike a few lessons about women. Absolutely fearless, he never missed an opportunity to use his smoothness on a member of the opposite sex. He'd approach any woman, any time, in any situation and try to impose his cunning charm on her. More often than not, he walked away with either a phone number or the woman.

He and Shelly spent the day telling us about their firm and the acts they managed. Amazingly, Don Rickles was one of their clients. They told us that Shelly would be working on the Hollywood side of things—TV, movies, fan magazines and the like—while Mel and Joe would be working on tours, on New York television and on the recording side of our career. Mel told us about their East Coast version of Shelly, Hermie Dressel. Hermie was a former drummer with the Woody Herman Band, a comical character whom we quickly accepted spiritually as "the sixth Kingsman."

Mel was aware that a member of their team needed to come up to Portland and get the once-over from our families, just like Bill Lee had done a few months earlier. Although we liked Mel, we connected and identified with Shelly in a much more brotherly way. His quick wit and big heart instantly drew all of us to him. Before the day was over, we were pretty well convinced Scandore and Shayne was the firm we wanted to be with.

Shelly and Mel went with us for the taping of the *Bandstand* show. Shelly knew everyone and everyone knew Shelly. Mel, meanwhile, spent most of his time with the executive suits. *American Bandstand* was taped at ABC and, before we left the studio that day, Shelly had worked his magic and booked us on a new rock 'n' roll television show on ABC called *Shindig*. He informed us we'd have to fly back to LA in a few weeks to tape our *Shindig* appearance.

Dick Clark was friendly and gracious. He asked about the words to "Louie Louie," expressing concern about us saying something on his show that might create a stir. We assured him the lyrics to "Louie"

Author on the drums, 1966

were quite tame and nothing to worry about. It was easy to see why so many musicians liked and respected him. He personally saw to it that his staff looked after us and treated us well. They made us feel like we were far more important than, in fact, we really were.

This being our first appearance on TV, we had quite a lot to learn in a very short time. The *Bandstand* crew showed us how to read the cue lights (which told us which camera was currently live), how to perform with less movement (so that the camera could remain steady and not induce motion sickness in viewers) and how to position our instruments for solos (so that the camera man could zoom in on the action). They explained additionally what we were to do in certain parts of the performance. Taping *American Bandstand* and working with the crew was a kick and, of course, it didn't hurt to meet our favorite female regulars who danced on the show.

With all of that excitement behind us, Shelly drove us to LAX. A few days later, he joined us in Portland, where his trial by fire went much the same as Bill's had gone earlier. Our families all loved him, for he had a special, endearing way about him. He could pick just the right things to put down, delivering non-stop lines that kept all of us holding our sides in laughter without ever offending. Initially out of affection for Shelly, we signed on with Scandore and Shayne and soon enjoyed rich rewards.

Over the previous eight months, we'd worked almost non-stop; over the next two years, we continued to work almost non-stop as well, only smarter and better: our performance fees increased, our tour schedule filled up with big-city, multi-act, high-visibility shows, our TV appearances multiplied to the point of becoming commonplace, and many other good things happened, mostly due to the professionalism and expertise of the staff at Scandore and Shayne. By the time the 1964 holiday season arrived, we'd appeared on several *Shindigs*, on *The Lloyd Thaxton Show*, on another *Bandstand* and on numerous local TV shows. We'd even found time to record a third album. We were well pleased with our choice for new management—a choice made at Bill Lee's urging.

VERSE 19

IT was approaching September and we were back on the road following the Beach Boy tour when my Uncle Art called my mother to let her know my car had arrived and would be waiting for me when I got home. Once she told me the good news, I called Uncle weekly for updates on its makeover. I didn't understand half of what he told me was being done, but it was fun feeling a part of the process. My excitement was building, and I couldn't wait to get home.

As soon as our tour ended, I hopped the first Greyhound I could for Olympia. Uncle Art picked me up there and drove me the last 14 miles to Shelton while I shared some of my road experiences and he talked about the car. I was a novice driver when it came to high performance machines, and he warned me to be careful—he didn't want to see me get into trouble trying to do foolish things I couldn't handle. At the Mel's Chevrolet dealership, he cunningly had my SS sitting in his showroom with all the bright spotlights shining off the gleaming red surface of the sexy looking car. It was love at first sight.

"Wow!" I said in shock as I walked into the showroom. "What a beauty!"

"Yeah, she turned out really nicely," he answered. He wore a vast smile and had the look of a proud papa in his eyes. You know that special look a father gets when he watches you when you gaze upon his newborn child for the first time?—he had it.

"Shall we light her up and take her out for a spin?" he asked, beaming.

"Oh, yeah!" I answered.

"Here are the keys," he said, dangling them in front of me.

As I reached for the keys, he closed his fist around them.

"Do you know how to drive a stick?" he asked.

"No, not yet," I answered, "but how hard can it be?"

Concerned about his showroom as well as my car, he answered, "Maybe I'd better pull her out of the showroom and let you take it from there."

"Good idea," I agreed.

He got in and started her up, while I stood to the side watching and listening.

Varooooom! the powerful red car sounded in a deep thunderous roar. *Varooooom! Varooooom!*

He pumped the gas as he looked out the rolled down window, wearing that unmistakable proud papa grin and seeking approval. Via a big grin, wordlessly I gave it.

"I split the manifold and put duals on her," he yelled over the roar.

I was almost afraid of the loud, deep-sounding machine. I walked around to the front of the car feeling an indelible, unerasable smile working its way onto my face. I followed Uncle Art as he backed her out through the double doors that separated the showroom from the rest of the dealership. The roar of the car fell dramatically when he finally reached the outside world.

"Get in," he said. "I'll take you out and show you what she'll do."

I jumped in, and he drove slowly through town. I could tell it was cool to drive that much power that slowly. People turned their heads at the shiny new red thundering race car as it slithered down Main Street, USA with the ease of a great jungle cat. When we reached the edge of town, Uncle stomped the accelerator to the floor. The car rose up and took off, pinning my head against the headrest. Amazing! With effortless skill, he speed shifted through the gears, squealing the tires with each powerful shift. A few miles out of town, he stopped the car in the middle of the road.

"What do you think?" he asked.

"Unbelievable!" I answered, trying to swallow my heart.

"You want to take it from here?" he said.

I wasn't sure I could, but I jumped out and ran around the car anyway. I slid behind the wheel, tingling with excitement and anticipation.

"Do you know what positraction is?" Uncle started.

"No, never heard of it," I answered.

"Well, it gives you more traction when you take off. It keeps the wheels from spinning by compensating for…"

He hesitated, seeing the puzzled look on my neophyte face.

"…It puts the power to both rear wheels for a better take off and less wheel spin," he said.

"Just take off, you'll see. The pedal on the left is the clutch. Push it in with your foot and start her up, put her in gear, give her some gas and let the clutch out."

Doing as he said, I pushed in the clutch, started her up, pushed the shifter handle forward and let out the clutch. The car lunged forward, giving our heads a tweak, and the engine immediately died.

"You have to give her more gas than that!" he said, laughing. "Try again."

Embarrassed, I again pushed in the clutch, started her up, pushed the shifter handle forward and did as I saw him do earlier, letting the clutch out as I pushed the gas pedal to the floor. This time, I was going to show that machine who was boss! Then the strangest thing happened. As I pushed the pedal to the floor, *nothing* happened. All I could hear was the roar of the engine as I pumped the gas. My uncle started rolling with laughter. As I continued to pump the gas, the car became enveloped in smoke—so much smoke, I couldn't see out the front window.

What's wrong with my new car? I asked myself.

Varooooom! Varooooom!

Surely I couldn't have broken my new car already, I thought.

Varooooom! Varooooom!

"Let off the gas a little," he yelled. "You're burning the tires off of her."

As I let off the gas, the tires caught hold of the hot pavement and we took off like a rocket. The tires made a sound that I'd never heard before. I'd expected to hear a screeching, but it was more like a zipping noise. I'd never driven a stick before, so I didn't know when to shift. As we cleared the smoke we were doing about 40.

"STOP!" Uncle yelled excitedly.

I hit the breaks, but forgot to push the clutch in, so as we screeched to a stop, the engine died again. I was petrified.

"Wow!" I said. "That was amazing! What happened?"

Uncle Art couldn't stop laughing.

"You were burnin' the tires off the darn thing!" he exclaimed. "You were just sitting there, spinning!"

"I was?" I asked innocently.

"That's what all of the smoke was" he continued, laughing. "You had the wheels spinning so fast, they wouldn't grip the pavement."

Using his sleeve, he wiped the tears of laughter from his eyes. Then the smell of burning tires caught up with us. It was noxious.

"Am I going to be able to drive this thing?" I asked.

"Yeah!" he laughed. "We just have to teach you how to drive a stick before you scare me half to death like that again."

Patiently, Uncle spent the next few hours suffering through head-snapping lunges and dash-grabbing stops until I could finally drive without requiring my future passengers to wear neck braces. For the next few days we worked on my hot rod driving skills and, by the end of the weekend, I not only could drive the car normally, but I'd learned how to speed shift and set the car up for drag racing. He gave me a crash course in how not to crash. Of course, starting on hills remained a major challenge for some time to come. Eventually, with the aid of a good emergency brake, I mastered that task as well. The head-turning car was amazingly fast and outrageously fun to drive. Uncle made me promise to limit my speed driving to the drag strip and keep it down on the streets—a promise I mostly kept.

The drive back to Portland brought a feeling of great independence. I was confident enough to feel I was in control of the little red rocket. (Thank God, I didn't have to stop on any hills between Shelton and Portland.)

EVERY town across America had a local teen hang out back then—and probably still does today, for that matter. Usually it came in the form of a drive-in filled with cars and kids. *The* place to hang in Portland was a drive-in named Yaw's. I'd never been into frequenting the local teen hot spots or hanging out just to be hanging out. As I stated earlier, I was into music as a youth and, through my high school years, I felt that socializing with a bunch of teenagers just doing nothing was a giant waste of time. However, on this occasion, as I drove back to Portland, Yaw's was the first place I wanted to take my new ride.

As I drove into the teen-filled drive-in, I could clearly see my car was the rage. I cruised through at Uncle's cool speed—as slowly as my car would idle without dying—and parked my awesome roaring machine right in front of the entrance. It took less than a minute for several of my classmates to recognize me and swarm my car, wanting to see the motor and asking questions to which I had no good answers. The word was out: I was a Kingsmen, I had the money, I had the car, I had the fame. Suddenly I was Mr. Popular, Mr. Where It's At, Mr. Happening, Mr. Cool.

Although I'd maintained a rather quiet role in high school, now, with fame, I'd become the center of attention. It felt strange to be treated by my peers at home the same way I was treated by teens on the road. From then on, it was too easy. I hate to admit it but, sadly, at 18 I started believing my own PR and was becoming a *bona fide* famous teenage idiot. Others saw me as cool, so I started seeing myself as cool, too. All I needed now was to get my period and I would be *completely* cool.

Author's 1965 Chevrolet Chevelle Malibu Super Sport 327 V-8

VERSE 20

FOR our next tour, we once again took the old reliables: our Pontiac Bonneville Safari station wagon and our Ford Econoline van. But, especially after our Beach Boys tour, we'd become convinced that traveling by bus would be much more comfortable and practical. Considering my dad's long career with Greyhound, I was given the task of calling him up and asking him to help us find a bus in good condition to purchase.

Instead of starting in the Midwest, as most of our previous tours had done, Bob had us playing in the Northwest for a week before working our way east. The first few gigs were short runs, and the routing made it easy for Lynn's wife Karen to join us for a few days. We were to play a gig in Bend, Oregon, an easy three-hour drive from Portland, and Lynn and Karen decided to drive over together using their own car.

We all noticed and thought it strange that the FBI was absent from all our Northwest dates. Playing a concert without the men in the grey flannel suits being present and taking notes felt odd. We hadn't seen any of Hoover's agents for so long, we began to think maybe they'd dropped their investigation.

I rode in the van with Jimmy-John (Jim's new star name), and Mike and Norm followed us in the Pontiac. Barry had been in Yakima and joined us in Bend that afternoon. As we drove into the parking lot of the town Armory, Barry met us with an odd smile on his face, shaking his head in disbelief.

"We've played a lot of crazy places before and been on a lot a of weird stages, but I don't think you guys are going to be ready for this one," said Barry, scratching his head.

"What's the deal?" laughed Norm as he climbed out of the

station wagon.

"They're using the wrestling ring for the stage, mats and all!" snickered Barry.

"Are you kidding me? I gotta see this!" said the curious Norm.

The Bend Armory was vintage Army blueprint material, identical to every other armory in the United States. The cement floor, metal ceiling and walls made it a challenging place to play. The standard musician joke was, "The echo was so bad in the armories, you could continue dancing to the music for 30 minutes after the band went home."

When I hopped up on the ring and landed, it felt like I was on a trampoline, and it took three or four rebounds before I stopped bouncing.

"Oh, no!" laughed Norm. "This is going to be bizarre. The instruments will be all over the place!"

Forever in search of fun, we all had to take turns testing the springy ring floor. By the time Lynn and Karen arrived, we had most of the ring set up, and I was trying to nail my drums to the bouncing make-shift stage. After getting over the shock of such a comical place to perform, Lynn told us that, in an effort to make a statement to the record company, he and Karen had written some new lyrics to the tune of "Big Boy Pete" while on their trip to Bend. Lynn thought that perhaps by recording a spoof, we could send a message to the record company and they'd finally let us have some freedom in the recording process.

Heretofore, Jerry and Stanley chose selections from our shows to record for our albums. They didn't seem to care what the recordings sounded like, nor did they care if the performances were less than perfect. We wanted to take a lesson from the Beach Boys and record new material, keeping quality of sound and level of performance in mind in order to better match the capabilities and demands of the technically-evolving radio market. When we heard them, we all thought Lynn and Karen's lyrics were hilarious and couldn't wait to get into the studio to teach our record producers a lesson.

That evening, we bounced and ricocheted off one another all night long—a moving, three-rope experience—without inflicting too much damage on the equipment or ourselves. On the plus side, I came away from the Bend Armory having developed and perfected a new technique for playing my drums while chasing them across a bouncing stage. It's a technique I've never used since, although, should an earthquake ever strike during a Kingsmen performance, I'm sure it will prove handy.

After signing autographs and answering all the usual questions about "Louie Louie," we finally got our equipment loaded as the echo of the music slowly decayed in the reverberating acoustical nightmare.

Planning to drive back to Portland, Norm and Mike and Barry hit the road as soon as the equipment was loaded. Lynn lingered at the armory, settling accounts with the promoter, while Karen stood outside by her car visiting with Jimmy-John and me. We were having a pretty good time joking about the stage and their new lyrics to "Big Boy Pete" when Karen turned serious.

"Is Lynn drinking out on the road?" she asked with obvious concern.

"Why do you ask?" I answered, hoping to avoid her question.

"Well, he seems to be... almost needing a couple of drinks every night, and I'm wondering if this is something he just does at home or if this is getting to be a habitual thing that I should be worried about."

I could tell it was a difficult subject for her to breach.

"Well, to tell you the truth," I said, "we've been a little worried about him ourselves. But he's been a ton better since we hired Mel to take over some of the responsibilities of the band. We all thought he was having a few drinks because he was away from you, and maybe because of having to deal with all of the pressures of the road."

"If it doesn't continue to get better, or if starts to get any worse, will you let me know?" she sincerely asked. "I'm a little worried about him."

Trying to lighten the mood, the ever-smiling GI Joe Jimmy-John jokingly interjected, "Hell, I'll just tell him I'll beat the crap out of him if he has another drink—if you want me to!"

"I'll have to get back to you on that one, James," Karen said, patronizing Jim and laughing. "I promise, I'll definitely let you know if I need you to take such a drastic action."

Just then, Lynn came out of the Armory.

"I'll let you know how it's going," I said quickly.

"Good," Karen said, smiling. "I hope everything keeps going well."

She covered our conversation nicely with Lynn and, as Jimmy-John and I drove back to Portland, we agreed to tell the other guys about our conversation with her. We loved Lynn and were concerned and puzzled as to what was triggering his self-destructive behavior; we were too young and immature to know how to help him with his growing problem.

SEVERAL weeks later, we found ourselves in a two-track recording studio in Seattle, recording more of the same crap covers that Jerry Dennon thought were proven sellers. As the session was coming to an end, Lynn pulled out of his briefcase the lyrics that he and Karen first showed us in Bend. This gave vitality and new energy to the mundane and disappointing Gestapo-like atmosphere.

"Hey, Jerry, I've got an idea for a novelty record," Lynn said, smiling.

"Nutty!" responded Jerry. ["Nutty" was Jerry's pet phrase and his general response to everything.] "Let's take a look at it."

Knowing it was a joke, the rest of us cast each other playful glances as Jerry read Lynn's lyrics.

"Nutty!" said Jerry, laughing. "'The Jolly Green Giant'—I like it! These lyrics are really very cleverly written. Did you write this, Lynn?"

"Yeah!"

"What's the music like?" asked the enthusiastic record producer.

Lynn explained the lyrics were to be sung to the tune of "Big Boy Pete," a 1958 hit by The Olympics. To further the hoax, Lynn told Jerry that we'd been performing this version of "Big Boy Pete" in our shows for weeks, and that it was going over well with audiences. Surprised by the enterprising Mr. Easton, his excitement bubbling over, Jerry sent us back into the studio to cut the track before we packed up and left for home.

Knowing the joke was on Jerry, and that we'd be making a statement to him and Scepter/Wand, we literally ran into the studio, filled with a great deal of impromptu impetuosity. We banged and crashed our way through the comical tune in typical Kingsmen fashion, making sure that everything was louder than everything else at all times. Once we finished the music track, we broke into raucous laughter and couldn't wait to hear the playback. Since this was a two-track studio, we recorded all of the music on one track and all of the vocals on the other. Lynn grabbed a tambourine and played it as he and Mike added the duet vocals while Barry, our simulated bass singer, added the "yea ye yow wa"s which were traditionally performed between vocal lines on "Big Boy Pete."

Laughing all the time, Norm and I watched and listened to the trio from the control room. Wearing their headphones, they clearly were having a ball singing the comical lyrics. Lynn shook the tambourine and hit it against his leg as he and Mike sang about the famous, giant green veggie-pushing character. Intentionally or not, they cracked us up.

> *You've heard about the Jolly Green Giant.*
> *Yea ye yow wa*
> *He's so big and green.*
> *Yea ye yow wa*
> *He stand's there laughin' with his hands on his hips...*

Well, you get the picture.

They were about halfway through the masterpiece when, all of a sudden, Barry started interrupted everyone.

"Stop!" he yelled. "Stop the tape! Stop it!"

Carnie, the engineer, quickly stopped the tape, and Jerry pushed the button on the control board that allows the control room to talk to the performers out in the studio.

"What's the trouble, Barry?" he asked.

Barry was laughing so hard, he couldn't answer Jerry immediately. Slowly, between gasps, he was able to communicate his inspiration.

"I have an idea!" he announced.

His laughter was infecting us like a virus, and soon we all lost it.

"Why don't I say different vegetables instead of the 'yea yee yow wa's?'" Barry suggested.

"Nutty!" laughed Jerry.

"Let's do it!" said Lynn.

We all went for his idea instantly, it added to the joke so nicely. The dynamics here were hilarious: we were laughing not only because the song was so comical, but because the more ridiculous the joke grew, the more Jerry—thinking we were serious—swallowed the bait.

"Hey!" said Barry. "Give me a minute to make a list of vegetables. I don't want to run out of veggies halfway through this festival of vegetables!"

"JOLLY GREEN GIANT" RECORDING SESSION,
AUDIO RECORDING, SEATTLE—1964
Left to right: *Jimmy-John, Lynn, Jerry Dennon, Mike, Karney Barton (engineer)*

We started throwing out suggestions, some of them bizarre, like rutabaga and egg plant. The less common the veggie, the more Barry liked it, and the harder we laughed.

Carnie started rolling the tape once again, and Barry kept us in stitches, proclaiming broccoli, spinach, artichoke hearts and the like instead of saying "Yea ye yow wa." Inspired by Barry's vegetable offerings, Lynn and Mike fell to the floor laughing once Barry declared "and Beans" at the end of the song.

Jerry and Carnie were in tears, so out of control I thought they were going to be sick. We enjoyed the adventure several more times through repeated playbacks until we were no longer capable of laughing any more. As we packed up our equipment, Lynn said it best: "Let's see what Scepter thinks about that!"

"What do you think, Jer?" asked Norm.

"Nutty!" answered Jerry with a big grin on his face. "Nutty."

We had a great time during the 180-mile trip home, certain that when Scepter heard our latest musical entrée, they'd call up Mel in protest and then, perhaps, we could finally have a say in the recording process.

VERSE 21

A few weeks later, Shelly called to inform us that we'd be coming back to Hollywood just after the holidays. Only this time, it would be—hold on to your hats!—to film a Frankie and Annette Beach Party movie, *How to Stuff a Wild Bikini*. Wow, were we impressed—not only with Shelly, but with ourselves as well. He said that we'd be in LA for at least a week shooting the film and that, while we were there, we were going to tape another episode of *Shindig*. Asked who was starring in the movie, Shelly started listing the Hollywood luminaries we'd be rubbing elbows with: Mickey Rooney, Annette Funicello, Dwayne Hickman, Frankie Avalon, Elizabeth Montgomery, Buster Keaton, Brian Donlevy, Harvey Lembeck—the impressive list seemed endless and left us joyously star-struck.

Bushels full of memories came attached to some of those names. I was raised on the *Mickey Mouse Club* and, like 99 percent of boys my age in America, I'd also had a childhood crush on Annette. And now I was actually going to meet her! Short in height, Mickey Rooney stood about as tall as any star you could name in the film industry. The fact that he was in the film impressed my family the most. Elizabeth Montgomery starred on *Bewitched*, then a top-rated TV show, Buster Keaton was a show biz legend, and Frankie Avalon had long been one of America's most popular teen idols/crooners (although he'd long since passed out of his teenage years).

Shelly told us we were going to have a cameo in the movie. Discovering that none of us had a clue as to what a cameo was he explained, after a few comical hicksville/Don Rickles-type put downs, that we were supposed to be a band playing in the teen club that Frankie and Annette frequented. We were going perform one song by ourselves, in the club, with all the Beach Party kids dancing crazily. After that, Annette's character, "Dee Dee," was going to join us on stage to sing a second song. We were to have no lines or acting parts in the movie.

Never having seen a Beach Party movie, I started looking for theaters that were showing them. (Remember, this was 1964, long before VHS or DVD technology, an age that worshiped eight-track tapes as the greatest audio innovation ever.) I tried to find movies with afternoon showings, but most all of them played in drive-ins at night. I managed to see one or two of them, anyway, and got the general idea of what they were about (straight-arrow boy meets straight-arrow girl/girls run around in bikinis/dirty old men leer and lust/virtue triumphs in the end/no drugs, no real sex, just boys and girls singing and dancing and playing on the beach). Predictably, Mike claimed—or should I say, *bragged*—that although he hadn't seen any of the teen epics, he'd *heard* them all.

Trying to maximize our time in LA, Shelly thought it would be a good idea if we scheduled a meeting with Ernie Leaner, our regional record distributor. He said that reps from all over the country would be in LA for a convention that same week, and that it would be a good opportunity for us to get to know the people who worked in the trenches. He advised us it was time we started playing a little politics that could help build our career.

"Besides," he said, "you're going there to work, not to play!"

Shelly also informed us that he'd set up an appointment with Raphael, a high fashion photographer in Beverly Hills. We learned that Scandore and Shayne agreed with the majority of Kingsmen about the poor quality of our existing promotional pictures. Mike, Barry, Norm and I were ecstatic about this news; Lynn was not, but he lost the argument. *Finally*, we could retire the hated "Lynn Easton and the Kingsmen" picture. Shelly said that the first time he saw that photo, he wondered whether we'd stopped by the Hollywood Wax Museum and had them do our make-up. How else to explain the scary-looking image? As we talked amongst ourselves, we realized that Dick St. John had been right—hiring professional managers who understood what steps to take and how to keep a career moving forward was indeed the correct thing for us to do.

Although the Hollywood Center Motel was no image builder, due to its central location and cut-rate prices, we once again decided to stay at our beloved "home away from home." When we checked in, we discovered that Paul Revere and the Raiders were already enjoying the deluxe accommodations offered by this showcase property (*i.e.*, they had indoor plumbing that usually worked). Mike and Lynn had known Paul's group for years and were delighted to share a couple of adjoining rooms with the always-ready-to-party Raiders. Within a few hours, both bands were treating each other like brothers and doing crazy, mischievous things involving pool chairs and wet towels.

The Raiders were barely bubbling under at the time and were in Hollywood to take a shot at turning the corner to the big time. ["Bubbling under" is a music industry term referring to a record whose sales are just below the point of winning a place on *Billboard*'s Top 100 list.] The determined Raiders would leave the amenity-challenged motel in the morning around the same time we did and spend the day beating the bushes in a tenacious effort to develop relationships that would be the key to unlocking the magical doors of show biz. At the end of the day, both bands reconvened around the pool to relive their latest adventures while downing a few beers and laughing at the Hollywood mogul-types we had to deal with. Sharing time and experiences like that made it a fun few weeks for both bands.

FOR our first day on the set, Shelly picked us up in his instantly admired white '62 Thunderbird convertible a few hours before we were supposed to report. Having decided to wear all black with yellow waistcoats in the movie, we packed our garb the night before in individual hang bags. Our guitars and bags easily fit in Shelly's oversized trunk. He had the top down, making it easy for us to see the sights and enjoy the exhilarating drive up to the front gate of American International Pictures film studios.

As we approached the famous entrance, a security guard emerged from the postage stamp-sized guardhouse. After making sure we were on his list of expected celebrities, he gave us an envelope containing our passes. Shelly joked with the man and did his best to make a big deal out of us, informing him that we'd be on the set for the following week. If you drew attention to yourself the first time you met people like the guard, Shelly reasoned, you wouldn't get hassled in the future if those people already knew who you were. Sounded good to me! Shelly held our hands that day, teaching us the protocols we needed to know to operate successfully on a motion picture lot. Some of the rules: Never open a studio door when the red light is on; Never ask a guy pushing a spotlight for directions; Never talk while the cameras are rolling; and Never, *never ever* open a dressing room or trailer door without knocking first.

The AIP studio was awesomely huge, easily larger than a football field. Padding covered the several-stories-high walls, and movie sets sat side by side throughout the busy and clutter-filled film factory.

American International Pictures had made a name for itself in the '50s turning out such drive-in movie classics as *Bucket of Blood* and *I Was a Teenage Werewolf*. Home to legendary B-movie director Roger Corman (*Attack of the Crab Monsters* and many other gems of the genre), AIP ventured in new directions in the early '60s, upgrading its image in the public eye. One of those new directions was a series of films—*The Fall of the House of Usher, The Raven, The Pit and the Pendulum* and others—based on the works of Edgar Allen Poe and starring Vincent Price. Another was a series of Beach Party movies—*Beach Party, Bikini Beach, Beach Party Bingo* and others—based on an innocent fantasy vision of life created by Hollywood dreamweavers and starring Frankie Avalon and Annette Funicello and a long list of old-school Hollywood icons (Mickey Rooney and Buster Keaton among them). The movies AIP churned out may not always have won the favor of high fallutin', big-name film critics, but they were wildly popular with American teens, which is exactly what we Kingsmen were and precisely the demographic group we understood best. In our world, you could hardly get more Hollywood than AIP.

After locating our dressing rooms and receiving our shooting schedule, we had some time to burn, and I decided to take a walk around the lot and see some of the hallowed ground that was off limits to everyone save those fortunate few who worked on or behind the silver screen (or those privileged few like me that had an artist pass).

Cutting between a couple of studio buildings, I came upon a three-

or-four space parking area. An elderly white-haired gentleman was just pulling into one of the parking spaces in a brand new, baby blue, four-door Lincoln Continental convertible with matching baby blue leather interior. I froze in my tracks, mouth wide open, savoring the beautiful, unusual work of Detroit art.

"I've never seen a more beautiful car," I told the man as he got out of his slice of heaven on wheels. "Was this a custom order? I didn't know Lincoln made cars this shade of blue."

"Yes, actually, it *was* a custom order," answered the well-dressed gentleman, beaming with pride. "It took quite a while for me to get Lincoln to make this car for me, but when it arrived, I was quite pleased."

Being young, enthusiastic and curious, I asked if I could check out his one-of-a-kind automobile.

"Sure," said the friendly gentleman, "jump behind the wheel if you like."

In less than an instant, I was sitting behind the baby blue wheel. The smell of the soft supple leather was divine, and the carpeting was plush and deep to the touch. Everything in the luxury car color-matched everything else perfectly.

Getting out of his car, I offered the man my hand in friendship. "My name is Dick."

"Glad to know you, Dick," he replied. "My friends call me Jim."

"Hey, Jim," I said as we shook hands.

"Where are you from?" he asked, smiling.

"I'm from Portland, Oregon," I replied. "Where are you from?"

"I live here in LA," he answered. "What brings you all the way from Portland, Oregon to AIP?"

"I'm going to be in a movie with Frankie and Annette," I proudly said. "Do you know who they are?"

"I think so, yes," he smiled.

"Yeah, their movies are geared for a pretty young crowd," I said, thinking he was probably not young enough to know who Frankie and Annette were. "But Mickey Rooney is in the movie, too, and I bet you know who he is!"

"I sure do!" said Jim. "What's the name of this movie of yours?"

"*How to Stuff a Wild Bikini*," I answered, laughing. "It's kind of a funny title, but it's a Beach Party movie. I'm not a star in the movie or anything like that. I'm in a rock 'n' roll band, and we're doing what they call a cameo spot in the movie. Do you know what a cameo is?"

"Yes, I do, Dick," he answered.

"I just learned what a cameo was," I said. "What brings you here, Jim?"

I continued to look over his car as I awaited his reply.

"I had some business to take care of," he answered, "so I thought I'd try to get to it today."

"Oh, what studio are you going to?"

"I'm not going to a studio. I'm going to the business offices."

"Well, you should see a studio while you're here. It's an amazing sight that everyone should see."

"You think so?"

Jim was a kind, grandfatherly type of man, and I thought I'd make his day. After all, he took the time to share his car with me.

"Take a look at this," I said as I showed him my artist pass. "I can go any place I want to go with this thing, and I can invite any guest I want to go with me, too. When you're finished with your business, if you have time, just walk over to Studio 4. Ask for me, and I'll introduce you to some movie stars and show you around the place. Who knows when you might have a chance like this again."

"I'll see what I can do," said the man, sounding genuinely grateful.

Thinking I'd better get back to the set, I said good-bye to Jim, and we went our separate ways. When I met up with the other guys, I told them about Jim and his baby-blue Lincoln. Mike was a Lincoln lover and was currently in the market for a gold four-door and really wanted to see the unique automobile.

Knowing an easy mark when he saw one, Shelly got a laugh from the guys at my expense.

"Golly gee, Dickie," he said, "anybody else would've, oh, I don't know, maybe used this opportunity to invite a girl to impress her into the sack. But you, you putz, you invite a grandpa!"

"Lil' Dickie's not a man yet, Shelly," Lynn said, laughing. "He hasn't had his period yet. It's better if he stays with the grandpas for a while."

"Did I hear you correctly, or is it something in the Oregon water?"

Shelly said, laughing and blinking his eyes in disbelief.

Everybody was cracking up at Shelly's comment when the stage manager pounded on our dressing room door, calling us to the set.

As we followed the stage manager to the sound stage, Mike whispered to Norm, "Shelly almost busted us."

"Yeah, we'd better tell him about the period thing right away, before he blows it for us," said Mike, causing them to giggle as they walked.

The stage manager took us to the set, where he introduced us to the director of the film, William Asher. After the usual exchange of pleasantries, Mr. Asher gave each of us a copy of the script and, sitting in a circle, he began reading through the pages with us, directing our performance. Talk about feeling special and cool, it was like a scene from a movie.

Mr. Asher explained his plans for filming our musical sequences and showed us how he would like us to set up on stage. He wanted Mike, Lynn and Norm to be in front of Barry and me. His plan was to do several takes of each song. First he was going to film the five of us as we performed the first song. Then he was going to change the set up (which meant changing camera angles and lighting) and film just Barry and me performing both songs because we couldn't be seen very well from the first set of camera angles and he wanted to get some unobstructed shots of us for the editors.

Extremely nice to us and a true professional, Mr. Asher said we'd meet most of the principals when we came back to do our cameo. He asked to take a look at the wardrobe we were planning to wear for the cameo, and I volunteered to fetch my outfit for him. Thrilled and excited to be in the middle of this movie adventure, I was barely able to keep contact with the floor as I walked back to the dressing room to retrieve my yellow-and-black costume.

According to the script, one of us was to introduce "Dee Dee" (Annette) between songs. This was a speaking part, and Mr. Asher asked whether any of us had ever had any acting experience. Lynn said that in high school he'd taken drama and been in several plays, so Mr. Asher gave him the part and a whole two days to learn his line. Lynn spent that time working the line with a thousand different emotional readings. He was really nervous and understandably didn't want to flub his acting debut. By the end, to a man, we knew his line as well as he did and were going mental at his over-rehearsing.

The following morning, we were to prerecord the tracks to the songs we were performing in the movie. Mr. Asher's assistant gave Shelly the directions to the recording studio. The AD [assistant director] told us that if they were able to stay on their shooting schedule, we'd be filming our scenes in the movie in two or three days—after the tracks were recorded. We'd be officially on call over the next few days, and he needed to make sure that we'd be reachable.

WITH us scheduled to record the tracks for the movie at 4 PM the following afternoon, Shelly set up a morning appointment for us with the record distributors. We decided to wear our black Kingsmen sweaters, an unfortunate move for me. When Shelly picked us up to take us to the meeting and saw the monogram on my sweater reading "The Kingsmen Dick," it inspired a day's worth of comedic material for Shelly and a day's worth of embarrassment for me.

Shelly had us howling as we entered the distributor's offices. Inside, he used the printing on our sweaters to break the ice and make the many nationwide record reps feel comfortable around us. As we stood before them, he introduced us one by one to the smiling crowd, pointing out that our mommies had made it easy for them to tell us apart by sewing our names on our sweaters.

"Gentleman, as you can see," Shelley said, "by his cute little name tag, this is The Kingsmen Lynn, this is The Kingsmen Mike, this is The Kingsmen Barry, this is The Kingsmen Norm and last, but certainly not least, I give you The Kingsmen Dick."

That brought the house down and color to my cheeks. Seeing where he was heading by the time he introduced Mike, I played along with the humiliation.

"I hope I become your favorite member of The Kingsmen!" I said when introduced, raising my hands like a prizefighter and stepping forward.

Once again, the room erupted in laughter. Our good-natured

joking neutralized the awkwardness usually found in these kinds of meetings and made it much easier for the reps to approach us. As we visited with them, Ernie, the hosting distributor, surprised us.

"We're wild about your new single and think it's going to be a monster hit!" he said, handing Lynn a 45. "Can I get you boys to autograph it for me? I want to hang it on the wall in my office."

"New single?" questioned a confused Lynn.

"*What* new single?" added a surprised Mike as he looked over Lynn's shoulder.

"'The Jolly Green Giant,' of course. Didn't you know it was going to be your next single?"

We stood there in silent shock, our jaws scraping the floor.

"Oh, no!" said Barry at last. "We were saving it for a special occasion!"

We were incredulous. The suits in New York hadn't gotten the joke we sent them in protest. Instead, they'd released the cornucopia of musical innuendos, thinking it was a serious record. We realized then they might *never* get it. Deluged with accolades from the reps about our clever new party record, we began to think maybe *we* were the ones stuck in the Dark Ages who didn't get it.

To our great astonishment, that record screamed up the charts, soon eclipsing the popularity of "Louie Louie." We left the meeting venting our concerns about the record company with Shelly, who was less than sympathetic. He liked "The Jolly Green Giant" and thought it was going to be a number one record for us. He added that, since the song was about the giant trying to get laid, it would create a resurgence of the "Louie Louie" controversy.

Boy, was he right. The Libby Corporation East Coast Division started setting up giant blow-up statues of their character at the entrances to our concerts in the Midwest and sending truckloads of canned vegetables to give away to the kids as they left. Having no sense of humor, and failing to see the value of the free exposure we were giving them, Libby's West Coast Division sued us for allegedly defaming their character. And the FBI, facing increased pressure, intensified their efforts to prove that "Louie Louie" was indeed obscene.

It took months to get it all straightened out, but eventually, Libby's West Coast Division joined the marketing-conscious East in supporting the record, thereby aiding and abetting our star-crossed rise to fame. In the oddest twist of fate of all, thanks to everything else going on, even the omnipresent FBI agents got into the act. After standing in front of the PA cabinets and taking notes all night, the boys in grey now joined us in passing out cans of Green Giant food to departing fans, helping to make the exiting process a little more orderly. From time to time, we exchanged small talk with the G-men, and they seemed to enjoy the change of pace. I wonder how much of that chit-chat made it into the reports that landed on J. Edgar's desk? I began half-detecting sympathy in some of the agents.

In an effort to take advantage of the surging popularity of our new hit, the record company released our third album, creatively titled "Volume 3" and featuring the despised first photo on the back cover (sometimes it's better to be lucky than good).

We left the record distributor meet-and-greet feeling pessimistic

Jolly Green Giant doll presentation
at Lake Hills Roller Rink,
Bellevue, Washington, 1965. Left to right: *Mike, Barry, Lynn, J.G. Giant,* DJ Pat O'Day of KJR-AM, *Lil' Dickie, Norm*

and rather down. We'd expected "The Jolly Green Giant" to flop and had counted on its failure to put us in the driver's seat, but that's not how things were working out. Thankfully, Shelly succeeded in getting us back on track attitude-wise by the start of our recording session that afternoon. Hoping still for the song's failure, we continued to enjoy our movie-making experience for a few more days.

The studio we used for the pre-recording was impressive. They had three-track recorders, enabling us to record the music in stereo and record the vocals and solos on the third track. What a luxury! We were well-rehearsed before we left Portland, and it didn't take long to lay down our tracks for the film.

We were given an early call to be on the set the following morning. The studio sent a limo to the motel, creating quite a stir among our fellow economically-aware, transient musician boarders. It was the first time any of us had been in a limo. The long luxury car came complete with a telephone, an eight track tape player, a power window between the driver and passenger compartments, an AM/FM radio, a sun roof and, to top it all off, a full bar.

Shelly met us at the studio and waited with us as the shooting fell behind schedule. They were trying to film a motorcycle stunt, and it was taking longer than expected. The AD told us we were free to wander the lot, but to check back with him every hour or so. I decided to go to the commissary and get a bite to eat. I couldn't get anyone to go with me, so I went alone. The guys were sticking around in hopes of meeting a few of the stars who were also on call and patiently waiting somewhere for the club scene to begin.

As I stood in the commissary line, I saw Jim sitting alone at a table by the wall of the cafeteria. I paid for my lunch and walked over to his table.

"Hey, Jim," I said, "are you expecting anyone to join you for lunch?"

"No," he answered, looking pleased to see me. "Please, sit down. I'd welcome the company."

We laughed and joked about the general goings on at AIP and I once again invited him to visit our studio. He told me he knew he wouldn't be able to visit that particular afternoon but that he may have some time in a few days and would do his best to find me then. I told him about Mike wanting to see his Lincoln, and he said he'd be more than happy to show it to him anytime.

Upon my return to the studio, the guys met me with some

degree of anxiety in their demeanor. We'd been dismissed for the day, and they'd been looking for me everywhere. I asked if it had dawned on them that I might be where I said I was going to be, in the commissary, but no one seemed to remember my asking them to join me for a bite to eat. Mike said he checked the commissary, but didn't see me. I told them I was sitting by the wall with my friend Jim who owned the blue Lincoln.

Shelly told me next time to make sure *he* knew where I was because the others were too star-struck to have their wits about them. He explained that since we'd been dismissed early, he'd called Raphael to see if he could take a few studio shots. Raphael was free, and Shelly wanted to get us to his studio as soon as possible. Obedient servants that we were, we packed up at once and had the limo drop us there.

We all liked Raphael at once. He made us feel comfortable, confident and relaxed during the photo session, like a true professional would, and was open to our suggestions. His studio was airy and bright, offering a much different experience from what our first encounter with a professional photographer was like. We told him about the movie we were doing and that we'd be in town for another week, taping *Shindig*. If he had the time, we said, we could meet him for another session to make sure he got everything he wanted. Our work that day completed, Raphael told Shelly he wanted to take some outdoor shots of us, and Shelly scheduled another day with him and also invited him to photograph the *Shindig* show. They were friends, and Raphael was willing to work a little harder and go the extra mile for Shelly.

THE following morning, the studio limo picked us up at our motel and took us to AIP for an early call. When we arrived on the set, the place was buzzing with action. They'd planned to get to us today, but the AD explained they were going to shoot the motorcycle crash stunt first, within the next few hours. As soon as that was finished, they'd reset the cameras and film our scenes. He encouraged us to hang around, saying this was something not to be missed.

We watched as they set up several extra cameras as insurance policies—in case something happened to one, they wanted to have several back ups. We listened as the stunt man went over the choreography of his feat again and again—a wise idea, for the studio wanted to get it just right and, more importantly, he'd be risking life and limb.

We were excited by what we saw and heard while, at the same time, disappointed by the delay—disappointed, that is, until Shelly told us that, as per our contract that he'd negotiated with the production company, we were making an extra $2,500 a day in overtime penalties. The studio was already three days behind and, despite promises to the contrary, it didn't look like they were going to get to our scenes for another few days at least. *Ka-ching, ka-ching, ka-ching.* That clinking sound we heard in the distance was that of a cash register adding up our extra earnings. We quickly decided that production delays were good things after all.

Of the hundreds of people who converged on the set to watch the motorcycle stunt, very few were principal actors in the movie; most were dancers, stagehands and extras. By late afternoon, all was ready for shooting the dramatic single-take scene. Tension mounted as we heard the stunt man revving his engine somewhere in the far reaches of the studio, readying for takeoff. Unseen, motorcycle and rider sounded like they were hundreds of feet away.

Varooooom! Varooooom! Varooooom!

The studio's sound-proofing only partially muffled the swelling screams. The distant reverberations reminded me vaguely of my new Malibu's roar.

With everything set to his liking, Mr. Asher abruptly gave the cue, "Cameras!"

With cameras rolling, the cinematographer yelled "Speed!"

With no turning back, Mr. Asher yelled "Action!"

With loud reports, bellowing engine and screeching tire shouted "Here he comes!" and, like an oncoming missile, the motorcycle hurtled toward us behind a cacophonous blast of sound.

Seconds later, like Evel Knievel, cycle and stunt man exploded through the wall of the set. A startling crash separated the two and sent the rider cart-wheeling through the air. When he returned to earth, a deep expanse of padding cushioned his landing. As the

Photograph taken by Raphael during our stay in LA shooting How to Stuff a Wild Bikini

stunt man raised his arms in victory, onlookers applauded, filled with admiration for the man and relieved that he was unharmed.

ANOTHER two days passed before the AD called Shelly and told him they were finally ready for us. Once again, the limo picked us up and delivered us to the lot. Walking into the studio, we noticed a group of people clustered around Mr. Asher, heads down, scripts in hand, engaged in animated conversation. Hearing us enter, they all looked up, and I immediately recognized several famous faces.

"Hey, Kingsmen, come over here!" our director called out enthusiastically. "I want you to meet a few of the cast!"

"This is our leading lady," he began, "Annette Funicello. Annette, I'd like you to meet The Kingsmen. This is Mike, Lynn, Barry, Norm and Dick."

"Hi, Annette, I'm Dick Peterson," I said nervously when it came my turn to address her.

"Dick, it's so nice to meet you," she answered graciously, reaching out and shaking my hand.

At her touch, I felt a thrill I can compare to this day only with what I felt when Penny Harper sat down next to me in the Gig Harbor movie house in fifth grade. How appropriate. My fifth grade year was exactly the same time I was nursing my boyhood fantasy crush on Annette during her Mickey Mouse Club days. From Penny Harper's cotton dress to Annette Funicello's hand—I was moving up in the world!

Meeting people like Annette, whom I'd always thought of in bigger-than-life terms, I felt excited and thrilled on the one hand and embarrassed and intimidated on the other. They were all in costume and had been working out the scene they were about to shoot. Annette's wardrobe was especially loose-fitting and not particularly flattering. We had been told she was pregnant and her wardrobe was designed to hide her delicate condition. *"If Annette can have sex,"* I thought at the time, *"my day will surely come!"*

"And this is Harvey Lembeck," Mr. Asher continued.

"I can't believe I'm meetin' da Kingsmen," Harvey said with a smile, his New York accent sounding like Von Zipper. Shaking Mike's hand, he added, "Finally, I get to know the real words to 'Louie Louie!' Don't I, fellas?"

In a softer voice that all could hear but played to a sense of respect for Annette, he added, "But you should wait until a more private time because I don't tink Miss Annette should be hearin' such tings."

Everyone laughed and instantly the tension and intimidation I'd been feeling disappeared.

Being a true comedian, Mickey Rooney couldn't resist raising the bar on Harvey in the spirit of one-upsmanship.

"You can tell the real words to 'Louie Louie' to Harvey," he said, "but you'll have to write them down for me. I'm friends with J. Edgar Hoover, and I know it would mean so much to him."

"Oh, by the way," he added, saluting us and bowing slightly, then warmly shaking our hands, "I'm Mickey Rooney. Pleased to meet you guys."

While Mickey's comments added to the friendly atmosphere, a come-back from the sweet and smiling and quick-witted Annette put her male co-stars in their place.

"Just remember, boys," she said, "if there are any words in that song that you don't understand, just come see me and I'll be happy to explain them to you."

Considering that she was with child at the time, and the likelihood that her condition was not the result of immaculate conception, my favorite Mouseketeer must have known *something* about doing the deed.

Mr. Asher had just finished introducing us to Duane ("Dobie Gillis") Hickman, when TV's most famous nose appeared.

"I'd like you all to meet my wife, Elizabeth," the director said, turning toward an instantly recognizable woman. "You might know her as Elizabeth Montgomery, but she's Mrs. Asher to me."

He was right about that. Until that moment, none of us had even dreamed she was married in real life; on her TV show, yes, to Darrin, but that was only make-believe. I waited in anticipation for her to twitch her nose just like her Samantha character did on *Bewitched*, but apparently that was just part of her on-screen persona, not something she practiced in civilian life. One more show biz illusion shattered!

We watched and learned as they finished shooting the scene they'd been working on since before we arrived. Mr. Asher finally got the performance he was looking for and said "print" to the AD.

"Print!" his assistant yelled. "Okay, that's it! Time to set up for the club scene."

That was *our* scene, and we watched with added interest while the crew, as though guided by an unseen divine hand, shuffled lights, cameras, walls and props, magically transforming the set into a new version of reality faster than I would ever have believed possible had I not seen it with my own eyes. After a few moments of this, an assistant woke us from our collective trance and led us to a room resembling a beauty salon where a team of make-up artists transformed us in record time into tanned, blemish-free leading men. Next, we reported to wardrobe, where our black-and-yellow stage outfits hung neatly on racks, pressed and camera-ready.

Nattily attired, looking something like five bumble bees, we buzzed through our scenes without a hitch. Annette sang wonderfully with us, and Lynn delivered his line to Mr. Asher's satisfaction in only two takes. Having endured his incessant rehearsals for two days, we'd expected something more and wondered, *Is that all there is?*

As I came off of the set, I saw my buddy Jim standing next to Elizabeth Montgomery. Worried that he might be feeling slightly out of place among so many famous stars, I walked directly over to him, thinking I could rescue him from any discomfort he was suffering. Having spent the better part of the day getting acquainted with cast and crew, I figured I'd do the honors and introduce him around to everyone.

"That looked like fun!" he said with a big smile on his face.

"It was *really* fun," I responded as I shook his hand.

"You guys were great!" Elizabeth said, beaming.

"Elizabeth, may I introduce you to my friend Jim?" I offered in an effort to make his visit to the studio a memorable one.

"Oh, thanks!" she said, giggling. "We've already met."

As she was talking, Mickey walked by and I gently grabbed his arm.

"Mickey," I said, "do you have a second to meet my friend Jim?"

"Jim!" Mickey cried, sounding genuinely surprised. "I didn't see you standing there. How's the family?"

Mickey and Jim exchanged a friendly hug, leaving me somewhat confused.

What's going on? I asked myself. *Everyone seems to know Jim.*

As Mickey and Elizabeth exchanged pleasantries with Jim, Shelly approached our friendly circle.

"Shelly," I said. "I want you to meet my friend Jim."

Shelly went immediately into his Don Rickles routine.

"Jim?" he said with great emphasis. "This is the 'Jim' you've been talking about for the last week? You dummy, don't you know who this is?"

"I'm sorry," he said directly to Jim. "He's from the sticks in Oregon, a direct relative of Jed Clampett's, you know. He doesn't get out much."

Everyone was laughing at his act.

"Happy to know you… Jim," Shelly said in Ricklesesque disbelief.

"Believe me, any friend of Dick's is a friend of mine!" said Jim.

"This is James H. Nicholson," Shelly said to me. "THE James H. Nicholson, you dummy. You don't mean to tell me you don't you know who James H. Nicholson is?"

I had no idea who James H. Nicholson was or why I should. My first thought was, he was some old retired actor whose name and face I should've recognized.

"Did you used to be a movie star?" I asked, giving Shelly new ammo for his Rickles comedy routine.

"You putz!" he exclaimed. "You hockey puck! Jim's the owner of AIP! He produces everything that comes out of this palace!"

Pointing to a tall director's chair standing nearby, Shelly continued.

"See this chair?" he said, "It says right here, 'JAMES H. NICHOLSON.' That's *your* Jim, dummy! There's one of these on every soundstage."

"This guy's had us all watching for a guy named Jim," Shelly said, pointing at me, "so he can show him around a movie set and maybe even introduce him to a few stars!"

"Really?" I questioned, still clueless, as Shelly once again interrupted.

"Alright everyone," he said, as though in charge, "get back to work! We have a film to shoot here."

ANNETTE & THE KINGSMEN
Left to right: *Norm, Lynn, Annette, Mike*

Still laughing, everyone started going their separate directions, leaving Shelly and me alone with Jim.

"Why didn't you tell me who you were?" I asked, curious to know.

Jim thought for a second before speaking.

"I enjoyed the way you were treating me," he finally said, "and I didn't want my position to affect the way you treated me. I just liked having a friend that didn't expect to gain anything from me."

"Yeah," I said, "but the yokel way I went on about introducing you to some stars and showing you the place where they make movies—you must have thought I was a hick."

"No, no, not at all," Jim responded. "I looked at that as innocent, energetic kindness, qualities you should strive to never lose, my young friend."

"Seeing our studio through your eyes," he went on, "has been refreshing for me and has renewed my perspective. That's why I came to see the filming of your scenes today. I think I enjoyed it as much as you. Sometimes, Dick, we get so caught up in what we're doing, we lose sight of the positive impact and effect we have on people."

"Unfortunately," he said, smiling and taking my hand, "I have to get back to my office. I'm already late for a meeting, but please don't let my position affect our friendship, will you young man?"

"Yeah," I answered with a grin, "if you can look past my being one of the famous Kingsmen, I can look past you being a big time movie mogul."

"I'm sure I'll see you again before you leave," he said with a smile. "Besides, we still have to show your friend my car."

"We have to come back tomorrow for something," I said. "I'll make sure I look you up before we leave."

As Jim walked away, Shelly put his arm around me.

"Jim? Jim? I better not let you outa my sight. You can be dangerous."

I did show Mike Jim's car the following day and was able to say a last good-bye to Jim. I thought I'd try to see him at least once every time we were in LA. However, although we talked several times on the phone, we somehow never managed to find the time for a personal visit.Unfortunately, so it is in the demanding world of show biz.

WE spent the remainder of that week working with Raphael and taping *Shindig*. During that span, Raphael succeeded in taking a number of photographs we later used for promotional purposes and on album covers. He photographed us on the campus of UCLA, and one of those images appeared on our fourth album, "The Kingsmen on Campus." One of his shots taken on the *Shindig* set was subsequently used as a promo picture. And, during one of our breaks at ABC, had us go out to the *Young and the Restless* set for a brief photo session on their beach, resulting in a picture that was used on our "Greatest hits" album. We were delighted with the results of our work-packed week with Raphael.

Meanwhile, taping another *Shindig* was like spending a few days with old pals. We'd become friends with a few of the Shindig Dancers and hung out with them on a few of our off days. Glen Campbell was still playing guitar in the house band with Billy Preston, Hal Blaine and Jerry Cole, and The Blossoms were still singing background, and seeing them again was fun. The only difference in the show was the absence of The Righteous Brothers, who'd had a monster hit with "You've Lost that Lovin' Feelin'" and were out on tour and no longer with the show.

This being our third time on *Shindig*, we already knew our way around the set, and what to do when, so we were able to help some of the new guests find their way. We performed two songs, including that masterpiece of fun, "The Jolly Green Giant." We still disliked the song, but Shelly insisted that a chance to perform a current hit song on *Shindig* was a marketing opportunity too good to pass up. And, of course, he was right.

Having a like mind for marketing, Norm shipped down a couple of his amps for the black and white television show. Sales of Sunn amps were increasing exponentially, and he was smartly pushing and pressing to take advantage of every marketing opportunity that came along—and a national television show was definitely a major opportunity.

Our December '64 visit to LA was an awesome, fun-filled, lucrative two weeks. I'd managed to rub elbows with movie and television stars, recording artists, a fashion photographer, the owner of a major motion picture studio and bus loads of record distributors—all of this while getting to know Shelly Berger. I found myself thinking, *Life can't possibly get any better than this."*

Photo by Rafael taken on set of *Shindig* during performance of "Jolly Green Giant"
Left to right: *Author, Barry, Norm, Mike, Lynn*

VERSE 22

LEAVING LA behind, we. returned to our normal abnormal life of touring the country between TV shows and major events. It didn't take long for us to fall back into our usual routines: Norm selling amps and grating on Lynn, Lynn tipping the bottle and irritating Norm, Mike chasing the young girls, Jimmy-John providing non-stop buck-toothed entertainment, Barry trying to spiritually connect with intellectual and cerebral maidens wherever he could find them, the FBI again frequenting our sold-out shows, endless symphonic concerts still playing in my head and I remaining utterly clueless to the ways of the real world surrounding me. Despite and because of all that, we were having a blast.

Several of us were hanging out in one of our rooms, watching TV at the Holiday Inn in Lawrence, Kansas. We were about to leave for a performance at the famous Tee Pee, a popular University of Kansas hangout. In the hallowed tradition of a Top 10 party school, 500 rowdy 3.2 beer-drinking Jayhawks used to pack themselves into that small club, originally designed to hold maybe 100 warm bodies at best. A night at the Tee Pee invariably turned into a wild, lusty, fun-filled, non-stop party, and that establishment became a favorite stop of ours where we performed a number of times.

Through the always-open door, Lynn came running into the room with exciting news.

"We're playing a concert with Ray Charles!" he announced.

We were all huge Ray Charles fans and jumped to our feet with excitement. The barrage of questions began.

"When?" "Where?" "What kind of show?" "How long do we get to play?" "Do we get to meet him?"

Lynn revealed it was a college concert date in Louisville a few weeks off. Knowing the date was out there kept us energized as we counted down the days until what we dubbed "Ray Day."

When the big night finally arrived, we were out of our minds with excitement as we took the stage as Ray's opening act. Normally, it's the duty of an opening act to work the crowd into a frenzy in anticipation of the headliner, and we did our best to do just that. As we retreated backstage after our encore, we passed Ray, the Raeletts and his band as they prepared to go on. We tarried briefly in our dressing rooms, just long enough to drop off our gear and towel off the perspiration from our performance. Then we hastened to a prime viewing spot offstage left to watch a true musical genius at work.

The crowd went crazy as Ray, wearing a brightly-colored sequin jacket and his signature shades and smile, was introduced and settled in at center stage before the keyboard of his gleaming grand piano. It took maybe a minute for us to realize this performer needed no opener to warm things up for him as he launched into a spell-binding performance that eclipsed anything I'd ever seen before—and nearly everything I've seen since. A recent hit of his was one of his best recordings ever, "Busted." I can still hear him singing the opening lines:

My bills are all due and the baby needs shoes and I'm busted
Cotton is down to a quarter a pound, but I'm busted
I got a cow that went dry and a hen that won't lay
A big stack of bills that gets bigger each day
The county's gonna haul my belongings away cause I'm busted.

Awestruck by this radiant musician, we were quickly reduced to mere shadows standing in the wings. It was magical being a part of a Ray Charles concert for one unforgettable night.

That same year (1965), we performed together with yet another transcendent musical genius in a most unlikely setting. We were booked to play a debutante party in Milwaukee for the daughter of the owners of the Schlitz Brewing Company. When we arrived at their estate, we were directed to the backyard—a regally landscaped expanse covering many acres, a garden masterpiece befitting the barons of "The Beer that Made Milwaukee Famous." There we found a gigantic white tent pitched in the middle of a broad lawn. Within, two stages were set up side by side. One stage was waiting to be filled with the musical gear of the Kingsmen; the other was already filled with the instruments and piano and personnel of Duke Ellington and His Orchestra. The Duke himself was leading the rehearsal.

Plans for the evening's social function called for us and the Duke to trade sets all night long. When the party animals from Portland, Oregon played, young men in their rented tuxes and young women in their newly-purchased formals packed the dance floor. When the Duke played, parents and chaperones in their evening finery took over, while star-struck Kingsmen filled the wings, hanging on every note of "Satin Doll," thrilled by every chord of "Take the A Train," transported by the haunting splendor of "Mood Indigo." In my pre-Kingsmen days—barely a year-and-a-half past—jazz had been my passion, along with classical music, not rock 'n' roll. As the Duke and his big band cooked past the boiling point, it felt like heaven on earth to me. Equally memorable were the intermissions, when I had several opportunities to talk at length with Duke personally—a thrill beyond description.

Ray Charles in the land of thoroughbreds and mint juleps, Duke Ellington in the land of brats and lager beer—two matchless musical geniuses, two unforgettable shows, two milestone nights for the boys from the City of Roses.

WE'D been out for a little more than a month when, on our daily call to Scandore and Shayne, Hermie told Lynn we'd be coming back to New York City in a few months to appear on *Hullabaloo*, a popular weekly rock 'n' roll TV show broadcast in color. In addition to that exciting news, Hermie informed Lynn that our "Louie Louie" album had topped a million in sales and that Scepter/Wand wanted to throw a gold album presentation party for us while we were in town. They intended to make the party a high-visibility media event to help with our national PR. Planning started immediately and, although the big event was still months away, we received progress reports almost daily. The Rolling Stones and Brenda Lee—both favorites of ours—were scheduled to appear with us on *Hullabaloo* and were added to the invitee list.

With money rolling in, we no longer had to travel by car and van. Now sporting a retired Greyhound bus we affectionately named "Herkirmer"—already our third bus in a line of road casualties—we found ourselves playing our usual one-nighters, crisscrossing the country while the never-ending saga of the dirty words followed us from town to town. It reached the point where, since no one believed us about the words to "Louie Louie," we started making up stories about the controversial recording and the unusual circumstances under which it was recorded. Some of those stories were so good, they lasted a few weeks before we invented a new tale for the relentless-but-gullible press.

We kept track of our performances and days off that year. From New Years Day, January 1, 1965 through New Years Eve, December 31, 1965, we worked a total of 352 days, taking only 13 days off—an average of one free day every four weeks. Many, many times we played multiple shows on a single day, sometimes at separate locations, and it would not be an exaggeration (or much of one) to say we performed 500 shows that year. Some publication—I don't recall which one—named us the top touring rock 'n' roll act of 1965. During one frenzied stretch, we set attendance records 56 straight nights at 56 different venues. I'll venture a guess that only a handful of bands at best can make a similar claim.

I don't remember ever playing that year to anything less than a packed house. Of course, we owed much of our success to the notoriety brought on by "Louie Louie," but that only partly explains our popularity. In many cases, we returned to the same venue multiple times over a several year period, and every time we sold out. Honest Abe Lincoln once said, "You can fool all of the people some of the time, and some of the people all of the time, but you can't fool all of the people all of the time." The same might be said of rock 'n' roll fans. People wouldn't have kept coming to our shows in such numbers had we not been doing *something* right. We had one heck of a roll on the concert circuit, and it wasn't all because of dirty lyrics or smoke and mirrors.

When you get right down to it, we were pretty darn good entertainers. If you bought a ticket to a Kingsmen concert, you knew you were going to have a good time, and having a good time is at the very heart of rock 'n' roll. One critic that never bothered talking with any of us before writing his book dismissed all of that as "the minor league B-circuit." With all due respect, I beg to differ. It was good-time rock 'n' roll at its best. There's nothing B-league about that. It's what the music is all about.

In order to consistently deliver those good times while maintaining the hectic pace we did, we needed mobility and flexibility. Herkimer gave us both. With some creative customizing, Herkie was transformed from a standard-issue Greyhound bus into a hotel on wheels. First, we had all of the seats removed, save for the first three rows. The open area in back was then divided into six eight-foot long spaces, three on each side. All of us—Lynn, Mike, Barry, Norm, Jimmy-John and me—were assigned our own spaces to do with as we pleased. Each of us had a custom bed with built-in storage underneath (like a captain's bed) and an individual wooden locker for our hanging wardrobes installed side-by-side at the back of the bus. All of our equipment and extra gear easily fit in the luggage compartments below. With the additional use of the overhead bins, we were able to travel in relative style and comfort.

Herkimer got her name from a pump jockey who was working in a gas station we stopped at somewhere in the Midwest. We'd purchased the bus in New York, and one of the stops on the bus line's route was the town of Herkimer. Indulging in our sick sense of humor, we left the scrolling city destination name in the window on the front of the bus, on Herkimer. Curious about our identity, the pump jockey asked if we were a rock band, and Mike answered in the affirmative.

"I figured you was," the astute, oil pushin', beer lovin' fuel engineer answered. "I even knowd who you fellers are!"

"Oh yeah?" Mike responded, indulging the gasoline fume-inhaling character.

Understand now, we had my mother paint "Kingsmen" in two-foot high electric blue letters on both sides of our bus. Knowing this, we were not at all surprised when the peanut-butter-stuck-between-his-teeth attendant claimed he knew who we were. And then, he delivered the ultimate line.

"Awe, there ain't no foolin' you guys," he said. "I seen it on the front of yer bus. Ya'll are Herkimer's Hermits, ain't cha?"

Mike looked over at us in shock, then turned back toward the smiling attendant.

"Why yes, yes we are!" he said with a smile. "Exactly! We're Herkimer's Hermits."

Hearing that, Barry sprayed the Coke he was drinking into the air, while the rest of us howled with laughter.

The man was thrilled with his discovery. After playing with the 22-year-old elementary school graduate, we ended up signing one of the brilliant detective's road maps for his girlfriend. He had us sign, "To Martha Lou, from Herkimer's Hermits." In recognition of that moment, "HERKIMER" was left in the window of the bus for the remainder of her life.

WE were enjoying traveling in the comfort of a roomy bus to sold out concert after sold out concert when we started hearing about Kingsmen shows we were not scheduled to play. Initially, we thought

Herkimer III

the reports were referring to the gospel group The King's Men, who, as I mentioned earlier, had been singing at religious gatherings for years. As the weeks passed, however, we started seeing actual posters that read "THE KINGSMEN" and listed the place and date of the show. Even more disturbing, these posters included the words: "Featuring their hits 'Jolly Green Giant,' 'Money,' 'Little Latin Lupe Lu' and 'Louie Louie.'" Stunned, we alerted Mel and Bob immediately.

Playing detective, Bob called a few of the promoters to gather information about these bogus shows. He discovered that several promoters for whom we'd previously worked had booked this bogus group, thinking they were re-booking us. They were quite surprised when a totally different band than us showed up. Even worse, the new group sounded awful. One of the promoters said he'd been told by their agent that this was the "true" Kingsmen band and that *we* were the imposters.

When Bob called Mel and told him what his research had uncovered, Mel and Joe were furious.

Bob gave Mel the phone number of the agent in Oregon that was booking this mystery band. Mel called the man, pretending he was interested in booking *his* Kingsmen. Before the conversation ended, he managed to get their touring schedule and convince the agent to send him their promotional material. The agent told Mel that Jack Ely was the lead singer on *all* of the Kingsmen's hits and had left the group recently after recording the records and started his own band. Further, the agent went on to claim, they had a cease-and-desist order against us issued by a federal court.

Mel hired Miles Lori, a high profile litigation attorney in New York City. Investigating the matter, Miles discovered that Jack, after dropping out of school and entering the army, had been discharged before his tour of duty was up for unspecified reasons. Returning to civilian life, Jack noticed our success and, breaching his contract with us, formed his own Kingsmen, found an agent and started touring. His agent actually called WMA to get our touring schedule so he could avoid the areas of the country where we were working, thereby lessening their chances of being caught. All of this was happening nearly three years after the song was recorded.

We were surprised to learn it was Jack who was deceiving the public. We had no problem with him advertising himself as "formerly with The Kingsmen." He was. We didn't even have a problem with him advertising himself as "the lead voice on 'Louie Louie.'" He was that, too. But he was doing much more than that: he was capitalizing on the other hits we'd had without him and on the name we'd been building since his departure. His posters and PR material emphasized not only "Louie Louie", "Money" and "Little Latin Lu Pe Lu" but "Jolly Green Giant" as *his* current hit, and that was neither factually true nor ethically right.

It's the way of the entertainment world—most bands change members at some point in their history. The Stones have changed members, The Beach Boys have changed members, even bands like Van Halen, Paul Revere and the Raiders and Chicago have all changed members, some of them several times. Sooner or later, personnel changes happen to almost every band. Even so, leaving a band doesn't give someone the right to start a new band with the same name.

We asked our fan club to gather all the information they could find regarding this other group and forward it to Miles. Meanwhile, Miles sent the bogus group's agent several threatening letters, with no response. Within a few weeks, we had all of the evidence we needed to take them to court. Upon filing an action with the Oregon courts, Miles saw to it that through the AP and UPI press services we would land again on the front pages of America's newspapers. "KINGSMEN NEED PERRY MASON" screamed the headline that streamed across the wire that day, followed by a complete article explaining the case.

A few months later the case went to trial. Miles was admitted to the Oregon bar through an Oregon firm and was brilliant in court as attorney for the plaintiffs. Loaded with evidence of Jack's misdeeds, he opened the case and immediately began pummeling the defendant and his counsel. The posters and other evidence were overwhelming, and it wasn't long before Jack's lawyer approached Miles, offering to settle the case according to the terms we'd offered in the letters that Miles first sent.

Those terms specified that Jack could not use the name "The Kingsmen," that all of his PR would be limited to saying that Jack was "formerly of The Kingsmen" and that that notice had to be in letters more than 25 percent the size of his name. On his end, Jack had a real problem with Lynn and didn't want him lip-syncing the vocals to the 45 on television shows. We had no objections to that. Lynn was supposed to be on the drums, anyway, and I was supposed to be doing the vocals to "Louie." Miles therefore drew up a clause in the settlement agreement stipulating that Lynn could no longer lip-sync to "Louie Louie." With the advent of Union rules, pre-recording became standard practice shortly thereafter and lip-syncing became mostly a thing of the past.

Finally, Jack wanted a gold record for "Louie Louie," which we also felt he should have. Accordingly, we had Scepter/Wand send him a copy of the original gold record with his name inscribed on the plaque. Jack soon changed the name of his band to "The Courtmen," and they were out of business in no time. Later, we caught Jack trying to breach the settlement agreement several more times. Eventually, under the threat of further legal action, he finally quit using our name once and for all.

Today, happily, the differences between Jack and The Kingsmen are history. We've all moved to higher ground and currently enjoy a good relationship. Together, we've spent considerable time soul-searching, clearing out the debris of the past and working on a better future for all of us. I'm sure that's what Louie would have wanted.

VERSE 23

WE'D been working our way up the Eastern Seaboard toward New England for several weeks and were about to have a rare three days off. As we sat around our dressing room shooting the breeze before a sound check, Lynn excused himself, explaining it was time for him to make his daily call to the offices of Scandore and Shayne in New York.

From the privacy of an empty dressing room, he dialed their number and spoke briefly with the receptionist, who immediately put him on hold. After a minute or so, Mel came on the line, and he and Lynn proceeded through their review of the news of the day. As their exchange neared its end, Mel abruptly switched subjects.

"Lynn," he said, "Joe and I want you guys to come to New York for a few days to discuss some pressing business matters that we need to address."

"What sort of 'matters?'" Lynn inquired.

"I can't discuss it over the phone," Mel answered. "It's something that's best discussed face to face. Trust me. We need you here."

"Yeah," Lynn replied, "but what do we do about Herkimer? We can't just park the bus on the streets of New York City for three days. Besides, it'll be impossible to find a spot. Why don't you meet us somewhere in New Jersey? Or, how 'bout some other suburb?"

"Hold on a minute, kid," Mel said, putting the receiver down on his desk with a plastic-sounding thud.

Lynn held on as told. In the background he could hear Mel carrying on an animated conversation with someone. The sound stopped and Mel picked up the phone again. Except it wasn't Mel this time, it was Joe Scandore, the front half of Scandore and Shayne.

"Hey, Lynn," said an unfamiliar voice, "this is Joe Scandore. How ya doin'?"

"Fine!" was all the surprised Kingsman could manage to say. This was the first time he'd ever spoken to *the* Joe Scandore.

"That's good," Joe said before directly getting to the point. "Look, kid, don't worry about your bus. You just get here. I'll have the boys take care of your bus."

There was a brief pause, and Lynn could hear Joe saying something to Mel—he couldn't quite make out what. Then Joe spoke again.

"Here, Lynn," he said, "I'm giving the phone back to Mel. You guys work it out. I want to see all of you boys here in New York on Monday."

Mel came back on the line, and in a few short moments, their conversation was over. Hanging up the receiver, Lynn hurried back to our dressing room.

"I just spoke with Joe," he announced upon entering.

"Wow, are you kidding me?" interrupted Norm. "You *actually spoke* with Joe?"

"What was the mystery man like?" I asked.

We hadn't met Joe yet and were all curious about him. Until now, we'd always spoken with either Hermie or Shelly—never with Joe—but it always seemed like Joe had the final say when it came to making any decision. We figured he was the senior partner in the firm, although nothing was ever said to that effect.

"Well," said Lynn, sort of puzzled, trying to answer my question, "I don't know. Picture a New York, Italian, mobster-sounding type guy and that would be what Joe kind of sounded like."

"Big surprise!" joked Barry. "With a name like Scandore, who would've thought he was Italian?"

"Joe says he'll have his boys handle Herkimer," Lynn continued, sidestepping Barry's remark. "He says we shouldn't worry about it."

Despite Joe's assurances, we remained a bit skeptical.

FOLLOWING directions Hermie had given him, JJ steered Herkimer to a warehouse located close to Bloomfield Street on the banks of the Hudson River. The warehouse manager was expecting us and directed him to park her in a space inside the building that a group of longshoremen had just finished clearing. Leaving our beloved Herkimer to fend for herself, assured by the manager that she'd be well taken care of, we were driven to a hotel close to Scandore and Shayne. After getting settled, we walked a few short blocks in the electrified air of the Big Apple to their office at 850 Seventh Avenue, a stone's throw from Carnegie Hall.

A smiling Hermie came out to meet us when we arrived, and we sat with him for a while, trading fun road stories with the savvy, veteran jazz drummer. He was halfway through one of his stories when a secretary appeared and summoned us into Joe's office. Despite it being daytime, it took a moment for our eyes to adjust to the muted lighting within.

Walnut-paneled walls with elaborate wainscotting framed tiers of library-like bookshelves, and large draped windows offered commanding views of the streets and people of New York. Ornate oriental rugs, expensive rolled leather furniture and an imposing meeting table with hand-carved legs added nicely to the richness of the room. Everything about that plush and grandiose space bespoke power and wealth.

When Hermie announced our arrival, a portly, expensively-dressed man pushed back the chair from his desk and stood, removing his wire-rimmed glasses, gracefully holding out both arms in a gesture of welcome and saying, "Finally, my boys are here!"

Beaming, he bear-hugged us one by one like we were prodigal sons returned, taking the time to acknowledge each one of us individually. Clearly, Joe knew more about Lynn and Mike and Barry and Norm and Dick than we did about him. It was overwhelming, no doubt intentionally so, and left me feeling more intimidated than welcome.

Joe's manner and appearance reminded me of Rod Steiger. Even better, although *The Godfather* was still years away as a novel and movie, Joe would've made the perfect Don Vito Corleone. He would've sounded a bit different than Brando, though—compared with the latter's mumbled growl, Joe would've delivered his lines with a much higher pitch to his voice. Still, the overall effect would've been much the same. Completing the package, Joe had a strange, noticeable dent in his forehead, several inches long, as though he'd been struck with a three-quarter inch pipe just above his eyebrow traversing his forehead into his gray, receding hairline.

With the first meeting pleasantries waning, he invited us to sit at his conference table, sent his secretary off for some thirst quenchers and went right to work. Speaking slowly and carefully, pausing at times to gather his thoughts while seeking just the right terminology, Joe began.

"I wanted you boys to come here for two reasons," he said. "One, we've been reviewing your contracts with Scepter/Wand and feel it's time to...*renegotiate* your deal."

"Can you do that?" I asked.

"Let's just say we are currently in a position to 'create' a new relationship with Florence."

"What's wrong with the recording contract?" asked Lynn.

Joe looked at him and smiled.

"As it exists today," he said, "your contract is a two-and-a-half percent deal, which you split with Jerry Dennon. That's unacceptable. We think we can get you six or seven percent, *without* Mr. Dennon."

"Wow! Are you kidding me?" asked Norm.

"When it comes to business, I never kid around," answered Joe, sounding as though he'd taken Norm's reaction as a statement of distrust.

"But our contract isn't with Scepter," Mike interjected, "it's with Jerry. How's that going to work?"

"Don't worry about Jerry," Joe said, unperturbed. "We have that...'situation' well under control. Jerry will be taken care of."

Mel and Hermie said nothing, Mel just puffing on his cigar, Hermie watching us. It appeared as though they been instructed to speak only if and when Joe directed them to do so.

"Our meeting with Florence is at 10 o'clock tomorrow morning," Joe informed us. "Hermie will pick you up at your hotel tomorrow at 9:30 sharp. Be waiting for him in the lobby. Is that clear?"

We just sat there and looked at each other, feeling uncomfortable.

"Yes, sir!"

"He will escort you to Scepter/Wand. Once you arrive, you will warmly greet Florence and, when I direct you to, you will sit outside of Florence's office on the bench by her secretary's desk. Mel and I will be the only ones taking the meeting with Florence. Incidentally, she doesn't know that you're in town and doesn't expect you to be attending the meeting tomorrow. So expect her...ah...to be...ah...surprised when she sees you."

Joe sat for a moment, looking down at the polished wooden table in thought. Looking up again, he went on.

"Florence is a smart lady. I anticipate you will see a look of concern on her face. Don't let that worry you."

Flicking his cigarette ashes in the ashtray, Lynn asked, "So, what does she think you're meeting about?"

"Hermie?" said Joe.

Instantly responding to Joe, Hermie spoke as though on cue.

"Florence thinks we're going to show her some new photos and discuss recording you guys there, in Scepter's studio."

With each new exchange, it became more apparent that Joe had orchestrated this well-thought-out ballet and was personally directing every movement of the creative choreography.

"Now, this is very important," Joe said forcefully, pointing his finger at us. "Once I close the door to Florence's office, except to say 'no' to anything offered you, You will not speak to anyone until I open the door. Then, every time the door opens, you will say, 'Yeah, dat's right, Joe!' and nothing more. Are we clear on that?"

"Yeah, dat's right, Joe!" Mike said, finding humor in the situation. We all laughed at Mike's quick wit, all of us, that is, save for Joe. Patient and unsmiling, he waited for silence to return.

"You are not to move from that bench until one of us comes out of her office and gets you," said the mastermind with a slight grin.

This guy's got to be kidding! "I thought to myself.

We all got the picture. We were to say nothing but "Yeah, dat's right, Joe!" unless we wanted to show a lack of respect toward Joe, which he clearly wouldn't tolerate. As to what would happen if we didn't follow his directions exactly, none of us were curious or brave or foolish enough to find out.

"No matter what," Joe said, "we must show unity if we want to succeed. Do I have your support?"

"Yes, sir!" we responded in sober unison.

For a moment, Joe appeared to gather his thoughts. then he continued.

"Now, with that understood, let's move on. The next thing is, we want you to become a corporation. There are many reasons why this is a good practice, and Hermie and Mel will fill you in on those details. We want you to incorporate here, in New York, and Hermie will have those papers for your signatures before you leave. There are several things you will need to decide with Hermie. You will be five equal owners of the corporation, but all of the transactions and funds will flow through our office. Everything will flow through your corporation. So Hermie, if you will show the boys to your office and take care of the rest of these details, Mel and I will arrange a celebration of their new recording contract for the boys for tomorrow evening."

Planning a victory party a day before his meeting with Florence illustrated Joe's conviction that he was going to be successful, and his confidence quickly infected all of us. There was no question in my mind that the following night, we would indeed be celebrating a new contract. But would Florence and her people, now giving us two-and-a-half percent, still like us? We were having fun the way things were, and we were all concerned about losing our relationship with Scepter/Wand.

Hermie stood, and we followed suit. Instantly, Joe transformed himself back into the warm and friendly man we'd met when we first walked into his office. Once we arrived in Hermie's office, he told us it was time for us to stop dividing all of the profits and to start taking salaries from a corporation. They wanted to put something away for our future and make sure that we had something in the bank when our days in the sun were over. We discussed what our wages should be and the different benefits we might want to consider. Strangely, none of us spoke about Joe in Hermie's office. We talked with Hermie about anything and everything *except* Joe as we threw out crazy names for the new corporation and decided on the makeup of its board of directors.

Hermie introduced us to their accountant—or was he a cook? In any case, he was to handle the books for us. There's that old joke about the firm that wanted to hire a new accountant. They asked all three finalists the same question, "How much is two plus two?" The first two candidates answered "Four!" While the third candidate closed all the windows, locked the door, disconnected the phone, leaned over and whispered, "How much would you like it to be?" Guess which candidate Scandore and Shayne hired?

Hermie next introduced us to their in-house music publisher, who wanted us to run all of our publishing through him instead of making Jerry Dennon rich — excuse me, I mean, instead of continuing to use Jerry's publishing company. Looking back on the whole affair, I think we did as they directed because we saw the impact they were having on our career and truly trusted them. It wasn't just intimidation.

That evening, we were all sitting in Mike's room, feet up on the bed, chewing the fat and watching TV, when the conversation worked its way around to our earlier meeting with Joe. None of us knew quite what to think about him, except we all agreed that he was undoubtedly in control of Scandore and Shayne. He was a little scary to us, too, but, as Lynn pointed out, "It's better to have him with us than agin' us." We saw Joe as a stereotypical New York Italian tough guy, just like the characters we'd seen many times in the movies. (Many of our impressions of New York were based not on reality but on what we'd seen in the movies — as demonstrated before by Lynn's tipping encounters with a New York cabbie and a Brooklyn bellhop and now again by how we dealt with Joe's implied threats.) We reasoned that Joe was most likely the money behind their firm and that it was just his personality that gave us the impression he'd rub us out if we crossed him.

As directed, we were all in the lobby of the hotel at 9:30 AM when Hermie arrived. He was in a good mood and made the morning walk down the street to the Scepter building a jovial jaunt. Joe and Mel showed up for the impending slaughter dressed to kill, and I now know that describing their attire as such is entirely appropriate. Mel made sure that the eight of us had an elevator to ourselves when he *politely* informed the woman waiting beside us in the lobby that our elevator was full and politely suggested she catch the next car. As we ascended to the Scepter/Wand floor, Joe moved to the front of the elevator and turned to look at us. With an evil smirk, he reminded us that whenever he opened the door to Florence's office during their meeting with her, we were to say, "Yeah, dat's right Joe!" and nothing more.

From the moment the elevator doors opened upon our arrival until the moment they closed at our departure, it was as though we were watching a movie for the second time. Joe had laid out every line, every move, every reaction perfectly, in advance, leaving nothing to chance. He was a man who didn't like surprises, a man who despised things he couldn't control.

Florence and Marvin were surprised and happy to see us. You could clearly see the concern on Florence's face when Joe told us to wait outside her office until he invited us to join them. She'd been around the block more than a few times, and she knew something unexpected was about to happen. We sat on the bench and watched Mel slowly close the frosted glass-and-wood door to Florence's office. He was grinning at us like a lion about to eat his favorite Christian and winked just before the latch clicked into position, securing privacy for the one-sided match about to take place inside.

As Joe had predicted, Florence's secretary offered us beverages and ashtrays as the sparring began, offers which, according to script, we politely refused. Within a few minutes, Florence started to yell. Her shouting not only surprised us, it started us worrying as well. Although we couldn't understand what was being said, we could easily tell she was growing more and more upset. I thought, *Is this the end of our recording career? Is Joe going to blow it for us? Does Joe know what he's doing?* I should've asked myself, *Do we know what we're doing?*

Pretending to type, Florence's secretary kept looking up at us, obviously uncomfortable with the situation. Periodically, she asked if we were sure she couldn't get us something while we waited.

The door suddenly opened, jolting us to attention.

"Ain't dat right, boys?" Joe asked, loudly and emphatically.

"Yeah, dat's right, Joe!" we answered in unison.

Immediately the door closed.

We shared worried looks, while Florence's secretary wore a what-the-hell-is-going-on expression on her face. Silently, we shrugged our shoulders and shook our heads, as if to say, "We have no idea!"

The yelling resumed until, once again, the door swung open.

"Ain't dat right, boys?" Joe called out.

"Yeah, dat's right, Joe!" we sang like trained parrots.

The yelling continued, louder than ever. Now, through Florence's office door window, we could see clouded shapes of people moving around in the war room.

Repeatedly, the door opened.

Repeatedly, we heard, "Ain't dat right, boys?"

Repeatedly, we answered as one, "Yeah, dat's right, Joe!"

Without warning, the yelling ceased, followed by a quiet what seemed to last an eternity. We looked up, looked down, looked left, looked right, but mostly looked at each other, wondering about our destiny, saying nothing.

When the door finally, slowly opened, Mel and Hermie were beaming as Joe invited us in. Marvin sat silently on the window ledge, and Florence sat behind her desk, looking worn out. She greeted us with a disconcerting smile as we reluctantly entered the room.

"Boys," said Joe, "in an effort to extend the length of your successful relationship with Scepter/Wand, and as a show of faith in your future, Florence has decided to offer a generous new contract, an offer we cannot refuse. Before we leave, Florence would like to say a few words to you."

Florence stood, appearing reluctant.

"Congratulations, Kingsmen," she said. An acquiescent smile came over her face as she looked at Joe and complained, "Now, can we go make some more hits so I can afford this deal?"

Everyone laughed uncomfortably at that, and the palpable tension eased. We cordially shook hands with Florence and Marvin and were quickly herded out of their offices and into an elevator Hermie had waiting for us.

As an individual, I may have been hopelessly naïve in matters regarding sex and adult life in general, but, in this particular business matter, I was not alone. As a group, in time, we were all proven to be neophytes. When it came to doing business, you were easily plucked, pitted and eaten alive whenever you had to deal with Joe.

At that moment, however, we were all dieing to know what had taken place in that office. We jabbered giddily as we descended in the elevator, until Joe put a stop to it.

"Quiet, boys!" he ordered. "Not here. Wait until later."

Joe didn't want anyone to talk about the negotiations with Florence until he was sure we couldn't be overheard. He directed us to a deli a few doors down from our hotel, where he said we could discuss the new deal with Florence over lunch. Once our orders were taken, Joe took the floor. We were on the edge of our seats.

"Boys, when we went in, we were thinking maybe we'd bump your percentage up to six, maybe seven percent. After the initial shock that lead to her yelling all those unpleasantries at us, she gave in and offered five percent tops!"

We were elated with the news and started celebrating. Joe stopped us with a wave of the hand.

"I told her we wanted twelve or we were removing our act from her roster. Then she really went crazy. She was all over the room."

If he didn't have it before, Joe had our undivided attention now.

"Finally," he went on, "she came up to seven and we came down to nine. Then she went to eight, while we held firmly at nine. At last, thanks to a little, shall we say, persuasion, we got her to agree to nine for you boys and an additional two percent for Jerry."

Nine percent! We were stunned, elated beyond belief, out of control. Once we calmed down a bit, Norm *had* to know what Joe said to Florence that made her change her mind and give up an industry record 11 percent.

"Once she pulled out her sales figures in an effort to prove she couldn't possibly afford any more than seven percent" Joe said, "I simply told her if she gave us 11 percent, I could increase her sales by more than 400 percent."

"How could you promise that?" questioned Lynn as we continued celebrating.

Joe laughed and slowly rubbed his hands together.

"I told her I knew some guys upstate that were selling more of her records than she was, and that if she made the deal for 11 percent, I could make a call and my acquaintances would stop bootlegging, or should I say producing, *all* of Scepter's records. I told her not only would *your* records increase by 400 percent, *her overall sales* would increase by over 400 percent!"

We five Kingsmen laughed, thinking Joe was pulling Florence's leg; Mel, Hermie and Joe laughed, knowing it was true.

Mel and Joe left us to our celebrating to get together the necessary paperwork for Florence; Hermie stayed until we were finished with lunch. Before dropping us at our hotel, he gave us the dope on Joe's plans for our evening.

"I'll pick you up in front of your hotel promptly at eight," he said. "We're having dinner at The Elegant. It's a supper club Joe owns. Make sure you're cleaned up and ready. It's going to be some celebration."

For the rest of the afternoon we chortled over our good fortune. We'd been making good money at one percent; nine percent was going to make us all rich! We flew high—maybe, like Icarus, too high—that day, thinking about all of the possibilities, counting our chickens before they hatched.

When we walked out of the hotel that night, Hermie was waiting for us in a long black shiny limo. Hermie always had a drink in his hand and another old road story for us from his touring days with Woody Herman, and tonight was no exception. He kept us amused with his anecdotes on our ride across town to The Elegant.

When we arrived, it was clear we were expected. An overwhelming number of people were milling around out front, waiting for us. Joe greeted us as we stepped from the limo, and we followed his lead as, like Moses, he parted the sea of people. We slowly advanced through the crowd, stopping now and then so Joe could introduce us to some of his many friends. I felt like a champion prize fighter being led to the ring to defend his title, like an Oscar nominee on his way in to the awards ceremony, like the President being led to the House rostrum to deliver his State of the Union speech—star treatment all the way.

As we were being seated at our table, Lynn whispered into my ear.

"Do you notice anything strange about the security in this place?"

"No," I answered quietly. "What do you mean?"

"They're all dressed in black suits, black shirts and white ties," he returned.

"So, what does that mean?" I questioned.

"That's the kind of stuff mobsters wear in the movies," he whispered. "You don't suppose Joe was actually telling the truth this afternoon, do you?"

"Naw," I answered in disbelief. "I think he's just a rich Italian guy. Italians kind of dress that way in New York. But, you're right, there does seem to be a huge Guido factor about."

Lynn and I looked at each other.

"We better leave it alone," we said in unison.

The club was not well lit when we first entered. It was kind of dark, in fact. But once the stage lit up for John Davidson's show, you could see rather well. The cutlery and china were of the highest quality, and the service from curbside through dessert was first class in every way. Joe and his staff saw to our every need, anticipated our every desire. He enjoyed reigning over this swanky nightclub, where he was king.

Hermie always referred to shots of whiskey as "big orange drinks," and he and Lynn consumed an orchard's worth of oranges that evening. Neither was feeling any pain early the next morning when our limo dropped us off back at our hotel.

To this day, I can't say for sure whether the figures at Scandore and Shayne were actually involved with the underworld. Some people I've known have made their living off of flaunting their "family ties," real or imagined. The fakers count on you not checking them out; the real ones—well, the real ones don't flaunt it; they have more effective ways to get their message across.

Joe never flaunted underworld ties; just his presence, just his manner left you feeling he must've had them. I do know that Joe was well-connected in many quarters and well-liked in any world in which he found it necessary to travel. He had a special talent for being able to talk to and work with anyone on any level. Whether you were royalty or a bum, if you had an encounter with Joe, you felt like it was a treat, even when he left with all of the sweets in his pocket.

WE accomplished quite a lot in the few days we were in New York: a new recording contract negotiated, incorporation papers signed and filed, an accountant enlisted to *look after* our money, an opportunity offered to write music. We were pleased with the results and couldn't wait to return to the Big Apple. Joe showed us a great time and had significantly enhanced our business—we thought. We developed a unique fondness for Joe Scandore and his colorful Italian manner.

THE BEST OF "MISTA D'S" INFAMOUS PHOTOGRAPHS
Standing, left to right: *Author, Norm, Lynn, Mike*
Seated: Barry

VERSE 24

FOLLOWING a performance in Hartford, we drove Herk through the rolling hills of Connecticut, finally arriving at the Howard Johnson's in Chicopee, Massachusetts in the wee small hours of the morning. I was rooming with Jimmy-John, and we were fast asleep when a sudden, rude and heavy pounding on our door woke us up.

Sleepy eyed, JJ answered the door. Two men in grey suits were standing before him.

"Are you Dick Peterson?" asked the white-haired gentleman on the right.

Thinking I might be in some sort of trouble, and with a Marine's sense of protection, JJ answered through his protruding teeth, "Who wants to know?"

"I'm Special Agent Big Important G-man with the FBI," said the man forcefully, presenting his badge, "and I was told I would find Dick Peterson in this room."

"I'm Dick Peterson," I said as I finished pulling on my trousers. Startled and terrified, I asked, "What's the FBI want with me?"

"You have five minutes to get to the Atlantic Room on the first floor," the man said. "We will answer all of your questions once you arrive."

With that, the two gentlemen walked away.

If Special Agent BIG-man was trying to intimidate me, he succeeded. I finished getting dressed and left JJ in a nervous tizzy. As I started down the hall, Mike and Norm emerged from their room. They, too, had been invited to visit the Atlantic Room for a sit-down with J. Edgar Hoover's personal emissaries.

"So, you finally did it, aye Lil' Dickie?" said Norm laughingly.

"Did what?" I asked nervously.

"Just kidding!" answered Norm. "Is there something you're hiding we should know about?"

"You don't think they want to ask us about Joe, do you?" Mike asked, adding a whole new dimension to my worries.

"Hey, we don't know anything about Joe," Norm counseled. "He's just our manager. Only tell these guys what you know, don't tell them what you think. Just be honest, and everything will be just fine. I think it's got to have something to do with 'Louie Louie.'"

Lynn and Barry were already sitting at the conference table with the two FBI men when we walked into the room. I thought it weird how the G-men all looked alike. They had on nearly identical grey suits, they wore the same grey hairstyle, they even sat the same way. We'd seen so many of these clones at our concerts, I started to wonder whether FBI agents were in actuality not true human beings but rather some sort of standard government issue robot. Humans or robots, flesh-and-blood or metal-and-electronics, they were scary.

I don't remember the agents' names, so I will refer to them according to the manner their attitude reflected.

Special Agent Big Important G-man ("Special Agent BIG-man" for short), whom you've already met, spoke first as he passed his FBI business cards around the table,

"I'm Special Agent Big Important G-man and this is Agent Can Ruin A Person (I'll just call him by his acronym, "Agent CRAP"). We're investigating allegations that have been made regarding your recording of 'Louie Louie.' You have a right to consult with an attorney before you make any statements, and you are not compelled to make any statements. However, any statements you do make can and will be used against you in a court of law. Do you understand what I have just said?"

So, it's 'Louie' they're interested in, I thought, *not Joe. Good!* Knowing that provided me a small measure of relief. I was certain there was nothing about "Louie Louie" that broke any law; I wasn't so certain about Joe.

"Yes, sir!" five voices answered as one.

"For the record, would you all identify yourselves?"

We each gave our name and its correct spelling as Agent CRAP kept a record of everything we and Special Agent BIG-man said.

Looking at Lynn, Special Agent BIG-man said, "Since you're the leader of the group, I'll talk to you first."

Hadn't he just advised us we could consult with an attorney before saying anything? Didn't matter. He started asking Lynn questions anyway. Over the remaining course of the interrogation, no mention of any kind was made concerning having an attorney present.

"You're Lynn Easton?" inquired Special Agent BIG-man.

"Yes, sir, I am," answered Lynn politely.

I was shaking in my slippers as Agent CRAP took notes.

"Where do you live, Mr. Easton?"

"I live in Portland, Oregon."

"You're the leader of the musical recording group The Kingsmen?"

"Yes, sir, I am."

"What can you tell me about your recording of 'Louie Louie?'"

Every time he opened his mouth and uttered a word, Special Agent BIG-man came across as condescending. "Nice" and "considerate" and "friendly" were nowhere to be found in his vocabulary.

"Well, I know that for the last year-and-a-half, certain people have professed to hearing obscene words on the record."

"Are there any obscene words on the record?"

"As far as I'm concerned, the words they claim to hear simply don't exist on the recording."

"You were present at the recording session?"

"Yes I was."

"Where did you make this recording?"

"We recorded it on the West Coast over two years ago, in Portland."

"What lyrics did you use?"

"We used the same words Richard Berry wrote."

"Do you remember if any of you made any conscious effort to include any obscene words in the recording?"

"We only practiced the song a few times before we recorded it with vocals. There was absolutely no deliberate attempt to include any obscene words on the recording."

"Well, how do you account for the popularity for the recording?"

1.
FEDERAL BUREAU OF INVESTIGATION

Date 9/7/65

Portland, Oregon, was advised of the identity of the interviewing agent. He was advised that he could consult an attorney before making any statement, that he did not have to make any statement, and that any statement he did make could be used against him in court.

▓▓▓▓▓ volunteered the following information:

He identified himself as a member of the vocal group, the "Kingsmen". He said he has been aware for over a year that certain persons profess to hear obscene words in the group's recording of the song, "Louie Louie" but so far as he is concerned the words they claim to hear simply do not exist on that record. He said the recording was originally done on the west coast over a year ago and the group simply selected a standard version of the lyrics. With a short practice session and certainly no deliberate attempt to include any obscene or suggested wording the initial tape recording was made.

The original recording sold poorly for several months on the west coast and was later recorded on the Wand label in New York. Some months after that label went on sale, the talk of obscenity in the recording arose. He said to put an end to this and to establish their own position, the Wand Corporation forwarded a record to the Federal Communications Commission at Washington, D.C., and it is his belief that the Commission replied they observed no obscenity in the unintelligible wording. The Corporation later offered a $1000 reward to anyone who could substantiate the reported obscenity.

▓▓▓▓▓ there was no deliberate attempt to include any obscenity in the recording and it is his belief only those who want to hear such things can read it into the vocal. He said he has heard others point out where the suggested obscenity exists in the recording but cannot make out what they suggest appears.

On 8/25/65 at Chicopee, Massachusetts File # Boston 145-385
Detroit 145-420

by SA ▓▓▓▓▓ Date dictated 9/1/65

- 13 -

One of 5 FBI reports that refer to our individual interviews. Printed through the Freedom of information/ Privacy Act Section 20324-5520

"It was very poorly recorded. When we first released 'Louie Louie,' it only sold a few copies before it died. It wasn't until almost 10 months later that we heard there was a question about the lyrics. And it wasn't until the controversy about the lyrics came up that the record took off. I think Scepter/Wand sent a few copies to the FCC, but I think the FCC told our record company that they found the record poorly recorded and the lyrics unintelligible."

After a moment of silence, Lynn continued.

"I know that the record company has offered a $10,000 reward to anyone who can prove there are obscenities on the recording. I think people can read anything they want into it."

"Okay," said Special Agent BIG-man. "Can we assume that you would all make the same or similar statements in this regard?"

"Yes, sir!" we all chimed in perfect harmony.

Looking at Agent CRAP, Special Agent BIG-man asked, "Can you think of anything more?"

"No, that should do it."

"Thank you gentlemen for your time. You are free to leave."

"Well, what happens now?" asked Lynn.

"You go back to your rooms."

"No, I mean with the investigation?"

"Oh! We turn our files over to the central office, and they'll notify the FCC. They'll deal with it from there. Mr. Hoover has taken a personal interest in this matter, so once he has all of the information he feels he needs, he'll turn it over to the FCC and they'll hold a hearing. Depending on the outcome of that hearing, a decision will be made about what, if any, further action needs to be taken."

Lynn shook his head slowly up and down, indicating he understood. The two agents got up and left without saying another word. We went to Lynn's room and called Hermie to tell him about the interrogation. Although interested, he told us not to worry about it, that the investigation would be over soon.

"Did they ask anything about Joe or any of us?" he inquired anxiously.

"No," answered Lynn. "Why would they?"

"Just wondering," said Hermie.

A few weeks later, we were once again on our way to New York City, this time for our gold album party and our appearance on *Hullabaloo* with the Rolling Stones and Brenda Lee. For weeks, Scepter/Wand and our team of managers had been working every angle, trying to attract media attention to the event. Wanting us to project the image of a big-time rock band, Joe'd rented the entire 32nd floor of the Warwick Hotel for us during our special media week in the city.

Lynn's wife Karen flew out for the extravaganza as well as Barry's future wife, Desha. We couldn't wait to show off our accommodations to them and to one and all. Owning the entire floor, each of us could pick any room we liked. We could run up and down the halls screaming if we wanted, and do it bare-beamed and buck-naked if we wanted that, too — and who would complain? But we didn't. A few years later, Led Zeppelin would set the standard for rock 'n' roll hotel mayhem, but this was 1965 and we were The Kingsmen, and we missed our chance to earn a place in the rock 'n' roll Hall of Infamy. No drugs, no hookers, no fights, no flying televisions, no fires, no spanking of a groupie's bare bottom with a dead fish — we were no fun at all by the new standards of rock 'n' roll exuberance that would soon prevail. Yet, by our more modest standards, we had the time of our lives that week.

Our first day in the city, we were to tape *Hullabaloo*. Wally Amos picked us up in an NBC limo and took us to the television studio. Meeting Mick Jagger, Brian Jones and the rest of the Stones on the set was cool, but meeting Brenda Lee was a bigger thrill for me. The Stones were rising fast and had just released "Satisfaction," but they weren't yet legends. Brenda Lee to me was already a legend, and getting to know her was a thrill.

Halfway through rehearsals, cast and crew broke for lunch. We invited Brenda to join us on a quick run to Coney Island for some of those famous Coney Island hot dogs, and she jumped all over the chance. Brenda's spunk and good humor made it a perfect outing at the beach.

Back in the studio, the taping went well; outside the studio, thanks to the efforts of Wally, Joe, Mel, Scepter/Wand and all the rest of our team, we were interviewed constantly our whole time there. The press coverage they set up for our gold album event was unbelievable. We invited the cast and crew of *Hullabaloo* to the Warwick for an after-the-party party. There were people everywhere, waiting to see us, asking questions, asking for autographs, telling us how great we were—always something nice to hear, whether it was true or not. It was crazy and fun and we felt like we were the toast of the town. Joe and Mel had celebrity hotel parties planned every night for us.

Courtesy of Mike, we had an endorsement deal with Guild Guitar Company, whereby they gave him guitars in return for the promotional benefits they received from having Mike play their guitars on stage. On our second day in the Big Apple, Mike and I visited the Guild factory and picked out a few guitars for ourselves. They showed us an experimental one-of-a-kind guitar they'd built using pear wood for the back and sides. Finding it was too expensive, they decided not to make any more guitars using the hard-to-find hardwood. I fell in love with the sound the instrument made and wanted it badly. They told me I could have it, but that they wanted to keep it for the day in order to take some pictures. They said I could pick up the guitar the following day.

The next day, I was walking along, new guitar in hand, when something odd happened—the lights went out, all of them! Traffic lights, office lights, street lights, fluorescent lights, incandescent lights, neon lights—you name the light, it was out. It was as though someone had pulled the plug on New York and, indeed, that's exactly what happened. The entire Northeastern US suddenly found itself without power. The Great Blackout of 1965 was on!

On my half-hour walk back to the hotel, I was astonished by how well New Yorkers handled the unexpected situation. Instead of spreading chaos and disorder, people everywhere were helping each other find their way.

As I walked in the front door of the hotel, Johnny Mathis was at the piano entertaining people who'd gathered in the candle-lit lobby. Seeing the crowd of stranded travelers, I instantly realized what that darkness meant for me: the elevators were out, and I was going to have to climb 32 flights of stairs, carrying two guitars, to get to my choice room. By the time I arrived on my floor, I was totally spent. Fortunately, we had party food everywhere to keep us fed. It would be more than a day before I was brave enough to attempt the stairs again.

Our party was scheduled for Club Arthur, a fashionable and chic New York hot spot at the time. The plan was to load our equipment into Club Arthur after we finished taping *Hullabaloo*. The bad boys from Portland would then provide the musical entertainment for the night, along with any guests who cared to join us on stage. The Great Blackout, however, delayed the party and ruined those plans. The delay meant that Brenda, the Stones, Dionne Warwick and most of the other high-profile celebrities who'd originally promised to come ended up as no-shows, and understandably so. With the odds stacked against them, our team did its best to salvage the situation, but momentum and excitement were lost. Joe managed to call in a few markers and fill Club Arthur with people, and Florence pulled a few strings and talked Angie Dickinson into presenting our gold albums. That attracted some media and excited us, but the expected swarm of paparazzi never materialized.

Hullabaloo, the interviews and the party (such as it was) gave us a big national PR boost. Nonetheless, we couldn't help but be a little disappointed. The team had worked so hard to pull the week together, only to be foiled by a freakish event totally out of their control. Whether an act of God or of Nature or of man or of all three, that cursed power failure definitely rained on our parade. Back on the road, we found ourselves doing one-nighters yet again and telling tales of our experiences during the Great Blackout of 1965.

A few weeks after the Blackout Shelly told me that he was leaving Scandore and Shayne. We were all saddened by the news. I had become close friends with Shelly and his family and I would call him from the road every few days to visit and catch up on the goings on out west in tinsel town. He was joining a management company that managed several superstars and he was really excited about his good fortune. He was like a brother to me and we kept in fairly close contact for a few years but once he started putting in 18 hour days for his new clients he had little time for chatting and we slowly lost contact.

VERSE 25

IT'S unnerving to receive a notice to appear in court. You can feel the blood rushing to your head and the sweat oooooozing from your armpits. Your heart seems like it's about to explode and you wonder what's going to happen to you but you can't really say—no one can. Such were my reactions whenever we were told an "invitation" had arrived at Scepter from the FBI or FCC concerning the investigation of "Louie Louie." For over two years, Specter/Wand's name was always on the "A" list, but the song was definitely ours, which I guess always made the Kingsmen accessories or something.

We'd had great fun playing off our bad boy image—an image we'd admittedly done precious little to earn. From day one, we'd known we were innocent of any wrong-doing, but went along with the game because, thanks to the lyrics controversy, teens everywhere were treating us like heroes. It mattered not how many times we told kids, parents, the press, promoters, fellow performers the lyrics on the record were not obscene. People pro and con remained convinced their version was the correct version of what they absolutely knew were dirty lyrics. All they wanted was for us to confirm they were in possession of the true words, as though that would impart to them a desperately needed cool.

Until now, it had all been a harmless, fun game, a chance to make great music with great friends. Denying rumors, answering accusations with a smile or simply stating "no comment" had always worked, without serious consequences. But now we were faced with a final ruling from a judge, and this was a different story. For the first time, I sensed we truly were in trouble. *What if the FBI or the FCC or whoever is judging the record doesn't believe us?* I thought. *No one else does.* The trick would be to prove ourselves right and our accusers wrong. But how? The words on the record were so garbled! The original lyrics, written to sound Jamaican, were just backward enough that almost anything anyone substituted for them would work. Which was the very reason there were so many different versions of the lyrics floating around, every one of which mysteriously seemed to fit with the record.

I've seen so many different versions of the lyrics over the years, I'm surprised the publishers haven't applied for an entry in the Guinness Book of World Records.

What do I mean when I say "Jamaican?" Take the second verse as an example:

> Me see Jamaica
> De moon above
> It won't be long
> Me see me love

Words in Jamaican English, especially in this song, don't always flow the same way American English does. For this reason, even when sung straight, the lyrics to "Louie Louie" sound garbled to the American ear. And if "Louie" 's lyrics are sung garbled—like they decidedly were by The Kingsmen that fateful April day in 1963—heaven help us! You then have free license to make whatever lyrics you like fit with the music, which is exactly what vast numbers of people did.

And so I wondered, *What will happen to us if those sitting in judgment buy into the dirty versions and don't believe us?*

Controversy causes people to take sides, and there was no middle ground when it came to The Kingsmen. We were heroes to those who thought we were getting away with something, and the source of great hatred to those who thought we were keeping some special dirty secret between us and the youth of America.

Our friends at Specter/Wand fought for as long as they could to keep the matter out of court. To them, the controversy was good for sales, and a final judgment in the case would most likely end the controversy, one way or another. They almost worried we might win and so, in an odd sort of way, did we. If we were vindicated, the press we were getting would soon fade away, along with our career.

ABOVE:
OUR GOLD ALBUM PRESENTATION, NEW YORK—1965
Left to right:
Mike, Norm, Angie Dickinson, Author, Barry, Lynn

LEFT:
THE ALBUM COVER

We were faced with a true dilemma, where neither choice was good. On the one hand, we wanted everyone to know we were not singing dirty lyrics—the rumors that we were, were embarrassing to us, to our friends, and to our families.

On the other hand, if it was found that we were singing obscenities, we might face penalties, fines and/or jail, and our touring and all the money that came with it would almost certainly end. "Pick your poison," the old saying goes. For over two years, we had avoided making that choice. Now, federal authorities were about to make it for us.

Since the investigation first began, every time Hermie or Mel or someone else at Scepter/Wand told us about another request from the FBI or the FCC for statements or documents or copies of the original tape regarding "Louie Louie," it scared us. We told everyone connected with the case we'd make ourselves available whenever they needed us. However, we were always told that Scepter/Wand's attorney's didn't want any of us to appear for any proceeding until or unless it was one in which we were named as defendants and facing prosecution. No doubt about it, statements like that always unnerved us. Thankfully, it was always the record company that was being summoned, not The Kingsmen individually or as a group.

At last, the day arrived when our fate was going to be decided in a final proceeding. The FBI and the FCC would be handing the US Attorney General the judge's finding, whatever it turned out to be. Hermie called Lynn and asked that we get a conference room at the hotel with several phones so he could talk to all of us at once. He was personally attending the proceeding and promised to call us as soon as a decision was rendered. We spent the whole afternoon sitting around, nervously waiting for the phones to ring. We were as edgy as Elizabeth Taylor's cat on a hot tin roof when Hermie finally called.

"Hello," said our leader.

"Hi, Lynn," said Hermie. "Are you all on the phone?"

We all answered individually in the affirmative, sounding like a herd of nervous school kids.

"I hope you're all sitting down," said Hermie.

"We are," we answered.

"We won!" he shouted. "They found in our favor and closed the government's investigation. We won! The bans have been lifted!"

If you've ever wondered what five rock 'n' rollers look like jumping for joy and slapping each other on the back, that moment would have been your chance. For a minute or two, we made absolute fools of ourselves, but we didn't care. "We won!" Once the dust had settled, we realized we didn't know exactly *what* we'd just won or what it meant to our popularity and careers.

"Wait a minute, guys," said Lynn, trying to reel us in and back to reality. "So, Hermie, did they find the record not obscene?"

"Not exactly," answered Hermie.

That got our attention.

"What do you mean, 'not exactly'?" asked Mike, listening on an extension.

"Yeah, what's the deal?" added Barry, listening on another phone.

Hermie could hardly contain his glee as he related to us the goings-on at the proceedings that day. We listened intently to his every word.

According to Hermie, the FBI presented a ton of evidence. They presented letters from parents from all over the country—California, Florida, Michigan, Alabama, Indiana, Illinois, everywhere—and every one of them offered a different version of the lyrics, all of them dirty. They presented documents from church groups, from Ladies Aid Societies, from students and schools. They presented statements collected during FBI field interviews with Richard Berry (the writer), Limax (the publisher), us (the villains), Scepter/Wand, Bob Ehlert, promoters, field agents that witnessed our shows—the list seemed endless. They presented correspondence from J. Edgar himself—letters he wrote to outraged do-gooders from every corner of the nation. They presented letters from state Attorneys General across the country demanding the record be banned and the Kingsmen be prosecuted for obscenities. They even presented correspondence between US Attorney General Robert Kennedy and J. Edgar Hoover that stated "something must be done about the record 'Louie Louie'."

The US Postal Service got into the act, questioning whether Scepter/Wand was involved in transporting obscene materials across state lines. And, of course, the FBI presented its own lab reports, chronicling their meticulous and repeated listenings to the record at various speeds, with every sound frequency alternately boosted or cut in an attempt to bring out the vocals and expose the lyrics.

Finally, after a great deal of heated debate over an individual's right to free speech versus the FCC's authority to regulate standards and practices, it boiled down to a request by the judge to listen to the recording himself. He would try to follow along with the Kingsmen's lyrics and compare them for himself with the many versions submitted as evidence by the FBI and the FCC.

If the judge found that the obscene version(s) of the lyrics matched the lyrics on the record, the FCC would ban the record nationwide and we would be open to prosecution. If not, the FCC would lift all existing bans and we would be off the hook.

According to Hermie, the judge had so many versions in front him, he couldn't tell which ones fit and which ones didn't. Over the phone, as best he could, Hermie reconstructed the dialogue he'd just listened to in the courtroom like atmosphere that day.

LET me tell you what I think," the moderator/judge said, surveying the courtroom.

I think that by giving this record so much attention, you've helped it achieve unwarranted success. This record is not a quality recording, this is not a great song and the performance is riddled with mistakes. Quite frankly, I cannot understand why anyone would ever want to buy this record. Without irrefutable evidence, I have to take these boys [us] at their word. You have given me so many different versions of the lyrics, your own evidence contradicts itself. Merely the fact that you make an accusation does not make it so. Not in this country. Not in my courtroom.

The jurist paused for a moment, removing his wire-rimmed glasses and rubbing his eyes, then went on.

"At this point, I'm inclined to believe you could make any words you want fit with the record—it's just a bunch of mumbo-jumbo."

The judge paused again, letting his words sink in. Speaking slowly and purposefully, he continued.

What I am deciding here today is strictly an issue of regulation.

Taking that into account, we have been asked to decide if this record falls within the legal definition, as set forth in FCC regulations, of "unacceptable material." If any of the obscene versions of the lyrics that I have been given—and for the record, they are numerous—are indeed the lyrics contained on the recording, then, I believe, they would more than fall within the FCC definition of "unacceptable material."

The judge fell silent for a moment, then began again.

I have listened to this... [he paused, shaking his head] "recording," if you can call it that, and, for the life of me, I still cannot understand why anyone would want to buy this thing. I suspect it has a great deal to do with the publicity this is getting and is not due to the quality of the record. But, that's not what we are here to decide. More importantly, I cannot make out any lyrics on this recording.

He paused again.

Evidently, I am not alone. Neither can any of the complainants! I mean, none of these versions can agree on what is being sung, if you want to call that singing.

We have listened to it at every speed and still I hear nothing concrete. So, what are we left with?

I cannot say that this record is not obscene, no more than I can say it is obscene. So, I have no choice. In the interest of fairness, I am going to stand by the FBI labs finding and I am going to deem this record unintelligible at any speed and lift the ban.

WHEN Hermie finished his account of the judge's decision, the five of us just sat there, motionless and silent. No one knew quite what to make of the judge's words.

"What does he mean by that," asked Lynn, "'unintelligible'?"

"Yeah, what does his decision mean?" asked Norm.

"Do we have to go through all of this again?" I added.

"No, you win, big time!" Hermie answered. "We couldn't have had a better decision if we'd written it ourselves.

We were still unclear about what "unintelligible" meant, and about what the ramifications might be.

"What are you talking about?" questioned Barry.

REPORT of the

FEDERAL BUREAU OF INVESTIGATION
WASHINGTON, D. C.

To: FBI, Detroit (145-420)
Re: UNSUB; 45 r.p.m. Recording "Louie Louie" POSSIBLE ITOM

Date: May 17, 1965
FBI File No. 145-2961
Lab. No. D-478135 AV

Specimens received 4/26/65

Q3   One WAND 45 r.p.m. recording bearing on one side the title "Louie Louie (Richard Berry) THE KINGSMEN"

ALSO SUBMITTED: Sheet of paper bearing typewritten words

Result of examination:

    Three additional copies of the phonograph record described above as specimen Q3 have been submitted to the Laboratory. One of the previous records was submitted by the Tampa Office with a letter dated 2/17/64 and captioned "UNSUB; Phonograph Record 'Louie Louie' Distributed By Limax Music, NYC; ITOM"; one record was submitted by the San Diego Office with a letter dated 3/17/64 and captioned "WAND, 1650 Broadway, New York, New York; ITOM"; and one of the previous records was submitted by the Indianapolis Office with a letter dated 3/27/64 and captioned "UNSUB; Phonograph Record Recorded By The Kingsmen Entitled 'Louie Louie'; ITOM."

    Because the lyrics of the recording "Louie Louie" could not be definitely determined in the Laboratory examination, it was not possible to determine whether this recording, Q3, is obscene.

    In accordance with your request, specimen Q3 is returned herewith. The "ALSO SUBMITTED" material is retained.

Letter from the FBI Lab, DC. 1965 Printed through the Freedom of information/Privacy Act section 202-324-5520

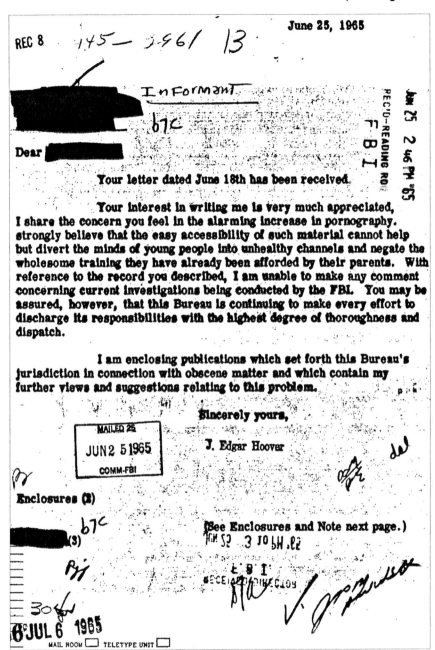

J. Edgar Hoover letter to an irate parent. 1965 Printed through the Freedom of information/Privacy Act section 202-324-5520

"Instead of saying 'Louie Louie' was or wasn't obscene," Hermie answered, "the judge deemed it 'unintelligible.' That means, he couldn't understand a damn thing on the record and he doesn't think anybody else can, either. So he lifted the ban. The rumors are still intact, 'Louie Louie' is still on the radio, and wait until you see the press we're going to get now. We play this right and we'll have a monster record on our hands—again. Everyone will think The Kingsmen have gotten away with it."

Once we understood what Hermie was telling us, we were elated. And soon, just as he predicted, "Louie Louie" started to climb the charts yet again and continued to sell crazily for years. Our bad-boy, no-comment personna remained intact in the eyes of the world.

Over 1,000 covers of "Louie" have now been recorded—with more no doubt to come—making it the second most recorded song in the history of rock 'n' roll. The pannel's decision that day gave the youth of America an icon that endures today, representing the vicarious victory of a collective act of defiance. "Louie Louie" no longer belongs to The Kingsmen, it belongs to the ages, and to each new generation that believes in having fun and thumbing their noses occasionally at convention and the status quo. (It didn't hurt either that, a few years later, John Belushi chose to sing a dirty version of "Louie Louie" in *Animal House*.) And still, to this day, people wonder what the real words are. The world of "Louie Louie" remains as it should be, "unintelligible at any speed."

VERSE 26

IT was a fairly common thing for the fans to take souvenirs, like the license plates or filler cap off our bus or anything else they could steal. We were on our way to a ballroom at an amusement park in Mt. Holyoke, Massachusetts. We were late for our engagement, and Jimmy-John was speeding through town trying to get us to the venue as quickly as he could when he was stopped by a city policeman.

"Damn it!" he yelled as he pulled the big silver-and-blue Herkimer Number Three over to the side of the road. JJ was fighting mad as he hopped out of the driver's seat and opened the door. The policeman met him at the side of the bus.

"May I see your driver's license and registration?" asked the officer nicely.

"What for?" complained the frustrated buck-toothed ex-jarhead as he took his license out of his wallet.

"Well, for one thing, you were going 55 in a 30-mile-an-hour speed zone. For another, I followed you through at least three red lights, and your bus has no plates, and you failed to come to a complete stop atno less than four stop signs!"

We hadn't been home in several months, and Jimmy'd forgotten that his driver's license had expired.

"I guess I could add driving without a current valid driver's license to the list," suggested the flustered cop as he looked at Jimmy-John's driver's license.

"Oh, yeah?" JJ responded. "Well, I know my rights, and you can't do this to me. I was a Varine [Marine] and I've been trained to drive every kind of vehicle there is!"

The confused officer just looked at the former Marine as Jimmy-John continued to semi-articulate his incomprehensible, screwy point while digging his grave deeper with every word.

Overhearing all of this, we started to worry that the cop was going to take Jimmy-John to jail, and we couldn't afford the time to go to a police station and deal with this predicament—we were already late as it was. So we voted for Mike to go out and address the officer. Hey, it was his cousin!

"Have you been drinking?" the policeman asked Jimmy-John.

"Hell, no, I haven't been drinking! What do you think this is?" answered Jimmy-John, raising his voice belligerently. "I have responsibilities and I don't have time for this. Don't you know who I have in this bus?"

"No, what are you talking about?" asked the baffled and frustrated cop. "I don't care if you were a 'Varine' or who you have in this illegal vehicle, or how late you are, or even what your mother's name is! I'm citing you for driving without a license, failing to stop at a stop sign, running a red light, driving an unlicensed vehicle and impersonating a human!"

"You can't do that!" exclaimed JJ.

"I can't?" responded the angry cop.

"No!" explained the exasperated Jimmy-John. "It will take too long, and furthermore, I have been trained to drive in all conditions, so I don't have to stop at stop signs, and I know when it's safe to squeeze through a red light!"

"Are you out of your mind, son?" asked the officer. "The law is the law, and in my town, there are no exceptions. Everybody stops for a red light, even a 'Varine!'"

"I have to get these guys to the amusement park. These guys are famous and they're late for their concert!"

"Are these the guys playing up at the park?" asked the officer, suddenly interested.

"What do you think I've been tryin' to tell you?" yelled our resident jarhead.

"Well, why didn't you say so instead of talking about all of this 'Varine' stuff! My daughter's at that concert waiting for you guys, and she's not going to be disappointed because her dad had to give you a bunch of tickets. Follow me, I'll get you there in a few minutes."

Mike didn't have time to say a word. He just turned around and quietly got back on the bus.

"Jimmy-John, you're amazing!" said Mike as JJ climbed behind the wheel.

"No," answered JJ, "I'm a Varine. They can't fool me!"

That kept us laughing all the way to the amusement park as the cop escorted us through town, lights flashing.

While we unloaded and set up, Mike, our nice guy and diplomat, talked with the cop and explained our situation to him. The officer finally calmed down and changed his attitude completely when Mike invited him to bring his daughter and her friends out to the bus to get autographs after the show. The cop accepted Mike's offer and, once the concert was finished, brought his daughter out to meet us. We played like we knew him well and gave her an autographed picture. Instantly, he became her hero. He even introduced his daughter to our "Varine," Jimmy-John.

As the months progressed, Norm spent more and more and more of his time on the phone with his brother and father talking business. Sunn had taken off like a skyrocket and, with every new phone call, the list of famous bands using its equipment grew longer and more impressive. Given Lynn's drinking and Norm's success, the tension that had been building between them for years was showing its face almost every day.

Whenever Lynn wasn't around, Norm brought up his drinking. He carried his protests further and further, finally insisting the time had come to take the leadership of the band out of Lynn's hands. He thought Lynn was hurting us with promoters and the press. Norm couldn't get past Lynn's "need to succeed" or his determination to be the most popular Kingsman, and Lynn couldn't get past Norm's standing up to him or his prodding us or his success with the girls and Sunn.

In the spring of 1967, we were about to play a concert on the East Coast when Norm, who was a little late, came hurrying into the dressing room after being on the phone. Seeing Norm, Lynn said something like, "Were you selling another amp or lying to another unsuspecting girl?"

His comment hit Norm exactly the wrong way.

"Go have a drink, you ass!" Norm snapped, bowing his back.

"What do you mean by that, Cyrano?" Lynn snapped back.

Norm gritted his teeth.

"What the hell are you talkin' about, you lush?" he challenged.

Lynn's thoughtless reprimand turned to anger.

"Everybody knows what you're doing on the road to get laid," he said, his voice shaking, "and about your bee-essing to Shannon about marrying her. You're not going to marry her. You're just feeding her the same line you feed all of your other gullible girls on the road just to get laid!"

Norm threw down his bag and flew at Lynn, fists swinging.

"Stop!" Mike screamed as he and Barry jumped between the fighters and grabbed them, stopping the senseless match before someone was needlessly hurt—physically. Emotionally and mentally, it was already too late.

As Barry pulled Norm away from Lynn, Norm yelled, "I don't need this crap from you and I'm not taking it any longer! You guys can keep on following this drunken idiot if you want to, but I quit!"

"Good riddance!" Lynn shouted back. "Asshole! Bass players are a dime a dozen!"

"I'm surprised you have a dime," shot back Norm, venom dripping from his words. "I thought all of your dimes went to calling bars to find the closest place to feed your habit."

Norm and Lynn had grown up in Portland, Oregon with two active volcanoes—Mount Hood to the east and Mount St. Helens to the north—looming on the horizon. In 1980, Mount St. Helens blew her top, with devastating effect; in 1967, Mount Easton and Mount Sundholm blew their tops on the same day, with devastating effect. Three years of pent-up frustration and anger on both sides were all released in that one explosive, double-barrelled outburst.

No matter what arguments we used, no matter what tactics we tried, we couldn't change Norm's mind. On the negative side, Lynn and his drinking were Norm's official excuses for leaving The Kingsmen. On the positive side, Sunn was Norm's real reason for leaving the band. Sunn amps had been his brainchild, and his baby was growing up fast. Like any proud father, he wanted to be there to watch and help and be a part of his progeny's life. By 1967, the company had long since ceased being a hobby. An international Who's Who of rock stars were using Sunn equipment, and the company needed, nay, *demanded* Norm's full-time attention. He made the only reasonable choice he had. A nasty fight with Lynn only hastened the inevitable. Norm angrily—and wisely—stuck to his guns and quit the band. It was time.

Although we soon hired another bassist—a talented musician who fit in perfectly with the four of us—to replace Norm, we deeply felt the loss. Oddly, in some ways, we had even more fun with Norm gone. But a fellow Musketeer can never truly be replaced—there's too much history to overcome—and, besides, when a player is replaced, the music changes, maybe only to a small degree, but it changes nonetheless. It took some time to adjust to the change, but we accepted it as part of a new day in the evolving history of our band.

IN 1967, if you were 18 or older and unmarried and not in school, you were a prime candidate for military service, by choice or not. Since we'd all given up college to tour, it was only a matter of time before the unmarried among us became eligible for the draft. Gold records meant nothing to the Army with a bloody war raging in Southeast Asia.

Lynn was married and had a child, so he was exempt. Single and out of school, Mike was the first Kingsman to receive his Notice to Appear, that dreaded, impersonal letter from the Selective Service with the infamous opening line, "Greetings."

Mike dutifully appeared for his draft physical, whereupon he discovered there were more benefits to being a rock star than mere unlimited access to accommodating young girls. He'd been playing his guitar so loud for so long, he'd largely destroyed the fine hairs of his inner ears. Citing his resulting deafness, the Army doctors declared Mike unfit to serve his country.

This was an era when draft-dodgers were escaping to Canada in droves, and young men who couldn't or wouldn't go north were trying everything they could think of to avoid military service. At about this time, *Newsweek* ran a feature story describing some of the tactics being employed. It concluded by quoting an Army officer who said, "If all else fails, wear a pair of black lace panties to your physical." To my knowledge, Mike didn't raid his girlfriend's lingerie drawer before his date with the medicos, but he did just happen to spend the entire evening before his physical in a pool swimming with JJ, leaving his ears acutely plugged. Mike was lucky that way, though: He always seemed to step on the one pile of crap that didn't stink.

Because of an asthmatic childhood condition, I was given 4 F status, which meant I would be among the last in the universe to be called up.

Barry sweated out his approaching notice. He was a peacenik at heart and totally against the Army and the war. He started seeing a psychiatrist some time earlier to build up a medical history, hoping the file would exempt him from service. As further protection from Army life, he and Desha planned to be married. One time in New York, Barry showed us the file that he had from his psychiatrist. It concluded, "After many weeks of evaluation, it is my professional opinion that Mr. Curtis is mentally unfit to serve in the Army." (Barry didn't need to consult a shrink to figure that out. Any one of his fellow Kingsmen would gladly and truthfully have testified to that effect.)

He who hesitates is lost. Before Barry could marry, he received his Notice to Appear. He arrived at the induction center with his psychiatric file in hand and a confirmed date when he was to be married. Seeing that, the Army doctors harrumphed, threw away his file, ignored his date at the altar and drafted him instantly. Figuring he might skip the country or marry if given the chance, they denied him the customary day or two with which to put his affairs in order and shipped him straight to Southern California without letting him make so much as a phone call. Bare spent six weeks in basic training, after which he and Desha *were* married. As soon as he graduated from ground school, the Army shipped him to Vietnam.

Losing Barry to the Army was completely unexpected, and we had no plan ready for replacing him. We only had a few days in which to find a new keyboardist, which we managed to do, but we worried about Barry every day for the next two years. During that time, we toured and recorded with two different keyboard players and three different bass players, wishing and hoping and waiting for Barry's return.

Life plays funny tricks on us sometimes. Of all of the Kingsmen, Barry was by far the least likely candidate for military service, intellectually and spiritually—a genuine pacifist in the best sense of the word. Yet, he was the only one of us Five Musketeers to serve.

After Barry left, Lynn lasted a little over a year. Pressures from our traveling and his drinking took their toll on this talented young man. Once carefree and energetic, he'd turned morose and apathetic. In an effort to save his life and marriage, we finally asked him to resign. That was a tough and emotional moment for all of us. Along with Mike, Lynn had been a founding member of the band and instrumental to our success. He'd been a Kingsman for over a decade, from the untroubled days when he played bongos and Mike played acoustic guitar and they both sang folk songs, through the chaotic recording of "Louie Louie" and the FBI's feverish pursuit of the song's true lyrics, to the post-hearing era when song and group reached iconic status.

No longer a Kingsman, Lynn had a few trying and troublesome years still to come. To his credit, and thanks to his tenacity, he triumphed over all of his personal demons and pulled his life back together. With the help and support of his family and friends, his fellow Musketeers, AA, a sailboat and his faith, our former-and-forever leader found his way back home. Today, his fun-loving, friendly, well-loved personality flourishes in full measure.

WHAT Lynn went through was basically nothing more than being human, all too human under extraordinary circumstances. The rest of us went through many of the same things; we just handled fame and being on the road and all the rest differently. Which doesn't necessarily mean we were angels. At times, the other four of us were equally at fault for losing our perspective. The surfeit of adulation and money we received affected all of us in a negative way to some degree. Until you live through such an experience, you can't imagine what an overdose of money and fame and PR can do to you, especially if you're just seventeen, as I was at the outset of my Kingsman career, or barely nineteen, as my four band mates were when I joined them.

At first, we accepted the fame and money with innocence and some measure of embarrassment. It didn't take long, however, before we started believing our own PR. That's when the trouble starts and you begin to lose your identity and perspective. When you come to expect the adulation, when you take the money and constant boot-licking for granted, that's when you lose respect for things that matter and focus on satisfying your immediate desires. Everything—girls, cars, homes, fans—becomes a hamburger, an easily replaced Happy Meal. With a McDonald's on every block, when you get hungry you just stop and order another hamburger. With so many girls available, they all become just another girl. With so many makes of car to choose from, when you get tired of one or wreck it, you just head to the nearest dealership and buy another model—with cash. With homes never being quite large enough, when one grows too cramped, you trade up into something bigger with better views. When old fans lose interest in you, new fans always come along ready to idolize you and beg for your autograph. Whatever gets you through the day is your only line of sight. In the end, you're left blinded to reality, unprepared for the devastating day when it all comes to an unexpected end.

FINALE

WITH the passing of the '60s, our ability to work steadily lessened. Times and tastes were changing, and audiences turned to the next generation of rock bands for their musical kicks. A phrase then popular, "tune in and turn on," matched neither our style nor our values, and interest in us faded. We'd charted 23 records—though most of them barely made the Top 100—nine albums, four top hits, and two number ones, one of which, "Louie Louie," remains to this day easily one of the biggest records in rock 'n' roll history. We'd been on countless television shows and made innumerable friends while surviving five-plus years of life on the road. Despite all that, the industry was leaving us behind and national bookings were growing scarce. We began staying home in the Northwest where we could always find work.

With the end clearly in sight, we contacted the "accountant" in New York in charge of our corporation to plan for the less-fruitful days ahead. For years, we'd been told that our corporation was doing well. When we spoke to the accountant, however, he informed us that the corporation was broke. When we asked to audit the books, he told us they'd been lost in a fire. Our nest egg was gone, untold thousands of dollars had disappeared without a trace, and our erstwhile financial managers just shrugged their shoulders and turned their backs on us. With our resources suddenly limited, we were suddenly forced to focus on surviving.

The dreams of the extraordinary and secure future that were born from such a successful youth, and the energetic optimism we all carried were replace with doubt and despair. Having to face reality, we tried as best we could to put that disappointment out of mind. For the next few years, we tripped around the Northwest, playing wherever and whenever we could. Things changed almost overnight in 1978 when *Animal House* was released, featuring John Belushi singing "Louie Louie" at a wild Delta House frat party early in the film and The Kingsmen's version playing in the movie and during the credits at the film's end. Director John Landis called "Louie" "the anthem for raucous behavior," and truer words were never spoken. Courtesy of *Animal House*, we found ourselves transformed from a bunch of "has-beens" scrambling for their next gig into a "classic" rock group back in wide demand. We started working nationally again and, when the Oldies craze arrived, it brought with it a welcome opportunity to continue working for as long as we cared. As *Animal House* became one of the highest-grossing films of all time, we noticed that nary a penny in royalties from "Louie"'s use, nor any of our recordings, came our way. *Very strange!* "we thought.

THEY say that in publishing you never finish writing a book, you just print it. With these pages growing large in number, I need to stop soon with my Kingsmen road stories. Otherwise, I'll end up going to press with a tome the size of *War and Peace*. To fill the time between now and when the presses roll, I'm going to jump ahead from the '70s into the 1990s.

It was 1992, and we'd just finished a free outdoor concert in a downtown public park in Rockford, Illinois. As we were signing autographs that beautiful summer evening, I heard a loud voice say, "I was in a famous rock 'n' roll band once!" I looked up and saw an unshaven, unbathed homeless man standing before me, holding on to a shopping cart full of his possessions and trying to get my attention.

I didn't give the man a second of my time and tried to get him to move on down the sidewalk. Most of the autograph seekers around me were young kids, and I didn't want him disturbing them.

Instead of moving, he held his ground and continued to chant, over and over, "Hey, man, I was in a famous rock 'n' roll band once! Hey, man, I was in a famous rock 'n' roll band once! Hey, man, I was in a famous rock 'n' roll band once!..."

"Hey, fella, could you just move along?" I said, growing increasingly irritated and disrespectful, "Can't you see, I'm a little busy here?"

Still, he wouldn't leave. Just then, I had an idea.

"Why don't you go talk to that guy over there?" I said to the derelict, pointing to Barry. "He's our resident old rock 'n' roll aficionado, and I'm sure he'd just love to talk to you."

"Okay, thanks!" said the drifter politely as he wheeled his stuff over to Barry. "I appreciate your kindness, sir."

I continued to sign things for the kids until all of the autograph seekers were taken care of. As we were getting into the 15-passenger van that was to carry us back to our hotel, Barry said, "Did any of you meet the guy who used to play sax in Little Richard's band?"

"You mean the bum with the shopping cart full of stuff?" I answered.

"Yeah, he was a really cool guy!" said Barry enthusiastically.

"He was!?" I questioned.

"Yeah! I don't know if it was the real guy or not. I mean, I didn't check his ID or anything, but he sure knew all of the right names of the guys that were in Richard's band back in the '50s."

"You're joking!" I replied, starting to feel guilty.

"Well, he certainly had all of his facts straight," replied Barry. "If he wasn't in Little Richard's band, he sure fooled me!"

I felt awful. At that moment, I realized I'd been a complete jerk, that I was all of the things I hated, all of the things I'd vowed never to become.

I tried to picture myself in that homeless man's position, and the more I thought about it, the angrier I became. *How could a guy be in a famous rock 'n' roll band that sold that many records and end up broke?* I'd heard the records he'd performed on countless times—played on the radio, featured in television ads, included in movie sound tracks. *Who's making all of the money?* Suddenly, I realized someone besides us was raking in a fortune off of all of *our* records. That thought started to weigh on me night and day. Two of my best friends and life-long band mates were barely scratching out a living, and none of us had been paid a penny in over 20 years for the use of "Louie Louie" or any of our other songs.

I'd worked hard all of my life and, although not wealthy, I was fairly comfortable at the time, financially speaking. My house was almost paid for, and I had no debt to speak of. So I talked with my wife Paige about trying to make right the situation with our records and royalties before a Kingsman found himself standing behind a shopping cart carrying all of *his* possessions telling some arrogant rock 'n' roller like me, "Hey, man, I was in a famous rock 'n' roll band once!"

Paige suggested that I call Laura Ben-Porat. Laura was a brilliant, highly respected lawyer living in Southern California and practicing with Gibson, Dunn & Crutcher, one of the top legal firms in the world. Laura had been Paige's best friend since high school and her maid of honor in our wedding.

I put a call in to Laura and, after I explained to her my plight, we discussed the different legal options I might pursue. Within a few days, she phoned me back. She'd come up with an ingenious legal theory she felt just might fly if we could find the case law to support her argument. She also advised me that Gibson, Dunn were far too expensive for me to afford and that it would be more cost-effective if I could find a lawyer willing to take my case on a contingency basis.

Laura's theory involved filing for rescission of the original contract. Although the statute of limitations for the State of California, where we filed our case, allowed us to sue for royalties dating back no more than four years, she believed we had grounds to rescind (cancel) our agreement, which would give us ownership of all of our masters. If we owned those, we'd then be entitled to *all* of the money generated by them and not just the royalties (which we weren't being paid anyway). By law, she pointed out, if you signed a contract with another party and they committed a material breach by not living up to any of its provisions, you had the right to void that contract.

The contract in question was the one negotiated by Joe Scandore that we'd signed with Florence and Marvin at Scepter/Wand's New York offices in 1968—the same document that promised us nine percent of the song's future licensing fees and royalties and profits and Jerry Dennon two percent of the same. In the ensuing years, ownership rights to "Louie Louie" and 105 other Kingsmen songs had passed on from Scepter/Wand to a Nashville-based company, GML, Inc. (The initials stood for Gayron "Moe" Lytle, principal owner and a frequent target of royalty-related lawsuits from artists such as The Shirelles, Hank Ballard and Gene Pitney.) Our suit—and several resultant counter-suits—involved GML and two related companies, Highland Music and Gusto Records, Inc.

While studying our original contract with Scepter/Wand, Laura noticed a provision stating that our record company was obligated *in perpetuity* to account to us for all royalties due, as well as to pay them. It also stipulated that our obligation to them ended if and when the contract expired. By not having paid us a penny in the past four years (in the past *30* years, in fact, as their own lawyer admitted in US District Court in 1998), and not having accounted for any of the royalties received during that time, the record company had created a material breach, which in turn gave us the right to cancel the contract, thereby ending any obligations we had to them and giving us control of the masters. The specific provisions of the four-year statute of limitations were key to Laura's argument. Under them, our contract—although renewed annually—was forever only a four-year contract. Because the record company had neither paid us nor provided an accounting during the previous four-year period, we could rescind.

We discussed potential lawyers, and she suggested talking with Cheryl Hodgson. Cheryl and I had worked together previously in a successful action by the band to take back ownership of the "Louie Louie" and Kingsmen names and trademarks. She'd done a great job for us then, and her "let's take on the world and right a wrong" kind of attitude and personality were perfect for dealing with the sorts of challenges we'd face in our new suit.

I called Cheryl, and we talked about the pros and cons of taking on the mysterious Missouri corporation that owned our masters. She was gung ho about trying to set a precedent with the case, but felt that her legal practice lacked the resources needed to take on such a sophisticated and time-consuming action. She said she wanted to talk with a lawyer friend of hers and see whether he might be interested in having his firm join her in the action. Their added manpower and his court experience, she believed, would greatly improve our chances for success. After several discussions, we decided to proceed together as a team—Cheryl's and her friend's firms and yours truly on behalf of The Kingsmen.

I filed the suit in all of our names; with a win, everyone would be entitled to their fair share of royalties and other earnings. Knowing the financial strength of the expected plaintiff, I proposed taking sole responsibility for all of the costs, provided that Cheryl and I were given free rein to run with the case as we thought best. With nothing to lose and everything to gain, everyone agreed to our terms, and we moved forward with the case.

In countless hours of research, Cheryl unearthed a precedent, *Nolan v Nolan*, that not only supported our argument but became the cornerstone of our case. With her partners, she put together a solid legal argument. None of us anticipated, however, the no-holds-barred ruthlessness of GML or their resourcefulness in exploiting our judicial system. The defendants countered our suit by filing lawsuits of their own against me in several different states where they had operations. As a result, plaintiff became defendant and defendant plaintiff; in time, things grew so confused, a US Circuit Court judge described our case as "procedurally convoluted."

GML's strategy was shrewd and financially beyond my means to counter. By filing a suit against me in New York, for example (which was one of their tactics), they forced me to answer their suit or lose by default. Were that to happen, GML could then take their judgment from the New York court, where they'd filed against me, to the federal court in California, where I'd filed against them, and have my case dismissed, citing their judgment against me in a different state regarding the same matter. If I were to answer their suit and avert an underhanded, bitter defeat, I would need to hire an attorney who was a member of the New York State bar. That would require paying a retainer.

In our legal system, an attorney practicing in one state can't argue a case in another state unless he or she has passed the bar in that state. Common practice is to hire a local firm and have your attorney handle the matter through their practice. The local firm becomes the firm of record, and they must oversee all of the legal work filed and be present at all legal proceedings—all of which is billable.

GML already had legal representation in place in several different states where they operated and worked through these to file their suits, making the process a simple one for them. For me, it was an entirely different matter: I couldn't afford to start hiring attorneys all over the US and, I think, GML knew it. Thankfully, I had allies. The thought of losing by default, of someone manipulating the legal system, of being denied our day in court, angered the now-determined Ms. Hodgson. Cheryl flew to New York and enlisted the help of a local attorney friend. After months of sweat and aggravation, they managed to a convince a New York judge to stay her decision in the suit filed against me by GML until the federal court in California had rendered its decision (the judge handed Cheryl her victory based on the prior filing date of our pending suit in California).

That was a huge win for us. We now had a stay of judgment from a New York judge that we could take to judges in any other states where GML tried to file actions against me and ask them to also defer to the California court's decision. It returned the ball game to our home field—not, however, without adding significantly to my legal expenses.

When the judge rendered his decision, it rescinded our recording contract and returned ownership of our masters to us. *We won!* we thought briefly, but our fight wasn't over yet, not by a long shot. What should've been a knock-out punch proved to be only the end of round one and the beginning of a prolonged legal nightmare.

When you win a judgment, you're supposed to prepare a document declaring to the court all of the things you think you've just won. If the judge agrees with your document, he signs the judgment, making it his order; if the judge thinks you've made claims that haven't been argued or proved, he can amend your document as he sees fit.

When you win a judgment, it isn't a matter of simply taking back your property. You must first declare to the court all of the rights, titles and interests that comprise your property, as well as any copies that may exist of your property and the rights, titles, and interests that belong to those copies, as well as any licenses granted or owned by your property. Successfully drawing up such a document, one that gets everything right, is what separates true lawyers from common advocates.

If your counsel neglects to include *every* aspect of your rights in this document, he leaves the door open for the people you've just defeated to continue using your property and reap the rewards of its use without paying you a cent. Plus, if your advocate fails to cross every "*t*" and dot every "*i*" during your legal proceedings, the opposition can exploit those loop holes in their appeals and overturn or greatly delay your victory.

Laura was thrilled when I phoned her with the good news. As our conversation continued, she prepared me for what to expect next, cautioning me to make absolutely certain that the document of judgment was complete. It was still my case, despite the fact that my lawyers were preparing the document; it was my responsibility and no one else's to look after this most important phase of the proceeding.

Cheryl was well aware of the importance of this document and told me she was waiting as we spoke for her partners to hand her a copy of the first draft. She promised to fax the document to me as soon as she received it. Then we'd go over it together with a fine-toothed comb to make sure everything known to man was covered. You only get one chance in such matters, and once you've filed your judgment, you can't take it back or amend it. Knowing this, we were determined to get it right.

Cheryl's partners, thinking the draft of the document they had in hand was complete, filed the judgment with the court without seeking her input and sent her a copy only afterward. Their document fell far short of the mark, creating a mess and guaranteeing me several more years of nightmares. Immediately, GML filed new lawsuits against me—none in California—and began filing appeals to the decision just rendered.

Usually, it is the loser that appeals a judgment and the terms contained therein. In our case, however, GML's attorneys loved the document Cheryl's colleagues drafted. She had to go before the judge and essentially appeal the document of judgment our own team had prepared. It wasn't pretty. Although the judge was on our side, he knew that if he allowed us to amend our document after it had been filed, his decision would be overturned in a higher court.

With no other choice, he denied the appeal, and a new legal battle was begun. Because of this blunder, I encountered a great deal of pressure from the band, who now had something to gain. They demanded that I fire our counsel and file a malpractice suit against them. Although largely innocent, Cheryl got caught in the middle.

I went through a succession of new attorneys and lost track of how many actions we were fighting. Finally, as my last resort and best hope, I hired Gibson, Dunn and Crutcher. A powerful worldwide firm, they had offices and manpower in most of the states where we were battling. With them as my advocates, I felt I might have a chance. Scott Edelman became the lead attorney handling my case. He warned me it was going to take years of time and piles of money for his team to unravel the legal mess I was in. I was prepared to fight the battle but not to withstand the financial hammer about to fall on my world.

ENCORE

SCOTT and Laura had been working on my case for almost a year. Following a series of meetings with them in Southern California, I was flying home to Portland when I suddenly found myself staring out the window at the distant Sierra Nevadas, numb from the endless ordeal and fighting back tears of despair. In a few hours, I would have to face my family bearing only bad news.

At the outset of the case, my original counsel had told me this would be a rather simple and inexpensive lawsuit costing "maybe 30 grand, tops." Thirty thousand dollars sounded like a lot of money to Paige and me. Nonetheless, after some brief soul searching, we decided to invest the money and fight to right a wrong. A victory had the potential of not only changing our lives, but of dramatically affecting the lives of my best friends and sending reverberations throughout an entire industry.

That optimism now seemed naïve and remote. As my plane winged northward, thoughts of how this supposedly simple lawsuit had spun out of control and taken over my life consumed me. I'd been drained of all hope and funds and wondered when if ever I'd recover. My legal bills had reached an unfathomable sum, and that promised light at the end of the tunnel was most likely a runaway financial train that would soon crash into my world and obliterate what little I had left.

With Scott and Laura and their team of lawyers, I was now fighting a multitude of cases. Five months earlier, as my legal bill approached $80,000, Scott had told me I'd have to come up with at least $200,000 within six months or they'd be forced by their partners to withdraw from my case.

Knowing that Scott had been victorious for us in proceeding after proceeding, I'd hoped that his firm would stick with me to the end, deferring their payment until then, confident that when this was finally over, funds from the inevitable judgment in my favor would more than cover their fees.

As I was leaving our meeting earlier that day, Scott had asked how my fund-raising efforts were coming along. I told him I was leaving no stone unturned, working daily on the problem. He alerted me that his partners were putting a great deal of pressure on him and expressed hope that I would be able to find the necessary funds within the next month, allowing them to continue representing me. Although disappointed, I couldn't blame him. They'd been fronting my costs for nearly a year. Laura had warned me in our first conversation about the case that they were too expensive for me to afford. She was about to be proven right.

Watching the patchwork of croplands pass below, I reminisced about simpler times filled with innocence and hope and wondered how Lil' Dickie from Gig Harbor could ever have gotten himself into a mess like this. The jolt of my plane touching down finally woke me from my journey back in time. Driving home, I found myself laughing out loud as comical memories of the past surfaced. Walking in the front door, I was attacked by two overly enthusiastic children bowling me over and showering me with kisses and talking a thousand miles an hour about their week. My daughter Teal rattled on about her ballet classes. Leaving my arms, she demonstrated the new positions she'd learned while I was in LA. At the same time, my son Karris had his hands on my cheeks, pulling my head away from Teal in an effort to tell me about the fort they'd built together down by the creek. To top it off, our Australian Shepherd Fa was dropping her tennis ball next to me, demanding that I throw the blasted thing so she could fetch it. The chaos was at once wonderful and emotionally wrenching. Just then, Paige came out of the kitchen and asked me how my meetings went. How was I going to tell her we were on the verge of losing everything?

"You kids go play and let me talk with your papa for a few minutes," she said smiling, wiping her hands on her apron. "Okay?"

The two whirling dervishes gave me hugs and scampered off to play. I got up off the floor and put my arms around Paige. She could sense the sadness in my touch as I hugged her.

"So, it didn't go too well, huh?" she asked.

"As far as the lawsuit goes, there's no way I can legally lose," I answered, "but Gibson, Dunn can't back off from their position. I have less than a month to come up with $200,000 or they withdraw from the case."

"What happens then?" she asked.

"I default, I lose the case and I owe over $200,000 to Gibson, Dunn and Crutcher."

"Come on, let's go into the kitchen. I have dinner on."

I followed Paige into the kitchen.

"So, what are we going to do next?" she asked as she walked over to the stove top.

"I guess just keep doing what we've been doing for the last five months," I answered, tired and dejected, "keep faxing and calling corporations, superstars, and the richest people in the world asking for their help. There's so much at stake here for so many people. Until Scott withdraws, I'll just keep pressing and praying. There's nothing else I can do."

"You've been doing that for months and not one person has called or faxed back. What makes you think someone's going to help you now?"

She was right, of course, but I had no choice. If I could only get these people to see how this judgment affected their future, surely they'd help. I continued to send and re-send faxes to countless people and corporations that I knew had something to gain were I to win. I'd been asking for help from them for months, but breaking through multi-layered corporate veils and management buffers was proving to be an impossible task. Daily, I sent faxes to superstars and their management companies, explaining that my precedent-setting suit would ultimately affect the many unpaid—and in some cases, starving—rock 'n' roll acts that had paved the way for their success. Still, my phone didn't ring and my fax machine remained silent. All the while, I spoke with either Scott or Laura nearly every day as they faithfully worked on my many cases.

Finally, D-day arrived, on a Friday. Scott called in the afternoon with the sad news that, effective at 5 PM, Gibson, Dunn was officially withdrawing from my cases.

All morning, I'd been faxing doomsday messages in a desperate, last ditch effort to get someone, *anyone* to respond. After the disappointing call from Scott, I gave up sending faxes and sat down at the dinning room table with Paige.

"Looks like we lose," I said, my eyes starting to tear.

"Well, you gave it a good try," she said through tears of her own, trying to encourage me. "We can sell the house and try something else."

It had taken us five years to build our dream house with our own hands and it killed me to ask her to give it up. At that moment, the phone rang, momentarily relieving the strain. I picked up the receiver.

"Is Dick in?" an unfamiliar voice asked.

"This is Dick," I answered. "Who's this?"

He told me his name, and I was surprised beyond belief. [He has since asked to remain anonymous, so I will call him "Mr. X."]

"I've been getting faxes from you for months," he said, "and this morning I got a fax saying 'today is doomsday.' What's this all about?"

"Unfortunately, you're a little late," I said hopelessly. "I wish you'd called yesterday."

"Indulge me and give me just the high points," he insisted.

One more time, I told my tale.

"I won a precedent-setting lawsuit that makes it possible for a recording artist to rescind their contracts and own their masters if they're not paid the royalties they're due. However, without financial assistance, I can no longer defend my victory. The opposition has appealed the judgment granted to me by federal court and, through a series of events, I now have several related lawsuits to defend. My adversary's tactic has been to financially break me and force me into default. Today, in about an hour, they will have accomplished their goal."

"I see from your fax that this action encompasses intellectual property. Is this true?"

"Yes, sir, it does, and it affects real property rights as well."

"Can you be in my office Monday by 10 in the morning to meet with a few of my people?"

"Sure, but what good will that do? I go into default in less than an hour, and there's nothing I can do about it."

"You have no idea what I can do," Mr. X countered with a laugh. "Stay on the line and give my assistant whatever information she requires, and I'll see you Monday morning at 10."

His assistant came on the line and asked me for Scott's number, saying she'd get everything she needed from him. Hanging up the phone, I told Paige about the call. Like me, she thought it puzzling but welcome.

At quarter to five, Scott called.

"I just got a call from Mr. X," he said excitedly. "How on earth do you know him?"

I explained to my astonished counsel the things I'd been doing to find financial support and told him that, encouraged by some of my friends, Mr. X had responded to my final plea for help.

"That's amazing!" he said. "Well, the good news is, I've talked with everyone here and, because of the interest from Mr. X, we're going to postpone the filing of the notice of withdrawal until Monday. We have a lot of work to do before your meeting with Mr. X. With the kind of resources he can provide, if we can get him on board, there's nothing on this earth that will be able to stop you. You'll win, my man!"

Scott's energy level was the highest I'd ever heard from him.

"But we have to convince his team first that you can't lose," he continued. "Our job this weekend is to send his attorneys the original judgment rendered by Judge Keller, the papers filed on appeal, our answers and motions on all of the related actions, and an overview of our legal strategies going forward."

"Sounds like a lot of work," I answered, wiggling a thumbs-up at Paige who was standing nearby, devouring my every word, trying to make out what Scott was saying. "Is there anything I can do to help?"

"Laura and I will be communicating with his attorneys all weekend to bring them up to speed on our progress."

"Is there any way you and Laura can attend the meeting with me?" I asked.

"Unfortunately, no. I'm in court that afternoon. We'll be taking the meeting with you by speaker phone. We'll answer their questions that way and go over the legal aspects of your cases. You'll be there in person, and it's important for you to take an active roll in the discussions. You need to let them see who and what are behind these litigations."

"I'll do my best, Scott," I said with happy determination.

"I have every confidence you will!" he said. "Let's get to work!"

When I hung up the phone, Paige and I jumped up and danced around the kitchen with a renewed sense of optimism. As we celebrated, I filled her in on the details of the conversation she'd been unable to hear. All weekend long, Laura, Scott and I jumped through the numerous hoops my potential angel's counsel had placed in front of us.

I was to appear at Mr. X's office at 10 AM Monday morning, and our success depended on my being there on time. With the luck I'd been having, I worried that something might happen—planes could be delayed, freeways might be grid-locked, who knows? As an insurance policy, Paige and I decided I should leave Sunday evening.

To continue, with all fairness to Mr. X, I have combined a few events to better protect his identity.

I couldn't sleep at all that night, I was so nervous knowing how many people were depending on me. I went over my presentation again and again in my mind, tossing and turning in my hotel room bed until the curtains slowly turned from grey to full color as the sun rose behind them. I arrived in the parking lot of Mr. X's building 45 minutes early and sat in my rental car going over the legal documents I'd brought with me.

A no-nonsense security guard, sitting at a desk resembling a spaceship's computerized monitoring station, met me in the lobby of the building. A bank of closed circuit TV monitors and computer screens towered in front of him. The architecture was modern concrete—cold and sterile. I approached the man feeling confident; he spoke first.

"What's your name and who are you here to see?" he said with authority.

"I have a 10 o'clock appointment with Mr. X," I answered.

"What's your name?" he asked with a stone face.

"Dick Peterson."

He picked up his phone and rang the appropriate party to announce my arrival. While waiting for my clearance, he pointed to a sheet in front of me and told me to sign in. He then hung up the phone, gave me a visitor's badge and told me which elevator to take and which floor to get off. I felt my confidence waning and intimidation setting in.

When the elevator doors opened at the appropriate floor, a receptionist greeted me. She, too, sat behind a series of monitors and phones.

"I have a 10 o'clock with Mr. X," I said, my confidence returning.

"Your name?" questioned the smiling, pleasant, dark-haired girl.

"Oh, yeah," I laughed, feeling only slightly mindless, "Dick Peterson."

Like the guard in the lobby, when she picked up the phone and spoke, she sounded skeptical that I was expected. I thought to myself, "I'd better get my mind together and start thinking or I'm going to blow it!"

"Through that door and down the hall," she said, pointing, "third door on the left. Wait there."

She pushed a button on her desk and the door opened in front of me. The hall was solid concrete with recessed lights set in the ceiling that created lonely pools of light on the floor every 10 feet or so. No pictures on the wall, no carpeting on the floor, just cold concrete. As I approached the third door on the left, it opened. I thought someone inside had opened it for me; instead, I discovered that it was a remote-controlled door that some unseen person had activated. I assumed the receptionist had been watching my every move via hidden camera and had pushed the button that opened it for me. It was spooky.

I walked into a spectacular-but-empty conference room. The long shiny wooden table was at least three inches thick and had been hewn from one solid piece of what looked like cherry wood at no doubt incredible expense. Fourteen elegant, high-backed black leather chairs sat around the table. Arrayed on the table were seven yellow tablets with pencils lying beside them, standing ready for note taking. Five tablets sat on one side of the table, one had been placed at the end of the table and the remaining tablet rested in the middle of the table opposite the group of five. I assumed—correctly—that solitary tablet was for me. The walls were raised panel hardwood that matched the table perfectly, the floor a combination of imported stone and exquisite carpet.

As I sat down in the chair in front of the single tablet, the door opened. A well-dressed, middle-aged woman came in, introduced herself and showed me the accommodations. If I needed a drink, she explained, I could push a panel on the wall to reveal a built-in, double-wide refrigerator stocked with snacks and every non-alcoholic drink imaginable. If I needed a phone, there was a remote dialer I could take to my chair. She pointed out that the room was equipped with computers, a movie screen, and an entertainment center. After telling me that I would be joined in a few minutes by "the others," she left the room. Now

I was truly intimidated and nervous. I sat for a moment, trying to look past the power I was about to confront and focus on my task.

The door opened again and the room filled with busy people introducing themselves to me and taking off their expensive jackets and draping them across the backs of their leather chairs. Overwhelmed, I tried my best to remember their names, but as quickly as they were uttered, their names stopped short of the defiant memory cells I had desperately called on for help. Two women and three men sat down across from me, opening their briefcases and flooding the table with stacks of documents. The men all wore custom tailored suits and 30,000 thread count white linen shirts with gold cuff links. I was definitely out of my element, but I liked the neighborhood.

The man sitting in the center of the five introduced himself as Mr. X's attorney. Looking straight at me, he spoke into the air.

"Scott? Are you there?"

From speakers hidden somewhere in the room, Scott's voice sounded sharp and clear.

"Yes, I'm here with Laura and a few of our associates, and we are ready to answer any questions you may have. Has Mr. Peterson arrived?"

"Yes, I'm here," I interjected, my voice cracking.

"Well," said Mr. X's attorney, "with your permission, Scott, we'd like to dive right into this and see what we can accomplish for Mr. Peterson."

I thought they might wait until Mr. X arrived, but they began their interrogation without him. It was clear from their questions that they'd spent a lot of time preparing for the meeting. Their probing was thorough and judicial. I patiently listened for over half an hour as the two teams talked with each other. The attorney's associates were continually feeding him previously-prepared written questions and documents, and Scott and Laura were fielding each question with the skill and agility of Alex Rodriguez chasing down a routine grounder at third.

Once the attorney was satisfied that Scott and Laura had adequately answered all of their questions, he thanked them for their time and patience and told them he and his associates would talk with Mr. X, give him their recommendation, and notify me of Mr. X's decision.

Scott requested that I call him once I was on my way home. With that, the call ended.

The attorney's associates started packing their briefcases as he informed me that his office would leave a message on my pager later that day regarding their decision. That was all it took for me to lose my feelings of intimidation and awe.

I have no idea from where the fearless bravery came. His statement hit the right nerve, and I blurted, "Oh no you don't! You haven't heard what I have to say yet!"

"Excuse me?" said the puzzled attorney as he froze in his tracks.

"Look," I said with passion and a little anger, "I've been sitting here for almost an hour listening to you high-priced attorneys discuss my case, and I appreciate the interest you've taken, but you haven't heard from me yet! Listen, this isn't about a pile of legal documents, it's about people. It's great that you guys sift through all of this legal stuff, but I came all this way thinking I was going to have an opportunity to explain my situation to Mr. X, and he doesn't even have the courtesy to show up for the meeting!"

"In all fairness to Mr. X," the attorney answered calmly, "he's had all of us working through the weekend on your behalf, and at a great deal of expense I might add."

"Money? It's not about the money!" I countered. "Not many times in my life am I going to be given the opportunity to sit in front of a group of high caliber people like you that can change so many lives, and you think I'm going to walk out of here without even being heard? No way! It's not going to take five minutes of your time to hear what I have to say. Five minutes. Is five minutes is going to hurt you? Are you that busy?"

A voice came over the same speakers on which we'd been listening to Scott and Laura.

"Sit down and let him speak."

"Yes, sir!" obeyed the attorney as he and his colleagues sat back down.

"Is that you, Mr. X?" I asked.

"Yes," said the disembodied voice.

"So, you've been listening?" I tried to affirm defiantly.

"I've tuned in from time to time, yes," answered the wise-sounding, calm voice. "As I'm sure you can imagine, I have quite a few things on my plate, and a $200,000 deal is not exactly a priority for me. With all due respect to you and your needs, Mr. Peterson, I spend more than that in an evening just taking a few friends to a Broadway play!"

"All I need is five minutes. If you're going to listen for five minutes, why don't you do it in here?" I challenged.

"I'll be right in," said the busy, wealthy man.

As we awaited his arrival, Mr. X's team of legal giants sat across from me, smiling and raising their eyebrows in disbelief. Within seconds, the door opened and I immediately recognized the famous man.

Standing out of respect, I offered my hand and said, "Hi, I'm Dick Peterson. Thanks for seeing me."

"I'm W," he said, shaking my hand. [I will use "*w*" as Mr. X's first name since "*w*" comes just before "*x*."]

Looking at his watch, he sternly continued, "and you've just used 15 seconds of your time."

"Okay," I said, "here goes…"

I took a deep breath and continued.

"This case isn't about you helping me, it's about you helping all of the people standing behind me waiting for me to finally win this suit. There are thousands of recording artists who are nearly starving because they're not being paid royalties by the companies getting rich off their work. When I win this case, those artists will be able to simply file an inexpensive suit and use our case law to reclaim ownership of their records."

I could see through his poker face as he glanced at his watch to let me know my time was running. "Yeah, I already know all of this" he was thinking.

"Okay, so here's my proposition. I have a house in Oregon that appraises for around $500,000. Take it! If you say no to me today, I'm going lose it anyway. I may as well guarantee your loan with it. Just buy me enough time to sell it so I can continue with this suit."

My proposition wasn't appealing to his heart, so I upped the ante.

"And I'm willing to throw in my share of the masters. You can have my percentage of the ownership. If you don't help me, I won't have them anyway. At least this way, we won't lose the case. The way I look at it, personally, I've already lost, but that doesn't mean that every one has to lose, too."

"How do you figure you've lost?" he asked, curious.

"Well, I owe Gibson, Dunn over $200,000. If they file a withdrawal, I will lose my cases by default and eventually they'll sue me for payment and I'll lose my home, the lawsuits and the masters."

Then I had an idea, like an inspiration sent from heaven. A few weeks earlier, I'd discussed the possibility of forming a foundation by using some of our future royalties to help recording artists recover their masters. Now I threw it on the table.

"When I win, I intend to form The Louie Louie Foundation to help pay attorney's fees for artists that need assistance in filing their cases."

"Stop right there!" said the suddenly attentive Mr. X.

My heart was racing. I feared my time had run out.

"You have just cured my problem," said the smiling Mr. X.

"How so?" I asked.

"I was going to say no to you until you mentioned the foundation idea."

"You were?" I responded with a lump in my throat.

"Not because I don't want to help you—I do," he said, rubbing his hands together. "But you have no idea how much negative PR I deal with every day,"

Switching gears, he looked at his counsel.

"Legally, will he win?" he asked.

"I have no doubt he will," answered his attorney.

Turning in my direction, Mr. X spoke directly to me.

"No one hears about the good things we do here," he said. "We can do a hundred different good things for people, and no one notices; but turn one person down and that's the craziness that's all over the press. If I help you and other artists hear about it and come to me for help, and I turn them down for any reason, that's what you're going to read about in the paper. It will eventually be my fault that they are homeless and broke. Now, however, if someone calls in need of help, we can simply say that we support a foundation that addresses their situation and refer them to you. It will be up to you to deal with them. Everybody wins!"

He looked at a woman sitting at the end of the table who'd been silently taking notes throughout the meeting.

"Cut Mr. Peterson a check for $200,000," he instructed her. Smiling, he added, "He has some bills to pay."

My eyes started to tear, and I could feel goose bumps on my arms and hot flashes up my back.

His lawyers instantly objected.

"You can't do that!" Mr. X's head attorney said. "We'll have to prepare loan documents and have him sign them before you release any funds."

Mr. X looked at the attorney in disbelief.

"I can do what I please, it's my money," he emphatically stated. "Write him the check now!"

As though stone deaf, his lawyer persisted.

"I'll call Scott and inform him about your decision. They can wait a few days to get their payment."

Pointing at me, Mr. X responded curtly.

"I know this guy. I've had an entire weekend to look into him. Don't you think I know who I'm dealing with here? Give him the money. He's not going anywhere!"

He looked at me and grinned.

"You'll sign the papers when they're ready, won't you?" he said.

"Absolutely!" I assured him.

As his assistant got up to leave, he stopped her.

"No, wait!" he said. She stopped and looked at the contemplative Mr. X.

"Write it for $300,000," he directed. He looked at me and said with a smile, "Believe me, $200,000 isn't enough. And if you need any more, just call me. We'll work it out."

Raising his hand and stopping the lady yet again, he said, "Oh, throw in an extra 20 K so he can get that foundation started."

Mr. X stood.

"It was a pleasure meeting you, he said as I fought back tears. "It's kind of a kick in the head meeting one of the Kingsmen. When I was in college, we used to dance to 'Louie Louie' and try to figure out the words. Someday you'll have to tell me the real words to that song, I wish you luck. This is a good thing you're doing. And, you were right!"

"I was?" I questioned. "About what?"

"You only needed five minutes," he said, laughing as he left the room.

I immediately called Paige first, and Scott second, with the wonderful, case-saving news.

Mr. X's kindness enabled me to win all of the GML actions and appeals and settle the malpractice suit. It took an additional three years to finish the cases, and I did have to ask Mr. X for an additional sum, which he gave gladly and without hesitation. My final legal tab? It took over $1,300,000 to win this precedent-setting case, but we won, and my fellow Musketeers joyfully celebrated the victory with me.

As it turned out, we did have to sell our house and radically change our lifestyle to service our debt. I didn't have to form the Louie Louie Foundation. Once I won, attorneys came out of the woodwork everywhere offering their services to help artists in need. We sifted through the sharks and created a network of reputable lawyers to represent artists living in their general areas. With all of the hardships the suit created, there were many times I wished I'd never started this crazy and emotionally draining action. But once I filed the suit, it never crossed my mind to quit. There was too much at stake for too many.

It's strange and wonderful to me how The Kingsmen, with "Louie Louie," came from such controversial beginnings to survive though the fun, heartaches, personal tragedies, rumors and investigations, to ultimately prevail, not only with this precedent-setting decision that changed our industry, but, of equal importance to me, to prevail in our brotherhood as well. Lynn did triumphantly pull his life together and I love and respect my fellow Musketeer. Norm is sailing and living somewhere in the Western Hemisphere but calling me for up-dates from time to time. Mike, Barry and I are still performing together and joined by two of the Kings greatest Musketeers, Steve Peterson and Todd McPherson.

Today, I continue to hit a stage somewhere in the USA with my fellow Kingsmen on weekends. I am more than fortunate to be forever connected with the Kingsmen, to be a part of this crazy history and to be able to continue to have a blast playing music with my fellow Musketeers for the endless party that is still rocking to "Louie Louie" and our out of control, unintelligible musical style of everyone playing everything louder than everyone else.

Oh, I almost forgot! Would you like to hear one more story, one about me finally getting my period and waking up to the real world? You know, the one with girls in it? No? Had enough? You sure? It's a great story. Okay, then, I'll share it with you another time. Go have a sandwich.

"Me gotta go now. Let's go!"

Barry, Author, Mike—1976
FOREVER COMPADRES

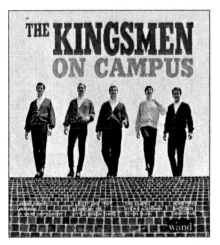

TO readers still waiting for the "true" lyrics to "Louie Louie" to be revealed in these pages, hopefully you understand by now that those words reside not on any song book page or web site but in your imaginations. They are anything and whatever you want them to be, good or bad, off-color or lily-white, comprehensible or not. Choose your own lyrics, therefore, and have some fun doing it. "Who's to say who's wrong or who's right?" Certainly not this writer, and I'm sure that Louie himself would agree were he to be asked. Some mysteries of the universe are best left ineffable.

As consolation prize, if you turn the page you will find the lyrics to another Kingsmen classic, "Jolly Green Giant." For parents or grandparents trying to get Little Johnny and Little Susie to eat their veggies, these immortal words by Lynn Easton, with horticultural embellishments by Barry Curtis, may someday come in handy.

JOLLY GREEN GIANT

In duh valley of duh jolly... (Ho - ho - ho)

Heard about the Jolly Green Giant (potatoes)
He's so big and mean (artichoke hearts)
He stands there laughin' with his hands on his hips
And then he hits you with a can of beans

He lives down there in his valley (Brussels sprouts)
The cat stands tall and green (spinach)
Well, he ain't no prize, and there's no women his size
And that's why the cat's so mean

One day he left His valley pad
I mean to say This cat was mad
Now lookin 'round He wasn't gone long
And then he ran into an Amazon

Well, this changed his whole complexion (broccoli)
He had never seen such a beautiful sight (corn)
Well, he looked at her
And she looked at him
And she almost passed out from fright

He looked at her Thought, "what a dilly"
He touched her once She slapped him silly
This was something He had never sensed
He looked at her As she commenced
Now listen, pal This ain't no fluke
I can't see goin' with a big green kook"

You've heard about the Jolly Green Giant (eggplant)
Don't let his troubles cross your mind (celery stalks)
He couldn't get Sally, so went back to his valley
The cat was color-blind
(Carrots, and beans)

After reading the verse 8 Jim, my editor, was inspired to write the following ode:

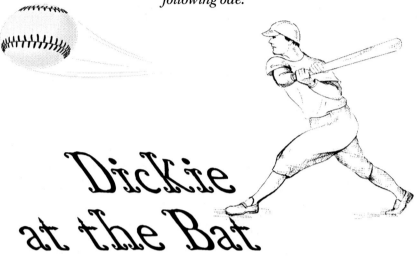

Dickie at the Bat

WHAT could be more all-American than baseball on a summer day on the sandlots of Gig Harbor? Unless, of course, you're talking about Ernest L. Thayer's timeless ode to the sport, "Casey at the Bat." With apologies to the long-departed Mr. Thayer, and to fans of baseball and poetry everywhere, we offer here a Gig Harbor take on Thayer's poem.

The outlook wasn't brilliant for the Harbor nine that day,
The score stood four to two, with but one inning more to play.
The underdog Leftover Bunch was down to their last frame.
A pall-like silence fell upon the patrons of the game.

A straggling few got up to go feeling deep despair.
The rest clung to that hope which springs eternal there.
They thought, "if only Dickie could but get a whack at that.
We'd put up even money now, with Dickie at the bat"

Steve Wilkerson would be up first, with Lester Frye to come,
two trusty, stalwart batters who knew how to hit it some.
Fans prayed the two would both come through and give them cause to shout.
Fans crossed their fingers, hoping neither one would make an out.

But Finholm followed Frye, then came Colby—Pity's Sake!—
and the former was a hoodoo, while the latter was a cake.
So upon that stricken multitude, grim melancholy sat;
for there seemed but little chance of Dickie getting to the bat.

But Steve let drive a double, to the wonderment of all.
And Lester, batting second, was stricken by the ball.
And when the dust had lifted, and men saw what had occurred,
Les took first and Steve took second, a base away from third.

Finholm heard the call, "Strike three!" and Colby swung and missed.
Harbor fans all held their breath; the opposition hissed.
One last chance, and Herb Cook's boys would send to bat their best:
Terror of the sandlots, Dickie! Pride of the Northwest?

Then from two hundred throats and more there rose a lusty yell;
it rumbled through the valley, it rattled in the dell;
it pounded through on the mountain and recoiled upon the flat;
for Dickie, Lil' Dickie, was advancing to the bat.

There was ease in Dickie's manner as he stepped into his place,
there was pride in Dickie's bearing and a smile lit Dickie's face.
And when, responding to the cheers, he lightly doffed his hat,
no stranger in the crowd could doubt t'was Dickie at the bat.

Two hundred eyes were on him as he rubbed his hands with dirt.
Two hundred tongues applauded when he wiped them on his shirt.
Then, while the writhing pitcher ground the ball into his hip,
defiance flashed in Dickie's eye, a sneer curled Dickie's lip.

*And now the leather-covered sphere came hurtling through the air,
and Dickie stood a-watching it in haughty grandeur there.
Hard at the sturdy batsman the ball directly sped—
"That's just my style!" cried Dickie. "I'll take a whack!" he said.*

*From the benches, black with people, there went up a monstrous roar,
like the beating of the storm waves on a stern and distant shore.
"Catch it! Catch the baseball!" shouted someone on the stand,
as the dunn sphere flew far o'r the center fielder's outstretched hand.*

*With a smile as wide as Texas Lil' Dickie's visage shone,
fans screamed in rising tumult while three runners scurried on.
Steve Wilkerson scored first, and close behind him Lester flew
around third base, across home plate, to tie the score with two.*

*Fraud!" cried his maddened rivals, and echo answered "Fraud!"
But one scornful look from Dickie and the audience was awed.
They saw his face grow stern and cold, they saw his muscles strain,
And they knew that Dickie wouldn't let his teammates down again.*

*Around third base and on toward home Dickie madly dashed;
when suddenly, to great surprise, his brother's diaper flashed.
Into the air the garment flew, as Dickie crossed the plate.
Home run! Game over! Victory! A time to celebrate!*

*The Harborites all swarmed the field and Dickie's teammates cheered.
The opposition slunk away, their threat no longer feared.
And on the wind, above the noise, a mother's voice rang clear:
"Oh, Dickie, darling Dickie, you've dropped your diaper here!"*

*Oh, somewhere in this favored land the sun is shining bright.
The band is playing somewhere, and somewhere hearts are light.
And, somewhere men are laughing, and little children play.
And joy reigns in Gig Harbor, Lil' Dickie's saved the day.*

Jim Ojala

All praises be to our Lord for his gracious gift of eternal life offered to all and the blessings he has generously given me.

Printed in the United States
51103LVS00003B/56